Also by Sheneska Jackson

Caught Up in the Rapture
Li'l Mama's Rules

Blessings

A NOVEL

Blessings

A NOVEL

Sheneska Jackson

SIMON & SCHUSTER

SIMON & SCHUSTER
Rockefeller Center
1230 Avenue of the Americas
New York, NY 10020

SIMON & SCHUSTER and colophon are registered trademarks
of Simon & Schuster Inc.

Designed by Deirdre C. Amthor

Manufactured in the United States of America

ISBN 0-684-85035-4

Acknowledgments

When I am still and quiet and allow myself a moment to reflect, I am often amazed by the beautiful blessings that have manifested in my life. My blessings come in many forms, but none more precious than my mother, Miss Etna, who is my number one fan. Thank you Eugene, George, Marcell, Kristen, and all the rest of the family for your love, support, and kind words. Big ups to the crew: Sheila, Melissa, Nondice, and the whole gang for keeping me young, grounded, and laughing. Thank you to my Dynamic Duo, Mary Ann Naples and Denise Stinson, for understanding that there is a message and method behind the madness. And thank you to the readers who enjoy my work and stick by me — I work for you.

I am so blessed to be able to do what I do. I am loved and I know it. And that feeling, in and of itself, is the greatest blessing of all.

From the depths — Sheneska.

I thank Him because I *know* He *is*.

Blessings

A NOVEL

1

In this life there are mysteries that will never be fully understood by mere mortals. Questions that when pondered extensively can leave the average human psyche in such a state of disarray that normal brain activity stalls, leaving the ponderer of such questions wallowing in a mass of confusion, aimlessly searching for the unknown, and ultimately leading to a state of mental chaos and cerebral shut-down. Unfortunately, as we all know, there are some questions that are better left unanswered. Questions such as Does God really exist? Is there life after death? Which came first? The chicken or the egg?

Indeed these questions can certainly leave one's mind hopelessly frazzled and disheveled. But there is an even larger question at hand today. A mystery that has eluded the genius of scholars, scientists, and political pundits alike. A question that has dogged the earth for hundreds of years, and even to this day we are nowhere near a breakthrough in this timeless riddle. The question is a serious one. The question is mind boggling. The question is this: Why? *For the love of God!* **Why does it take so long for a woman to get her hair done at the beauty shop?**

Many have tried to unravel this mystery, but none have succeeded. Some of the theories to explain this phenomenon include tardiness on the part of the client, overbooking of appointments, and a general lackadaisical attitude on the part of the beautician. Still, the answer to this question has escaped us. We may never get to the bottom of this dilemma, but if we are truly committed to bringing about change we must first tackle the obvious, most irritating, and most unscrupulous element of the equation. And that is this: Beauticians talk too damn much.

Oh yes, it is a natural fact that beauticians love to run their mouths. No matter where you live, be it North, South, East, or West, it doesn't matter. Where there are beauticians there is chatter. And on this day, in the bustling city of Inglewood, California, inside the small but well-kept beauty salon on the corner of Centinela and LaBrea, the natural facts were in effect.

"I just can't believe he could do something like that," Faye said, shaking her head as she ripped open a bag of silky straight weaving hair. "Do *you* think he did it?"

"Hell no, I don't *think* he did it," Zuma answered as she meticulously pulled the end of a rat-tail comb through her client's thick hair, creating a perfect one-inch side part. "I *know* he did it."

"Don't say that," Faye said, pulling the one hundred percent human hair from its bag and shaking it out. "I believe he's innocent. You saw the trial. He didn't look like a killer."

"Well I don't know what trial you were watching, but all I know is this: His blood didn't just get up and *walk* over to that crime scene. He was there, he did it, he's guilty as sin, and that's all I have to say about that."

"*Stop it!*" Faye squeaked, the words stinging her ears as if she was the one accused of murder. "He was set up! And to be perfectly honest, I for one am glad that he got off. It's about time we won something around here. We didn't get any justice with Rodney King," she said, a bit surprised by the rising tone of her voice. She paused and brought it down a notch. "That not-guilty verdict was a victory for all of us. We won this time."

"*We won?*" Zuma said and stuck the comb into her client's hair. She turned to face Faye head-on and put her hands on her hips. "What did *we* win?" she asked, flinging her hand through the air. "I have yet to see my O. J. prize, honey. *Please.* We won?" She sucked her teeth. "I've just about had it up to here with everybody assuming that *all* black people think O. J. Simpson is innocent. Unh-uh, not me. I know he did it. He did it. He did it. *He did it!*"

"Well, you weren't looking too unhappy when the verdicts came down," Faye reminded Zuma and raised her hand in the air, rationally. "You were sitting right here in this shop jumping up and down with everybody else when we found out O. J. had been set free."

"Hell yeah, I was jumping up and down. But I wasn't jumping for O. J.," she said, and smirked. "I was jumping for Johnnie Cochran. Now that's one bad man. People may not like his tactics, but he was just doing what any other good attorney is supposed to do — support his client at all costs and *win*. Shoot, Johnnie Cochran is a damn hero and if he had been white, people would have been begging for him to run for president by now," she said, and pointed a finger for emphasis. "Shit, Johnnie Cochran is the man, but O. J.?" she said, and curled her lips. "Fuck O. J."

"*Zuma*," Faye said, wincing at her use of foul language.

"*Faye*," Zuma said, not giving a damn.

"Well, I still don't think he did it. He may *know* who did it. But he didn't do it himself."

"Hell yeah, he knows who did it. *He did it!*"

"A man like that cannot kill two people. It's physically impossible," Faye rationalized. "How is O. J. going to kill *two* people with *one* knife? I mean, what was the second person doing while O. J. was stabbing the first? Waiting in line talking about, 'Cut me next, O. J. Cut me'?" Faye paused, surprised by the laughter that statement had generated, but she wasn't trying to be funny. "No," she continued. "There's no way a man like that can kill two people."

"A man like *that*? A man like *what*?"

"A rich black man like O. J. Simpson has no reason to be killing anybody. O. J. Simpson is black and any black man going up against this racist judicial system in America has got my support."

"O. J. Simpson ain't *black*. He ain't nothing but another rich, stuck-up white boy. He ain't never used none of his money to help out black folk," she said, and pointed at Faye. "When have you ever heard about O. J. doing something to help out the black community?" she said, and waited briefly for a response, but Faye was dumbfounded. "O. J. hasn't done shit for me," Zuma said with fire. "Shoot. Where was some O. J. when I was in need? Where was some O. J. when my car was being repossessed? Hell, where was some O. J. when my broke ass couldn't pay my light bill last week? Shoot, support O. J? O. J. can kiss my black ass. And I mean that. *Shiiit*."

It had been two years since the verdicts had come down in the O. J. Simpson trial, but the Juice was still a hot topic at Blessings. Blessings was the spot, the place where everybody came for a little *pleasant* conversation.

Never mind that Blessings was a beauty shop. The way people ranted and raved throughout the place, it could easily have been mistaken for a town hall meeting arena. While women with nappy heads waited patiently on the faux leather sofa for hours and sisters with half-wet locks bent over shampoo bowls scratching their dandruff, the conversation between the two beauticians brewed on. Once again the subject had turned to the Juice, and as usual, the conversation was heated. So heated, that even the time-conscious clients had to get in on it.

"I know one thing," the lady with blond-streaked hair yelled as she poked her head from beneath the dryer. "If nothing at all, O. J. Simpson is a wife beater. Y'all saw those pictures of Nicole. She didn't beat herself up," she said, then slammed the lid of the dryer back over her head.

"O. J. said he never hit that woman and I believe him," a lady with a head full of loose braids said as she sat in the corner of the faux leather sofa. Her words seemed to ignite the blond-streaked lady's nerves as she poked her head from beneath the dryer again.

"Y'all kill me," she shouted over the rumblings of the old machine she sat underneath. "You women support O. J. like he was some sorta god." She looked sideways toward the lady sitting under the dryer next to her. "I know some of y'all have had your butts beaten by a black man," she said and squinted her eyes at her neighbor, "so don't tell me that O. J. isn't capable of beating his wife. I don't care how rich he is or was, he's still a wife beater."

The lady sitting next to her gasped as she rolled her eyes and pulled her skirt tail down to hide the black-and-blue bruise that stained her round thigh. She crossed her legs and hoped the conversation would end. But it didn't.

"O. J. was framed," another lady called out from the shampoo bowl. Her brown locks were covered in conditioner and as she lifted her head from the bowl, water dripped down the sides of her face. "Those crooked, racist cops set O. J. up. It was a C-O-N-spiracy."

The woman with the loose braids jumped in again. "That's right. That damn Mark Fuhrman ain't no good. This whole thing was a setup from the get-go," she said, scooping a handful of braids out of her face. "Did you hear those tapes he made? Nigger, nigger, nigger. He didn't have no business being on the police force, let alone being a part of the trial."

The blond-streaked lady had nothing to say about that so she just pulled down the lid of her dryer and sat back. But that didn't end the conversation. Another woman with a head of freshly blow-dried hair slammed the *Essence* magazine she'd been reading onto the counter in front of her. As she turned around to confront the lady with the loose braids her long hair whipped across her face just like one of those girls in the shampoo commercials on TV. "Now, I'm not trying to defend Mark Fuhrman, but the man was a cop. He was just doing his job. So what if he said all that mess on those tapes? That don't mean he framed O. J. Simpson."

"Fuhrman is a red-necked racist. Anybody who could talk about black people the way he did is capable of anything."

"Oh," Shampoo Commercial said. "And I guess you've never uttered a racist word in your whole entire life, huh?" She swung her head around to confront the lady at the shampoo bowl. "I was in here last week when you walked in here bitching and complaining about the *Beaner* who cut you off and almost made you crash into a tree. Now, does that make you racist against all Hispanic people?"

The lady at the shampoo bowl stuttered and wrapped the white towel that was around her neck over her damp hair as she sat back and shut up.

"And you," Shampoo Commercial said, turning to the woman with loose braids again, her hair whipping through the air. "Remember last month when we were in here talking about the civil rights movement? You said all white people are devils and that you wouldn't care if they all disappeared off the face of the earth." She tilted her head to the side. "Does that make you a racist? Just because you said those words, does that mean you're capable of framing somebody just because they are white?"

The blond-streaked lady realized Shampoo Commercial was on her side and regained enough confidence to poke her head from beneath the dryer again. "I said it before and I'll say it again—O. J. Simpson is guilty as sin," she chanted like a cheerleader and gave a thumbs-up to Shampoo Commercial. "We've got a killer on the streets," she said as she lost her grip on the dryer's lid and it smacked her on top of her head. She winced, but didn't lose a beat. "And another thing," she said as the dryer's automatic timer buzzed. "That stupid jury in the criminal trial ought to be shamed of themselves."

The bruised woman sitting under the dryer next to her gasped again, but this time she pulled the lid of the dryer from over her head and turned right around to face her opponent. "I've been silent long enough," she said, and pulled her skirt tail down again to hide the black-and-blue mark on her thigh. "Don't go blaming those black people on that jury. They did their jobs. It's not their fault that the prosecution couldn't prove its case beyond a reasonable doubt."

Shampoo Commercial stood up from her seat to walk over to the hair dryer section so she could get in on this phase of the conversation. "No," she said defiantly, "those jurors did not do their jobs."

"Oh yes they did," Loose Braids said as she too walked over to the dryer section. "Those folks ought to be commended. They were locked up for almost a damn year. Away from their families and everything."

"Hell, I should be so lucky," Blond Streaked interrupted. "I've been looking for an excuse to get away from my family for years." She and Shampoo Commercial chuckled over that. But Loose Braids and the bruised woman were not in the mood for laughing.

"I get so tired of people coming down on that jury." Loose Braids sighed. "Just because they were black and happened to come back with a not guilty verdict, everybody wants to call them stupid. As if a black jury isn't fit to handle a case like this." Bruised nodded as Loose Braids continued. "That black jury made the right decision," she said and pointed directly at the blond-streaked woman. "O. J. Simpson is innocent."

"First of all," Blond Streaked said as she removed the dryer from above her head and stood to her feet. She was all of five foot nothing, but as she looked up at Loose Braids her stance was like that of a giant. "You best get your finger out of my face," she said, eyeing Loose Braids until the finger she pointed had eased its way down. "And second of all, I call those black jurors stupid because they are. They did not do their fucking jobs. They listened to over nine months of testimony and reached their verdict in three hours? Ain't no way in the world you can call that doing your job. They were supposed to *deliberate*. Have you ever looked up the word *deliberate* in the dictionary?"

Shampoo Commercial took over from there. "Deliberate means to slowly and methodically come to a decision," she said, moving closer to Loose Braids and speaking as if she were talking to a two-year-old. "Deliberate means to weigh *all* the evidence. To consider it *carefully*. How could that jury consider nine months' worth of testimony in three hours? They did not do their jobs," she said, stressing each and every word of her final sentence.

"Yes they did!" Bruised shouted and pushed the dryer lid away from her head again.

"No they didn't!" Blond Streaked and Shampoo Commercial said in unison.

"Yes they did!" Loose Braids groaned.

"No they—"

"*Hey, hey, hey!*" a voice shouted from the other side of the shop, forcing the debaters to pause. They all caught their collective breaths as they turned to catch a glimpse of the woman walking their way. "What in the world is going on over here?" the tall, pristine woman asked as she moved between the feuding ladies. She graced the debaters with a smile so pleasant that they all began to feel a bit awkward about the way they had let their conversation get out of hand.

"Sorry," Loose Braids said as she slowly walked back to the sofa and took a seat. "I guess we got a bit too caught up in our conversation."

"Sorry," Blond Streaked said as she sat back down beneath the hair dryer next to Bruised.

"Yeah, I'm sorry too," Shampoo Commercial said as she headed back to her chair and picked up her *Essence* magazine. "We didn't mean to get so loud. It's just that *some* people have some very screwed-up ways of thinking."

"Excuse me?" Bruised said and raised an eyebrow.

"Now, now, ladies," the tall woman said calmly yet authoritatively.

"Sorry," Bruised said and faked a smile toward Shampoo Commercial. "I guess you're right. I mean you ought to know with that big ass bowling ball you call a head. With a dome that big I guess you're qualified to think for all of us."

Loose Braids snickered as Shampoo Commercial rolled her eyes, but before another word could be uttered, the tall lady with the soothing smile spoke up. "Everybody just calm down," she said. "This is a beauty shop, not a battlefield," she scolded, and frowned for a second. She looked over her shoulder at Faye and Zuma and squinted her eyes at her fellow beauticians. "See what you guys started?" she said as both Faye and Zuma shrugged their shoulders and smirked. The tall woman looked around the shop at all the disgruntled customers and realized she had to do something quick. Unhappy customers were definitely bad for business. "Hey," she said, clapping her hands together and flashing her smile around to all the ladies. "I've got a joke," she announced, then took a deep gulp before she continued.

Faye and Zuma shot each other a look, but that didn't stop the jokester from putting on her show. "Okay," she said, grinning. "Here we go. . . . What do you get when you cross an elephant with a rhinoceros?"

Faye and Zuma rolled their eyes and sighed. The disgruntled debaters didn't even raise an eyebrow as they looked curiously at one another.

"Okay, we give up," Zuma squawked as she walked behind the client sitting at her hair station and waited for the punch line.

"Elephino!" the tall jokester said and grinned. "Get it? Hell if I know . . . *Ele-phi-no* . . . Hell if I know! . . . Get it?"

They didn't.

Still everyone gave her a polite chuckle, which was all the tall woman needed to feel satisfied. She stood in the middle of the shop and smiled to herself. Once again she had brought order back to the chaotic shop. So what if no one understood her joke. No one ever understood her jokes. The point was that she had returned the atmosphere back to its proper state of bliss. Keeping the peace was her duty. She owned the place. Her name was Patricia Brown.

Pat looked around at the shop she'd owned now for five years and decided to pick up a broom. The floor was covered in matted, dirty hair from a previous client who had her shoulder-length coif chopped off to a chin-length bob. She sighed as she swept through the shop, smiling at the customers who politely moved their feet out of the way for her. It was Friday evening and as usual the place was packed with women looking to get "did up" for the weekend. She was proud of her shop and the women who frequented it. Be they businesswomen who came in every week to keep up their professional appearances, broke women who had scraped together just enough money minus a tip for the occasional splurge, or the teenage ghetto fabulous girls who'd conned their boyfriends into giving them some cash to get their hair *did*. The nature of the client didn't matter to Pat. She loved them all.

Pat didn't see hair styling as a form of retail beauty. She saw it as a form of therapy. She was often amazed at what a good hairstyle could do for a person's self-esteem. It was almost miraculous. She'd named her shop Blessings, because that's what she wanted to create. She and the two other women who worked with her could take any average-looking woman off the streets and turn her into a diva with the flip of a hot comb. They were practically miracle workers. Hooking up hair was the ultimate blessing, Pat thought, and one of the easiest ways to make women feel better about themselves.

As she glided her broom across the floor toward the bathroom, Pat stopped for a minute and stuck her head in to take a peek at herself in the mirror. She ran her hand over her freshly styled hair that Zuma had trimmed for her earlier that day. She tucked a single curlicue that Zuma had left dangling over her eye behind her ear and smoothed it down. Zuma was always trying to give Pat's hair a bit of pizzazz, but pizzazz wasn't Pat's style. She was the conservative type. A prim and proper Christian woman whose only vice was her penchant for telling an occasional dirty joke. Pat was tall and slender with an understated beauty that didn't need to be beefed up with silly fashion fads or here-today-gone-tomorrow hairdos. Pat was content with herself and happy, and as she gave herself a final once-over in the mirror, she plastered the smile back onto her face, looked over her shoulder at the fully crowded shop, then continued sweeping.

When she had finally gathered up all the hair with the dustpan and trashed it, she sat down in a chair in the back of the shop and let out a sigh of relief as she gazed around. This was the first time Pat had been off her feet all day, and even though she still had a slew of heads to finish, she couldn't resist stealing a couple minutes of solitary relaxation. She glanced at her friends, Faye and Zuma, as they worked feverishly on their clients' heads. It was already getting dark outside and still her shop was packed with people. She knew she wouldn't get home before midnight tonight, but that was the norm on Fridays. She always kept the shop open late on the weekends to meet the demands of her ever-increasing clientele. Fridays and Saturdays were the days her shop made the most money and although the weekend was always hectic, she performed her duties with great pride. Yes, she was overworked, but that was a price she was willing to pay for success. More than anything, Pat was proud. Blessings was her baby. Her very own beauty shop. Her very own business. Her husband had bought the shop for her, but she had made it her own. Not only was she a wife, she was an entrepreneur now, and her life had taken on new meaning. And that was a blessing in and of itself.

To outsiders looking in, Pat had the perfect relationship with her man. He was rich by black folks' standards, meaning he owned a home, had a nice car, good job, and no apparent addictions. He loved Pat to death and gave her everything she ever wanted. But there was one thing that Pat's husband could not give her. He was a good man, but he wasn't God. He couldn't part the seas, turn water into wine, or heal the sick. So for now Pat had to make the most of the things her husband did give her, the most important thing in her life — her beauty shop.

Blessings was located in Inglewood, California, a small, predominantly black area of Los Angeles that for the most part was considered a pretty good city. It wasn't as ritzy as West Los Angeles, but it didn't have the negative reputation of South Central even though it was only a stone's throw away. Inglewood was the perfect location to start up a small black business, but it was obvious to Pat when she first began looking for a location for her shop that she wasn't the only one who thought like that. There were so many other beauty shops in the area that Pat had been cautious about opening another right in the midst of all the competition. But Pat knew one thing. Black women like to look cute. Black women spend more money on hair, clothes, and entertainment than any other race of people. A black woman could have a refrigerator with nothing in it but a bag of bread, but if it came down to getting her hair done or going grocery shopping . . . well, let's just say she'd be eating wish sandwiches until her next paycheck.

With that in mind, Pat decided to go ahead and open her shop in Inglewood despite the competition and because she didn't want to work too far away from her home in Ladera Heights, the black Beverly Hills. Driving was not one of Pat's favorite things to do and with Inglewood being the next city over, she decided to throw caution to the wind and go with her instincts. Besides, Pat had a plan to get over on all the other beauty salons in the Inglewood area. It was a gimmick, she knew, still she gave it her best shot. Her plan? To post a sign right in the front of the shop's window that was sure to get everyone's attention. The sign was simple and to the point: *Get your hair done in two hours or less or the service is free — Guaranteed.*

Needless to say, with the wait at most other salons in the area being upwards of three hours, Pat's sign attracted a huge amount of attention and gave her the leg up on the competition that she needed. Still, the gimmick only worked for a couple of months. The first weeks were wonderful. The sign caught the eyes of many women and clients began to trickle in slowly but surely. But by the second month, the darn sign began to work too well and soon Blessings was filled to the brim with so many clients that there was no way possible for Pat to keep her guarantee. There was no way she could get to all her customers in less than two hours working by herself.

She thought she had found the answer to the problem when she hired a part-time shampoo girl to help her out for a while. But even the two of them working together was not enough of a solution and on several occasions Pat found herself doing more heads for free than she could afford. Needless to say, the sign had to come down and with no gimmick, Blessings became just another run-of-the-mill beauty salon in an area already congested with too many. A few die-hard clients who were pleased with the way Pat handled their hair stayed with her, but most of the clients dwindled away, especially after a shop named Off the Hook Hair opened up just two blocks away. Off the Hook Hair specialized in all the latest hair designs, and though Pat did consider herself to be an okay beautician, especially considering the fact that she'd only had her license for less than a year, she knew she could never compete with the stylists Off the Hook Hair had to offer. So, slowly but surely, Pat's business began to go under.

That first year Blessings was in business was a nightmare that Pat would certainly rather forget, she thought to herself as she stretched out her legs in the back of the shop. Looking around the shop now, though, it was hard to believe that Blessings had almost gone out of business in that first year. Now Blessings was considered one of the best hair salons in the city. People came from as far away as the San Fernando Valley to get their hair done at Pat's shop and business was, as they say, booming. Of course the days of the two-hour guarantee were long gone. Now if you come into Blessings by ten, you're lucky to get out by five — on a good day. It was just one of those things. No one knows why it takes so long to get their hair done, they just accept it. They make a day out of it. And knowing that it can be rather taxing sometimes to wait over four hours to get one's hair done, Pat figured she could at least give the women who came to her shop a relaxing atmosphere. From the outside, Blessings looked like any other beauty shop. The two huge windows in front were trimmed in pink and stenciled with prices and advertising specials as well as a big, black woman with a full head of crimson hair and of course a large pink neon sign that blinked "Blessings." But inside, Blessings had all the comforts of home. There was a big-screen television complete with VCR, a sound system, a mini refrigerator and microwave oven for those who brought in food, a nice comfortable sofa, and mounds and mounds of magazines to distract the clients from their long wait. The shop was relatively small with only three hair stations, two shampoo bowls, two hair dryer seats, and one newly purchased manicuring station that Pat had bought last month because she wanted to expand. Just last week, she'd had the painters out restenciling the front window from Blessings Hair Salon to Blessings Hair and Nails. And it wouldn't stop there. Pat had even bigger plans for expansion. Soon she'd add on waxing and massaging, and as soon as the renters next door decide to shut down their fledgling hardware store, she planned on purchasing it too, knocking out the wall that separated the two suites and adding on an aerobics studio. But those plans would have to wait for a year or three. Right now, hair and nails were all Pat could handle.

With the addition of the manicuring station, Pat had plans of going back to beauty school to get her manicuring license. She hadn't planned on doing nails herself, but since the red and white Help Wanted sign that hung on the front door hadn't been answered she really had no choice. Pat had it hard enough doing hair alone and adding manicurist to her title was not a welcome designation for her. But she had gone ahead and purchased the manicure station and she couldn't let it go to waste. So on top of doing hair, booking appointments, greeting customers, answering phones, keeping the place clean, and managing the books, Pat would soon be taking on even more responsibility. But Pat wouldn't complain. No, no. She'd do whatever it took to make her business the best it could be. Blessings was her baby and she would never let it go under. She remembered how awful she felt that first year of business when the lack of clientele almost forced her to close down her shop. The thought of losing what she'd worked so hard to create was almost too painful to remember. But that was a very long time ago, Pat assured herself as she got up from her seat in the back of the room and walked up front toward her hair station. She beckoned her blond-streaked client to join her and as she watched her scramble from beneath the hair dryer she pasted on a smile and tapped the seat of her chair. "Come on, darling," she said to her client as she watched her sit down in front of her. She placed her foot on the lever at the bottom of the seat and pumped four times until her client was elevated to the proper height. "Spirals or an up-do?" Pat asked as her client gave her a perplexed look. "Spirals," Pat decided and plugged in her curling wand. Pat took in a deep sigh as she combed through her client's hair and waited for the wand to heat up. She looked around the shop, knowing it would be hours before she could get off her feet again, but still she didn't complain. She'd take a jam-packed salon over an empty one any day. She'd seen her share of empty seats that first year of business and she vowed never to go through that experience again. And as long as she had her secret weapon she never would. Pat's secret weapon would keep her in business for the rest of her life. That secret weapon went by the name of Zuma, Pat thought to herself as she shot her friend a quick glance. Blessings wouldn't be half the shop it was today if it weren't for Zuma. Zuma was the diva of all hair stylists in the L.A. area. Pat knew it, the customers knew it, and you better believe Zuma knew it too.

"Flip on the radio," Zuma yelled to Pat without even looking in her direction. And, like an obedient pet, Pat obliged.

Those who didn't know Zuma would swear she was the bossiest bitch they'd ever met. But that was just Zuma's way. The "please" in the statement was an understood thing that didn't need to be said. Sort of like the silent g in the word *fight*.

When Pat hit the radio switch, a smooth jazzy beat rolled through the air, and as if stung by a bee, Zuma paused dramatically and stared at Pat as if she'd just seen a ghost.

"What?" Pat exclaimed as she returned to her hair station and returned Zuma's glare.

"*Aw shit*," Zuma said, closing her eyes.

"What!" Pat said nervously watching Zuma and wondering if she was about to have some sort of physical breakdown.

"That's my jam!" Zuma shouted and finally snapped her fingers and bobbed her head to the beat of the music. "That's that Erykah Badu cut," she said, and nudged her client, who could care less. Her client had been in the shop now for four hours and all she wanted Zuma to do was fix her hair so she could get the hell out of there and go home. Damn Erik Dubois or whoever the hell that was on the radio.

Though Zuma's client was nearing her pissed-off point, Zuma didn't pay her any attention. "*Oh on and on and on and on*," she sang and danced her way over to Pat. Zuma knew Pat wasn't a fan of hip-hop, but she had at least gotten her older pal to respect Erykah Badu's music. In fact, Pat and Faye were the two most hip-hop-impaired people Zuma had ever met. Even though they were only a few years older than her, she often found herself breaking down the simplest of terms to them just so she could be understood. It had taken almost two weeks for Pat and Faye to understand what Zuma meant when she called something "the shit." Once Pat had walked in the shop wearing a brand-new pair of shoes which Zuma enthusiastically referred to as "the shit," and Pat's feelings had been so hurt that she almost cried. Until, that is, Zuma explained that she was merely complimenting her.

It had taken Pat a while to get used to Zuma's eccentric, eclectic ways. Zuma was part homegirl, part African princess, and part businesswoman with just a touch of snobbery on the side. There were many things about Zuma that Pat didn't understand. Like how she could claim to be Muslim and still eat pepperoni pizza. How the mirror at her hair station could be filled with motivational sayings like the one that read, "All that I need is already in me" yet Zuma seemingly was always in search of some unobtainable thing. Or how Zuma's most commonly used phrase was "My money is funny and my credit won't get it," yet Pat knew from the books that Zuma was pulling in gobs of money by the week, more than she and Faye put together as a matter of fact. Zuma was a piece of work, but just like a raggedy old blanket, she had a way of endearing herself to all who crossed her path. Zuma was the type of person you hated the first time you met her, but after a few days getting to know her, you'd wonder how you could have ever been so wrong.

"*My cipher keeps moving like a rolling stone,*" Zuma sang as she danced her way over to Pat, grabbed her by the hand, and spun her around. Zuma snatched up an empty bottle of water and held it to her mouth as she swayed around the room as if she were Ms. Badu herself. The rest of the women seemed to come alive with Zuma's impromptu performance and before long the entire shop was chanting, "*On and on and on and on.*"

Even Pat got in on the groove for a moment. She stuck her hand in the air and moved it from side to side just enough to show that she had rhythm, but not so much as to bring any attention to herself. But Pat could spare only a minute's worth of time, and when she caught a glimpse of Zuma's pissed-off customer, who, unlike everyone else, was not too thrilled with the shop's sudden lapse into *Soul Train* fever, she reached out for Zuma and pulled her close to her chest. "If you don't get back to your client she's gonna have a cow. You're moving so slow today, you're gonna have to speed up to stop," she whispered.

Zuma rolled her eyes, bumped Pat on the hip, then headed back to her hair station. Zuma was as slow as the day is long, but *damn*, could she hook up some hair. She was a celebrity of sorts in the hair community. Her appointments were booked up for months in advance, which in shop talk meant she had a following. Zuma didn't care that it took her forever to finish a client's hair. She didn't care how much her clients sighed, rolled their eyes, or tapped their fingers impatiently. She knew that once her clients saw the finished product, they'd worship her forever. Hell, she was Zuma. Couldn't nobody do the do like Zuma could.

Long before Zuma ever came to work at Blessings, Pat had heard of her. Everybody knew Zuma. She was the infamous top stylist at Off the Hook Hair known best for her outrageous couture hair designs, which she showed off at Off the Hook's annual hair and fashion show. Pat had attended one of their shows during the first year she had opened Blessings. At the time Blessings was in a financial slump and Pat figured she should go check out the competition, get a few ideas on how she could make her hairstyles better, and maybe even steal a few hair designs for herself.

When Pat attended the show at Off the Hook, she sat in the back of the huge salon hoping no one would notice her. Not that they'd know who she was anyway, considering that Blessings had no following whatsoever. Still, she sat incognito in the back of the room watching the wonderful, nonstop display of fashion and hair designs as models strolled through the shop, spinning around, swinging their heads, and showing off their hairstyles from every angle. Aside from a few intricate finger-wave designs, Zuma's creations stole the show that year. She opened her collection with a simple flat ironed geisha bob, moved on to an abstract braided and spiraled up-do and the pièce de résistance—a motorized windmill. Yes, *motorized*. Pat couldn't believe her eyes when she saw Zuma's final hair model take the stage. The confident model walked out wearing what seemed to be two simple ponytails on the sides of her head. But when she reached the end of the stage the tails began to slowly move upward, and when they reached the top of her head they began to spin around and around. The crowd went crazy as they watched this girl's hair spinning like a roller coaster, and when the darn hair lit up with multicolored bulbs the crowd could barely contain itself.

Though she knew no one would ever be caught dead wearing their hair in such a gaudy style, Pat could see why Zuma was L.A.'s top hair stylist. She took hair to a different level. She made it an art.

Pat had thought going to that hair show would give her the added motivation she needed to stick with her own shop and make it an even better establishment. But in actuality all that came of it was a sense of depression. There was no way Pat could compete with Off the Hook Hair. Their reputation was too established and their stylists were on the cunning edge. And the fact that they were only a few blocks away from Blessings made matters worse.

After Pat left the show, she realized she didn't have a fighting chance of keeping her business alive, and the more she thought about it, the more she realized there was really only one thing left for her to do—quit. She had toyed for weeks with the idea of closing down her shop, but the thought of giving up just didn't sit well with Pat. She knew the odds were stacked against her, still she couldn't throw in the towel. She knew there had to be a way, *some* way to hold on to her business. Pat often sat alone in the shop long after closing time on her knees, praying for God to give her the strength to keep on keeping on. She'd pray until her knees were sore, then get up and pray some more. But after a month or two of this, God still had not answered her and all Pat had to show for her prayers were two knobby knees and an empty bank account. Still Pat was sure of one thing—God was no liar. Ask and you shall receive was what the Bible said, and by faith, Pat knew that one day when God was good and ready He would answer her prayer. It took a while, but verily, verily, the day finally came.

Pat had been nearly knocked off her feet when the young woman with a head full of tiny twists popped up at the shop one morning. The woman had been carrying an oversized hair bag filled with curlers, combs, brushes, dryers, and clippers. She'd walked right into the shop and over to a hair station without so much as a "hey, how ya doing" to Pat. She simply plopped down her hair bag, raised her eyes and said, "Can you use another beautician?"

"Do I know you?" Pat asked, cautiously, peering at the girl with the Afrocentric hair and relaxed, baggy attire. She tried to place her face, but though it was familiar she couldn't remember where she'd seen her before.

"You ought to," the woman replied and placed her hand on her hip. "Know me, that is," she added as she looked at Pat with an elitist air so arrogant and unwelcome that Pat's otherwise cool demeanor became stiff. "So can you use another beautician or what?"

Being a refined woman herself, Pat was not impressed by this stranger's presumptuous attitude, which she chalked up to a lack of home training and official church rearing. She was even less impressed when the woman, who appeared at least five years her junior, began unpacking her bag and setting up her utensils on the counter. If Pat was not mistaken, this was still *her* shop. But judging by the actions of this young girl in torn jeans with a pair of obvious knock-off Chanel earrings hanging from her lobes, it was hard to tell who was running things. It was a rarity for Pat to raise her temper, but this girl was pushing it. Who does she think she is, Pat thought, and stared at her sideways. And that's when it hit her. She *did* know this woman. She'd seen her at the Off the Hook Hair show, but for the life of her she couldn't remember her name, until . . . "You, you're . . ."

"Yes, I am," Zuma said, without even looking at Pat. She pulled out a notebook from her bag, opened it up, and began taking out small pieces of paper and sticking them on the mirror in front of her.

Yes, Pat knew this woman, but what she didn't know was what the woman was doing in her shop and why she was pasting these scrappy pieces of paper on the mirror. Papers that read, "No weapon formed against me shall ever prosper," and "Whatever you can believe and conceive you can achieve." Pat didn't know what was going on, but there was one thing she did know, or at least she thought she did. "Don't you style over there at Off the Hook Hair?"

The woman sucked her teeth and sighed. "That is past tense, honey. Get it straight or leave it alone," she said, then began mumbling to herself so rapidly that Pat almost assumed the girl was going insane. The only words she could make out were "bitch" and "fucking with the wrong woman" and "better recognize."

Pat scratched her head as she eyed the woman, watching as she mumbled on and on, becoming more and more upset with each utterance. She didn't know how to react in this situation so she decided to remain calm and fish around for more information. "Did you get fired?" she asked, then immediately realized she asked the wrong question when the woman stopped mumbling and glared into her eyes.

"Fired?" she huffed and jerked her head to the side. "No, baby. Don't get it mixed up. I *quit*. Okay?" She pointed a finger in the air for emphasis. "See, that bitch Connie thinks she's slick. But little do she know I wrote the book on slick. I know all the tricks. Shit. She better recognize."

"Connie?" Pat questioned with a wince.

"Yeah. She owns Off the Hook and I guess she thought she owned me too, but I had to wake her to a few things," she said and sucked her teeth. "Girl, let me tell you what happened," she said, shifting her weight to one side and cozying up to Pat as if they were old buddies. "Do you know that tramp had the nerve to come up in my face yesterday talking about she was going to raise her commission on me? Shit, I told her she must have lost her damn mind," she said and pulled on one of the tiny twists that filled her head. "Hell, she was already getting thirty percent of what I made, then she gonna say she want forty-five? Oh hell no. That's bondage. I told that bitch I would rent my hair station for eight hundred dollars a month, no commission, take it or leave it."

"I guess she refused, huh?" Pat asked as she picked up a bottle the woman had tipped over as she ranted about her former employer.

"Naw," she said matter of factly. "I went off on her so bad that she backed down. I had to show her who was really the boss. She had fucked with the wrong woman, honey. I guess she was asleep, but I had to wake her up."

"Well, if she agreed to your terms, why did you leave?"

"Because she pissed me the fuck off," she scoffed. "She shouldn't have even come at me like that in the first place, demanding more money and shit. Ain't nobody over there bringing in more clientele than I was. But was that good enough for Connie? No. She had to be greedy and start talking that forty-five percent shit like I was some new Jill straight out of beauty school. Shit. Fuck her. Fuck that bitch. I don't give a fuck. I'm gone. *Do ya miss me?*" she yelled at the top of her lungs.

Whoa, Pat thought to herself and took a step back. She didn't know whether to laugh or be scared, so she just stood there watching the woman, silently preparing to run for her life if it came down to that.

The woman eased off her anger long enough to pause and take a good look at Pat for the first time. She smiled briefly, realizing her attitude was getting the best of her as it often did. It didn't faze her. Zuma believed in being real and expressing herself. Still, the look on Pat's face told her that she needed to chill out. So she took a deep breath, braced herself, and began afresh. "Look. I don't mean to bust up in your shop like I'm running things, but I can't continue to work for Connie and that's just the way it is," she explained as pleasantly as she could at the moment. "Anyway, I live right around the corner from here on Eucalyptus and I pass by your shop every day." She took a quick look around the empty, stale place and played with her hair twists. "I know how business is doing," she said with a pitiful grimace on her face.

"It's pretty terrible."

"You said it, I didn't."

An embarrassed silence hung between the two women. Business was terrible and whoever actually said it didn't matter — it was the truth. Business was worse than terrible, it sucked, and as Pat stood facing the presumptuous, hot-tempered woman she was sure of one thing. God had answered her prayer. This woman was the talk of the town in the world of hair. She had name recognition and could bring in the clients. She also obviously had a chip on her shoulder, a bad attitude, and a hint of conceit, but every gem has at least one flaw, Pat concluded.

"Anyway," the woman continued, "I can get a job anywhere I want and that's the truth," she said, giving the shop the once-over again. She curled her top lip as her gaze returned to Pat. "But," she sighed, "since this shop is so close to my apartment . . ."

"You're hired," Pat interrupted, realizing the great opportunity that stood before her and not wanting to waste another minute.

"And you're a very lucky lady," the woman said and batted her eyes. She smiled and extended her hand to Pat. "Zuma Price."

"Pat Brown," she said and returned the smile. "Welcome to Blessings."

Ever since that day Blessings had been swamped. Gone were the days of slouching around the shop, hoping, wishing, and praying that one, just one potential customer would poke her head through the door. Now Pat had to handle the fall-off customers Zuma couldn't get to because she was too swamped, as well as the few regulars she already had. But Pat didn't complain. A packed shop meant a packed bank account, and oh, what a blessing that was.

"Can we turn that music off for a minute please?" a plump brown face asked as she brushed by Pat to get back to her hair station. "My customer's got a headache," Faye said as she fluffed out the newly tightened weave she'd just sewn into her client's hair.

Pat excused herself from her own client and dashed to turn off the radio before joining Faye at her station. She stood behind the wide woman and leaned over her shoulder. "You haven't had a break all day, have you?"

"I've done two weaves, an African corn row, and that woman with the loose braids is next," she said as she spun her client around in her seat and handed her a mirror so she could examine the back of her head. "I'm gonna have to take a minute to eat before I start on the next one."

"No problem," Pat said and looked around the crowded shop. It was nine-thirty and still the place was jammed. But Pat knew Faye needed a break. Faye was as nice and polite as anyone could be, but when she was working on an empty stomach, she could get a bit testy. "You want me to run out to Popeye's and pick you up something?"

"No thanks," Faye said, wiping sweat off her forehead. "I've got some greens and tortillas warming up in the microwave."

Greens and tortillas, Pat thought, and winced. What a combination. But Faye was always bringing in strange combinations like that to eat. Yesterday it had been pig's feet with a side of Spanish rice and beans. Go figure, Pat thought as she watched Faye collect three hundred dollars from her customer, slip it into her jumbled cleavage, then hustle over to the microwave in the back of the room.

Faye Cruz was Pat's best friend and closest confidante. She was closer in age to her than Zuma so naturally they were tighter. Faye had been working at Blessings for just under four years now as the shop's one and only hair braider and weave specialist. Faye had been braiding hair ever since she was in elementary school, but she'd never thought she was capable of making money at it until after her husband died, leaving her with zero income and two mouths to feed. Faye had never worked a full-time job in her life until she came into the shop four years ago. And when she first walked through the door and found Pat in the back of the room dusting off countertops she nearly freaked and ran right back out the door. But it was too late. Pat had already gotten a glimpse of her and there was nothing left for Faye to do but exactly what she'd come there to do — ask for a job.

Faye was a whole two years younger than Pat, but if you saw the two together you'd swear Faye was old enough to be Pat's mother. It wasn't that Faye was ugly or had wrinkles or warts and such. It was just that she didn't do anything with herself. Thanks to her half-black, half-Mexican heritage, Faye had a head full of long and wavy hair that reached all the way down to her waist. Many women would love to have a head full of healthy hair like that, but all Faye ever did with it was pull it back and plait it in one long French braid that dangled down her back. You'd never find a ring in her ear or on her finger and the only jewelry she ever wore was the gold-plated face of the Virgin Mary that hung on a once gold, now rusted silver chain around her neck. She never, ever wore a drop of makeup so thank God she had smooth, glowing skin. Still, even the most natural face could use a spruce of lipstick every now and again. But the thing that most added to her aging appearance was the extra eighty-five pounds she carried on her frame. To see her walk, you'd swear she had arthritis by the slow way in which she moved around, her thick thighs blocking one another as she waddled. The extra weight not only added years to her face, it also added years to her mind. Faye couldn't remember which had come first — had she lost interest in herself, then gained all the weight or did she gain the weight, then lose interest. The only thing she was sure of was that she no longer cared. Why concern herself with trying to look good? Men weren't attracted to her anymore. Why concern herself with trying to lose weight? She couldn't do it anyway. She'd been on every diet known to man — Weight Watchers, Jenny Craig, Pritikin, the cabbage soup diet, the apple diet, the one meal a day pile anything you want on one plate and no more diet — none of them ever worked. So why concern herself at all? Faye was what she was. A thirty-three-year-old, five-foot-two, two-hundred-and-ten-pound woman. Why fight it?

But at moments like the one she experienced the night she walked into the shop to meet Pat, Faye wished she could instantly snap her fingers and make all her weight go away. She hated first sightings. Without fail, the first thing people did when they saw her was look her up and down and shake their heads. Then they'd pretend not to see her or, if forced to make her acquaintance, pretend as if the fact that she was large made no difference to them. But Faye knew her size affected people. People often dealt with Pat and her weight just as they would deal with a person who had a bad case of halitosis. They'd try to be nice and ignore it, but they knew it was there. There was no way you could miss it. Whoever came in contact with her had to deal with her problem and though they tried to act like they didn't notice it, she knew for a fact they did.

Faye tried not to let the curious way in which Pat gawked at her bother her on that first night they met. After all, it was nighttime, Pat was closing up, and in walked a complete stranger. Faye would have gawked too if she was in Pat's position. Still, Faye knew the peculiar look on Pat's face was more about her size than the fact that she was an unknown.

Faye had squeezed herself into her one and only church dress and jammed her swollen feet into a pair of white pumps. She approached Pat with the confidence anyone else would show when confronting a possible employer, but when she opened her mouth to state her purpose the only sound audible was that of her cries. "I need a job," she wailed and threw her hands over her face.

At first Pat had thought the woman was crazy. She backed away for a second and watched as the woman's stomach jiggled, pushing in and out, shoulders heaving up and down, her mouth seemingly stuck in the open position. But soon Pat's apprehension turned to compassion. She searched the countertops for a box of tissue, but couldn't find one.

Luckily Faye had come prepared. She opened up the tiny white patent leather purse she carried and searched around, pulling out her wallet, a rosary, and finally a crumpled tissue that looked like it had been used before. "I'm sorry, I'm sorry," Faye whimpered, wiping the sides of her face and trying to control herself. "It's just that I *need* a job and, and . . . I don't know where else to go." She dabbed at her nose and took a deep breath, knowing she was not making the great first impression that she had set out to display. She hadn't intended to beg or to cry, but she could not help herself. She was desperate. She had children. Mouths to feed. She needed money. "I've been braiding hair since I was ten," she spat out. "I do weaves, I, well . . . I'm not too good with chemicals, but I can help out on washing and conditioning, or if you just need someone to clean up the place . . ."

"Slow down," Pat said, more concerned with the woman's mental state than her verbal résumé.

"You don't understand. I *need* a job. I've got two children, my husband died and . . . and . . ."

"Ssh," Pat purred. "It's going to be all right," she said. "Everything's going to work out fine," she said, eyeing the rosary the woman still clutched in her hand. "Have you been using that?" she asked and touched the row of beads and the woman's hand. "Prayer works."

"I know," Faye said, suddenly finding strength in the woman's touch. The last time she'd gone to confession the pastor had told her she had to be strong. He told her to pray for strength, seek it out and meditate in it. She did. Still, when her mind was lulled into thoughts of her dead husband, seeing him slumped over, bleeding blood so red . . . "Oh God," Faye screamed as the tears began to flow again.

Pat felt so bad for the stranger that she took her in her arms right then and there and alone in the empty shop the two strangers held on to each other, neither one wanting to be the first to let go.

Two blessings were received that night. Faye found a job and Pat found a new friend.

Faye popped three quarters into the soda machine and retrieved her diet Sprite. As big as she was, she didn't know why she always opted for diet instead of regular, but she figured it was the least she could do. She took her bowl of greens and flour tortillas over to the sofa and sat down next to the woman with the loose braids. "I'll be with you in about ten minutes," she told her next client, then began to dig into her first meal of the day if you don't count the entire bag of Chips Ahoy she'd gone through at her hair station.

"What are you eating?" Loose Braids asked Faye just as she plopped a spoon full of greens in the center of her tortilla and rolled it up like a burrito. Faye bit into her cuisine and winced. She'd forgotten the salsa. But it was too late and she was too hungry to stop to go back to the refrigerator and get it. As she swallowed she turned to the woman and explained.

"Collard greens and tortillas," she told Loose Braids. "My mom used to cook this for my dad all the time. Would you like to taste?"

"No thank you," Loose Braids said, unaware of the frightful grimace she held on her face as she watched Faye chow down. "How did you come up with a combination like collard greens and tortillas?"

"When your mom is black and from the South and your father is a straight, traditional Mexican you find many different ways of compromising."

"Interesting," Loose Braids said, then quickly turned away.

As Faye swallowed another mouthful of her dinner she could feel all eyes turning on her. She couldn't understand why folks always liked to watch fat people eat. They stared at her as if she was doing something wrong. As if she were a diagnosed cancer patient smoking a cigarette. If there had been anywhere else for Faye to go she would have vanished. But since there wasn't she did the next best thing and tried to divert everyone's attention somewhere else. "So did we ever finish that conversation on O. J.?" she asked, politely covering her mouth as she spoke.

"Yes," Pat shouted quickly, not wanting to get all that started up again. She thought she'd closed the book on that conversation earlier, but Faye had defiantly opened it up again.

"Guilty!" Zuma sang as she sprayed her client's hair with oil sheen, then flagged her hand in front of her face as the cloudy fog engulfed her.

"Guilty," Pat's client chimed in and with that, Pat threw her hands in the air and walked off toward the rest room. She had been holding it for a long time and since she didn't want to hear another word about O. J. she decided to go handle her business, hoping against all hope that when she came back out the conversation would be finished for good.

"I say he's not guilty," Loose Braids said, and nodded to Faye as she downed another load of greens and tortillas.

Faye put her hand over her stuffed mouth before she spoke again. "I'm with you," she said, then swallowed.

"Look," Zuma shouted as she took the money her client held out for her and walked behind the woman toward the front door. "None of us will ever truly know whether O. J. did it or not," she said and paused to say a quick good-bye to her client. "But I'll tell you one thing—none of this mess would have ever gotten started if O. J. had been a true brother and stayed away from those white women."

"I know that's right," Pat's client said as she waited patiently for Pat to come back from the rest room.

"You ain't never told a lie," Loose Braids admitted and pursed her lips. "But when a black man gets a little money what's the first thing he does?"

"Runs over to the other side," Zuma said, and shook her head.

If there was one thing practically all the women in the shop could agree on, it was the fact that no black man should be married to a white woman. Not when there were so many single, eligible, intelligent, and attractive black women such as themselves to pick from.

Faye was the only one who didn't agree with this logic. She thought the women sounded just as racist and stupid as a white man who'd say his daughter could never date a nigger. Faye saw nothing wrong with black men dating or marrying white women. Love was love, regardless of color or culture, and if it weren't for interracial marriages, Faye wouldn't be alive today. Her black mother and Mexican father were the perfect example of color-blind love. Sure they had their cultural differences, but their love was stronger than any conflict that could ever arise between them. Not even their differences in religion could tear them apart. Faye's mother was Southern Baptist and her father a devout Catholic. But never did they argue over opposing ideologies or conflicting doctrines. The bottom line was that they both loved the Lord so they simply shared religions. One month they'd attend St. Joseph's cathedral, the next, Wholly Waters. Their differences added spice to their lives, not animosity. Faye could still remember the lazy Saturday nights she'd watch her mother and father sashaying to Aretha Franklin one minute, then doing the cha-cha to Antonio Carlos Jobim the next. One night her mother would prepare neck bones and corn bread, the next night she'd make mole and manzanas rellenas. Their love wasn't about color, it was about acceptance, give and take, honesty and compromise. Those were the biggest lessons Faye learned from her parents. They never sat down and gave her a lecture about it. She just picked it up from the way she saw them living and loving. They taught her what true love was all about and Antoine, her beloved husband, taught her all the rest. But now they were all gone and the only love Faye knew now was the sacrificial, selfless love a mother has for her children. Romantic love was a town too far away for Faye to visit again. But if she ever got the opportunity to go there she wouldn't let the mere color of someone's skin keep her from it.

Faye hadn't realized her thoughts had drifted so far away until Zuma's booming voice roared through the air and snapped her back to the present.

"Honey, it's not just the athletes and the actors who are chasing white girls anymore," she said incredulously. "Now these everyday broke, run-of-the-mill brothers are dumping the black queens for the *Baywatch* babes."

"And what's so wrong with that?" Faye asked and pushed her plate away. "If two people fall in love, why shouldn't they be together?"

"Because it's not about love," Zuma said quickly. "To black men, white girls are like special trophies. They look at us like we're cheap knock-offs of what a woman should be. Since we don't have the hair, the nose, the small tooty behinds, somehow we aren't worth as much."

"Black men have been brainwashed," Loose Braids said, and turned to face Faye. "Everything they see in this society tells them that white is right and black is wrong and they believe it. That's why they go after white girls. Because they think they are better than us."

"But that's not every case," Faye said, and shook her head. "Sometimes it's really about love. Take Marcia Clark and Chris Darden, for instance."

"They fucking?" Zuma asked.

"*Zuma*," Faye said and winced. "Don't be so crass."

"Well are they?"

"Well, Marcia says they weren't, but Darden seemed to disagree," Loose Braids said. "And that's exactly what I'm talking about. Why Chris got to be all on the white girls' tip? A sister would love to be with a man like that. I know I'd take that big bald head of his and love him right," she said, and snapped her fingers to let everyone know she *meant* that.

"But that's what I mean. Maybe it was love for Chris. I mean he and Marcia were together all day, every day, for months. Can't you see how he could fall for her?" Faye said, flagging her hands in the air.

But her opponents were not willing to give in to her point of view.

"Blacks should stick with blacks and that's all I've got to say," Zuma said with finality, but Faye wasn't going to let it go.

"Look at us," Faye continued as she pointed to each woman around the room. "Look at all the different shades of brown we have in here. Not one of us can say we are one hundred percent pure black. The races have been mixing since the beginning of time," she said, then pointed directly at Zuma. "Look at you," she said as Zuma froze. "You're lighter than most white people. You ought to be thankful for race mixing or else you wouldn't be here."

Zuma squinted her eyes and seemed to boil with anger. "Thankful? Yeah right," she said and threw her hands in the air. "Thank you, Mr. Slave Owner, for creeping into the shed house and raping my black ancestors. Thank you ever so kindly," she said, then ran a hand through her twisted hair. "That's nothing to be thankful for, Faye."

"Well you're here, aren't you?" Faye asked, directly. "And so am I," she said, and pointed to herself as she stood up. "I'm thankful my Mexican father fell in love with my black mother. If he had thought like you guys I wouldn't be here today," she said with an increased intensity. "I myself married a Mexican because I fell in love with a Mexican," she said, defensively. "You can't stop love because it doesn't come wrapped in the package you're most accustomed to."

"No," Zuma interrupted. "You married a Mexican because you're part Mexican yourself. You can't even understand what us black women go through. Do you really know how it feels to be passed over by a black man? You don't know what the black woman's struggle is all about."

The loose, deep, caramel-colored skin on Faye's arm dangled as she lifted her arm high above her head. "Who cares if I'm half Mexican? With skin this dark I got called nigger so many times growing up that I forgot all about being Mexican. So don't act like just because you claim to be so *Muslim* and pro-black that you're the only one in here who knows about the struggle."

"Damn, Señorita," Zuma said, realizing how personally Faye was taking this conversation. "I didn't mean to hurt your feelings. Come on, Mami," she said, hurrying over to Faye with her arms outstretched. "Dame un besso," she said, puckering her lips and making kissy sounds.

"That's not funny, Zuma," Faye said and pushed her away, then shyly looked around the room full of ladies. It was rare for Faye to raise her voice, but sometimes Zuma could really get under her skin.

"Well, don't get your panties in a knot," Zuma said.

"Don't you worry about my chones, brrruja," Faye shot back.

"What did you just call me?"

"Nothing," Faye said coyly and sat back down.

"Don't be speaking that Spanish shit behind my back," Zuma warned.

"Cayate."

"No, you shut up," Zuma said, nodding her head.

"Whatever," Faye said, giving up.

"Fine," Zuma said and backed her way to her hair station.

"Good," Faye said louder.

"Great," Zuma scolded.

"Beautiful."

"Dandy."

This would be a good time for one of Pat's jokes, but she was still locked away in the rest room. The tension in the air was so thick between Zuma and Faye that the other ladies in the shop sat silently on edge, unsure if the scene they were watching was a fake argument or the real thing. But Faye and Zuma both knew were they stood. They'd always had this ongoing animosity toward one another, bickering back and forth over silly things. Sometimes it seemed they took opposite sides on a subject just to keep an argument churning. Or at least Zuma would. With the way Zuma picked away at Faye's nerves, one would assume she hated the woman. But that wasn't the case at all. There was love between Faye and Zuma. They could both feel it and sometimes it even showed. Like the times when Faye's car would break down and Zuma would go out of her way to pick her up for work. Or the times Zuma would run out of change for the soda machine and ask Faye if she could break a dollar. Their relationship was an unusual one, but unusual wasn't a bad thing. Just odd.

"Look," Zuma said as she sat down at her hair station. "All I'm saying is that black women are just as good as white women and brothers need to recognize that. I may not have hair all down my back or a pointy nose or a flat behind, but I'm just as beautiful as any white women in this world," she said, rolling her eyes. She took both of her hands and ran them over her face, through her hair, then across her chest as if she were the starring vixen in a porno flick. "Look at all this loveliness," she said, and licked out her tongue so ridiculously that it caused Faye to hang her head in embarrassment. "You tell me what white woman could compete with this?" she said, trying to hold back a giggle.

And with that, a hush fell over the room. It seemed as though the sentence Zuma spoke had performed a magic all its own. At once, every eye in the shop focused on the front entrance and the strange woman who appeared in the doorway. Zuma was the last to focus her attention, but when she noticed the silence in the room she followed the glares of all the other women until she too was eyeing the doorway and the woman with straight blond hair and eyes the color of the sky who stood there. None of the brown faces in the shop uttered another word, but the vibe could be heard loud and clear.

What the hell is she doing here?

Sandy Dew McReiney stood in the doorway, tossing back each and every stare that came her way. The tension in the room was thick enough to bite into, and for a split second Sandy had thought about turning right around and going back home. Then again, she was used to this kind of reception. She'd been through it all her life, but that didn't make it any more bearable. She walked into the beauty shop and stood next to the reception desk knowing full well that every eye was upon her, but that no one would bother to speak. She could hear the whispers the ladies shot back and forth between themselves. *What she want in here? She must be lost.*

Sandy shifted her weight from side to side, wishing she'd gone bare instead of putting on the thong bikini underwear that was beginning to irritate her butt. Slyly, she slid her hand behind her back and grabbed the thin string through her Lycra leggings and yanked it to one side. She smirked as she tapped the three and a half inch heels of her stilettos, still waiting for someone, anyone, to say something to her.

They hate me because I'm white, she thought, a theory that had haunted her nearly all her life. She was always the minority, the only white in the bunch. She and her mother had always lived in predominantly black neighborhoods until her mother up and moved them to her new boyfriend's house in the San Fernando Valley when Sandy was sixteen. She hated that city and couldn't wait to get out of there. She had felt so out of place, so void of flavor out there amongst the upwardly mobile white folks who rolled the Ventura Boulevard with their car tops down. A Valley girl was something Sandy was not cut out to be, and on her seventeenth birthday she left her mother and moved back to Los Angeles on her own. The move wasn't only because she hated the Valley. The fact that her mom's boyfriend kept sneaking into her bedroom at night had a lot to do with it too. Still, in her heart, Sandy was black and felt more comfortable being a part of the black culture. She wasn't country or rock and roll. She was hip-hop smoothed out on the R&B tip. She was hot links and baked beans. She was *Ebony* magazine, forget *Vogue* and *Cosmopolitan*. She was black, through and through, only you couldn't tell that by looking at her. You could catch a glimpse of it when she spoke, though. Her speech was laden with the slang of the streets, the hip sayings of the day, the "Yo, what's up's" and the "Just chillin's." On more than one occasion Sandy had been accused of trying to act black or trying to talk black. But Sandy wasn't *trying* anything. She acted and talked the way she'd been taught. The way all the other kids spoke in the neighborhoods she grew up in. It wasn't an act to show how down she was. It was her true self. Straight, no chaser.

Sandy turned away from the reception desk and looked through the crowd of brown faces for one that seemed halfway polite. She sucked her teeth, knowing still that no one would even smile her way. Forget these broads, Sandy thought, and ran a hand through her long blond hair. She'd done that on purpose. If there was one thing she knew black women hated her for more than her skin, it was her hair. Yes, Sandy thought as she needlessly flung her hair from side to side. It's all mine, no weave, no chemicals, just mine. Long, naturally blond and manageable. Jealous? She smiled to herself as her audience turned up their noses and rolled their eyes. Well, fuck y'all too, Sandy thought, tiring of the silent treatment. She looked through the crowd of faces again and cleared her throat. "Is anybody running this place or am I standing here for my health?" she asked in her deepest, most aggravated voice.

Instead of an answer all she received were more intense stares. Stares that if audible would say, "No, she didn't," or "She's got her nerve."

Sandy sighed and put her hand on her hip in preparation to speak again, but this time with more fervor. Just then a door in the back of the room opened and out came Pat. She breezed through the shop and stopped at Zuma's hair station. "Remind me to order some more toilet paper from the warehouse tomorrow," she said hurriedly, wiping her damp hands on a paper towel. "Did you hear me, Zuma?" she asked, but got no response. She looked at Zuma carefully, then around the shop at the other patrons. "What's going on?" she said, then let the stares of everyone else point her in the right direction. "Oh, we've got another customer," Pat said and headed toward the reception desk. "Hi, what can I do for you?" she said to Sandy with a big smile.

Just then the phone rang out and Pat bent herself over the desk to pick it up.

"Excuse me for a second," she said to Sandy as she put the phone to her ear.

Sandy waited patiently for Pat to finish her conversation. By that time most of the other women had ceased staring at her—except for Zuma. Fed up, Sandy began to stare right back at her. The two locked eyes for what seemed to be hours, neither one of them wanting to blink or dare to be the one to look away first.

When Pat hung up the phone she placed her hand on Sandy's shoulder. "I'll be right with you in a minute, darling," she said, and rushed over to her hair station where she'd left her last client. Just then the phone rang out again and Pat pleaded for patience from her client and ran back to pick it up. She gave Sandy another "I'll be right with you," then put the phone to her ear and pulled out her appointment book. She made a notation, then hung up the phone, only to have it ring a split second later. She smiled regretfully at Sandy and picked up the phone again. "It's for you," she screamed to Faye and laid the phone on her shoulder.

Faye had already taken Loose Braids to her hair station and began unraveling her long, frazzled hair. "Take a message, please," she shouted back, too caught up in the business of hair to stop for the phone.

Pat did her duty, hung up the phone, then looked around the shop. It was almost ten o'clock and the place was still packed. Zuma had two heads left, Faye was working on her last, but that was a braid job and would take at least another two hours. And in addition, there was her own client she'd left at her own station. Pat's nerves were on the verge of exploding and when the phone rang out for the fourth time in less than two minutes she screamed. "What is this?" she shouted and snatched up the phone — *again*.

Sandy continued to wait patiently as she glanced at Pat, watching her book another appointment and concluding that she liked the tall woman even though she did think she smiled just a bit too much. Anyone who smiled that much has got to be truly unhappy about something, Sandy thought to herself. Still, her first impression of Pat was cool. As for the rest of them, she thought, and turned to face the others in the room — they can all kiss my white, freckled behind.

She boldly stared over toward Zuma again and found her still staring back.

"So what were we talking about earlier?" Zuma said, obviously talking to Faye, but refusing to take her eyes off Sandy.

Faye looked over at Sandy with apprehension and squeaked out, "I don't remember."

"I do," Loose Braids said confidently. "We were talking about all those white women stealing our black men."

"Don't start any mess," Faye interceded, and gave Zuma a cautioning glare.

"The mess has been started already," Zuma said, still glaring at the white intruder. "All I'm saying is that if these white women weren't so conniving maybe the brothers would marry us."

"I heard that," Loose Braids said. "Have you seen the way white women throw themselves at our men? Pathetic."

"Mmm-hmm. They need to get their own men and stay away from ours."

"My mother always told my brother," Loose Braids added, "if she can't use your comb, don't bring her home."

That comment ignited a chuckle throughout the shop. Even the fair-minded Faye had to laugh, but just for a second. "That's enough, you guys," Faye said sternly. "Let's be nice," she said and smiled apologetically toward Sandy.

"Oh don't mind me," Sandy retorted confidently, then looked back at Zuma. "Maybe if the black man was being taken care of he wouldn't have to look outside his own kingdom for a good woman."

Oh. It was on then.

Zuma's mouth dropped wide open and again all eyes returned to the white girl with the attitude, and though no one said a direct word to her the comments were loud and clear. "That bitch gon' get her ass beat up in here," she heard someone say.

"Well, come on with it," Sandy said, too bold and too proud to hide behind a whisper.

Pat put down the phone and picked up on the taut strain lingering through the room again. "Something wrong?" she said, not knowing fully what was going on. Then she paused for a moment and it hit her. Pat shook her head, knowing this was a *color thang* and felt sorry for the black women who were so insecure with themselves that the mere presence of a white woman could put them on edge. She was too much of a Christian to be ruled by race. As far as she was concerned the white girl standing beside her was just as much her sister as the darkest woman in the room. After all, everyone is a child of God, Pat thought. Still, she knew she had to do something to break the ice. "I've got a joke for you all," she said as she stepped from behind the reception desk, oblivious to the sighs the other women blew out. "Why did Buckwheat wash his clothes in Tide?"

Faye, her partner in peacemaking, was the only one who was paying attention. "Why?"

"Because it was too cold to wash his clothes out-Tide. Get it? Out-Tide, *outside?*"

"Got it," Zuma huffed with a frown.

Pat's joke had not brought peace, but it did shift the waves. She glanced over toward Zuma, then to Sandy. "Okay," she said pleasantly. "What can I do for you? You need an appointment, hair, braids? How can I help you, honey?"

"Well, I —"

"Excuse me again, sweetie," Pat said and reached for the phone for the umpteenth time. She told whoever it was to hold, then turned her attention back to Sandy. "Sorry about that. It's just that we're so busy around here."

"That's a good thing, ain't it?" Sandy said, and leaned her elbow on the reception desk.

"Yes, I guess it is. But no more interruptions. How can I help you?" Pat said and opened up her appointment book.

"Oh, I ain't here for no appointment," Sandy explained. "Actually, I wanted to know if you could use a little help around the shop."

Pat blinked her eyes rapidly. "Help, honey?"

"Yeah. I do nails," she said, and motioned towards the manicuring station. "I just got my license last week and I've been eyeing that Help Wanted sign on your front door for the past month, hoping it would still be there when I graduated."

"Is that right?" Pat said, obviously caught off guard. This was the last thing she'd expected the woman to say. She looked her over more carefully, examining the painfully high heels the woman wore, the extra tight leggings and the fitted T-shirt. She certainly didn't look like a manicurist, Pat thought. Then again, just what does a manicurist look like, she questioned herself. Then Pat looked down at the woman's hands and nearly squawked. Her nails were so chewed and battered that Pat could have sworn the woman used them to buff bricks. You call yourself a manicurist, Pat thought. Then almost as if psychic, the woman pulled out her graduation certificate from the Inglewood School of Beauty.

"Here you go," Sandy said and handed the certificate to Pat and watched as she looked it over. "I do it all. Acrylic, porcelain, pedicures— the whole hook-up. I got my license right here at the beauty school on Broadway."

"Uh-huh," Pat said, bewildered, and as Sandy watched the confusion on Pat's face she became defensive.

"Uh-huh," Sandy mimicked. "What? Is there a problem?"

"No," Pat said, and plastered a smile onto her face.

"So what's the deal? I mean, don't you need help around here? Isn't that what you got that sign in the window for?"

"Well yes, but—"

"But what? Is it because I'm white?" Sandy snapped, realizing that Pat was just like every other black woman she'd met. Prejudiced.

"Now hold on, honey. Don't start none, won't be none," Pat said with authority. "Your color has nothing to do with this. It's just that I wasn't prepared for this. Do you know it's almost ten o'clock at night? Most people who are serious about employment go job hunting in the daytime."

"Well, excuse me for having a three-year-old and a ten-month-old to look after, okay. This was the only time I could get away. And what's the difference? The shop is still open."

Pat paused and smiled really hard. She wanted to be sure that this woman knew she was not trying to be unfair. It was just that she didn't know what to say. "I'm gonna have to give this some thought," she said as the woman eyed her suspiciously. "What's your name?"

"Sandy," she huffed. "Sandy Dew McReiney."

"What a pretty name," she said and offered her hand. "I'm Pat," she said as they touched palms. "As you can see," she said, and held out her other hand toward the group of ladies in the room, "I'm pretty swamped right now, so why don't you come back tomorrow morning before we get too busy and we can talk about this further."

Sandy curled her top lip and shifted all her weight to one leg. "Come back, huh?"

"I'm not brushing you off, honey. Just come back in the morning when I'll have some time to really consider this. Can you do that?"

"Yeah, I can do that. *If* you're on the real."

Pat glanced over at Zuma, wishing she had her there to interpret for her. But after a slight pondering she realized *on the real* must mean truthful. "Yes I am," Pat said, so happy she'd gotten it. "I'll see you tomorrow," she said, and tapped Sandy's shoulder.

"Peace," Sandy said as she backed her way to the door. She gave Zuma one last stare, then swung her long blond hair and went on her way.

"Good riddance," Zuma shouted as the door closed. "What the hell did she want anyway?"

"Mind your own business," Pat said as she headed back to her hair station, still looking over Sandy's manicurist certificate. "We'll talk later."

"Mmm-hmm," Zuma said as she eyed Pat like a hawk. "We'll talk all right."

It was a quarter to midnight when Faye closed the door behind the shop's last customer and locked it. Pat sat behind the reception desk, counting the day's receipts and recording them on the finance page of her day book. Zuma stood beside the shop's window, peering out into the black night, rubbing her hands through a thick pink solution, trying to get off the burgundy cellophane she'd applied to her last customer's hair. It had been a long day for all the ladies and in less than seven hours they'd all have to start over again.

"What time's my first appointment?" Zuma asked Pat as she walked over to the reception desk.

Pat moved her day book aside and opened the appointment book to Saturday. "You've got a seven-thirty relaxer touch-up and an eight o'clock press and curl. Then at nine-fifteen —"

"Okay, okay," Zuma said, holding up a hand and letting out a sigh.

"What about me?" Faye asked and joined the girls.

"You've got an eight o'clock, but she wants tiny, individual braids so you know what that means."

"Six hours if I'm lucky."

"Yep," Pat said, and slid her finger down the page of the book. "Then at three, you've got a weave, and at five you've got —"

"I know. *Another* weave."

"That's right," Pat said as she moved her finger across the page to check on her own schedule. She found that she had a seven-thirty blow and curl, an eight-thirty virgin relaxer, a nine-fifteen finger wave, and *oh*, she thought and slammed the book shut. What a long day laid ahead of her. She always knew that her business would be a success, but she had never imagined it to this degree. Over the past three years, the shop had taken over her life. Not that she had much of a life before. It was just she and her husband, and to be totally honest, with the problems their relationship had been going through lately, it was better for her to stay busy at work than to go home and deal with him.

Still, she wished she had more time on her hands to spend doing the things she'd like to do — like sleep, or watch a movie, read a book, or her most favorite pastime of all — doing absolutely nothing. But time was a luxury for her at this point in her life and she could do little to change that fact. *Unless*, she thought as she sat behind her desk and leaned back into her chair. *Unless* . . .

"What you over there daydreaming about?" Zuma asked, heading back to her hair station to straighten up her counter.

Pat got up from her seat and walked to the middle of the shop to face Zuma. She beckoned for Faye, who was busy gathering up long pieces of hair extensions, to stop what she was doing. "I've got a question for you both," she said to the ladies, and put a finger to the side of her cheek. "You remember that girl who stopped by tonight?"

"The white girl?" Faye asked, laying her extensions across the back of a chair.

Zuma curled up her lip. "What about her?"

"Well," Pat started and began to pace the floor. "She was looking for a job and I was figuring—"

"Oh hell no," Zuma interrupted. She plopped her hair bag down in a chair. "She ain't working off in here. No, no. I don't like her attitude."

"You don't even know the girl," Faye said, and crossed the floor to Zuma's station.

"I may not know her name, but I know her game."

"*Zuma.*"

"*Faye,*" she mocked back.

"*Ladies!*" Pat said, stopping it before it could get started. "I think we could use the help. It doesn't make any sense for us to still be in this shop at midnight. We need someone to pick up the slack."

"Well, is she qualified?" Faye asked.

"She just graduated with a manicurist's license. I was thinking she could start off with nails, then help out with washing and conditioning. Doesn't take too much expertise to wash someone's hair."

"I don't need no help," Zuma huffed.

"You're slower than a crippled snail, Zuma," Faye said, then looked around the shop. "I know I could use someone to help me take down braids."

"And she could help out with the phones and booking appointments too," Pat said and put her hands on her hips, satisfied with the way things were coming together in her head.

"I don't like her," Zuma snapped, and continued clearing off her counter. "She's got too much attitude for me."

"Look who's talking," Faye said, and laughed.

"Well, there can only be one diva around this joint, and I've already claimed that title."

"Well, there is only one owner of this joint," Faye said as she went back to arranging her hair extensions. "It's your decision, Pat."

"I know," Pat said. She walked over to Zuma and put her hand on her shoulder as a gesture of peace. "I told the girl to come back tomorrow so I'd have time to think things over."

"Hmm," Zuma moaned. "I hope you make the right decision."

"Oh, Zuma," Faye grunted. "You don't like her just because she's white. I swear you are the most racist person I've ever seen in all my days."

"I am not racist," Zuma quipped. "I am pro-black. There's a difference."

"Oh really?"

"Yes, really."

"Whatever."

"Whatever back to you."

"Fine."

"Good."

"Perfect."

"Excellent."

"Stop it!" Pat shouted and turned to walk back to the reception desk.

"But—" Zuma said, only to be stopped.

"Zip it. Button it. Lock it, and throw away the key," Pat insisted as she sat down behind the desk, missing the snarl Zuma pitched in her direction.

Faye took a bundle of weaving hair, tied it in a knot, and placed it back into its package. Then she picked up her old battered satchel and tossed the hair inside with the rest of the unused fake locks and moved it to the side. She gathered up a collection of magazines her clients had left at her hair station and took them back to the magazine rack near the sofa. As she put them down she peered at the crumpled magazine on top and shook her head. "That poor baby," she said, eyeing the cover of the *National Enquirer* with grief.

"What you boo-hooing about over there?" Zuma asked. "The little girl in Colorado. You know, the beauty queen. What a shame," she said staring at the sweet face on the wrinkled paper.

"Oh yeah, what's her name? Janet, Jesse?" she asked as she walked closer to Faye.

"JonBenet Ramsey," Faye said and turned the *National Enquirer* around to show Zuma the picture."

"Fuck that little white girl," Zuma said and snatched the paper from Faye's hand.

Faye gasped at Zuma and snatched the paper back. "What are you talking about? This is a tragedy. That girl was only eight years old when somebody raped and killed her."

"Fuck her!" Zuma said, raising her voice.

"You've got a problem," Faye said, disgusted with Zuma's attitude.

"Girl, this stuff happens every day in the black community and nobody gives a motherfuck," Zuma spit out. "But just because this girl was white and rich she's getting all this national coverage. How come they didn't make a big to-do about that little baby in Compton who got shot playing in its front yard last week? Huh? I'll tell you why, because the baby was black. And what about that child out there in Chicago, uh, uh . . . Baby

X?" she said, snapping her fingers. "Why didn't that get national attention? Because nobody cares when a black child dies, that's why. But let a little white baby bite it and the whole fucking world goes crazy."

"There you go with that black, white mess again. You need to get over it, Zuma. Every life is a sacred life."

"Except when you're black," Zuma retorted as she sprayed Windex on her station's mirror and went at it with a paper towel. "Black babies are dying around here left and right, and nobody gives a damn. Fuck 'em. Just let 'em die. They weren't going to be anything anyway."

"Well, it's the black people who are killing the black children, Zuma. They are dying because of gangs and drug dealing. Black-on-black crime, Zuma. That's what's going on."

"You don't have to preach to me," Zuma said, with an innocent air. "I know the deal. But let me ask you this. If white kids were killing each other through gangs or drugs, do you think this government would let that go on?"

"I—"

"Hell no," Zuma shouted. "The president would be on the TV every day. Drugs would be off the streets. Guns would be gone."

"Whatever, Zuma," Faye sighed. "It's too late at night to be politicizing."

" 'Cause you know I'm right."

"Fine," Faye said, waving her off.

"Yeah, fine."

"Great."

"Wonderful."

"Oh mi cabeza."

"Don't start that Spanish shit."

"Pat, would you please tell Zuma to be quiet, por favor," Faye said as she plopped down in her seat and massaged the sides of her head. When she got no answer from Pat, she turned around to see what was going on.

Pat had long since removed herself from Faye and Zuma's discussion. She couldn't bare the topic. Faye and Zuma gave each other a look and decided it was time to shut up for real. They both busied themselves with their preparations to leave, both knowing that they had slipped into a discussion that was too much for Pat to deal with. Pat never joined in on discussions about children. The topic only bought her sadness.

Children were the one thing missing in Pat's life. She had everything else. A loving husband, a beautiful home, her own business. But the one thing she wanted the most was the one thing that she had been denied.

When she and her husband married ten years ago, the first thing she had done was toss out her birth control pills. She'd expected to be pregnant within months, but after two years of trying she'd gotten no results. Next came a visit to her doctor, then tests and more tests, then a diagnosis. Pat was infertile.

When Pat first learned of her infertility she became so despondent that for a while her husband had seriously considered checking her into a psychiatric hospital. To say she was depressed was an understatement. Pat had felt so low that she could not see herself up. Her husband had tried to comfort her, but there was no way he could. He didn't understand what she felt. She couldn't explain it. She was barren. She felt less than a woman, less than a human being. She had all the parts God had given her, they were all in the right places, but they would not, could not do their jobs. Not being able to have a baby was like having nineteen dollars in the bank and trying to use the ATM machine. It was so frustrating that at times Pat would get so angry that she'd beat the walls until the angst inside subsided, leaving only an empty feeling so hollow that Pat thought she'd never be able to be happy again.

It wasn't until Pat's husband bought her the beauty shop that Pat began to come alive again. The shop had given her an outlet, a place to pour her attention, a project to fill her mind. It was just the gift she needed. He'd do anything to save his wife from the terrifying depression he'd watched slowly take her over. Still, to this day the relationship between Pat and Mark had never returned to the way it had been when they first got married, and to be honest the blame lay mostly on the shoulders of Pat. She knew Mark loved and supported her in everything she did, still somehow she felt unworthy of that love. Unworthy of him. Instead of moving closer to her husband in her time of pain and need, Pat began to push him away. It wasn't that she blamed him for the fact that she couldn't have a baby. His sperm were fine. It was Pat who had the problem. Still, it was her husband, the closest person to her, who bore the brunt of her discontent.

Of the three ladies, only Faye had been blessed with children. Zuma was nearing the age of thirty and was still without a child, but unlike Pat, all of Zuma's parts were in working condition. The only reason she had no children was because she couldn't find the proper father to impregnate her. For her, too, children were the only thing missing in her life. She had been wanting a child ever since she was twenty-one years old, but she wanted to do it the right way. She'd seen too many women in her lifetime, fooling around with loser after loser, only to wind up pregnant and be left alone to raise the child as a single mother. She didn't want that for herself. She wanted a husband, a man who could support her and her baby. But after years of searching for Mr. Right, she'd come up empty.

Still, her desire for a child was strong and five years ago she decided it was time to stop waiting for a man to come into her life and give her the things she needed. Zuma planned to be pregnant by the time she turned thirty. It was a goal she'd set for herself five years ago and with her thirtieth birthday less than a month away she was right on schedule. Zuma had a master plan and she was working it to her advantage. She knew what she was doing and one day very soon she'd have a child. A child that would take away the pain of the secret she'd been keeping for so many years.

"It's time for me to get outta here," Zuma said, and flung her hair bag over her shoulder.

"I'm outta here too," Faye added, and did the same.

Pat grabbed her purse from underneath the reception desk and sat it on top. She searched it for her car keys and pulled them out just as Faye walked up and grabbed the phone from beside her.

"Come on, Faye," Zuma shouted as she waited at the front door for the other ladies. It was Faye's paranoid insistence that they all walk out together for safety reasons, yet she was holding everyone up. "Who you calling anyway? You ain't got no man."

"Besa mi culo, brrruja," Faye wanted to shout. But telling Zuma to kiss her ass was too unkind, so she ignored her pest and waited for someone to pick up at her home. She wanted to remind her older daughter to unlock the top latch on the front door so that she could get in, but when the phone picked up on the other end, it was not her daughter's voice who greeted her.

"Hello," the voice squeaked playfully.

"Christopher," Faye said. "What are you still doing up?"

"Nothing."

"Boy, it's midnight. You know you ought to be in bed. I told Antoinette you were to be asleep by nine o'clock," Faye huffed and pursed her lips together. "Put that girl on the phone."

"She's not here, Mami."

Instantly, Faye panicked. "She's not what?"

"She's been gone since the *Power Rangers* went off TV. But I've been a good boy, Mami. I've been taking care of myself," Faye's son said with pride. "I'm hungry, though," he whimpered. "I tried to reach the raviolis in the cabinet, but I fell off the chair."

"Oh Dios," Faye said quickly and put her hand over her eyes. "Are you all right, mijo? Did you hurt yourself?"

"Unh-unh."

"All right, baby. I'm on my way. Are the doors locked, the windows closed?"

"Yep."

"All right. I'm coming home," Faye said, and slammed down the phone as tears of frustration welled up in her eyes. "I'm gonna skin that girl alive," she shouted and rushed as quickly as her thick legs would let her. Her sixteen-year-old daughter had left her six-year-old son at home by himself. *Again.*

"Let's go," she shouted to Pat and Zuma as she walked out the door, mumbling to herself.

Pat and Zuma gave each other a look, knowing by now that the only time Faye got upset was when her daughter screwed up. Pat flipped off the lights and walked out behind Zuma, then locked the door.

"Another day come and gone," Zuma said, and walked into the parking lot beside Pat as they both watched Faye slam the door of her car and speed off.

"Yes," Pat said, as she stuck her key in the car door. "And what a blessed day it was."

2

Faye pulled her beat-up four-door into the driveway of her small, boxy house and yanked the keys from the ignition. She'd driven the three miles from the shop down Manchester like a bat out of hell as horrible thoughts swarmed through her mind about what could happen to her young son at home all by himself. Like many streets in Inglewood, theirs was well-kept and clean, but that didn't stop the violence and the crime from sneaking in. Mrs. Johnson, her seventy-four-year-old neighbor from two doors down, had had her home burglarized just three weeks earlier, and Faye's own home had even been hit last year just before Christmas. They had stolen every gift beneath the tree and were about to snatch the television set, but it must have been too heavy, Faye had figured. She had found it lying on its side in front of the doorway when she'd come home from work. Without even stepping foot inside the house she began to cry uncontrollably. Faye had saved over a thousand dollars, which she had spent on a slew of lavish gifts for her children last year, and to have it all taken away just two weeks before Christmas was nearly enough to break her. Pat and Zuma had loaned her enough money to replace most of the gifts, but that didn't take away the feeling of violation Faye felt over having the gifts she'd bought with her own hard-earned money stripped away from her by some low-life degenerate.

Although Faye only rented her house, she still felt the sting of the ever-decreasing property values in her neighborhood. More and more, the good, hardworking black folks who made Inglewood the outstanding community it had grown to be in the eighties were moving out and on to greener, safer pastures. And, slowly but surely, gangs were creeping into the once outstanding community. Drugs were seeping out of the woodwork and a new, trifling crop of residents was moving in. The type of residents even black folk themselves referred to as niggas. Her son was not safe alone in that house by himself. No one was safe around here anymore.

But this was not the first time Faye's daughter had pulled a stunt like this and left her six-year-old son at home alone. Faye had told her daughter over and over again that she needed to be responsible and take care of her younger brother until Faye made it home from work. But talking to Antoinette was like talking to a brick wall. Everything Faye told her to do seemed to go in one ear and out the other and it was time, Faye thought as she walked onto her front porch, that Antoinette grew up. "This has got to stop," Faye mumbled to herself as she walked inside. "Antoinette has got to learn."

"Mami," Christopher squealed as he belted toward Faye and wrapped his arms around one of her thick thighs.

"Mejito," she replied and patted the top of his wavy, black hair, then slid her hand downward and tugged on his ponytail. Her son's hair was thick and long and ever since he was a baby, Faye refused to cut it. Instead, she kept his hair pulled back into a ponytail just as her husband had kept his own hair, and when her son looked up at her with those hazel eyes and greeted her with a smile, Faye tingled from his love, noticing as she always did just how much he looked liked his father. "Are you all right?" she asked as she peeled her eyes from her son and glanced around the room. It seemed every light in the house was on, not to mention both the TV and the radio. The boy must have been scared, Faye concluded, and looked down into her son's face again. "Are you sure you're all right?" she asked and stroked his cheek.

"Uh-huh," he said, and let go of her thigh. "I'm hungry, though, Mami. Can we go to 'Donald's?"

"McDonald's is closed, baby," she said, and made her way over to the radio and turned it off.

"But I'm hungry. I want 'Donald's."

"Please don't start whining," Faye said, frowning as she turned off one of the lights in the front room. She walked to the hallway and flicked off that light as well. "Now where is your sister?"

"I'm *hungry*."

Faye sighed and turned to her son. He was still in his school clothes, she noticed as she walked over to him and grabbed him by the hand. "Come on here, boy," she said and walked him to the kitchen.

Again she found the light on, plus a turned-over chair beside the counter where he must have fallen earlier. She picked up the chair and put it in its proper place, then reached into the open cabinet and pulled down a can of raviolis. "Get the can opener," she told him, but he'd already taken care of that part.

"Let me do it," he said and took the can from Faye and went to the kitchen table. Carefully, he opened the can as Faye had taught him, then grabbed a bowl off the counter and poured in the raviolis. Faye stood back and watched as her son took the bowl to the microwave and set the timer. He was such a good son, she thought, and smiled watching him eye the bowl as it spun around inside the microwave. Although Christopher was only six, Faye could already see that he had the makings of a responsible, intelligent adult. He was so dependable, so thoughtful, so much like his father and so very little like his sister.

"Did Antoinette say where she was going?" she asked him as he sat down at the table to finish waiting on his dinner.

"Unh-uh," he said and lifted his shoulders.

"You mean she just up and left without saying a word?" Faye asked incredulously. Then she realized this was Antoinette she was talking about and suddenly that scenario didn't seem so incredible anymore.

Christopher looked as if he was thinking really hard, then he held up a finger. "She did say something before she left, Mami."

"What?" Faye asked, hoping this would be the clue to where her daughter had snuck off to.

"She called me a punk," Christopher said and sulked. "She punched me in the arm too."

Faye sighed. "What else happened?"

"Well, I was watching *The Terminator* with Arnold Schwarzenegger on HBO," he said quite seriously. "Then she came in and turned the channel to MTV. Then I snatched the remote and turned it back, 'cause that wasn't fair, Mami. I was watching the TV first. Then she pushed me and called me a punk and I shoved her back and then she turned the TV again and I said, I'ma tell Mami on you, then she called me a punk again, and—"

"What happened after all that?"

"Then that boy came to the door."

That boy, Faye thought as her otherwise understated temper began to boil. She'd told Antoinette she wasn't to see *that boy* anymore. He was too damn old for her and though Antoinette had lied and said he was just sixteen, Faye hadn't been fooled. The boy was over six feet tall and at least two hundred pounds and unless he was eating Miracle Gro every night for dinner, there was no way he could have made it to that size by the age of sixteen.

Faye had seen the boy her daughter called Shock G just one time before. He'd come to the door one Sunday afternoon asking if Antoinette could come outside. Faye looked over the dark-skinned boy with the shaved head, loose-fitting clothes, and earrings in both ears, and fixed her mouth to say tell him to go away. But Antoinette had flown out of her room and to the front door so fast that all Faye could do was stand in the doorway and watch as her daughter cozied up beside the over-grown boy and batted her eyes, acting as if she was a full-grown woman instead of a sixteen-year-old girl who wasn't even mature enough to handle washing her own clothes without turning all the whites to pink and red.

When Antoinette found Faye snooping, she gave her a look that shouted *mind your own business*, and Faye closed the front door. But the overpro-tective mother in her would not allow her to walk away. She smashed her stomach to the door, stood on her tiptoes, and watched the two of them through the peephole. Their conversation was muffled, but there was no mistaking the sneaky hand the boy slid down Antoinette's back or the sly tongue that slipped out his mouth just as he leaned over to kiss her.

"That's enough," Faye said as she flung open the door and stared at her daughter. "Tell your company it's time to leave," she ordered.

"Ma," Antoinette yelled and screwed up her face so tight that she didn't even look the same anymore. Antoinette was normally a beautiful girl. She had taken on the same features as Faye, only unlike her mom, Antoinette was slim and trim. A slinky size 2 with just enough butt and hips to force her into a size 4. Her skin was deep brown and smooth, only with all the makeup she wore you could barely tell. Except for her hair, Antoinette looked straight black. Unlike Christopher, there were no traces of her Mexican heritage in Antoinette's facial features, and just like with Faye, people assumed she was one hundred percent black. At the shop, Faye would have to hold her tongue every time a woman said something disrespectful about Mexicans. If she were the Zuma type, she'd tell the woman to go fuck off, but Faye didn't let the stupid comments of others rile her up. It doesn't take much info to be ignorant, Faye believed. But self-control took power, something Faye exuded much of as she and her daughter faced off in front of Shock G.

"Can't you ever leave me alone?" Antoinette said, still contorting her face so that Faye could barely stand to look at her.

"It's time for you to come inside, young lady," she reiterated.

But Antoinette didn't budge. It wasn't until a more powerful voice spoke up that she paid any attention.

"Don't sweat it, babe," Shock G said, as Antoinette turned loving eyes on him. He chuckled as he backed away across the front lawn. "Yo, I'll check you tomorrow," he said as he nodded his good-bye to Antoinette without so much as a "so long" to Faye.

"I hate you," Antoinette said, as she stormed past Faye into the house. "You always looking over my shoulder," she huffed and went straight to her room.

"That boy is too old for you," Faye said, following behind her, catching up just as the bedroom door slammed shut in her face.

"He's sixteen!"

"*Antoinette*," Faye shouted through the door. "I know better than that."

"He *is*. And we weren't doing nothing anyway."

"He's too old for you and you are not to see him again," Faye said, refusing to go around and around with her youngster. "Do you hear me? Little girls your age shouldn't be dating anyway."

"I'm sixteen and a half. I'm almost grown."

Faye shook her head and shut her eyes. "Look Antoinette, I had better not hear tale of you seeing that boy again. Do you hear? . . . Do you hear me?"

"Yeah. *Daaang*."

And that was the end of that commotion — or so Faye had thought.

"Look, Mami, look," Christopher's voice squeaked, forcing Faye to pay attention. She pushed away her thoughts and turned to her son to find him smiling up at her with his eyelids turned inside out.

"Christopher," she scolded. "What did I tell you about that?" she asked as he playfully unflipped his lids. "One day your eyes are going to get stuck like that," she said and shook a finger at him. "Now what happened after that boy came to the door?" she said, continuing on with more important matters.

"Antoinette took him to her room, then I turned the channel back to *The Terminator*," he said, jumping up as the microwave timer went off.

"She took him to her room?" Faye shouted.

"Uh-huh," Christopher said, poking his finger into the bowl to see if it was hot. "Ay."

"Be careful," she warned as he carried the piping hot bowl back to the table. She leaned backward and grabbed a spoon out of the drawer behind her and handed it to him. "So what happened next?"

Christopher dug into his raviolis, then blew on them so hard that a few fell off his spoon and back into the bowl. He stuck what was left into his mouth and began to speak as he chewed. "They stayed in the room for a long time . . . until Arnold Schwarzenegger went off . . . then they came out and Antoinette hit me in the back of my head and said she would be right back. Then they left."

"That was it?"

"Uh-huh."

"She hasn't been back since?"

He shook his head.

"She hasn't called?"

"Nope."

Damn, Faye thought and got up from the table. She immediately went to the phone and picked it up. But who was she going to call? She didn't know the number of that boy and she couldn't call the police. She glanced at the clock on the wall and found it was going on one o'clock in the morning. She had no idea where her sixteen-year-old daughter was and there was nothing she could do.

"Is Antoinette gonna get it?" her son asked, already finished with half his bowl of raviolis.

"Don't you worry about Antoinette. I'll take care of her," she said as she stood tapping the receiver of the phone, her thoughts and emotions so scattered that she could barely think straight.

It took Christopher all of four minutes to complete his meal and when he was done Faye picked up his bowl and took it over to the sink. "You go get out of those clothes and take a bath," she told him, and started a bucket of dishwater.

"But I'm tired, Mami," he whined.

"Did you hear what I just said?"

"But there's no school tomorrow."

"I don't care, boy," she yelled. "Don't argue with me. Just do as I said."

" 'Kay," Christopher whined and huffed out of the kitchen.

Faye regretted raising her voice and as she watched her son walk away with a bowed head, her guilt only grew stronger. She had taken the anger she was feeling toward Antoinette out on him and that wasn't fair. But Faye was so frazzled that she couldn't help it. What am I gonna do with that girl? she thought over and over again as she stood in front of the sink. She had heard children tended to rebel during their teens, but this was getting ridiculous. Antoinette had a mind all her own and though Faye had tried and tried to talk some sense into that thick head of hers, nothing seemed to be working. The last two report cards Antoinette had brought home were filled with D's and F's, her skirts were getting tighter and shorter and her attitude — oh Dios. It was foul. But what else could Faye do? She'd tried everything. Punishment, phone restrictions, talking and talking and talking, and nothing worked, she thought as she washed out the ravioli bowl, plus the mounds of other dishes that sat on the kitchen counter that Antoinette was supposed to have cleaned when she'd gotten home from school. I can't handle this all by myself, Faye thought as she turned off the water and wiped her hands on a dish cloth. She went to the cabinet and grabbed a pack of Oreos and opened them as she sat down at the kitchen table. Twelve cookies later, she realized that she was doing it again. Eating out of frustration. Faye wasn't hungry at all. In fact, her stomach still ached from being filled to the limit with collard greens and tortillas. Yet she couldn't stop stuffing herself. She'd been eating this way ever since Antoine had died. Whenever the pain got too great or the confusion too much to sort, Faye turned to food. Sweets were her favorites. They soothed her, gave her a feeling of comfort, eased her mind.

Since her husband's death six years ago, Faye's weight had escalated from 140 pounds to 210. Looking at her now, it was hard to believe that she had once been what guys with perfect Afros and plaid bell-bottom pants had called a fox. But that was back in the days before the kids and the stress. At her loveliest, Faye had been five foot two inches, 105 pounds. She had gotten up to 130 during her pregnancy with Antoinette, but just as soon as she dropped her load, she returned to a proper 110 pounds. While carrying Christopher, her weight topped out at 140, which on a frame of five feet two inches felt quite uncomfortable. But Faye hadn't been worried about the extra pounds at the time. She knew it would eventually disappear, plus Antoine certainly had no problem with it. Her husband's lust and desire for her seemed to escalate the bigger Faye became. Not that he wasn't completely taken with her when she was thin.

Faye's size didn't matter to Antoine. His love for her was too deep. Antoine was the kind of man who believed in strong affection. When he said, *I love you*, he didn't say it and walk away. He said it, then took your face into his hands and stared deep into you so that there could be no doubt that the words he'd spoken were true. He believed in hand holding, kissing every time someone walked through the door, complimenting, reassuring, and those all important surprise love attacks he'd throw on you from out of nowhere. Antoine was passion. And that is why Faye married him just two weeks after they met.

Faye had just graduated from high school and worked part-time directly across the street from the construction site where Antoine worked. She was the cashier at the 7-Eleven and every day for over a month, Antoine would walk across the street into the cool air-conditioned store where he'd spend his entire lunch break, escaping the heat. It took him more than a month before he spoke his first words to Faye. Before that, he'd simply come in, order a Slurpee, and drink it down slowly as he stood reading car magazines and the current editions of the *Recycler*. But when he did finally speak to Faye, he came straight to the point. "I wanna take you out," he told her one day as he waited for Faye to hand him his change.

Faye smiled and blushed, then said something stupid like "Huh," so Antoine made it crystal clear.

"I'll pick you up after work," he said, faking macho cool when he really wanted to blush himself.

"But you don't know when I get off."

"You come in at twelve, you get off at four," he corrected her and then slurped up a mouthful of his drink so quickly that he got freezer brain. "Ay," he said, grabbing his head and shaking it from side to side as his long ponytail whipped through the air.

"Here," Faye said, offering him her plastic bottle of water. "Drink it quick."

There was no way Antoine could be cool as he stood there grimacing, grasping his head and bouncing up and down, trying to stop the inside of his head from turning to ice. He took the bottle of water and put it to his lips and in seconds, his brain freeze subsided and he looked away from Faye in embarrassment.

Faye held back a giggle as she bent her neck, trying to get a glimpse of Antoine's face. "I'd love to go out with you," she told him and put a confident smile back on his lips.

"Cool," he said and slurped his drink again, this time more slowly. "I'll pick you up at four," he said, and made his way to the door. That was the first time he didn't spend his entire lunch inside the store. Faye guessed it was because he'd embarrassed himself with the freezer brain incident and she didn't want him to leave thinking he'd turned her off so she decided to boost up his ego just a taste. "I love your hair," she said, eyeing his ponytail until he turned to face her.

He smiled like he'd just pulled a trick on some unsuspecting someone and said, "Gracias, mi esposa." He gave Faye a wink, then opened up the door of the shop.

"You're welcome," she said smiling her own devilish smile. "But I'm not your wife."

"You speak Spanish?" he said and turned around.

Faye was sort of shocked. Hadn't he known that she was part Hispanic? Isn't that why he asked her out? "You didn't know I was Mexican?"

"You look black."

"Well, I am. Half and half."

"Cool," he said, and nodded as if he'd received some sort of bonus.

"So you like black girls, huh?"

"Yo creo en la oportunidad igual."

Faye held up a finger, confused. "Hold on. I'm not totally fluent," she said and giggled. "In English please."

"I'm . . . how do you say . . . an equal opportunity employer," he said, and winked his eye.

"Well, let freedom ring," she said, raising her eyebrows as they both stood staring at one another, marinating the something-something that brewed between them.

And from then on—it was on.

By the weekend, Faye had a ring, by the next Wednesday Antoine had taken his paycheck from the construction company and put up the first and last month's payment on their rental house, and by the following Friday, the two were standing in front of a judge at the downtown Municipal Court building. They didn't have the money or the ability to take time off from work for a honeymoon, but that didn't matter. Every night they'd spent together since they'd met had been a honeymoon and as fate would have it, the night after their wedding turned out to be more special than any other night of their short lives together. That night was the night they conceived their first child. The night they became parents.

Faye could not believe the fairy tale her life had become. She was the happiest she'd been in all her life, she was married to the only man she'd ever loved, and inside her, growing, was his child. Their child. Life was perfect.

The only slight glitch in their otherwise happy existence was the cold, almost blizzardlike rapport Faye had with Antoine's parents. Faye's parents had been wary of the quickness of Antoine's proposal too, but after meeting him and realizing that he was a good, hardworking, committed man, they soon turned their apprehension around and gave the couple their lifelong blessing. Antoine's parents were harder to sway, though. They were very traditional people, very strict and set in the ways and customs of their Mexican heritage. Neither spoke much English, though they'd been living in the States for over twenty years. They came to America for the better employment, not to escape their Mexican culture. Their biggest objection to Faye was that she was not completely Mexican and the fact that she wasn't totally fluent in Spanish didn't help either. They believed any Mexican who didn't speak the language was ignorant and worse—a traitor to their culture for embracing the customs and practices of America to the exclusion of Mexico. They never grew fond of Faye and considered her worse than a *gringa*. To them Faye was more despicable than the white people in America who wanted them and everyone else like them to run for the border and go back to Mexico—she was a black Mexican who didn't even know her roots—and in their eyes she and her whole family were worthless.

Faye's in-laws never got to know her well, but for the sake of their son's happiness they put up with her and even attended the wedding. Fortunately, Antoine had a mind of his own and once he made it up that he wanted to share his life with Faye, there was nothing his parents could do or say to stop him.

Nine months after saying "I do," little Antoinette came screaming into the lives of Faye and Antoine and like a one-eyed bandit she stole the heart of her father. Daddy's girl could do no wrong and both he and Faye spoiled their only child to death. Not with material things, for the Cruzes were not well off by any means, though Antoine worked twelve to sixteen hours a day. But the love they gave Antoinette was beyond compare. She was the center of their lives, their pride and joy, their blessing from God. And even though money was tight, Faye quit her part-time job at 7-Eleven and became a full-time mom. The Cruzes got by with little money and a ton of love until the end of their first year of marriage, when work seemed to slow up for Antoine.

Inflation and joblessness struck the country like a rim shot in the early eighties and the construction business was one of the first industries to feel the plunge. Life was not easy for the couple and their baby during that period. Often there were weeks between jobs for Antoine and on more occasions than he would have liked, he had to go to his parents and ask for extra money. Faye's parents were barely making it themselves and with her dad's bad back and her mother's diabetes, they spent most of their spare money on hospital visits, so asking them for a loan was out of the question. The only other alternative was Antoine's family. Faye knew how demeaning it was for Antoine to ask his mom and dad for a handout, but he did it whenever the couple ran into dire straits. It took a strong man to admit when he was in need, Faye knew, which is why her love for her husband grew even stronger during the rough times. She admired her man to the fullest and it made no difference to her that his pockets were deflated. What mattered was that he was her husband, that he loved her and their child, and that he was there for them even when the best he could do was turn to his mother and father for money.

But rough times never last for long and by the end of the eighties, the construction trade began to pick up again, and within a few years, Antoine was back on top, having saved up a good-sized bank account filled with off-limits money they both vowed never to touch unless they found themselves in a financial jam again. And in another two years, Antoine had saved up enough money and had become so stable that they both decided the time was right to add on to their family. Antoinette was nine years old and still the sweetest distraction in her father's eyes, but now the Cruz family wanted another child — a boy, more specifically — and in no time at all, Faye's belly was expanding with new life. And, just when they thought life could get no better, Antoine came home one evening with a big announcement.

"I got a promotion," he screamed as soon as he walked through the front door.

Faye walked out of the kitchen where she was just about to start on dinner and stood back, eyeing the overjoyed expression on her husband's face as he laughed and shouted again, "I got a promotion."

"What's a promotion, Daddy?" Antoinette had asked as she ran excitedly to her father and jumped into his arms.

"A promotion means you get to go to McDonald's more often," he told her as he kissed her mouth, then put her on the floor. She stood in front of her father as Faye walked up behind her, reaching around her to grab Antoine's face.

"A promotion?" Faye squealed. "I'm so proud of you," she said as she took him in her arms and Antoinette squeezed between them.

"You're looking at the new head foreman for Distance Construction," Antoine announced proudly. "That means more money, more benefits, more vacation . . ." Antoine's voice trailed away as he stood back from Faye, then leaned over to touch her stomach. "That means a better life for this little guy," he said, then smiled as he stood back up. "A better life for all of us."

"Yay," Antoinette screamed out, not really understanding all that was going on, but happy to see her father so thrilled just the same.

"We're going out to celebrate tonight," he told Faye as Antoinette screamed out with joy.

"Just the two of us?" Faye said, raising a devilish eyebrow and grinning.

"I think we can arrange that," Antoine said, returning his wife's come-on.

"I'm going too," Antoinette announced matter-of-factly.

"Not this time, mija," Faye said, rationally.

"No," Antoinette screamed. "I wanna go." She looked to her father for a sign of compromise in his eyes.

"Sorry, chiquita. Tonight's just for Papi and Mami."

"No," Antoinette whined and stomped her feet. She threw herself on the sofa and began to cry like a toddler whose favorite stuffed animal had been taken away.

But no one paid her much mind. All Faye and Antoine could think about was the good news he'd just dropped, the wonderful night out they were about to share, and the sensual, sexual evening that awaited them once they returned home.

Antoinette sat in the backseat of the car and cried all the way to Faye's parents' house and when her father came around to her door to let her out of the car, Antoinette grabbed hold of his hand and pleaded once more. "No, Papi. Don't leave me. I wanna go with you."

"Next time, mija," he told her, and walked her to her grandparents' door.

Faye watched out the window as Antoinette continued to whine and stare at her as if she were a mistress taking her beloved away. That was the first time Faye had felt hatred from her daughter and as she sat in the lonely kitchen now, halfway through her package of Oreos, she wondered as she always did if things would have turned out differently if Antoinette had gone out with them that night. Maybe her presence in the car would have made Antoine act differently. Maybe her presence could have saved her father's life.

When Antoine returned to the car, he leaned across the seat and kissed Faye so wildly that for a second Faye thought they'd be better off going back to the house and taking that kiss to its ultimate extreme instead of going out to celebrate at their favorite restaurant. But Antoine was so hyped about his promotion that Faye decided it was best to stick with their original plan. There'd be time for sexual celebration later, she was sure.

Antoine started up the car and zoomed down the street toward the 405 freeway. They were headed to the Chart House Restaurant in Redondo Beach, a place they hadn't been to since the night they'd gotten married. Money had been so tight lately that the two of them had not been able to share a night on the town in years, but all that was about to change, thanks to Antoine's promotion.

He spoke feverishly about his new role and how he'd finally been given the job he'd been slaving away for for years. He had been so into telling Faye the story that he nearly missed his exit off the freeway and at the last minute had to swerve across two lanes of traffic to get to the Redondo Beach off ramp.

"Ay, Papi," Faye screamed as she balanced herself by holding on to the door handle.

"Lo siento," he said, and also apologized to the driver of the car behind him by raising two fingers of peace into the air. But the driver behind Faye and Antoine was not satisfied with Antoine's apology. He leaned on his horn profusely and as Faye looked back at him out of the sideview mirror she could see the man give them the middle finger as his lips rattled nonstop, saying words Faye could only imagine had no resemblance to "Have a nice day."

Knowing he had been in the wrong, Antoine threw up the peace sign again as he too scoped out the man through his rearview mirror. But his gesture only seemed to upset the driver more and as they turned on to the surface street, the driver laid on the horn again. Antoine kept an eye on the irate driver as he drove on for four more blocks.

"Is he following us?" Faye asked, suddenly becoming antsy as she watched the car behind them swerve in and out of its lane.

"Ese es loco," Antoine said, now becoming upset. "What's your problem, man?" he yelled as he slowed the car toward a red light.

Faye's chest tightened as she watched the car behind them swerve out of its lane and pull alongside Antoine at the light.

"No," Faye warned as she watched Antoine roll down his window. "Let it go," she demanded. "Just turn off the street."

"Relax," he told her as the window on the car next to him slowly came down as well. "Yo, what's your problem, homes?" Antoine asked, full of machismo and hype.

An angry golden brown face much like Antoine's own stared right back at him. "What that deuce-deuce C like, fool?" he roared.

As Faye looked across her husband, she could tell that the Hispanic face looking back at her was that of a gang member and hastily she grabbed hold of her husband's shirt. "Let's go," she whispered, but Antoine paid her no mind. Instantly, Faye's head began to hurt. She put her hand over her stomach as she felt a strong kick bang inside her and her head pounded like a drum. Seconds later she felt another kick and almost screamed from the pain. It was as if her unborn baby knew what was going on. As if he were trying to put a stop the madness he felt brewing in the outer world. "Antoine," Faye whispered, "Antoine, let's go!"

"I don't know what you talking, man," he said as the guy in the other car began to growl. "I was just apologizing to you, man," he said, and held up two fingers again. "It's all about peace, homeboy," he said. "It's all about peace."

Faye's eyes seemed to lock in on the two fingers her husband waved in the air, then slowly, her eyes glided out the window to the man in the other car. She saw the rage in his eyes as he too watched Antoine's fingers. Did he think her husband was holding up some sort of gang sign? Is that what he thought?

Just then Faye got another kick from inside that was so powerful she had to look down at herself to make sure she was still intact. And in that split second, a tremendous boom filled the air. Faye shut her eyes and tightened her body as another boom rocked her earlobes. She felt the wetness on her hands and slowly opened her eyes to see deep red dots sprinkled over her lap. She could hear the screech and smell the burn of tires and as she looked straight ahead, she saw the other car dash away . . . and as she turned once more, she could see her husband's limp body slumped over the steering wheel. "Faye," he said in a voice so deep and hollow that Faye could barely understand. The sound scared Faye, to look at him scared her. This was not her husband. This man, covered in blood, slumped, in shock, shot — this was not her husband. "Love you," he said, his lips moving in slow motion. No, Faye thought . . . this could not be happening. This story, this fairy tale could not end this way. Not when it had been so beautiful and magical. Not when they loved each other so much.

"Make sure the kids remember me" were the last words Antoine spoke . . . or maybe he did say more, only Faye couldn't hear him. Her cries, screams, and yells were too loud.

Antoine's death was one of the first traffic killings in L.A. and with all the press coverage the incident received, other copycat freeway killings began to pop up across the city. It was a ridiculous time in L.A. history. No one could understand or believe that it was possible to lose one's life just because you cut someone off on the freeway or drove too slow in the fast lane. But Faye could believe it. She had seen it firsthand, had had her husband blown away in broad daylight right in front of her because he'd swerved in front of someone on the freeway and given him the peace sign.

There was no way to fully capture the depth of the loss Faye felt. Her husband, the love of her life, her sole provider, the man she had fully expected to spend decades with, was shot dead right beside her as his unborn son, a son he would never know, who would never know him, twirled around inside her stomach. Overwhelming desolation could only begin to describe Faye's feelings. Her life had been ruined, her future had been ruined, and things would never, ever be the same.

But the hard part had only just begun. Telling Antoinette was the hardest thing Faye ever had to do, so hard that she did not do it. She passed that burden on to her parents, and as she sat in the next room she could hear Antoinette go crazy. Her screams sounded as if they could crack cement, her bellows as if they could disturb setting stone. She had run out of the room and into the room Faye was sitting in at her mother's house. She looked at her from the doorway, then suddenly — "I hate you," she screamed at Faye. "This is all your fault. You took my papi away from me. You wouldn't let me go with you. I hate you."

That was the beginning of the end for Faye's relationship with Antoinette. Before her father's death, Antoinette had been the model child. Loving, polite, disciplined, with only a slight touch of the wickedness one could expect from most girls her age. But in the absence of Antoine, everything about her daughter changed.

And everything about Faye changed as well. The years following her husband's death were the most difficult of Faye's life. She had thought the worst was over, but she had been wrong. Not only had she lost the only man she ever loved, but she had also lost her only source of income. She had two children now, and though the bank account of emergency money Antoine had built up before he died came in handy, it didn't last very long. Soon, the need for money led Faye to Blessings and her first real job, but even after finding work, all of Faye's problems were not solved. She was still left with the emptiness of living life without her beloved Antoine, the only man she had ever been truly connected with. There was no one she could talk to about her feelings when she was alone at times like these. Sure, she had Pat and Zuma, but she still longed for more. For someone to come home to, for someone to watch Letterman with, for someone to hold her in the midnight hour. The only thing that could give her that feeling of ease now was food. So she ate. And she ate. And she ate. Eating didn't make the problems disappear, but at least it soothed her. Took her mind off the hurt for at least a little while.

Life would certainly be different if Antoine were still alive, Faye thought as she continued her vigil at the kitchen table, stuffing her mouth with cookies. If he were alive, Faye would have had a reason to lose all the baby fat she'd gained during her last pregnancy and she surely would have never let herself get this heavy and out of control. If he were alive, she'd have a reason to get up and put on makeup, a reason for living instead of just getting through day after day. And she would have help. She wouldn't have to go through this thing called parenting alone. She wouldn't be sitting here wondering where her teenage daughter was at one-thirty in the morning. Antoine would have never stood for this behavior. He would have laid down the law with Antoinette. He would have kept this family together. But he was gone and the burdens were all on Faye now.

She closed her cookie bag and got up from the table and went to her son's room, finding him sprawled across his twin bed in a pair of Spiderman pajamas. She lifted her son's small body and wrapped his cover over him, taking in the fresh smell of Ivory soap from his skin. She smoothed out the curls that lay across the top of his head and breathed in deeply, soaking up the bond she felt with him and for him. A bond that touched her deep inside. She'd protect him at any cost, do whatever it took to make him happy, she thought as she stroked the side of his face. She'd do the same for Antoinette too, she thought to herself as she left Christopher's room and crossed the hallway to her daughter's empty hideaway.

Faye and Antoine had shared this room before Christopher was born. It was the larger of the two bedrooms, so Faye had moved all of her daughter's things there and given the smaller room to her newborn baby. She took to sleeping on the living room floor until a couple of years ago, when she saved up enough money to buy a sofa sleeper for the front room. She walked through her daughter's room and sat down on the edge of her day bed and put her feet up. "Where are you, Antoinette?" she said and closed her eyes. It was now 1:45 and still she was not home. Sixteen years old, Faye thought, and shook her head. Sixteen and going on forty, she thought again, trying to picture the way her daughter looked before she'd gotten too grown for her britches. But when Faye closed her eyes all she could see was the off-putting girl her daughter had come to be. She remembered back two years ago, when Antoinette first started wearing makeup. She'd cut all her eyebrows off and penciled them back in with an arch so high that it made her looked like a witch. The clothes she wore were so tight that she looked more like a streetwalker than a high school kid. But at least her style of dress had changed recently. Now her daughter had done a complete 360 and took to sporting baggy jeans and oversized T-shirts. She often wore a Raiders cap, usually turned to the back, making her look just like a little thugette or rapper. Nothing like the prissy little girl who sat on her father's lap so many years ago.

Faye heard what sounded like a car pulling up to the front of the house, and immediately jumped up. She ran to the front window and carefully pulled the curtains back. She hadn't seen the car before but she recognized the driver. It was *that boy*, she discovered, then quickly let the curtains fall. She ran to the kitchen to turn out the lights, then back to her daughter's room as she heard the front door creep open and the sound of footsteps tiptoeing through the house. The footsteps paused every couple of seconds until they were right at the bedroom door. Through the dark she saw her daughter's hand feel around the wall in search of the light switch and when it was on her daughter slid through the door and into the brightly lit room.

"Mami!"

Busted, Faye thought, as she stood at the foot of the day bed staring into her daughter's astonished face. She was wearing a huge sweatsuit she'd never seen before and a pair of fresh white sneakers. Her lipstick was a dark, almost black shade and her eyes were covered so heavily in paint that Faye wondered how she could see out of them. "Where the heck have you been?"

"Whachoo doing in my room?" Antoinette asked, and pinned herself against the wall, not sure if she wanted to come in or run back out.

"It's nearly two o'clock in the morning, Antoinette. Where have you been?"

"Out."

"Out with whom?"

"My friends. Monique and them."

"I'll ask you one more time. With whom?"

"I said Monique and them."

"I saw you with that boy. He just dropped you off."

Antoinette stared strangely at her mother. "Then why'd you ask me?"

"Do I ask much of you?"

"What?"

"Do I ask much of you?" Faye repeated. "All I ask is for you to pick up your brother from school and watch him until I get home. Is that asking too much?"

"I ain't no baby-sitter. I ain't getting paid."

"I don't have to pay you. You're my daughter."

"Shut up," Antoinette mumbled, and looked down at the floor.

"What did you just say?"

"Nothing."

"I can't believe you just walked out of here and left your brother home by himself. Anything could have happened to that boy. He's only six."

"Is he still alive?"

"That's beside the point."

"Whatever."

"Don't you whatever me. Where have you been? Didn't I tell you I didn't want you hanging around that boy no more?"

"I hang around whoever I want to. You can't pick my friends."

"That's it," Faye said and stomped her foot. "You're on punishment," she said and immediately went to the nightstand and unplugged her daughter's phone.

"I don't give a fuck."

"What?"

"Nothing."

"What did you just say to me?"

"Nothing, Mami, dang."

Faye stormed over to her daughter and stood directly in her face. "And where did all these new clothes come from, huh? Did he buy you these things?"

"Yes he did," she answered coolly.

"Where did he get that kind of money if he's only sixteen?"

Her daughter didn't have an answer for that.

"Do you hear me talking to you?"

Still, there was no answer.

Faye grabbed her daughter and sat her down on the bed and began removing her clothes. "You're giving these things right back and you better not ever see that boy again."

Antoinette laughed as her mother tugged and pulled at her clothing. It was funny to her. Every time her mother got mad, it was funny. What could she really do to stop her anyway? Not a damn thing, Antoinette thought, as her mother stripped her of her pants and jacket, leaving her in a long T-shirt that came almost to her knees.

Faye balled the clothes up in her arm and threw them in the corner of the room. When she turned back to look at her daughter she stopped cold. She squinted at her daughter's arm and almost fell backward. "What the hell is that?"

"What does it look like?"

Faye looked closer and indeed it was what she thought it was. "A tattoo?"

Her daughter smiled and ran her hand over her right arm. The tattoo spelled *Shock* G in thick black letters and was anchored by a small red heart.

"You got that boy's name tattooed on you?"

"Yes I did."

Faye covered her mouth with her hand and shook her head. She couldn't say another word. Her body trembled as she stood watching her daughter, who obviously thought this whole thing was a joke. What could she possibly say to get through to her? She'd said everything, done everything, and still her daughter would not listen. Helplessness was the feeling that swarmed around Faye and she couldn't make the feeling go away. All she knew was that her daughter was slipping away from her. So she was on punishment? She'd put her on punishment before. It hadn't worked then and it wouldn't work now.

Faye bit down on her bottom lip. Her eyes drifted around the room and landed on a small photo of her late husband that sat upon Antoinette's dresser. Oh how I need you, she thought, almost becoming entranced.

"So whachoo gonna do now, Mami? Make me go to the doctor's and get it taken off?" Antoinette asked, still stroking her tattoo as if mocking her mother.

Faye turned to her daughter, then picked up the phone she'd taken from the wall. "I don't know what I'm going to do," she said softly as she headed for the door. She paused to say something else, then decided it was useless. As usual, her daughter had won, and Faye left the room feeling more like the child than the parent.

She walked away in defeat to the front room and put her daughter's phone in the closet. Then she went to her sofa sleeper and let it out. Next she hit the kitchen, and grabbed the half-eaten pack of Oreos and brought them back to her bed. She lay down as she stuck the first cookie in her mouth and closed her eyes as she chewed. By the fifth cookie, she could feel her blood pressure easing. By the seventh, she actually felt calm. By the ninth one, her eyelids became heavy and by the fourteenth . . . there was peace. Finally.

3

Quietly, Pat stepped through the double doors of her house and carefully shut them behind her. She gripped her keys tightly in her hand so that they wouldn't clank together, then slipped out of her shoes and left them by the entrance. Her mission as always was to be as quiet as possible. Her husband was a light sleeper and the slightest sound could awaken him. Pat definitely didn't want to do that. If Mark awoke they'd be forced to talk and talking to her husband was the last thing Pat wanted to do these days. She felt kind of guilty as she crept around the darkened house acting more like a burglar than a resident. She'd been avoiding her husband for months, blaming her lack of time for him on the busyness of the shop. But lately, even when Pat would make it home at a decent hour, she found ways of keeping her distance. She either had to go shopping or she was reading a book or there was some other excuse, all designed to limit the time she could spend with her husband. Mark's own work schedule helped in her distancing tactics too. He owned a string of apartment buildings in Long Beach, California, and seeing to them often kept him away from home long past dusk. But unlike Pat, Mark still tried to make time for the both of them. Just two weeks ago, he'd shown up at the shop all decked out in a tuxedo, carrying flowers, plus two tickets to see the Alvin Ailey dance troupe, which had come to town. The customers in the shop had all marveled at Pat's romantic man, wishing they too had a husband who cared about them as much as Mark seemed to care about Pat. But Pat was not so thrilled. She used the shop as an excuse and told her husband she could not get away. And when Zuma and Faye butted in to say they'd take care of the shop for the night, Pat quickly switched to Plan B, the old headache excuse. Zuma and Faye were stunned that Pat would refuse a date with her husband, but Pat knew what she was doing. She didn't want to be alone with him. She didn't want to fake it. Things were bad between her and her husband and a night with Alvin Ailey was not going to change that. Mark said he understood, which was his way. He always understood. He always accepted things the way they were. But Pat was different. There were many things she could not understand, many things she could not accept, and her body's inability to produce a child was one of the biggest. Mark had long since accepted the fact that they would never have children. He'd moved on with his life as if it were just one of those things. It was as if having a child meant nothing to him, or at least that's the way it felt to Pat. She'd never understand why her husband wanted to act like everything was going to be okay when Pat knew otherwise. Not being able to have a child was not okay with her. Her husband could be cool about it, accept it as just one of those things and move on, but Pat was angry. Angry at him for not feeling more and angry at herself for being inadequate as a woman.

Pat's mission to be quiet was almost foiled when she passed the dining room and saw two yellow balls glistening in the darkness. She gasped and fell against the wall as the eyes of her cat twinkled. "Kunta," she whispered, and flipped on the lights. Her fat black cat sat perched on the dining table amid what looked to be a candlelight setting for two. There was a candelabra in the middle of the table, two place settings, and two empty wine glasses. "Did Poppa make dinner for me?" she whispered to Kunta as she carried the cat out of the dining room and into the kitchen. She clutched Kunta under one arm, then opened the refrigerator and saw several Tupperware containers filled with food. Her husband had gone all out tonight. There was Caesar salad, onion soup, plus her favorite, penne pasta with pesto sauce. In the door bin was a bottle of Firestone wine and on the bottom shelf a bowl of strawberries and whipped cream.

Pat closed the refrigerator and sat Kunta on the center island of the kitchen. She pulled over a stool and sat beside her cat as she smoothed out his thick coat and Kunta purred with delight. Deeper feelings of guilt swept over Pat as she thought of all the wonderful things her husband had done over the years to keep her happy. If Pat said she wanted the moon, Mark's mind would begin plotting a way to get it for her. He even laughed at all her stupid jokes. Still, lately it seemed nothing he did had been enough. Mark wasn't the type of man women usually fall for. He wasn't suave or mysterious and he didn't have an extraordinary look about him unless you call looking like a nerd something special. What Mark was was kind, generous, and so thoughtful that one could easily label him a push-over. He was the kind of man every woman *said* she wanted, but always passed over because he wasn't *cool* enough. In fact, Mark was so nice that he'd bore most women, but Pat fell in love with him anyway. She wasn't most women. She was a woman who knew there was no future in dealing with men who felt it unsafe to let their feelings show. She wanted a man who loved her so deeply that it hurt him and in Mark she'd found that man. Still, nothing her husband could say or do these days could make up for the emptiness that Pat felt in her life. But it wasn't Mark's fault, she told herself. She was the defective one, the one whose body would not work properly.

"I'm not going to do this," Pat said to Kunta as she turned him around and stared into his yellow eyes. "I'm not going to think about this tonight."

But who was Pat fooling? All she ever did was think about how things used to be between her and Mark. How things could have been if only her body would allow her to give birth. Depressing as it was, she couldn't help but think about it.

Pat had her first inkling something was wrong when after six months of trying she had not become pregnant. So when two years passed and nothing happened she and Mark decided to go to a fertility expert. They were still practically newlyweds at the time, still full of hope and ambition for the future, and they figured whatever the problem, they'd find out, fix it, and move on to parenthood. There was no cause for alarm, they'd told themselves — at least not yet.

The first thing the doctor did was take a medical history of both of them. He asked them every question from height and weight to what was their most common sexual position. When their medical history gave no warning signs of what might be wrong, they moved on to the next phase, which was a fertility workup. Actually it was a series of four tests that would let Pat and Mark know what was keeping them from conceiving. The first test in the series was a semen analysis for Mark, and when the doctor handed him a plastic cup and told him to masturbate into it and return it to the nurse, he didn't even blink an eye. However awkward or humiliating it seemed, it was his duty.

Pat had followed him down to the room where the quasiscientific procedure was to take place. She stood outside the door for what seemed to be over fifteen minutes as she waited for her husband to complete his task. But after thirty minutes, she began to worry. She knocked on the door and put her face against it. "You okay in there?" she asked, wondering what was going on. Had he spilled his cup and had to start over or what?

"I'm okay," Mark huffed. "Just give me a minute."

"You've had thirty," Pat said and turned the knob on the door, but it was locked. "What's going on, Mark?" she asked as her worry began to escalate.

"*Nothing*," he strained.

"Well what's taking so long?"

"You know how I am when I'm under pressure."

Pat rolled her eyes and looked up at the ceiling. Mark had never performed well when he was under pressure. Even on their wedding night he'd conked out after three minutes. Mark was an excellent lover any other time. It was just when he felt he *had* to perform that he ran into trouble. "Open the door, Mark."

"No," he said quickly. "I can handle this. Go away."

"*Mark*, open this door."

"Stop. I'm embarrassed enough as it is."

"If you don't open this door, I'm gonna bang on it till security comes."

A few seconds later the door was flung open. "Get in here," he said as he pulled her by the arm and quickly shut the door behind him.

The room was dimly lit and scarcely furnished. There was just a chair, a table, and a box full of porno magazines. How cozy, Pat had thought as Mark sat down in the chair and let go of the top of his pants, which he had been holding.

"What's the matter, Mark?" Pat asked as she stared at her embarrassed husband.

"I told you, nothing. It's just going to take some time. This is serious business here."

"I know, Mark. And if you don't get some sperm into that cup we won't even be able to start the process."

Mark dropped his head in his hands. Why had Pat said that? It only caused him more anxiety. Pat looked across the room at her poor husband and sighed as she approached him. "How 'bout a little joke?" she said, and paid no attention when Mark shook his head. "What's Michael Jackson's idea of a perfect ten?" she said and raised her eyebrow. "Two five-year-olds," she said, and laughed a little bit too hard until she saw that her husband was not joining in the festivities. "Okay," she said, and moved closer to him. "Move out of the way," she said and knelt beside him.

"What are you doing?" he asked as Pat reached for his private part. "No, don't touch it," he said, and brushed her hand away. "You might mess it up or something."

"I'm just trying to help."

"But the doctor said I had to do it."

"What difference does it make whose hand is doing it?" Pat said through clenched teeth. "Just move out of my way and hold the cup in the ready position."

Pat grabbed hold of Mark as he held the cup below her hand. She stroked him up and down so quickly that Mark began to wince. Then she realized she had to slow down. She couldn't approach this like a job, it had to be more sensual. But their surroundings did nothing to heighten their sexual senses.

After two minutes, Mark began to sigh. "This isn't working."

"Well, close your eyes. Use your imagination," Pat said, and slowed down her movements. She unbuttoned her blouse with her free hand and pushed it back. "Look at me," she said as her husband opened his eyes and turned his head. He stared at her black lace bra, but still there was no emotion. No quickening of his heart rate, no panting, not even an "Ooo." She leaned over and kissed his stomach and still there was no reaction. This has got to be the most ridiculous thing I've ever done, Pat thought to herself as her hand slipped from his penis and landed on one of his testicles.

"There you go," Mark moaned, and closed his eyes. He grabbed hold of himself as Pat continued to stroke underneath. As her husband sat there enjoying the moment Pat glanced around the room. There had better not be any hidden cameras in here she thought as she felt the veins pop out on her husband's skin. "Here it comes, baby," Mark said as Pat removed her hand.

"The cup," she screamed as she backed away. "Hold up the cup!"

"Oh shit," Mark said as he adjusted the cup just in time to catch his fluid.

Pat couldn't hold back her laughter. The scene was too goofy to be true, but it was necessary, she thought, as she smiled toward her husband and blew him a kiss. "Good job, Superman."

"Ha, ha," he said as he carefully covered the cup and began pulling up his pants.

The next twenty-four hours were hell as they waited to find out what the results of the test would be. Mark could barely sleep through the night for wondering what the doctor would say the next day. "Maybe my little guys are deformed," he said to Pat as they lay in bed. "Maybe this is all my fault."

Though Pat had been thinking the same thing, she didn't let on. There was no cause for alarm, she kept telling herself — at least not yet. "Remember our vow?" she said, and rolled over onto her side to face him.

"We said we weren't going to worry," Mark said, and pulled her closer to him.

"That's right. We are not going to worry about this, Mark. Do you hear me?" she said, and reached out for his face. "Whatever the problem, we'll take care of it." She held on to her husband and felt him quivering. She hadn't expected him to get so shaken by all this. "It's just a simple semen analysis," she said as if it were a normal everyday thing. But they both knew it wasn't.

They were up at the crack of dawn and headed back to the doctor's office. They sat together hand in hand waiting for him to come in with the test results, and when the doctor walked through the door, Pat examined his face looking for an early clue of what he might say. But the doctor was calm. Too calm. So calm that by the time he sat down Pat and Mark were about to burst from all the expectation. "What's the verdict?" Pat asked, and scooted to the edge of her seat.

"I've got good news and I've got not so good news," Dr. Rathbatham said, and opened their medical chart.

Pat looked over at Mark and noticed him sweating.

"The good news," the doctor continued, "is that the results of the sperm analysis came back normal. Looks like your sperm are in excellent condition," he said, and smiled at Mark, who instantaneously let out a huge sigh. The doctor smiled and nodded at Mark's relief, but just as soon, his face took on a frown. "The not so good news is that the problem undoubtedly lies with you, Mrs. Brown."

Pat sat still as a rock and stared into the doctor's eyes.

"We will have to continue with the fertility workup, but now our focus will be on you."

Pat winced as a twinge of pain tapped the side of her head. She felt as if she were standing in a police line-up and had been picked out as the culprit. "Me," she said and put her hand to her chest. "Something's wrong with me?"

"We haven't found anything wrong with you, Mrs. Brown. In fact I've been examining the results of your medical history and pap smears from as far back as ten years and they all seem normal. What we have to do now is dig deeper and find out if there is something we may have overlooked."

Pat turned to her husband, then back to the doctor. "Remember what we said," Mark whispered to her and leaned in close. "We are not going to worry. We are going to find the problem and fix it."

Shut up, Pat thought to herself, and clenched her jaws together. She didn't want to hear all of that right now. All she could focus on was the fact that something must be wrong with her. *She*, not her husband, was the cause of all this.

From then on Pat felt alone. Mark gave her all the support she could expect, but the fact remained that whatever the problem, it was her problem. She had not meant to push Mark away, it had happened gradually. Though he said all the right things, like "We'll get through this," and "Everything's gonna be all right," she still felt so alone. She couldn't tell him how she really felt deep inside. She couldn't tell him how unwomanly she felt, how scared she was. So she kept her feelings to herself and did what she had to do.

For the next six months, Pat's life was ruled by the fertility workup process. It seemed every time she turned around there was another examination, another reason she had to be up at the crack of dawn, another purpose for her to place her feet in stirrups and have a doctor roam through her vagina. The first test she had to endure was for ovulation. She had to keep charts and graphs of her body temperature. Every day, it was the first thing she had to do in the morning. She couldn't even get up and go to the bathroom first. She lay there in bed and stuck a thermometer in her mouth, checked the results, usually ninety-eight degrees, then marked it down on a chart.

Next, she had to have the doctor check for progesterone in her ovaries by taking a blood test, and after that the doctor had to recheck her ovaries by endometrial biopsy. The doctor had said it wouldn't be painful. But any time someone opens your legs and passes a plastic tube into your uterus and sucks the lining out, you better believe it's got to at least sting. But after about a month, all the tests on her ovaries were completed, and still there was no sign of any cause for infertility. Her tests were all normal, which was a good sign, but it also meant that they had to continue testing.

The next phase of the workup was the postcoital test, which was just a fancy way of saying after sex. This test seemed easy enough at first, but having to have sex with your husband, then get up and go to the doctor without even washing down there was a bit awkward. But it was necessary for the doctor to remove a sample of mucus from her cervix. This test too was normal. Pat's cervix was fine and still the tests continued.

The final test Pat had to undergo was the tubal patency exam, in which the doctor took an X ray of her uterus and Fallopian tubes. Pat had thought this was going to be as simple as a chest X ray but she was fooled. She lay on the examining table and put her legs in stirrups as the doctor put a balloon inside her and inflated it. Though they'd given her an anesthetic, Pat still couldn't handle knowing what was going on inside her. And even after all this, the test came back normal. There seemed to be nothing wrong with Pat physically. But now, six more months had come and gone and still she had not been able to produce a child.

Sex with her husband was becoming more of an experiment than a romantic ritual. Spontaneity was a thing of the past. Now sex had to be scheduled. The timing had to be right, Pat's temperature had to be just so. . . . Everything had to be perfect. There were many times when Mark wanted to have sex just for the sake of doing it, but Pat was so stressed that she was rarely in the mood. Sex was not for pleasure anymore. It was simply a means to an end. An end that seemed further and further away as the months passed by.

Pat had scheduled a consultation with her doctor following her last fertility test so that he could give her his final opinion on whatever was causing her inability to conceive. Mark had wanted to be present but Pat had refused. She knew her husband wanted to support her, but she felt she had to do this by herself. She still felt this was only *her* problem. It was *her* body that wouldn't act right, so she went to her doctor's office alone and waited anxiously for his arrival.

"I've got good news and not so good news," the doctor said once again forcing Pat to remember the first time she'd heard him say those words. The first time he'd given her terrible news. "The good news is that we can find absolutely nothing inside your body that should prevent you from having a child. You've passed every test we've given you with flying colors, Mrs. Brown."

The doctor seemed to smile upon giving this news, but Pat was not so pleased. "Then what the hell is wrong with me? Why can't I get pregnant?"

"Well, it seems that we have a case of unexplained infertility. While we have performed all the state-of-the-art tests that are at our disposal there are some cases, like yours, that remain beyond our understanding."

"Are you telling me you don't know what's wrong with me?"

The doctor sighed and took off his glasses. "That's partly correct."

Pat gasped and stood straight up. "So why have I been coming here? Why have I been wasting my time?"

"It hasn't been a waste —"

"Yes it has. You've been probing me, x-raying me, having me make up stupid charts. And after all that you still don't have a clue?"

"Well, Mrs. Brown —"

"Well my ass," she exploded. "I've wasted over six months on all these high-tech tests and you sit here and tell me you don't know what's wrong with me," she said and threw up her hands. "You can send a man to the moon, but you can't tell me what the hell is going on inside my body?" She shook her head as she paced back and forth in front of the doctor's desk. "So you're telling me I have to just accept the fact that I can't have kids?"

"No, Mrs. Brown," the doctor said, and slowly put his glasses back on. "I'm not saying that at all."

"So where do I go from here? What's left for me to do that I haven't already done?"

"I could start you out by taking Clomid, which is a pill."

"Forget pills, doctor. I want to get pregnant," Pat screamed. "I want a baby."

"And I want you to have a baby."

"Then don't waste my time. What's my next move?"

"Well, we could skip the preliminary treatments and go straight to GIFT."

"GIFT," Pat said and frowned. "What's that?"

"Gamete Intra-Fallopian Transfer."

"English please," she insisted. "What does it do?"

"It's similar to in vitro fertilization."

Pat leaned over the doctor's desk and stared into the doctor's face. "*English.*"

"We take one of your eggs, fertilize it with your husband's sperm outside the body, then insert it into your Fallopian tube."

"And this will get me pregnant?"

"I can't promise that."

"Well, does it work?"

"Yes, but giving you statistics on its success rate wouldn't help. Every woman is unique and your case is very unique considering we don't even know what is actually causing your infertility."

"But there is a chance?"

"Yes, there is a chance, but the procedure is very expensive. It costs ten thousand dollars per procedure and if it doesn't take the first time we must start all over again, meaning another ten thousand dollars."

"I don't give a damn about money, doctor. I just want a child."

"And I want you to have a child."

"Then dammit, let's do it!"

Pat had gone straight home from the doctor's office after setting up her appointment for the GIFT procedure and signing papers promising over ten thousand dollars. Though she hadn't let on to her doctor that she was the least bit concerned about money, on the drive home she became nervous. Ten thousand dollars was a lot of money, especially since she had none of it herself. Pat was a housewife at the time. Mark made all the money, and though he'd set up a checking account for her, she'd still have to go through him to get her hands on that type of cash. She worried about how he'd react to learning how expensive the procedure would be. But Pat had her mind set. She wanted to have the procedure and nothing Mark could say could change her mind.

Mark was waiting for her at the door when she walked up, and the first anxious words out of his mouth were, "How'd it go?"

But the first words out of Pat's mouth were, "I need ten thousand dollars."

Mark looked lost as he closed the door and turned to Pat. "Huh," he said and put his hands on his hips.

"Look, Mark," Pat began as her eyes filled with tears. "I need ten thousand dollars," she said as she stood before him begging like a child. "The doctor said he doesn't know what's wrong with me. He said it's a case of unexplained infertility. Now I know we've already spent a bunch of money on these tests, but this is my last hope, Mark. The doctor wants me to have this, this thing," she said as she paused briefly to catch her breath. "He wants to take some of your sperm and implant my egg . . . or take my eggs and mix it with . . . Dammit, Mark," she said, exasperated. "I need ten thousand dollars."

"Pat," Mark began, but was cut off.

"No Mark. Just listen. This is my last chance."

"Pat —"

"Mark please," she cried and placed her hand over her stomach. "I want a baby so bad, Mark. I want a baby," she said, and clenched her fist.

"Pat," Mark said as he took his sobbing wife into his arms. "It's okay.

You can have the money," he said, and placed both his hands on the side of her face. "Do you hear me, Pat? It's okay. I'll give you anything you want. I'll sell one of the apartment buildings if I have to."

Pat's head dropped down as relief encompassed her. "Thank you, Mark," she sobbed as Mark held her tightly. "Thank you."

"Don't thank me," he said as he rubbed her back and tried to calm her down. "Don't you know we're in this together?"

Pat and Mark made love just for the hell of it that night, something they hadn't done in a long time. Well, Mark made love at least. Pat just lay there oooing and aahing while thoughts of cribs and bottles ran through her head. Pat had always known marrying Mark was one of the best moves she'd made in her life and that night she was absolutely convinced of that fact. As he lay there sleeping that night, Pat watched over him, and prayed in a way she had never prayed before. She thanked God that she was infertile and couldn't conceive, for she knew He was trying to teach her something. She thanked Him for the sorrow and anxiety she'd gone through for so long, knowing full well that one day His total immaculate plan would be revealed to her. She thanked God for Mark too and praised him for giving her a man with an understanding, a man who had figured out the true meaning of husband. She prayed long and hard that night, giving thanks, asking for nothing, and every night after, she did the same.

But after a whole year had passed, and after six attempts at the GIFT procedure had failed, Pat began to lose her faith. Mark had spent more than sixty thousand dollars and sold two apartment buildings in the process, and still Pat could not get pregnant. The bond between them began to weaken, and as every attempt to conceive fizzled, Pat closed herself off more and more. Mark had tried to talk to her, to break down her walls, but nothing he did or said could make her feel any better. At night she'd lie in bed crying, and during the day when Mark was away she'd lift up her gown and wrap a pillow around her stomach. She'd walked around the house for hours like that, imagining how it would feel to be pregnant. How it would feel to have a baby growing inside her. How it would feel to be called Mama.

After the sixth failed attempt and watching his wife slip deeper and deeper into depression, Mark tried to rectify the situation. For a couple of months Mark had begun to contemplate an extraordinary notion, and the more he thought, the more he knew he had to do what he was planning and put an end to the deep depression engulfing his wife. He'd come home from work early one evening and walked into the living room to find his wife asleep on the sofa. He shook her on the arm to wake her up and as he did this, he noticed the bulge beneath his wife's gown. "What is this?" he asked as Pat sprang up half awake. When she realized what was going on, she snatched the pillow from around her stomach and threw it to the floor. "What was that for?" Mark asked as he stared at the pillow, realizing how deeply disturbed his wife had become.

"Nothing," Pat said as she got up from the sofa and headed to the kitchen. "I didn't have time to cook yet," she said as she hurried around, hoping Mark wouldn't ask any more questions about the pillow.

"I don't care about dinner," Mark said as he showed up behind her. Pat shut her eyes tightly and leaned against the center island. When she reopened her eyes she found Mark right before her. Concern was written all over his face as he reached forward and put his hand over Pat's stomach. "It's not working," he said as Pat shut her eyes again. "It's just not working."

Pat knew where this conversation was leading. They had the same conversation after her third, fourth, and fifth attempts to get pregnant, and each and every time Pat had said the same thing. "I wanna try again. I know this is going to work." She reopened her eyes and found Mark shaking his head.

He looked her dead in the eyes and said, "No."

"Mark?" Pat said, feeling like a ten-year-old who'd been told she couldn't go out to play.

"No," he said again, and took his hand away from Pat's stomach.

Pat looked deeply in her husband's eyes looking for some sign of hope, some sign that would let her know that he didn't mean what he was saying. When she couldn't find that sign, the anger that was brewing inside her broke loose. "You just don't give a damn, do you?" she said and backed away from him. "You never cared about having a baby."

"How can you say that? I've always wanted a child just as much as you. But this isn't working. It's time you accepted that. It's time to move on to something different."

"No," Pat shouted so loud that it startled Mark. "I want a baby. I won't give up."

Mark's eyes filled with tears as he moved toward Pat and put his arms around her. But Pat didn't want to be consoled. She pushed him away so hard that he almost lost his balance. "I want a baby," she screamed, and lunged at Mark. Hysterically she pounded her fists against his chest as if that would make him understand her.

"Stop it, Pat," he said, trying to grasp her hands. He grabbed her by the wrists and pulled her close to him. "We've tried six times."

"I don't care."

"We've spent over sixty thousand dollars."

"So sell another apartment building. Sell the damn house if you have to, Mark. I don't care. I just want to have a baby."

"Pat," Mark called as she stood before him briskly shaking her head. "Will you listen to what I'm saying?" he asked, and waited for the glazed look in Pat's eyes to disappear. "You've got to admit this isn't working. We've got to move on. Try something else."

"There is nothing else."

"Yes there is," he said, and gripped Pat tightly. "We can adopt."

"What?" Pat asked, and squinted her eyes.

"We can adopt," Mark repeated as he let go of his wife's arms and waited for her response. "There are many children out there who need a home and loving parents," he said softly. "I know you wanted to have a child of your own. I know that. But think about it, Pat. Don't you want to be a mom? Does it really matter if the child comes from your body or not?"

The thought of adoption had never crossed Pat's mind before. She'd been so wrapped up in trying to get her body to do something it refused to do that she never considered taking another route. Pat didn't answer her husband's question that night. In fact it took her over a month to think about it, but when all was said and done, Pat realized that no matter how it came to be she wanted a baby in her life. And if her body couldn't do the trick, then maybe someone else's could.

Pat picked up Kunta and dropped him to the floor as she got up from the stool she'd been sitting on and flicked off the light switch. She walked out the kitchen and up the staircase to the second floor. She could hear Mark snoring even before she reached the bedroom. She thought about taking a shower before getting into bed, but knew that the sound of the water would awaken him. She quietly peeled out of her clothes and put on the flannel gown that lay on the chair beside the bed. Slowly she pulled back the covers and eased herself down on the mattress. She paused abruptly when Mark stopped snoring and curled himself into a tight ball. Seconds later, he was snoring again and Pat eased herself upon a pillow and closed her eyes.

She tried to go directly to sleep, but her thoughts had overtaken her again. Being infertile was at one point the most devastating thing that had happened in her life. But adoption had topped that. Making the decision to adopt hadn't come easily for Pat and instead of being a glimmer of hope it was a saddening realization. The realization that she'd given up any hope of ever having a child of her own. But the more she and Mark discussed it, the more Pat began to see adoption as her best and only choice of ever having a child.

Pat had wanted a newborn infant, which meant she had to find a woman who was already pregnant and willing to give up her child. She thought finding such a woman would be like looking for a needle in a haystack, but once she and Mark sat down with an adoption counselor she realized it wouldn't be so hard. The counselor had told her there were many women across the country and particularly in California who get pregnant all the time and for any number of reasons decide to give their babies up. The counselor had given them the names of all sorts of women's groups, clinics, and hospitals they could contact in order to find women wanting to give up their babies. The counselor also gave them a game plan. First they needed to find an adoption attorney to handle all the legal work, then they'd have to put together a résumé of sorts to send out to the various groups, clinics, and hospitals to let the expectant mothers know that they were looking for a child. And once they found a mother who was willing, all they had to do was wait, sign a few papers, and soon they'd have a child.

Pat had never known it could be so easy. Since the counselor stressed to her that sending out the letter to the groups was the most important aspect of the game plan, that's the first thing Pat and Mark embarked on. They went to a photographer and took pictures of themselves, figuring any expectant mother would want to know how the future parents of her child looked. Then they sat down together and wrote a letter: *Hi. We are Patricia and Mark. Mark is in real estate and Patricia is a homemaker. We have been happily married for five years, but our doctor has told us we will never be able to have a child of our own. So we are turning to adoption to make our dreams of having a child come true.*

They added more information about their home lives, then affixed their photo to the page and Xeroxed hundreds of copies, which they sent to hospitals and pregnant women's groups across the state and within that same month, Pat and Mark received the phone call that would change their lives. It was from a sweet-sounding young girl named Carmen Williams. She was seventeen years old and pregnant. She said she'd been given Pat's letter by one of the prenatal nurses at the clinic she'd gone to in downtown Los Angeles. Carmen and Pat spoke on the phone for over an hour that first day and by the end of the conversation Pat had learned that Carmen had gotten pregnant by a young guy who'd left her and that she didn't want to keep her baby, but because she and her parents were devout Catholics, she could not have an abortion. She wanted to do the right thing, she told Pat. She wanted to give her baby a good home.

Pat and Mark arranged to meet with Carmen the next day. Even over the phone, Pat could tell the girl was nervous about the whole situation, so she invited her over to the house instead of meeting her at some neutral, unfamiliar location. That way Carmen could see how Pat and Mark lived and put her mind to rest that her child would have a good home. Pat had called over her adoption attorney so that he could answer any questions she or Carmen might have regarding the adoption process. But when Carmen showed up at the door and came inside, she refused to say a word until the adoption attorney left.

"I don't want lawyers," Carmen had told Pat in private. "I just want to talk to you. I want to make sure my baby will have a good mom and dad."

Mark told the attorney to leave and for the next two hours the three of them got to know each other. They didn't talk much about Carmen's baby, they just talked about life. About books, movies they'd seen, food. It wasn't a stiff conversation. They just got to know one another as people, as friends, as human beings who could help one another out. And, by the end of the day, everyone realized they were making the right decision.

Over the next two months Pat kept in constant contact with Carmen. She would pick her up from her house and drive her to her prenatal appointments, then afterward they'd go to lunch or to the movies or walking around the mall. Pat paid all of Carmen's expenses and even gave her spending money on the side. It wasn't to bribe the girl, their friendship had grown too strong for that. The money was in case of an emergency or just in case Carmen woke up in the middle of the night and needed a pint of ice cream. After all, she was the mother of her future child. Pat didn't want her to lack anything.

As the big day came closer and closer, Pat began to fill Carmen in more and more on the adoption process. She still refused to speak to their adoption attorney, but by that time Pat was so adept with the process that she felt she could be the attorney herself. Since they were going through an independent adoption, the terms were flexible. Carmen had already told Pat that she didn't want to see the child after it was born. Pat would take custody of the newborn from the hospital and within six months she'd go to court and file the papers for full adoption. All Carmen had to do once the baby was born was sign her adoption consent paper and set everything in stone. The whole process was a no-brainer and the more Pat read up on the subject, the more she realized she didn't need an adoption attorney in the first place. She could handle the adoption and all the papers herself. She and Carmen were friends and if anything ever went wrong, they'd be able to work it out amongst themselves — or at least that's what Pat had thought until the week before Carmen was to give birth.

Pat had been awakened one night at eleven o'clock by the phone. It was Carmen. At first she'd thought Carmen was going into labor early and she needed to go to the hospital. But that wasn't it at all.

"I want to keep the baby with me for a while after it's born," Carmen had told Pat.

Pat frowned as her heart began to beat rapidly. "But you said it'd be too painful for you to see the baby after it's born. We'd already agreed that Mark and I would take the baby home from the hospital. What's changed, Carmen? What's going on?"

"You told me I had forty-five days after the baby was born to change my mind, didn't you?"

"You're changing your mind?"

"I didn't say that, Pat."

"Well what's going on, Carmen?"

"I just want to keep the baby with me for a while after it's born. Just a day or two . . . so my child will know who I am."

Pat kept Mark up all night worrying over that phone call. "She's probably just having last-minute guilt," Mark said. "But when she thinks about it she'll realize she's doing the best thing for the baby," he said, and held Pat tightly, trying to ease her weary mind.

Pat wished she could be as sure as Mark, but after all she'd gone through over the past years, she didn't want to take any chances. She woke up early the next morning and drove over to Carmen's. She needed to talk to her, to make her understand that she was indeed doing the right thing by giving her custody of her unborn child. She couldn't back out now, Pat thought as she got out of her car and headed to Carmen's door. Please, girl, don't back out now, she thought to herself as she waited for Carmen to answer the door. But when she finally showed up and opened the door, Carmen doubled over in pain.

"*Carmen,*" Pat shouted and bent over next to her.

"I think my water just broke," she said, startled. "I'm having the baby. I'm having the baby *now!*"

Pat wasted no time. She helped Carmen out the front door and to her car and raced her to the hospital. She stood right beside Carmen all decked out in hospital greens and held her hand all the way through the delivery, yelling out commands as if she were a drill sergeant. "*Push, breathe, breathe, push,*" Pat scolded. And after twelve hours of labor a precious baby boy came poking his head into the world. He was the most beautiful thing Pat had ever seen. He seemed so strong as his tiny clinched fists swung through the air and waved for everyone to see.

Pat couldn't believe her eyes. When the doctor held out the baby for Carmen she took him for a brief second, looked him over, and began to cry. "You take him," she said, and held him out for Pat.

Startled, Pat opened her arms. "Oh," she cried as she cradled the baby next to her chest. She looked down at his slanted eyes and poofy head and smiled through her tears. This is my son, she thought as her tears dropped down upon him. *This is my son.*

Pat hadn't wanted to give the baby to the nurse for washing, but reluctantly she did, then hurried out of her hospital greens and ran down to Carmen's room. While she waited for her to return, she phoned Mark and told him the good news. "We've got a son," she told him. "We've got a son."

She couldn't make out what Mark was saying. All she heard through his sobs was the sound of joy. The sound of peace, now that the battle was over.

"I've got to go," Pat said as she wiped her eyes and looked over toward the door of the room. As she hung up, a familiar-looking woman passed through the door. Pat tried to place the woman's face but couldn't, so she held out her hand and introduced herself. "Hi, I'm Pat Brown. You must be part of Carmen's family."

"Well, I guess you can put it like that," the woman said as the door opened up behind her again. "Carmen," the woman said as the nurse wheeled her into the room and over to the bed. "I rushed over as fast as I could," she said as she helped Carmen onto the bed and pulled the covers over her.

Carmen's eyes darted back and forth between the two women.

"So tell me. Is it a boy or a girl?"

"It's a boy."

"Oh my God," the woman said, and silently wept into her hands.

Pat grabbed a box of tissues from the table and offered them to the woman. "Thank you," she said, and grabbed a handful. "Oh by the way," she said as she wiped her eyes. "I'm Sharon Bobber," the woman said, and extended her hand to Pat.

"Sharon Bobber," Pat exclaimed and reached out. "From the Channel Eight evening news?"

"Yes," she said, and smiled at Pat.

"But what are you doing here?" Pat asked, and glanced curiously at Carmen. "I didn't know you two were related."

The woman smiled and took hold of Carmen's hand. "I'm here to take custody of Carmen's child."

"What?" Pat said, and stopped cold. "What's going on?"

"You haven't told her?" Sharon asked, turning to face Carmen.

Carmen's eyes closed as she shook her head.

"Told me what?" Pat said, her body instantly beginning to ache.

"I am adopting Carmen's baby."

"What?" she whispered softly, then with fury. "What!"

Sharon Bobber swallowed hard as she assessed Pat's reaction. "I'll leave you two alone," she said as she walked past Pat to the door. "I'm going to see my son."

"What's going on here?" Pat asked, unable to keep her body from shaking.

"I've decided to let Sharon Bobber adopt my child."

"What are you talking about? I'm adopting your child. We've already—"

"I haven't signed any papers, Pat. I've got forty-five days to make up my mind," Carmen said, rationally.

"But why?" Pat asked with a curiosity so raw it seemed her brain had been wiped clear of everything it had ever known. "Why are you doing this?"

"I got a letter from Sharon about a month after I met you. She was also looking for a child to adopt," Carmen said, and fiddled nervously with the sheets on the bed. "At first I told her I didn't want to let her adopt my child. She's always on assignment with the news station, she works long days, and she doesn't even have a husband."

"So why are you doing this? Mark and I can be the perfect parents for that little boy."

"I know," Carmen said, "but Sharon's going to send me to college. She bought me a car and she's gonna pay for my housing expenses for the next four years."

"That's bribery, Carmen."

"It's making a life for myself. I couldn't afford to go to college on my own. Now I can have a life and my baby can have one too."

"That's not making it, Carmen," Pat huffed. "That's mistaking it. If money is what you wanted all you had to do was say the word," Pat pleaded. "I can give you all those things too. Please, Carmen. I thought we were friends."

"I've already signed papers with her attorney. I've taken the money too."

Attorney, Pat thought as her anger moved closer to hysteria. "How could you do this?"

"I'm sorry, Pat," she squealed. "I had to do what was best for me."

"No," Pat said and grabbed Carmen's shoulder. "You can't do this to me. You cannot do this!"

It took Mark plus two nurses and a security guard to drag Pat out of that hospital. She had gone completely berserk and not even a shot of Valium could calm her down. A few years back she had read a story in a magazine about how celebrities and other influential people used their status to win in the adoption game. But that was before Pat had even considered adoption. She'd never thought something like this could happen to her. She never thought she would be denied a child just because her face wasn't on TV or because she didn't live an extraordinary lifestyle. But it had happened. Her baby had been taken away and given to that bitch on the news and once again Pat's hopes of having a child had been stricken down. For weeks, all Pat could do was lie in bed and drink soup. Her body had dwindled down to nothing and her mind was following closely behind.

Pat couldn't pinpoint the day she finally began to come out of her depression. She guessed it was because she never really got over it. To this day, the yearnings, the pain, the hopes and fears of having a child in her life still frequented Pat's mind. Often on nights like these, she felt she could easily slip back into her depressed state. Even after she got over the adoption ordeal, Pat didn't really begin to live again until Mark bought her the hair salon. It was only then that her mind filled with enough other business that she could block out her angst over losing a child. But on nights like this, Pat realized that she would never be completely over it. Never would she fully accept the fact that she would never be someone's mother.

Mark rolled over in bed and practically crushed Pat. She took a deep breath, hoping he'd stay asleep, but this time her luck had run out. "You're home," he said in a groggy voice. "Why didn't you wake me?"

"Go back to sleep," Pat said, and rolled away from him and closer to the edge of the bed.

"What time did you get in?"

"I don't know," Pat said, and faked a yawn, hoping he'd think she was too sleepy to carry on a conversation. Didn't work.

"I cooked dinner for you."

"Thanks," she said and pulled on the covers. "I'll take it to work for lunch tomorrow."

"Are you okay?" he asked, and slid closer to her and wrapped his arms around her waist.

"Yeah," she said quickly. "Just tired."

Her husband pressed his body against her and Pat could feel him growing. "I missed you," he said, and kissed the back of Pat's neck.

Pat lay still and closed her eyes tightly. Please don't ask for what you can't have, she thought. But Mark didn't hold back. And who could blame him? They hadn't had sex in four whole months. So Mark did what came naturally. He lifted the bottom of Pat's nightgown and felt his way up to her panties. His fingers fumbled around until they found their way beneath them and between her legs. Pat squirmed and repositioned her legs tightly together, but this didn't stop Mark. He tugged on her panties until they began to come down and cupped his hands between her legs again. If this was supposed to get her in the mood it wasn't working.

"Just stop, all right?" Pat said, no longer able to take his touching her. "Just go to sleep."

Mark sighed and took his hand away quickly. "It's been months, Pat."

"And?" she said as the anger inside her quickly rose to the top.

"I just want to be with my wife. I love you. I need you."

"It's late and I'm tired. I've got to get up early for work—"

"Come on, Pat," he said cutting her off.

"I'm just not in the mood."

"I can't believe this," he said and sighed like a let-down child, making Pat feel so guilty she couldn't stand it.

Pat pulled back the covers and lay flat on her back, letting out a harsh sigh of her own. "So go ahead, Mark. Get on top of me and do what you have to do. *Damn*," she said and spread her legs an exaggerated distance apart.

Mark stared at her for a moment then turned on his side and sighed again.

"Dammit, Mark. If you've got something to say, just say it."

He turned over to face her again and softly put his hand on her face. "I think we need to talk. I know you're still having a hard time dealing with—"

"No," Pat said, and shook her head. "Don't say it."

"I know it's difficult," he said in a soothing voice. "I know you want a baby, Pat. I know you're still hurting. But I'm your husband. You've got to talk to me. Don't shut me out. You've—"

"Mark!" Pat screamed, no longer able to take the sound of his voice. This was the very reason she'd tried to be so quiet and not wake him up. She knew it would come to this. She knew he'd want to *talk.* But she couldn't. Not now. "I just want to sleep. Okay? Will you please just let me *sleep.* Please!"

Mark knew there was no use. "Okay," he said, and threw himself down on the bed.

"Fine," she said and pulled up the covers.

"Fine," he said and yanked the covers back and sighed for the third, most irritating time. "You know," he said, then paused, "the way you act . . . sometimes . . . I . . . I think you want a divorce," he said offhandedly.

"Maybe I do," Pat said in a voice so stern and direct that it left nothing to be confused about.

She hadn't expected to say that. He hadn't expected to hear that.

Mark stared at his wife's back for a moment, then turned back on his side. "You don't mean that," he said as he closed his eyes and tried to go back to sleep.

"Maybe I do," Pat said as she stared at the wall in front of her.

The silence in the room lasted awhile before Mark sat up and turned on the light beside the bed. "Just exactly what are you saying?" he said and stared at Pat's back.

Pat didn't say another word though she knew her husband was waiting for a response. She didn't know if she was serious or just talking out of anger. But what she did know was that they couldn't go on like this for much longer. Something had to give. "Just go to sleep, Mark," she said, and pulled the covers tightly around her neck. "Forget about it."

"No, dammit," Mark said and snatched the covers back. "I want to know what you're saying."

Pat lay still for a couple of seconds, then slowly and calmly she sat up.

She looked at her husband, then got up from bed. "I'm going to sleep downstairs," she said as she headed for the door. But before she could get there, Mark was on her heels. He grabbed her arm and spun her around.

"Are you telling me you want a divorce?"

"Yes," Pat screamed, and snatched her arm away. "That's exactly what I'm telling you."

4

Zuma was up and dressed by six-thirty Saturday morning. She had already prayed to Allah, given her respect to the East, and now it was time to get on with her day. Still, she was bone tired, and if it hadn't been for the fact that she hadn't prayed and given respect for the past four days in a row, she would have slept in again. But Zuma had allowed herself to backslide far enough on her religious rituals. She had decided to switch from Christianity to Islam about a year ago for no other reason than she thought it was the right thing to do—the *black* thing to do. Still, she couldn't quite get used to the rigors of being Muslim. She could handle praying for a full hour nonstop, but she couldn't quite get with all the dietary changes being a Muslim forced upon her, especially the one about not eating pork. Pork had been such a constant in Zuma's culinary reper-toire that the thought of giving it up completely was like taking away a credit card from a shopaholic. To be honest, Zuma often slipped up and had a couple slices of bacon every once in a while, but she didn't really consider that cheating since the bacon she ate was made out of sixty percent turkey. Besides, she figured Allah was an understanding type of guy. There's no way in the world she could believe that on the day she met her maker he would grill her about such trivial things as whether or not she ate pork. There were greater sins for her to worry about, she figured. She'd made many a transgression in her day. So many that Allah could probably care less about her occasional splurge on pepperoni pizza. Still, Zuma vowed to herself that she'd be one hundred percent pork free by next year. That was surely enough time to wean her palate away from pig.

The other thing about being Muslim that Zuma couldn't quite get with was the fact that she had the obligation to turn over five percent of all her income to the religion, but it was better than Christianity's ritual of tithing ten percent, which to be honest is the most important reason Zuma changed religions in the first place. She was a businesswoman at heart, and it didn't take her long to figure out that being a Muslim was a whole lot cheaper than being Baptist. And though she wasn't quite a five percenter yet, she was getting there, and most importantly she spent all her money at black-owned businesses. That's what being Muslim was all about for Zuma. It was taking pride in her African heritage and supporting her brothers and sisters in the cause of life. Damn whether or not she ate the other white meat. There were more important aspects of being a Muslim than that.

Zuma set her Koran on her dresser as she looked in the mirror and fluffed out the twists on her head. She noticed she had bags underneath her eyes and tried to smooth them out, but as soon as she removed her fingers the puffs popped right back up. She yawned and tried to perk herself up by flinging her arms through the air, but she still needed an extra boost, an extra shot of energy to push her over the edge into the land of the fully awakened. She breezed out of her bedroom and into the living room of her apartment and stopped at the stereo. She pressed the track button on her CD system and waited for George Clinton and the P-Funk All-Stars to come blasting through the speakers. "*Flash light . . . red light,*" she sang as she bopped into the kitchen and opened the refrigerator. She pulled out a container of cut peaches and grabbed a fork as she jammed back into the living room and sat down on the sofa. She grabbed her hair bag from the floor and pulled out her change purse and began counting yesterday's tips. There was forty dollars and a couple of quarters, which she laid down on the table in front of her. That was pretty good, she thought, considering two of her clients had walked out of the shop without so much as a thank-you, let alone a tip. Zuma didn't like nontippers. She felt all the energy she put into creating a hair design should at least be compensated by a couple extra dollars on the side. But some people just don't have class, she thought to herself as peach juice dripped down onto the collar of her white T-shirt. She lifted the collar to her mouth and licked the juice off before stuffing her mouth with a forkful of fruit.

By the time she'd finished her breakfast, "Flash Light" had gone off and

"One Nation Under a Groove" had begun to play. Forget that it wasn't even 7 A.M. yet. Zuma didn't care as she shimmied up from the sofa and turned up the volume. *"Getting down just for the funk of it,"* she sang as she headed back to the kitchen. She put her empty peach container in the sink, then grabbed her empty Evian bottle and filled it with tapwater. Gotta get those eight glasses a day, she thought to herself as she capped the bottle, then took a sip.

As she walked back into the living room, she passed her answering machine, which sat on one of her end tables. She'd been so sleepy last night that she hadn't bothered checking her messages, so she pressed the playback button before sitting down again, then picked up the remote for the stereo system and turned down her jam. The next voice she heard as she crossed her legs was that of Taj.

"Zuma. You there? Pick up the phone. Pick up the *phone.* Zuma. Zuma. Zuma, I'm sorry, all right. All right . . ."

"Whatever," Zuma said and rolled her eyes, waiting for the next message. This time it was Robert.

"Hey, Zuma. What's up, doll face? Are you ever at home? What's a brother gotta do to get in touch with you? Hit me on my hip when you get this message. Ciao baby."

Ciao baby? How a Negro from the ghetto gonna be talking about Ciao baby? Brother, please, Zuma thought and waited for message number three.

"Zuma. *Zuma.* I know you're there. Pick up the phone. Pick up the fucking phone."

Taj was getting a bit perturbed. But who cares? Zuma rolled her eyes and waited. Next message.

"Hi, Zuma. This is Kristoff. Are we still on for Sunday? Looking forward to it. Give me a call."

If I have time, Zuma thought, and kicked her heels onto her coffee table and waited for the next message.

"Yo Zuma. Zuma. Pick up."

"Forget you, Taj," Zuma said, and got up to push the Erase button on the machine. That was the last message, and as Zuma returned to her sofa and turned up the sound on the stereo again she let out a long sigh. "All you guys can kiss my ass," she mumbled, and clicked her fingers to the sound of Knee Deep.

Taj, Robert, and Kristoff were the men in Zuma's life, and though they were all special to her in their own particular ways, none of them was worth a full investment of Zuma's time. Time to Zuma was a priceless commodity and she refused to waste it any longer on relationships that were going nowhere.

Taj was Zuma's longtime boyfriend whom she'd known ever since high school. Her relationship with Taj was one of those on again, off again, slightly obsessive-compulsive-could-be-fatal deals. Taj had been a player back in the day and on several occasions had traded in the commitment he'd given to Zuma for a one-night rendezvous with anything in a tight leather skirt and high heels. But now that Taj was pushing thirty he wanted to settle down. Only Zuma had had enough. She'd figured cheating was just in Taj's bones and no matter how he tried to tell her differently these days, she just wasn't buying it. To be honest, she really didn't know why she still talked to Taj considering all the bullshit she'd been through with him over the years. She had once loved Taj so much that she would have done anything to please him — and she did. But now her love for him had changed. The only reason she dealt with him now was because she felt sorry for him, and though Taj had been trying his damnedest to get her back, Zuma had no plans of ever having a serious relationship with him again. She'd been down that road with Taj and now it was time to move on. It had taken her a long time to get him out of her system and now that her mind was reprogrammed, she refused to let a virus like Taj break it down again.

Robert, on the other hand, was loyal to Zuma through and through. She and Robert had been going out for about a year, but there was one thing keeping her from really settling down with him. He was too damn overprotective. He always had to know where she was going and where she had been and what time she was coming back. Zuma wasn't the type of girl you could put on a schedule, and when her timing was the slightest bit off, Robert would fly into a rage. Though he never hit her, Zuma could foresee the day when she'd come home from work just a bit too late and he'd slam her into a wall. Zuma wasn't having that. Robert would always blame his overreactions on his love for Zuma. "I act this way because I'm just so crazy for you," he'd say. But no. *You're just crazy*, Zuma had concluded and put an end to their intimate relationship. Robert needed a woman who could be submissive and that was a character trait that Zuma did not carry.

Kristoff was the most sane of the three, but even he didn't have what it took to keep Zuma's interest. He was lousy in bed and even after months of trying to train him in the fine art of arousing her sexual passion, Kristoff could not pull it off. Zuma had thought about drawing him a diagram of her body and starring the exact places for him to touch that would get her hot, but that was taking things too far. If a thirty-year-old man could not figure out how to get her in the mood even after explicit instruction, then he wasn't worth the frustration. Zuma did a better job taking care of herself in the sex department. Besides, there were more important things on Zuma's mind these days than sex.

For all their faults and differences the three men in Zuma's life did have one thing in common. They all had money. That was a prerequisite for getting with Zuma. She was the diva of dividends, and unless a man had a solid bank account and enough generosity to spread some of that money in her direction, he wasn't fit to fool with. Zuma wasn't after men only for money but she believed that if she had a bill that needed to be paid, her man should be able to take care of it with no problem. Zuma preferred to look at it as sponsorship. The men in her life didn't give her money just for the hell of it, they were sponsoring a well-deserving woman in need. Just like parents sponsor their kids to college or a big corporation sponsors a charity event.

Still, by all conventional standards, Zuma was indeed greedy, and if you called her a gold-digger she didn't give a damn. You could call her what you wanted, but you'd never call her broke.

The truth of the matter was that Zuma made good money all by herself. She only had to pay Pat eight hundred dollars a month to rent her hair station at Blessings, which was nothing considering she pulled in over four thousand dollars a month, including tips. It had taken Zuma over ten years to build up the reputation and clientele to rake in that kind of money. As a hairdresser she was making more than most government workers and she didn't even have a college degree. But Zuma didn't waste her money on material things. She lived in a low-budget apartment, drove a simple blue Saturn, and all it took to fill up her wardrobe were a few pairs of Levi's and a couple packs of extra-large white cotton T-shirts. The rest of Zuma's money was in the bank or invested in mutual funds and CDs. Zuma knew how to handle money. Hers and that of others. More than a gold-digger, Zuma was a money hoarder. She collected it, saved it, and made it work for her. But Zuma's love of money wasn't some fanatical vice, it was all for a purpose. All a part of her master plan. A plan that one day would include what would be the love of her life — a beautiful child.

Zuma's master plan had been in effect for the past five years and so far it had been moving along quite smoothly. On her twenty-fifth birthday,

Zuma came to the realization that she needed to make a change in her life. She was working at Off the Hook Hair at the time and made almost as much money as she did now, but kept much less of it. Her lifestyle at the time was borderline psychotic. She spent money two times faster than she made it. She was sporting a candy apple red BMW sportscar, had sixteen different credit cards, all of which were over or close to the max, her wardrobe was laced with every designer label known to man, and her savings account — *please* — there was no savings account. Zuma was living the high life back in the day. She surrounded herself with all the material things that she thought would make her happy. But at the end of the day, as she lay in her brass bed in her then eleven-hundred-dollar-a-month apartment off Wilshire Boulevard, she realized something was missing in her life. She always knew what that thing was. It was something that she had wanted ever since she was in high school. That one thing was a child. That's why Zuma had come up with a master plan. It was all for her child. She wanted a baby desperately and when she had her baby she wanted to be in the position to take care of it completely. She wanted her baby to have the best of everything. She wanted her life to be in order. She wanted to be *ready*.

And now, five years later, with her thirtieth birthday just around the corner, Zuma was ready. She had started by downsizing her life in order to save money. She moved to Inglewood where the cost of housing was cheaper. She sold her BMW, cut up all her credit cards except for one, and sold all her designer labels at a huge sale she put on one day at Off the Hook. She then used that money to pay off all her outstanding bills, and to this day, the only money that left Zuma's hand was for apartment rent, shop rent, utilities, gasoline, and food. Where there was no bank account before, there was now a substantial one. Sixty-eight thousand dollars strong to be exact. And that wasn't all. As of last April Zuma had decided it was time for her to own her own shop. So ever since, she had been taking business correspondence classes in order to get her business license so that she could one day open a shop of her own. Her world was coming together.

Changing her life was not an easy task, but knowing why she was doing it made it easier. None of the changes Zuma had made were for herself. They were all designed to give a good life to the baby that she would one day call her own. She had seen the struggling mothers who came into the shop, all complaining about how tough it was to raise a child and bitching about how they wished they had done things differently. But Zuma would never be one of those ladies. The difference between them and her was that she planned. She knew what she wanted and she knew how to get it.

Zuma could barely hear the sound of the phone when it rang for the music that was filling the air. As she reached over to pick it up she glanced at the wall for the time. It was 6:55. "Hello," she said as she turned down the stereo with the remote.

"Zuma?"

Oh shit, she thought as the voice twanged in her ear. "What, Taj?"

"Why you didn't call me back?"

"I've been working," she said as she shook her head, hoping he'd make this quick.

"You get my message?"

"Yes, Taj."

"Well?"

"Well what?"

"I said I was sorry."

"I know," she said, remembering the silly argument they'd gotten into last Sunday. Taj had asked her to meet him at a restaurant, but Zuma had forgotten. She'd been so wrapped up in studying for her business correspondence classes that she missed the date. Taj had gotten upset and gone off. It was her only day off from the shop and he'd really wanted to be with her. But dating wasn't a part of Zuma's master plan and dating Taj wasn't even on her list of favorite things to do. She had apologized but that hadn't been good enough for him so he started an argument. Now he was calling to say he's sorry. They'd been through scenarios like this together for over fifteen years. The only difference now was that Zuma didn't give a damn. If Taj wanted to be her friend that was fine. But other than that, Zuma could care less.

"Zuma?"

"Yes, Taj."

"Why aren't you talking?"

"I really don't have much to say, Taj. I've got to go to work."

"So you're saying you don't have time for me?"

Here we go, Zuma thought to herself, and rolled her eyes.

"You be tripping, Zuma. You know a brother want to be with you, but you still won't stop tripping."

"I told you, Taj. We can't be together. Too much has gone on between us."

"That's your problem. You living in the past. Forget all that old shit. I'm talking about starting over, Zuma."

"I can't talk about this now. I have a seven-thirty at the shop."

"So what? You just gonna get off the phone?"

"I've gotta go."

"See how you do me?"

"Remember how you did me?"

"Whatever, Zuma," he said and hung up the phone in her face.

Taj was a trip. After all he'd put Zuma through over the years he expected her to just forgive and forget and move on. Since he was ready for a serious relationship now, he felt Zuma she be good to go. But Zuma had been through enough with Taj and she wasn't going back for more. Because of Taj she had done something that she would forever regret. Something that no matter how it went down could never be justified.

Zuma had fooled around with Taj on and off throughout high school, but it wasn't until after they had graduated and a few years had passed that they finally became a couple. At least Zuma had thought they were a couple. She knew Taj was seeing other girls but she still considered him to be her man. Taj had never been much for the girlfriend-boyfriend thing and Zuma knew that. But compared to the major player he'd been in high school Taj was a new man. He had matured rapidly, due for the most part to the new business he had started with his brother. By the age of twenty-two, Taj was part owner of a traveling car detailing company. He and his brother made big money going to people's homes and businesses to detail and wash their cars. The responsibility of owning a business had made Taj slow down with the ladies, but he still claimed he wasn't ready for a serious commitment with Zuma. But that was okay with her. At least he was moving in the right direction. She knew that it was just a matter of time before he settled down completely and Zuma had been willing to wait. But sometimes things don't go according to plan. Sometimes the snow comes down in June, sometimes the sun goes around the moon, and sometimes, oh yes, *sometimes* a condom breaks and you wind up pregnant.

Zuma had waited weeks before telling Taj that she was pregnant because she didn't know exactly how he'd react. The only thing she knew was that she was with child and the parameters of their relationship were about to change. She didn't know if she was happy about the pregnancy herself. She was only twenty-one at the time and motherhood was the furthest thing from her mind. She was barely out of beauty school and was nowhere near the hair design heroine that she was today, so money was scarce. Still, she wanted to do the right thing. She hadn't planned on becoming pregnant, but now that she was, she accepted it and vowed to do whatever it took to give her baby a good life. She knew Taj would not be pleased with the news that he'd soon become a dad. He wasn't even ready for a real relationship, let alone the responsibility of being a father. But Zuma believed Taj would do right by her and the baby. Even if he didn't want to settle down with her, she figured he'd still support her and her child. At least now he had a booming job and a steady cash flow. She knew he'd be upset at first, but soon he'd get over it. The fact of the matter was that he had no choice. She was pregnant with his child and there was no way to get around it.

Still Zuma had been nervous about breaking the news to him. So nervous in fact that she decided she didn't want to be alone with him when she told him. Instead she decided to tell him at Houston's, the busiest restaurant she could think of. At least there he couldn't throw a tantrum. She met him there on Friday night, the busiest of all. She fidgeted around all during dinner trying to figure out the proper way to tell him, as she sat across from him, eyeing his clean-shaven face, expertly groomed sideburns, nicely broad shoulders, and firm hands. But by the time the waiter had come to the table with their bill, she decided the best thing to do was just blurt it out.

"Taj," she said softly as he picked up the bill and looked it over. As she watched him reach into his pocket and pull out a wad of cash, she braced herself and let it out. "I'm pregnant."

Taj stopped cold and looked across the table at Zuma. His stare was so intense that Zuma began to get edgy. She cracked a nervous smile and raised her eyebrows. "I know it's the last thing you wanted to hear, but it's the truth." She waited for some type of response from Taj, but got nothing, so she continued to speak. "Look, Taj. I know you're not ready for a serious relationship and believe me, this is not some stunt to get you to marry me or anything like that. I just want you to do the right thing. This baby is half yours, you know." She thought that would ease Taj's mind a bit, but still she got no response from him. "Well, aren't you going to say something?"

Taj sighed and shook his head and instead looked over the dinner bill once again. He took the wad of money in his hand and pulled out two twenties and put them on top of the receipt. Then he counted out several

more twenties and put them on the table too. He placed his hands on
both stacks of money and pushed them to the middle of the table. Zuma
looked down at the stacks of money. One she knew was for the waiter, but
the other, which appeared to be several hundred dollars, was a puzzle.
She looked sideways at Taj with a question in her eyes.

"That's for you," he said, and stuffed the rest of his money wad back
into his pocket. "Handle your business."

Zuma pulled the money toward her and stared at it until she finally got
it. Oh, she thought, and smiled. Money to take care of the baby. But it
was too soon for that. Her insurance took care of the prenatal bills and it
was too early to start buying baby clothes and furniture. She pushed the
money back toward Taj. "Thanks," she said, feeling so glad that Taj would
do the right thing and support their child. "But I don't need any money
yet."

Taj drew his hand across his face, then pushed the money back to
Zuma. "Handle your business," he said again, but this time his voice was
more firm.

Zuma frowned as she pushed the money back again. "I said I don't
need any money right now. Thank you."

Again Taj pushed it back. "I don't want any babies, Zuma. So handle
your fucking business," he said as his voice grew louder and he looked
around to make sure he hadn't been overheard.

"So what are you saying?" she asked, knowing exactly what he was
saying. "What is this money for?"

Taj stared at her, refusing to put into words what he was actually saying.
But they both knew what he meant—Get an abortion.

Zuma picked up the money and threw it in Taj's face. "You low-life
fuckball," she screamed as heads turned and whispers began to brew. She
walked around the table, then leaned over in Taj's face. "I'm having this
baby, you sick fuck. And you are going to support it."

Zuma raced out of the restaurant and once she got into the parking lot
she slowed down. She waited at her car for Taj to join her, but when she
looked behind her, he was nowhere to be found. She thought for sure
he'd be on her heels if for no other reason than to finish the argument. But
for Taj, there was nothing else to say. He'd made it perfectly clear what his
position was going to be. Now it was up to Zuma to decide the rest.

A month had passed before Zuma saw Taj again. He'd made no effort
to get in contact with her and during that time all Zuma could think
about was how she could never raise a child all on her own. At the time,

she had just started doing hair and she was barely making any money at all. She didn't even have a home of her own. She was still living with her parents, whom she hadn't even told about her pregnancy. Though she was a grown woman she knew she wouldn't be able to handle a baby all on her own. She'd have to go on welfare, get WIC, find Section 8 housing, all of which meant that the baby growing inside her would be born into poverty. There was only one way she could have that baby and that was if Taj took his responsibility and helped her out.

Even though he hadn't bothered getting in touch with her since their fight at Houston's, Zuma decided to give him one last shot. She had to make him understand that he had to do his part. She had to make him understand that she wanted that baby. She showed up on the doorstep of his apartment and knocked, and though no one answered, she knew he was there. His car was parked right out front and the light in his bedroom was on. So Zuma continued to knock and when there was still no answer she began to pound. "I know you're in there, Taj," she screamed. "Open this fucking door."

A couple more minutes passed before the door came swinging open, but the body behind it was not that of Taj. It was a woman. She was tall and lanky and dressed in a robe. She said no words, but the look on her face told the whole story — *What do you want?*

"Where is Taj?"

"Why?"

Strike one, Zuma thought to herself, and took a deep breath. She knew this woman had to be Taj's girl of the moment and since she didn't have a beef with her she didn't want to get into an argument. "Is Taj home?"

"Who wants to know?"

Strike two. This woman had one more nasty remark to say before she got smacked, Zuma thought as she sized up the woman and picked out which eye she was going to smash her in if she got smart one more time. "Taj!" Zuma screamed and looked past the woman into the house. "Taj, if you don't get out here right now — "

"He's not here," the woman said, and that was about all Zuma was going to take from her.

She pushed the woman backward and stepped through the door. Thank God the woman stumbled to the floor or else Zuma would have been in for a fight. Instead she rushed through the front room and back to Taj's bedroom. She opened the door and closed it behind her as she heard the sound of the woman's footsteps coming after her.

"What the hell?" Taj said as he jumped his shirtless body up from bed just as the woman came bursting through the door. The woman lunged toward Zuma, but Taj held her back. "Hold on a minute," he said, trying to calm his woman down.

"You better put a leash on your dog," Zuma told Taj and stood safely behind him.

"Fuck you, bitch," the woman yelled out, and lunged again.

"Are you going to let her hit the mother of your child?" Zuma said as she backed her way toward the farthest wall in the room.

"Who is she?" the woman asked and brushed Taj's hands off her.

"His baby's mama," Zuma answered for him.

"Shut up, Zuma," Taj yelled over his shoulder as he pushed the woman toward the door of the room. "Just give me a minute to talk to her."

"Hell no. What do you need to talk to her for? I want her out of here."

"I ain't going nowhere," Zuma said.

"You better get her out of here."

"Don't you give me no orders," Taj told her, and pushed her out the door. "I said just give me a minute," he said as he closed the door in front of the woman's face.

"So is that your new girl?" Zuma asked as Taj turned around to face her. "Does she know that I'm carrying your child?" Zuma screamed more for the woman, who she knew was probably listening at the door. "Does she know you're about to become a *father?*"

"I'm not about to be no father, Zuma. I ain't ready for that right now," he said, calmly running a hand over his face.

"What do you mean you're not ready? You're grown, you've got a good job."

"I told you. I'm not having that now."

"And I told you I'm having this baby."

"Then you'll be doing it all by yourself."

This is not the way Zuma had expected this conversation to go, she thought to herself as she crossed her arms over her chest. "I can't do it all by myself."

"Then handle your business."

"Do you know what you're asking me to do? That's murder, Taj. *Murder.*"

"Girl, please. Women do that shit all the time. It ain't no big deal."

"It is a big deal to me. I'm not killing this baby. *Your* baby."

Taj threw up his hands and sat down on the bed.

"I can't believe you're acting this way."

"What you want me to do, Zuma? I'm not ready for this. And neither are you."

"So what? No one is ever really ready for children. But they accept the responsibility and do the best they can."

Taj shook his head and stared down at the floor in silence. For the first time, Zuma thought that maybe she was getting through to him. He patted the space beside him on the bed and motioned for Zuma to come sit down. He waited several more minutes before he finally spoke and this time he seemed to be more open. "How long have we been messing around?"

"Six years," Zuma recounted as she thought back to the first time they'd gone out in high school.

"And how many times have we broken up since we first got together?"

"A million and thirty-two," Zuma said sarcastically, wondering where this was all leading.

"And every time we break up, we get back together, don't we?"

"What's your point, Taj?"

"My point is that I always come back to you," he said and turned around to face her head-on. "I know one of these days we're probably going to be together forever. I can see myself with you when I get older. But I'm just not ready now."

"But I don't need you to be with me now. I just need you to say you'll be there for the baby."

"But that's not what I want. The time is not right. What I'm saying to you is that we need to wait. We need to wait until we're older, when we can be married and start a family. We need to do this the right way, Zuma. Now is just not the time," he stressed, then dropped his head into his hands.

Zuma looked Taj over, trying to figure out if he was truly serious. This was the first time he'd ever talked to her about the future. The first time he ever admitted that they even had a future together. She watched as he got up from the bed and walked over to his dresser. He opened it up and pulled out a wad of money and came back to the bed. "Someday, Zuma," he said, and placed a roll of bills in her hand. "Someday, but not now."

Zuma took the money and crumbled it up in her hand as tears began to flow from her eyes. Taj sat beside her and put a comforting arm over her shoulder. There they sat in silence for a very long time, neither one of them truly realizing the depth of the decision their silence was setting in stone. Zuma knew what she had to do now. There was no way to change Taj's mind.

Eventually, Zuma handled her business, but never again was she the same. Mentally, Zuma was nowhere near the woman she was today, and at the time, in the back of her twenty-one-year-old mind, she had thought that having an abortion would somehow bring her closer to Taj. That somehow it would show him that she was willing to do things his way. That she'd wait for him until the time was right when he'd given up all the other girls in his life and could focus on her and the future. But as the years passed and Zuma matured, reality came into view. What she had done was murder her baby, all for the sake of a man. And as the years passed by, the guilt she held over doing that grew stronger and stronger. The truth was that the abortion really fucked up Zuma's head. Through school, she had heard many girls talk about getting abortions like it was no big deal, like it was a form of birth control. But while it seemed to be no problem for some girls, Zuma was different. It wasn't that she was against a woman's right to choose, it was just that for herself, in her own mind, abortion was killing. And, on that day when she'd gone to the clinic, paid her money, and had her insides sucked out, in her mind she knew she had committed murder. Forget the politics of the situation. Forget what everyone else's views were. To Zuma, she had committed the biggest of sins, and hers was the only opinion that counted.

Though all that happened years ago, the memory of what she had done still plagued Zuma. It still kept her up at night, invaded her thoughts on otherwise peaceful days, and troubled her heart like nothing else had had the power to do. And now that Zuma was about to turn thirty she wanted more than ever to rectify the bad decision she'd made so long ago. She wanted to do the proper thing. She was ready to make it right. She was ready to be pregnant, to give birth, to bring forth life and cherish it. Only that way could she rectify the wrong she'd once done when she was so young and so stupid.

Zuma glanced at the clock on the wall and found it was seven o'clock. The shop was only ten minutes away, but she decided to get a move on anyway. She got up from the sofa, grabbed her water bottle, stuffed it into her hair bag, and headed for the door. She snatched up her keys from the top of the stereo and punched the CD off button at the same time, before opening the front door.

But just as she was about to step out, a huge, dark figure blocked her path and stepped in front of her.

Oh shit, she thought and rolled her eyes as she moved backward. "What are you doing here?"

Taj pushed his hard body against Zuma until he had moved her back far enough to step inside the apartment. He closed the door behind him, leaned against it, and eyed Zuma like she was made of glass, but he didn't say one word.

Zuma was totally unimpressed with Taj's spontaneous appearance. She wanted so badly to give him a piece of her mind, but she didn't have time to waste lecturing him again. So she simply pursed her lips and huffed. "I said, what are you doing here?" she asked and folded her arms over her chest. "Didn't I just tell you over the phone that I had to be down at the shop for a seven-thirty?"

Taj's only response was to lower his lids until his eyes became a couple of horizontal slits. He stared at Zuma this way in silence until Zuma could finally take no more. That little lustful gesture didn't work on Zuma anymore. There had been a time when if Taj had looked at her like that, Zuma would come busting out of her clothes.

"Move," she said, and nudged him away from the door, but Taj was no pushover. He grabbed Zuma's arm, turned her around, and pinned her against the wall. And still, he said nothing, only peered into her face in what Zuma concluded was some sort of romantic "sex me baby" trance. But whatever it was, it still wasn't working. Don't you know I'm over you, she wanted to say as Taj insisted with his silent come-ons. "Get off me, boy," she said, and twisted her body so that she was able to slide away from him. "I'm on my way to work, Taj," she said, and straightened out her T-shirt. "So unless you've got something to say, I wish you'd get the hell out of my way."

Taj breathed deeply, finally realizing that whatever he thought he was doing was not working out as he'd planned. So he took to his next line of defense — whining. "Why you gotta be like this?" he finally said, and placed his hand on his hips as he waited for Zuma to respond.

"Be like what?" she asked with irritation.

Taj sighed with roughness. "You know what I'm talking about, Zuma. Why you playing these games?"

"Games?" she said simply, and shook her head in confusion.

Her coolness seemed to push Taj over the edge. He spun around and put his hands on his head. "How long are you gonna make me wait before you give in?" he asked as frustration seemed to radiate from his pores. "You know I want to be with you now. You know I'm ready to settle down and I told you a long time ago when I got to this point you would be the only woman I'd want."

"You wanna be with me *now*," she stressed, and put her hand in the air. "Oh, okay. Let me see if I've got this straight," she said. "*You* are ready to be with me *now*, so therefore I should bow down and let you have me? Is that how it's supposed to work out?" she asked as her voice got louder. "Have you forgotten how long we've known each other, Taj?" she asked, and waited less than a second for the answer. "Fifteen years," she said, flashing five fingers three times. "*Fifteen.* If you wanted me so bad you could have had me by now, but *no*," she said and shook her head. "You wanted to be a *player*," she said, and took one step back and looked at Taj from head to toe. "And look at you now—thirty years old and all played out."

Taj laughed, mostly out of embarrassment, but also because he and Zuma had had this conversation many times before since he'd made it up in his mind that his player days were over. And the conversation was always the same. He'd come over, beg and plead, and Zuma would turn him down. The whole scenario had hurt his feelings the first couple of times they'd gone through it, but now it only made him laugh. For he knew in his heart and Zuma knew as well that she couldn't resist him forever. He had been her first and he knew how much weight that carried. It was only a matter of time, he figured. Only a matter of time. He moved in closer to Zuma and wrapped his arms around her waist, swaying ever so slightly from side to side like they used to do together back in high school at the Friday night dances. "That's right, baby," he said, rubbing her back. "Let it all out," he said, and leaned over to kiss her cheek, then her neck. "Tell me how much of a bad boy I've been. Tell me how much I've dogged you in the past. Go ahead, get it all out of your system," he said, as he placed kisses all over her neck.

"Stop it," Zuma warned, hating herself for liking the way Taj felt. His was such a familiar touch. He knew just how to please her, how to bring her to her knees, and when he moved his lips to her ears . . . "Stop, Taj," she insisted, and pushed him away.

Taj smiled, knowing he still had the power to break down Zuma, the diva with the heart of stone.

Zuma knew Taj thought he had won, but that wasn't the case at all and as she stood there watching him grinning from ear to ear she almost wanted to slap him silly. Did he really think she was that easy?

"You know we're going to be together one day, don't you?" he asked, so full of pride and victory.

"Never," Zuma said, directly

"We're going to get married."

"Please."

"Buy a house somewhere on top of a hill."

"Ha."

"Take vacations once a year — twice."

Zuma yawned.

"Have kids."

All movement seemed to stop. Zuma couldn't believe Taj had said that, and after the words came pouring out of his mouth even Taj had to stop cold, unable to believe he'd traveled into that forbidden territory. Zuma and Taj never spoke of children after the day she went down to the clinic and had the abortion. The subject was taboo. It was as if they both believed the fact that they never spoke about it would make its reality a lie. Taj never wanted to discuss it because he didn't want to hurt Zuma, and she never bought it up because she didn't want to remind him of how cruel he'd been even to have suggested such a thing as abortion. But she was the most cruel. Taj had only suggested, she was the one who'd gone through with it.

Suddenly, Zuma felt anger. Anger toward herself and anger toward Taj. And this anger, this feeling of self-contempt, this . . . this, this *thing* that had the ability to creep up in Zuma's emotions was the very thing that would not allow her to be with Taj ever again. Their history together was too plagued, and whether they spoke about it or not, the knowledge of what they'd both done would always hover over their relationship.

"I'm sorry," Taj said, bowing his head and stuffing his hands inside his pockets. "I didn't mean to bring that up."

"Bring what up?" Zuma said, playing the fool.

"You know," he said, and shut his eyes tightly.

"No, I don't know."

"I didn't mean . . . I mean . . . I shouldn't have said . . ."

Zuma wanted to hear him say it. She wanted him to bring up the subject of kids. She wanted to talk to him about it. She wanted to tell him how she felt so many years ago when she'd gone down to that clinic all by herself. She wanted him to know what it was like for her. But she didn't want to be the one to speak of it first. She wanted Taj to be the one. But as she stared at him, waiting for him to speak, she realized he was a weak man. He wouldn't dare speak of kids or abortion. He wouldn't dare bring up the past. He hadn't been man enough to accept the responsibility as a father nine years ago, and now he wasn't man enough to say what was on both their minds.

But Zuma wasn't weak. Not even a little bit.

"Did I tell you I was going to have a baby?" she blurted out in frustration. She stared at Taj as his eyes seemed to grow too large for their sockets, and suddenly she wondered if she should tell him. She hadn't told anybody else what she was planning to do. She had kept it a secret. But now . . .

"What did you say?" he asked. The jealousy and confusion in his voice was like music to Zuma's ears.

"I'm going to have a baby," she said again.

Taj's eyes darted to various parts of the room, then back to Zuma. "Are you trying to tell me you're seeing somebody else?"

"Nope."

He frowned and squinted at the same time. "What are you saying, Zuma?"

"I'm saying I'm going to have a baby."

"Well, as far as I know you still need a man to do that."

Zuma grinned devilishly, then shifted her hair bag on her shoulder and headed past Taj to the door. "I've got to go to work now," she said as she opened the door and stepped out.

"Wait a minute," Taj insisted, and ran out after her. "What are you trying to tell me, Zuma? What's this . . . this stuff you're talking?"

Weak bastard, she thought to herself as she locked her front door. He couldn't even say the words. *Baby. Pregnant.*

"Talk to me, Zuma," he said as he followed her down the front steps and out to the carport of her apartment building. "Talk to me."

By the time she reached her car and got in, the nagging sound of Taj's voice became too much for Zuma to bear. She had never exposed the realities of her master plan to another living soul, but today she was breaking the rules. "I'm getting artificially inseminated," she said as she sat in the driver's seat, looking up at Taj with confidence.

"You're getting artificially inseminated?" he said, then seemingly held his breath. And when he could hold it no longer he let it go and with it came the loudest howling laugh that Zuma had ever heard in all her life.

Taj had to bend over and grab his stomach to tame his overwhelming bout of snickering. But there was nothing funny to Zuma. Nothing funny at all. She had expected such a childish reaction from Taj. There was no way he could know how serious Zuma was. She hadn't expected him to understand. She hadn't expected him to realize that she wanted a baby so badly that she'd do anything to have one. She didn't expect him to care that for the last five years she'd been waiting and planning for just that, saving her money to cover the expenses. She didn't expect him to understand at all. She didn't expect anyone to understand, which is why she'd kept her plans a secret from everyone, including Faye and Pat.

"Wait a minute," Taj said, once he was able to catch his breath. "You mean to tell me that you are going to go down to some hospital and pay for some sperm from a guy you don't even know? That's how you're going to get pregnant?"

Zuma stared up at Taj and smirked. Exactly, she thought, but said nothing. She simply smiled, slammed the door of her car, started it up, and took off, leaving Taj hooting all by himself in the carport.

He just don't know, she said to herself as she drove toward Blessings. Artificial insemination was not a joke to her. She'd been reading and studying up on the process for years. Once she realized that she could not find a man suitable to be a father before she turned thirty, she began exploring her other options, and artificial insemination was the most sensible. Sure, she could have gotten pregnant by some of the men she knew, but if she did that she would be tied to them for life. They would always be around, trying to be involved, and she didn't want that. None of the men in her life were worthy of that privilege. If they were, Zuma would have been with them, gotten married to them. With artificial insemination, she was the one in control. She didn't have to answer to anybody. She could have a baby all by herself and take care of it all by herself. She was the only one she could depend on in this life. She was the only one who could make it happen.

Zuma had already taken the preliminary steps in the artificial insemination process and now she was going to move full speed ahead. Oh yes, by the age of thirty, Zuma would be pregnant. She'd have her life together and, most importantly, she'd have the baby she always wanted.

Zuma banged her hand on the steering wheel, so revved up by the fact that her plan was coming together so well that she couldn't control herself. "Get ready, world," she shouted as she hooked a left onto LaBrea. "I'm gonna be a mama."

5

Sandy's four-year-old son, David, had one more time to blow bubbles in his milk before Sandy would reach across the kitchen table and slap the shit out of him. She had told him as plainly as she could speak, "Stop blowing bubbles. *Stop blowing bubbles*," and still her bad-ass son refused to quit. He was always testing Sandy. Always pushing the edge. But little did he know, Sandy was already close to the edge, teetering on it, and if she had to reprimand his little bad ass one more time, she was going to knock his head off. She watched her son out of the corner of her eye, while she bounced her ten-month-old daughter, Dalila, on her knee. She was just waiting. Waiting for him to give her a reason. Waiting for him to push her final button.

"Mommy," David said playfully. "Can I go—"

"No," Sandy answered, before he could even get the sentence out of his mouth. No, you can't *do* shit, you can't *have* shit, and you can't *go* nowhere. Shit!

"But I—"

"Shut up, David," Sandy warned. "Just shut up and eat your damn breakfast," she said, and watched him roll his eyes at her. She felt like slapping him just for that, but her daughter got in the way. Dalila threw her wild hands on the table and whimpered, "Ba-ba," as she reached for her bottle and turned it over, spilling milk all across the yellow plastic place mat.

"Damn it," Sandy screamed, and smacked Dalila's little hand. "No," she said as she clutched the girl under her arm and snatched the bib from around her neck. "No, no, no," Sandy said as she soaked up the milk with the bib and her baby began to cry. She bounced the baby on her knee and rocked her from side to side, trying to get the little brat to shut the hell up. But nothing seemed to work. "Ssh," Sandy said as she looked down into Dalila's face. "*Ssh,*" she said again, and bounced the baby up and down. But the more she shushed, the louder Dalila became, and the louder Dalila became, the more pissed off Sandy grew. She pushed her chair back and cradled Dalila in her arms as she squeezed behind David's chair to get out of the tiny kitchen. "So you wanna cry all day?" she said as she walked to the back bedroom with her daughter. "You wanna cry?"

She opened the bedroom door, laid Dalila down in her crib, then walked right back out and slammed the door behind her. "Cry your ass to sleep then," Sandy said as she paused for a second in the hallway, trying to regain her cool. She blew out a mouthful of hot air, then walked back into the front room and stood at the screen door. She looked outside through the hundreds of tiny dirty holes in front of her face and put her hands on her hips. "Where the hell are you, Cerwin?" she mumbled to herself as she walked out and stood on the porch. She shielded her eyes from the sun as she looked both ways down the street. But she saw no signs of the man she'd been living with for the past seven years.

Sandy had thought she'd made herself perfectly clear to him last night when she told him she needed him to watch the kids while she went back down to Blessings to see about getting a job. "No problem," he told her, "I'll watch the kids." But Sandy should have known that was just a crock of shit. Anytime Cerwin said something was no problem that usually meant the opposite. But for the life of her she could not figure out where he could be. The club he owned didn't open till four-thirty in the evening and there was no place he could go on a Saturday morning except down to the racetrack or . . . or . . . No, Sandy thought. She knew there were any number of places Cerwin could be but she had promised herself she wouldn't let her mind think like that. Sandy had always been a jealous woman and the slightest irregularity could set her off. Last week when some unknown woman called the house and asked to speak to Cerwin Sandy nearly lost her mind. She'd dropped the receiver to the floor, moved the end table to unplug the phone, grabbed it by its base, and flung it across the room to where Cerwin sat. Cerwin had adjusted to Sandy's fits of jealousy over the years and by the time the phone was in the air, he had quickly ducked out of the way. It wasn't until later that day, after they'd argued for hours, that Cerwin had plugged the phone back in, only to have it ring and find out that the mysterious woman on the other end of the line was a saleswoman from the *L.A. Times* who'd called to get him to buy a weekly subscription. He knew Sandy wouldn't take his word for it so he told the girl to hold on and gave the phone to Sandy. He smiled victoriously as he saw the humiliation sneak up on her face. But that wasn't the first or last time Sandy let her jealousy and insecurity get the best of her.

She was always accusing Cerwin of infidelity and it seemed they argued on the subject at least three or four times a month. Usually, their arguments ended with Sandy's picking up a lamp or a pot or some other piece of household furniture and flinging it through the air at Cerwin and on some occasions she'd even make contact. At other times Sandy would just lunge at Cerwin with her bare hands. He never attacked her back though. Cerwin had become an expert at dipping and dodging and was usually able to restrain Sandy without hurting her. To be truthful, Cerwin was a monogamous man. He had been with Sandy for seven whole years and never once had he thought of leaving her for another woman. That was an idea that only Sandy held on to. In her own suspicious, insecure mind, she often brewed up false, crazy notions of Cerwin slipping off somewhere to be with some other chick, and it was at times like this, when Cerwin would disappear without a word, that Sandy's jealous tendencies loosened. "Lousy bastard," Sandy said as she checked both ways down the street for him again. She whipped around and went back through the screen door and stood behind it, peering through the tiny holes. Cerwin thinks he's slick, she thought to herself, and gritted her teeth. She wasn't no fool. In the business Cerwin was in, he had his pick of fine young tenders, and though he swore up and down to Sandy that she was the only woman in his life, she knew better. She *knew*. But hold on, Sandy said to herself. There's got to be an explanation for this, she thought. And Cerwin had better have one ready as soon as he got back home.

She took one last peek down the street, then turned away from the screen and walked back into the kitchen. As she squeezed past David's chair she smacked him on the side of the face. "What did I tell you about playing in your food?" she said, and watched as David slowly took his fingers out of his eggs. He shrugged his shoulders and put his hands in his lap. Sandy grabbed the sides of his face and squeezed. "What does that mean?" she said, and mimicked his shrug. "Can't you talk? What's your mouth for?" she said as she leaned over into his face. "Now what did I tell you about playing in your food?"

David's lips quivered as he spoke. "You said for me not to do it."

"Then why are you doing it?"

Again, David shrugged his shoulders, and Sandy squeezed on his jaws tighter. "Use your mouth."

"I don't know," he said as tears began to form in his eyes.

"I know you don't know," Sandy said as she let go of his face and popped him in the mouth. "Get on out of here," Sandy said as she yanked David out of his seat and flung him toward the front room. "Hardheaded little boy," she mumbled as she picked up his plate and put it in the sink. She sat down at the table again and felt the side of her coffee cup to see if it was still warm. She lifted the cup of decaf to her mouth and took a sip, hoping the familiar bitterness would calm her nerves. But just as she was about to relax, she winced at the sound of her name.

"Mommy," David called from the front room.

"What?"

"Can I go outside and play?"

"No, damn it," Sandy said quickly, then just as quickly reconsidered. Better he be outside than sitting around the house getting on her nerves. "Yeah," she shouted, and simultaneously heard the sound of her son's feet heading for the front door. How many times did she have to tell him to stop running in the house, she thought, then clenched her fist on the table as the walls shook. And how many times did she have to tell him to stop slamming that screen door? "Damn," Sandy mumbled, and took another sip of her decaf. That boy was just too damn hardheaded. He was just like his daddy she thought as she checked the clock on the wall and saw that it was already going on eleven. She had told Pat that she would be back at the shop before things got too hectic around there, but she was already too late. It was a Saturday and she knew Blessings would be packed by this time. Carelessly she pushed her coffee cup out of her way and cursed Cerwin in her mind. He had been the one who insisted she go to beauty school and get her license so she could get a wholesome job. And here he was fucking up her first attempt at making that happen by not being there to take care of the kids. She had thought about just leaving the kids at home by themselves, but if Cerwin came home before she got back and found them unattended he'd pop a blood vessel.

Sandy really wanted that job at Blessings. Not so much for herself, but because it was so important to Cerwin. Everything she did was to please that man. She even had kids just because he wanted them. Sandy hated children herself and had never before imagined being someone's mother until the day Cerwin brought it up. If she had had her way, she would have had her tubes tied long ago. But for Cerwin, she conceived her first child four years ago and though she had heard somewhere that motherhood was supposed to change you, she never felt any differently about children. She hated kids before she had them and she hated them right now. It was a total accident that she had gotten pregnant for the second time last year and oh how she wished she had just gone down to the clinic and gotten rid of it. But if Cerwin had found out she killed one of his little soldiers he would have aborted *her*. And still after two children, Sandy's outlook was still the same. She hated them. She could never tell that to another living soul, but oh, how true it was. The pain of childbirth could never compare to the torture of being a mother. All Sandy did all day long was run behind kids, wipe dirty noses, prepare bottles, change funky diapers, and wish like hell she had had the sense never to fall into this trap. Her only outlet had been her job, but Cerwin hadn't even wanted her doing that anymore even though he had given her her first job by hiring her at the club he owned. Seven years ago, being a stripper, or an exotic dancer, as Sandy preferred to call it, had been a turn-on for Cerwin. But now that she was the mother of his children it seemed the thought of having Sandy down at the club prancing across the stage and shaking her moneymaker was a bit too much for Cerwin. So he fired her last year, right after she told him she was pregnant with their second child.

Sandy had been so mad that she didn't know what to do. She had wanted to be a dancer all her life and even when she was pregnant with David she continued to dance. As a matter of fact, she made more money dancing pregnant than she did when she was as thin as a rail. It seemed the look of a fat woman in a g-string was a big turn-on down at Big C's Strip-O-Rama, and the men would throw her big bucks just for her to sashay over to them and let them feel her stomach as she shimmied up and down and twirled her hips. But the very thing that was making her pockets fat made Cerwin pissed. He had hinted around about the fact that he wanted her to stop dancing back then, but it wasn't until baby number two was on the way that he actually put his foot down.

Sandy had been sitting backstage at her makeup table chatting to a group of other dancers when Cerwin walked in and made his way through the crowd. "You're not going on tonight," he told her as the group of half-naked ladies got out of his way. Everybody knew when the boss man was upset and by the look in Cerwin's eyes Sandy could tell Cerwin was in no mood for debate. He was a tall, pale man with long, dirty blond hair that was receding just enough to draw undue attention to the knot that poked out atop his forehead. Cerwin was a whole twenty-three years older than Sandy and he looked the part. His large potbelly was firm and hung about two inches over the top of his pants and though Sandy had tried to give him a few fashion tips over the years, she could never make him buy pants large enough for his waist. Cerwin's appearance didn't concern him. All he cared about was his business and his children. Damn his hair and a larger size of pants. Those things had nothing to do with the man he was on the inside.

Sandy didn't complain too much about his looks, though. She loved Cerwin dearly, but even love couldn't keep her tame. "What do you mean I'm not going on tonight?" she asked as she turned to the mirror and began applying her fake eyelashes.

"I mean you aren't dancing tonight and as a matter of fact, you ain't dancing no other night."

"Don't start no mess, Cerwin," Sandy said quietly as she looked through the mirror and smiled like nothing was going on to the few women she saw peeking at her. "Dancing is my life. Of course I'm going on tonight."

Cerwin grabbed her by the arm and swung her around in her seat. "Whose name is that outside on the billboard?" he asked sternly. "It's me, Big C. This is my business. Now if you wanna get technical about the shit, your ass is fired. I ain't gonna have my woman going out there shaking her pregnant ass all around for everyone to see. Hell, you might shake the baby out too soon or something."

"How you gonna fire me? I'm the mother of your children."

"Don't make me have to say it again."

"Oh fuck you, Cerwin."

"Don't push me, Sandy," he said as he leaned over into her face.

The few women who had stuck close to the action cleared out. They were used to this kind of bickering between their boss and his girlfriend, but they didn't want to be in the way. Just in case things got a little out of control as they had on several previous occasions. It wasn't unusual for Cerwin to come storming backstage after one of Sandy's sets and start whooping and hollering because she had gotten too chummy with one of the customers. It was even less of a shock to see Sandy pick up a brush and chuck it at Cerwin's head. They argued like that all the time and usually Sandy was the victor. But that night, Cerwin was the forceful one. He'd come, he'd spoken, and that was all there was to it. He was putting his foot down, closing the chapter and locking the door. "You are not dancing anymore," he said to Sandy as he spun her back around in her chair to face the mirror. "You are a mother now and you are going to start acting like one. Your dancing days are over."

Cerwin slowly backed his way through the crowd of women to the red velvet curtain that acted as the door to the dressing room. As he walked out he turned to Sandy and pointed to the corner of the room. "Take my son, my baby that's in your stomach, and yourself back to the house," he said, and disappeared through the curtain.

"Fuck you, Cerwin," Sandy said as she looked over to the corner of the room where her three-year-old David sat in front of a portable TV. Since she only worked four hours a night, she'd bring her son down to the club with her and while she was onstage one of the other girls would watch him till she got back. She had a pretty good setup down at the club, but all of that, according to Cerwin, was about to change.

"Was he for real?" one of the girls named Freak N U asked as she sat down next to Sandy in front of the mirror. "He can't be for real. You make too much money to give up dancing, honey."

Sandy closed her eyes and shook her head. She was the most well-known dancer at Big C's and all the men emptied their wallets when she took to the stage. She was the only one of the girls who'd ever stripped while she was pregnant, which made her a novelty of sorts, a living legend. The men loved it when she shook her blond hair into their faces and batted her royal blue eyes as she slipped up and down the steel pole in the center of the stage. And she loved just being out there. Dancing had always been Sandy's passion ever since she was a little girl. Sandy would always try out for the dance troupes when she was attending school in the predominantly black neighborhood where she grew up. But she was always passed over. Even when she'd try out and seemingly performed better than all the other black dancers, she'd never be picked. It was a black thang, she knew. The only reason why they never picked her was because she was a white girl and they didn't want no "off-beat blonde" on stage with them. Still, she loved to perform and she'd dance for hours around her mother's house when she was there all alone. She'd pretend she was in the ballet, or a showgirl on the Vegas Strip. And until she'd met Cerwin seven years ago, she'd never been able to show off her skills on a real stage. But now that she had, she loved the feeling. Stripping wasn't exactly Sandy's dance of choice. She much preferred the smooth flow of modern jazz and ballet. Still, stripping was what was available and she had grown to love it. And furthermore, she wasn't going to give it up just because Cerwin said so, she thought to herself, then turned to face Freak N U. "I'm going out there," she said as she grabbed her lipstick and twisted it up.

"You bet not," Silky Smooth said as she came up and stood behind Sandy's chair. "Big C didn't look like he was fooling around, girl."

"He sho didn't," Cream said as she took a spot next to Silky. "Girl, you ought to just take your son and go home. Shoot, you don't need to be dancing anyway."

"I know I wouldn't be dancing if I was pregnant," Freak N U said as she piled a glob of green eye shadow on her eyes. "Why don't you just wait till after you have your baby. Maybe Big C will let you come back then."

"Hell no," Sandy said as she stood up from her chair and snatched off her robe. Her silver sequined bikini thong glistened under the light of the room. "Every damn thing I do is for Cerwin. He wanted me to move in with him and I did. He wanted me to get pregnant and I did. Well, what about what I wanna do? Shit, dancing is the only thing that I *can* do and I'm going to do it. Fuck Cerwin. He ain't my daddy," she said, and turned to Freak N U. "Is he my daddy?" she asked her.

"No."

"Is he my daddy?" she asked again, and turned to Cream.

"Nope."

"Yo, Silky," she said, squeezing lotion into her palm and rubbing it on her poofed-out stomach. "Is Cerwin my daddy?"

"Not that I'm aware of."

"I didn't think so," Sandy said, satisfied with the general consensus.

"But he's your man, girl," Cream said, and poked Sandy's belly button. "You better listen to your man."

"Whatever," Sandy said viciously, then really thought about what she was planning to do. She didn't want to get into a huge fight with Cerwin and she could sort of understand his point of view. Still, Cerwin was not the boss of her. Yes, she respected him, she had no choice. Cerwin had taken her in and given her a job when Sandy was at her most desperate. She had just left her mom back in the San Fernando Valley with her boyfriend, who had apparently thought Sandy and her mom were a two-for-one deal. At only eighteen years old, Sandy had grown tired of her mom's boyfriend's constant come-ons and had thrown all her necessities into a backpack and headed back to Los Angeles. She didn't know where she was going to sleep that night or if she would sleep at all. The only thing she knew when she stepped off the bus in front of Big C's Strip-O-Rama was that she needed a job. She had passed by the strip joint many times as a kid, but she had never imagined she'd one day be walking through its doors, asking for a job. But one afternoon while Sandy was still living with her mom and her horny boyfriend, Sandy had turned on the *Ricki Lake* show and saw that they were doing a program on strippers. She watched as the women danced across the stage and listened as Ricki's irate audience slammed the women, calling them whores and sluts and disgraces. But Sandy saw the women for what they really were. Dancers. She understood why they did what they did. Forget the money part of it, they did it because they loved to perform. Not everyone had the talent or the fortunate opportunity to perform with a reputable dance company. But when you have a passion for dancing, you take whatever opportunity comes your way. Sandy knew it had been risky coming down to a strip club in the heart of Inglewood looking for work. Still, when Sandy walked into the damp, musty building and saw the tall, pale man standing behind the bar, a sense of calm fell over her. It was as if she knew instinctively that this man would take care of her. And when she spoke to Cerwin for the first time face-to-face, she noticed something in his eyes. Something soft and careful, something that the fact that he was twenty-three years older than she couldn't overshadow. Cerwin didn't have to give her a chance, but he did. And from then on things between them just clicked. Within a month she was living in his house and after a few run-ins with his several girlfriends at the time, Sandy had earned the right to be his one and only. Sandy was completely in love with Cerwin, but on that night he forbade her to work at the club anymore, she wanted to kill him. More and more Cerwin had been ordering Sandy around. She always did whatever she could to please him, like cooking, cleaning, drawing his bath, massaging his feet. But as the years moved on, Cerwin was beginning to take these pleasures for granted. Sandy had believed it was always a woman's duty to take care of her man, but she wasn't no sucker. She took care of Cerwin because she wanted to, not because she had to. But the more she did for him the more he took advantage. Yes, Cerwin was old enough to be her daddy, but he wasn't her daddy, and he wasn't going to tell her what she could and could not do.

"Hand me my brush," Sandy said to Silky Smooth as she tugged on the front of her sequined thong and stepped into her matching heels.

"You're not really going out there, are you?" Silky asked as she handed Sandy a brush and stared at her in disbelief.

"Yes I am," Sandy said as she ran the brush through her hair, flipping it from side to side. She threw the brush down on the counter and leaned over in the mirror to check her makeup for the final time. Out front she could hear the music starting as the deejay came on the mic to announce the next dancer. "Luscious," she called over her shoulder, then turned around. "I'm taking your place tonight," she said as she began to walk toward the curtain.

"But wait a minute. I need my tips," Luscious said as she walked behind Sandy, then paused. Sandy turned to her and squinted her eyes and that was the end of that argument. Sandy was the boss's girl. Nobody fucked with her.

Sandy listened behind the curtain as the deejay yelled into his mic. "Come on, y'all. Take your hands out your pants and put 'em together for *Luscious.*"

As the music pumped up and the crowd roared, Sandy stood behind the curtain, wondering if she was doing the right thing by disobeying Cerwin. Maybe Cerwin would be too busy at the bar to notice she was onstage, she thought. But that's all that was — a thought, and a stupid one at that. Sandy knew the second she took to the stage the crowd would stand to their feet like always and chant her name. "White Chocolate," they'd all call out. "White Chocolate come dance for me." No way Cerwin wouldn't notice. But Sandy didn't care. She was tired of his telling her what to do. It was her damn life, and if she wanted to dance pregnant, then dammit she was gonna dance.

Sandy stuck her leg out through the curtain and kicked it in the air. She took it back, paused, then threw open the curtains and walked out. The crowd went nuts as Sandy walked center stage and took hold of the steel pole. She spun herself around, then let go and did the splits. She rolled on the floor until she was at the end of the stage, then perched herself on her knees. The man in front of her stuck a five-dollar bill into the zipper of his pants, which Sandy crawled after with no hesitation. She dropped and rolled until she was in front of another man, who held what appeared to be a twenty between his fingertips. Sandy spread her legs for him as he reached over to insert the money in the top of her thong. But the nasty little man went down too far and stole a little touch of the pudding. But that was all right. That free feel cost him twenty bucks, Sandy thought as she stood up to her feet and unhooked the back of her bikini top. "White Chocolate," the men screamed as she teased them with a quick peek, then covered herself back up. She sauntered to the other side of the stage and just when she was about to let her bra top fall to the floor a strong hand jerked her by the arm and through the air.

"What? Uh . . . *Cerwin!*" Sandy kicked her feet and pounded her fists on his back as she lay upside down over his shoulder. "Put me down," she screamed as a succession of boos filled the room.

Cerwin marched her straight to the back dressing room, scooped up David into his free arm, then walked right back out front, through the crowd of men to the entrance. There, he placed Sandy onto her feet and shoved his son into her arms. He pulled off his leather jacket and laid it across her shoulders. "The keys are in the pocket. Now take yourself home."

"No," Sandy said like a defiant child. "I'm not your slave, Cerwin. You don't own me. You can't tell me what I can and cannot do."

Well, that was all the backtalk Cerwin was going to put up with that night. He turned Sandy around sharply, opened the door, and pushed her out into the street. "Go home," he said with such finality that Sandy could no longer argue.

"I hate you," Sandy said as she backed her way to the parking lot. "I hate you," she screamed again as she opened the driver's side door of the Cadillac and threw her son across the front seat. David hit his head on the window and began crying, but Sandy paid him no mind. All she could focus on was her hatred of Cerwin. "I'm leaving you," she screamed as she started the car engine and banged her hand on the steering wheel. She watched him through the window of the car as he went back inside the club, and realized a few things very quickly. She had one child and another one on the way, she had just lost her job, had no real money saved, no place to go, and most importantly, she loved the man she hated. "Damn you, Cerwin," she said as she peeled out of the parking lot. "I wish I could leave you."

The next few months were boring as hell. Sandy spent her nights lying around the house growing fatter and fatter every minute and wishing she could be down at the club with Cerwin and her friends. Cerwin wouldn't get home until after three o'clock in the morning and as soon as he walked through the door Sandy would be in his face. "So what happened tonight? Was it packed? Did the girls rock?" But Cerwin would be so worn out that he didn't want to talk. All he'd tell her was that things were going okay, that everything was copacetic. But that wasn't good enough for Sandy. She wanted details. She felt so far removed from real life that the smallest things would excite her. She wanted to know everything, like starting from when Cerwin walked in the door and turned on the lights — *everything*. But talking about the club was the least of Cerwin's wants. All he wanted to do when he got home was hit the sack, where he'd stay until noon the next day, when Sandy would cook him up lunch and bring it to his bedside. If she was lucky she'd get to spend a few moments with him in bed before he had to get up and go back down to the club to set up for the four-thirty after-work crowd. But usually all Cerwin wanted to do was play with his son while Sandy sat watching them, wishing she could once again be the center of Cerwin's attention.

And recently these days, there had been even less time for Sandy to spend with her man. Cerwin had gotten the big idea a few months ago that he wanted to spruce up his club in an effort to bring in more customers. Sandy had thought it was such a stupid idea. It was a strip club, not a five-star restaurant. Who gave a fuck what color the damn place was or what kind of carpet was on the floor? But Cerwin's mind was set and for the past month all his extra time had gone into making renovations to Big C's. And the little time that he spent at home was either sleeping or playing with his kids. It had surprised Sandy how attentive and loving Cerwin was as a father. Having kids had made him more of a homebody. He loved his kids, loved playing with them, showing them things. And when Dalila came along, Cerwin became even more doting. Neither one of them had expected a girl. Certainly not Sandy. She wouldn't have cared if she miscarried. But after Dalila was born, Sandy began to see a softer side of Cerwin. He fussed over her like she was a princess. Whenever he was home he'd feed her, give her a bath, even change her stinky diapers. Sandy always appreciated the time Cerwin spent with their kids because it meant she could take a break. But to be truthful, as Sandy watched him with the kids she would sometimes feel a pang of jealousy. She didn't hate him for being a father, she just hated him for giving his kids more attention than he gave her. Before the kids, they spent all their time together, but since the kids, Sandy had to fight to be noticed. At least when she was working she could spend her evenings with the man she loved, but now all Sandy did was look after kids and wait her turn for attention.

Though Cerwin spent all the time he could with his kids, Sandy was still their sole caretaker. She spent her days catering to them and her nights alone. She felt worthless as a mother. Being a mother had no redeeming qualities to her. Dancing was the only thing that made her feel good about herself, but when she asked Cerwin if she could go back to work a few months ago, he answered her with a fierce stare. She knew that meant no, so instead she asked him about something else she'd been thinking about. Sitting at home all day and night gave Sandy time to think about a lot of things, in particular, what the hell she could do to get out of the house and away from her kids. She thought about waitressing, getting a job at the mall, or becoming a grocery clerk. But what appealed to her the most was the idea of working in a beauty shop. She had walked by Blessings on several occasions and always liked the atmosphere. It was always packed with women talking and getting pretty, and it reminded her so much of the strip club. So she asked Cerwin if he would give her the money to go to beauty school and much to her surprise she didn't have to ask twice. "It's about time you decided to do something with yourself," he said, and threw her his wallet.

Though learning to do nails was hard, Sandy loved going to beauty school because it gave her a chance to get away from those goddamn kids. While she went to school, Cerwin kept the kids and when it was time for him to go to work he'd take them with him and have one of the girls keep an eye on them. Then he'd take a break around eight o'clock and drop them back home with Sandy. Sandy had offered to pick the kids up from the club, but Cerwin didn't even want her near the club anymore. But that was okay with Sandy. From one to eight every day she had resumed the life of a real adult. She didn't have to wash any dirty faces, fix any lunches, or fill any bottles. She was free. But when she graduated two weeks ago, her life quickly returned back to normal, though not for long. Sandy had wasted no time going down to Blessings and asking for a job. She wanted that job really bad. So bad she could taste it. If she had to spend one more day in that house with those loud, crying, dirty kids she was going to lose her mind. And if it weren't for Cerwin, she'd be down at the shop right now talking to Pat and convincing her to give her a shot.

"Damn you, Cerwin," Sandy said as she got up from the table and looked over at the clock. "I go through all the trouble of getting a manicuring license and looking for a job and now I can't even go take care of my business because your stupid ass ain't home," she shouted into the empty kitchen. She picked up her coffee cup and put it into the sink and just as she was about to turn around she heard a loud noise outside. "Mommy," she heard her son call. The sound of tires screeched outside.

"Oh my God," Sandy gasped as a quick picture of her son lying under the wheel of a car shot through her brain. She whipped around and ran out the kitchen and through the screen door. "David," she shouted as she rushed down the stairs looking out into the middle of the street at the black truck that sat just inches from her son's frozen body. As she ran into the street, the driver of the truck stuck his head out the window and yelled, "You better get your son out the street, lady."

She grabbed David by his shirt and pushed him up on the sidewalk. "Get your ass in the house," she told him, then turned back to the truck and gave the driver a stiff middle finger. "Why don't you watch where the fuck you're driving?"

"Why don't you watch your kids," he said, then sped off down the street.

Sandy walked back up the steps, then paused as she put her hand on the screen door. How many times did she have to tell that boy to look both ways before he crossed the street? He just won't listen, she thought to herself as she yanked open the screen door and marched inside the house to the closet. She pulled down one of Cerwin's long leather belts and doubled it over in her hand. "David," she screamed as she turned around and saw her son cowering on the sofa. "Didn't I tell you to keep your little ass out the street?" she asked as she made her way over to him. "Didn't I tell you that?" she asked as she stood above him and raised the belt. "Didn't I?"

David shrugged his shoulders and that was all Sandy could take. She laid into him and between every word she spoke came the fire of the belt. "I'm-not-gonna-keep-telling-you-the-same-thing-over-and-over-and-over-again," she said as her son scrambled around trying unsuccessfully to avoid his whipping. "No-more-out-side-till-you-learn-how-to-stay-out-of-the-street," she said as she backed away from him and put the belt back into the closet. "And shut up all that crying," she said as she closed the closet door and turned back around to face him. "I said shut up, David," she said, standing in the middle of the room and pointing a stiff finger in his direction. But David was in too much pain to obey his mother's threats. Sandy quickly grabbed him by the arm and led him to the back bedroom. She opened the door where her daughter lay in her crib sleeping and as soon as she pushed David in, her daughter woke up and began her own parade of tears. Sandy stood in the doorway, watching her children and wishing they were not hers. She backed out of the room and slammed the door. Oh, how she wished she were childless, she thought to herself as she stood in the hallway, trying to calm herself down. But Cerwin had wanted kids so she obliged. And now she was paying the price.

Sandy slowly walked back into the front room and as she reached the screen door, she heard the sound of Cerwin's Cadillac. Finally, she thought, as she sighed with relief. Now she could go down to Blessings and get that job. As she waited for him to walk through the door, she ran to the closet and pulled down her purse. She whipped into the bathroom, ran a brush through her hair, then walked back toward the screen door.

Sandy stopped abruptly when she saw the two people walking up the steps. One of them was Cerwin, but that bitch beside him would have to be explained.

"Go on inside," Cerwin said to the girl as he held the screen door open for her.

Sandy raised her eyebrow as this strange woman came stepping into her home, looking around the place like she was about to set up shop. She was a young thing, tight body and perky breasts. Sandy felt the jealousy brewing as she looked over the woman, but she remained cool. There was an explanation behind this bitch, she was sure. Sandy didn't even blink an eye when the woman smiled her way and held out her hand to Sandy. But Sandy wasn't shaking hands today. She stared at the woman, then turned to Cerwin and put her hand on her hip.

"Where you been?"

"I had some business to take care of this morning. Renovations are kicking my ass."

"Uh-huh," Sandy said and turned to the woman. "Who this?"

"Where are the kids?" Cerwin asked and poked his head into the kitchen.

"I said, who this?"

"My name is Bronze," the woman said, and stuck out her hand again towards Sandy.

"I didn't ask you," Sandy said, calmly and slowly.

"Watch your attitude, Sandy," Cerwin said and offered the woman a seat. "I thought you said you had to go see about a job this morning."

"I do. But I couldn't go nowhere without someone here to take care of the kids."

"That's why Bronze is here," he said, and smiled toward the girl. "She's gonna be baby-sitting for today."

"She's gonna be what?"

"I said she's gonna be baby-sitting while you go out today," he reiterated. "And if you get the job, maybe we'll keep her on indefinitely."

"And what's wrong with you? Why can't you watch the kids?"

"You know we're painting the inside of the club and doing all that renovating shit."

"So take the kids down to the club with you."

"Naw. The club ain't no place for my kids. They need to stay right here in their own home. So Bronze is gonna look after them for a while."

"Bronze, huh," Sandy said and gave the lady another looking over. "You work down at the club or something?"

Bronze hesitated to speak, but then said, "I'm new. I'm only seventeen so Big C won't let me work yet. But I'll be eighteen in a few months. I'm just doing this for a few extra dollars. I love kids, so you don't have to worry. I'll take care of them for you real good."

"Well, make sure that's all you take care of," Sandy said, and walked over to Cerwin and stood directly in his face. "Baby-sitter, huh?" she asked as she gave him a quick peck on the cheek. "Baby-sitter my ass," she said as she walked out the door.

For a second there, Sandy thought about turning right back around, but she convinced herself not to. She wouldn't let her jealous nature get to her today, and besides, she wanted that job at Blessings really bad. It would give her something to do, make her some extra money, and most of all get her out of the house and away from her kids. Sandy couldn't let that opportunity pass. For once she'd have to trust Cerwin. He never cheated on her in the past so why should he start now? Cerwin loved Sandy and Sandy loved Cerwin, more than anything else in the world. More than herself and definitely more than her kids. No, she wouldn't let jealousy rule her today. Today she would do something for herself. She would go down to Blessings and beg for a job if she had to. Sandy needed a life, and today she was going to get one.

6

"So anyway, girl," Faye's client said to her as Faye pulled a comb through her head. "We get in bed, right. We're touching, feeling, you know — doing our thing, right."

"Yeah, yeah."

"And all of a sudden I feel something sharp on my leg."

"Something sharp?"

"Yeah, *girl.* So at first I don't pay it no mind, 'cause the kissing and the touching got me all distracted and shit. But then I feel it again, right. So I stop for a second and pull back the covers and I'll be *damned.*"

"What was it, girl?"

"It was that trifling Negro's toenails!"

"Oh my goodness. His *toenails?*"

"Yes, girl. I look over at this Negro's feet and they are just as crusty as they wanna be. Girl, I reach down and feel my leg and the damn thing is bleeding."

"*Uuuah.*"

"Girl, sheets all ripped up. I'm saying, this Negro's toenails look like they ain't been cut in years. Feet just crusty, ankles all ashy. Honey, feet look like they been dipped in acid. You hear me?"

"Child, *please.* So what did you do?"

"I kicked his nasty, rusty ass right on out."

"No you didn't."

"Yes I did, girl. If a man can't keep his feet in check ain't no telling what other parts of his body need help. Old rusty, stank bastard. Hell yeah, I threw his ass out."

Of all the days of the week, Saturdays always seemed to be the most eclectic at Blessings. And since most women had Saturdays off, it was also the most busy. But on Saturdays the women seemed to be more free. On Saturdays the hot topics at Blessings were never political or intellectual. There was no discussion of current events or trials or anything of a serious nature. On Saturdays the women let loose. They spoke about the topic that was nearest their heart — men. Yes, Saturdays were daylong male-bashing festivals. On this day, women shared their juicy stories about Friday night dates that went sour, the men in their lives who for one reason or another were just plain fuck-ups, and the trials and tribulations of putting up with the male species as a whole. On Saturdays the women got down to the real. And this Saturday was no exception.

Zuma tried to keep her client's head still as she went at it with a pair of scissors. But Zuma's client was too busy trying to turn around to listen to the ending of the crusty toenail story Faye's client was telling. Pat was busy at the shampoo bowl, and on the sofa sat another six ladies, all waiting patiently, talking lively and hoping their entire day wouldn't be wasted inside the shop.

"So did you go out with that guy from your job?" Zuma's client yelled over to Pat's client at the shampoo bowl.

Pat's client lifted her head slightly as water streaked down her face. "Honey," she said, and rolled her eyes. "That story ain't worth telling."

"Why?" Zuma and her client asked in unison.

"Last time you were in here you said you couldn't wait to get that man out the office and on a real date," Zuma added.

"Well, that was then, honey. I wish I had waited."

"So what happened?"

"Nothing, girl. We went out, came back to my place, and by that time I was like *ooo, la, la*. I mean the man was turning me on in each and every other way."

"Yeah, and?"

"So we get undressed, get into bed, and he starts doing his thing, right. You know grinding, moaning, and all that jazz, right."

"Right, right."

"So after about fifteen minutes I say, 'Look here, baby. Stop teasing me and put it in.' "

"Uh-huh."

"Honey, the bastard told me it was already in!"

"What? He was in and you couldn't feel it."

"Honey, the boy's dick was so tiny he couldn't come if you called him."

"Girl, you lying."

"Naw, honey. So I figured maybe it was just the position, you know. So I roll over and get on top . . . *still* couldn't feel a thing."

"Naw, girl."

"Yes, honey. After that I just rolled back over on my back and let him have at it. Little dick motherfucker," she said as Pat wrapped a towel around her wet hair. She raised up her pinkie finger and shook it in the air. "Honey, this is a giant compared to what that man had to offer."

Zuma and her client laughed uncontrollably as Pat tried to offer a new perspective.

"It's not the size that counts," Pat said and squeezed conditioner into her palm. "It's the motion of the ocean," she said as she massaged the white solution into her client's hair.

"Come on, Pat," her client said, and pursed her lips. "I'm damn near forty years old. My stuff ain't tight no more. You got to pack some power for me to feel you."

"Can't work the middle if your dick's too little," Zuma said as her client burst out laughing.

"Y'all need to quit," Pat said, and blushed. "Now what about you, Zuma?" she asked and looked over her shoulder. "What did you get into last night?"

"Child, I left here at midnight with you," Zuma said as she snipped at her client's hair with quickness and precision.

"Since when did that stop you from going out?"

"Child, I went home and went straight to bed."

"What?" Faye gasped.

"Taj stopped by this morning," Zuma said, and frowned. "But I told y'all before, I ain't wasting no more time on Taj, Robert, or Kristoff. Can't neither one of those Negroes give me anything but a headache. I'm tired of wasting my time."

Faye bundled a string of fake hair in her hand as she sewed it inch by inch into her client's head. "How many times do I have to tell you, Zuma? You've got to give it time. The right man will come along one day."

"Girl, I'll be thirty years old in a couple weeks. I've given it time. I'd just as soon be by myself than to settle for a man who can't give me all that I need."

"Listen to you. You're the baby of the shop. You talk like you're fifty years old. You've got time, girl. You gotta be patient."

Patient, Zuma thought to herself as she laid down her scissors and fingered through her client's asymmetrical hair design. Patience was something Zuma didn't have. She knew what she wanted and she knew what she had to do to get it. Forget a man. That was no longer part of her master plan. And after her conversation with Taj this morning she was now even more convinced of what she had to do. She'd already gone down to the Century City Hospital and begun the artificial insemination process. She'd given them her medical history, gone through a physical exam, filled out all the forms, and even had the donor's sperm picked out for her. They had given her the option of picking out the donor sperm herself, but Zuma knew she couldn't handle that. She didn't want to go searching through books and pictures and personal histories, looking for the perfect father. She was too picky for that. If she'd gone that route, it would have taken her years to pick out the perfect father for her baby. So Zuma decided to leave that decision up to the doctors. She had complete faith in them. She'd read through every pamphlet the Century City Hospital had to offer on its artificial insemination program and she'd even done some private research on her own at the library one evening when she'd gone to check out a book for her business correspondence class. She knew the hospital was the best insemination institute in the country. They were experts and only accepted donated sperm from intelligent, physically examined men who were mostly interns from medical schools across the country and college students. The Century City Hospital was elite and Zuma realized just how elite when she found out the price for one insemination ran between fifteen and twenty thousand dollars. But that was a price she had long planned for. Twenty thousand dollars would only bring her bank account down to forty-eight thousand, still enough money left over to open up her own beauty salon once she finished with her business correspondence classes. Zuma's master plan was coming together like a magnet to metal, and now the only thing left for her to do was go in for the actual insemination. No, Zuma thought as she glanced across the room at Faye, there was no time to be patient. In less than two weeks, she would be thirty years old and, Allah willing, with child.

"What are you giggling about?" Faye asked, breaking into a half smile herself as she watched Zuma.

"Nothing," she said quickly and put on a stone face. Zuma had never said a word to Faye about wanting to have a baby. Faye was too fair-minded and dignified. If she told her she'd planned on getting artificially insemi-nated, she'd have a cow. *That's not the proper way,* she could hear Faye say. *You should wait to get married. Don't be in such a rush.* Zuma wasn't trying to hear all that. She would never be able to make Faye understand how important having a baby was to her unless she also told her about the baby she'd aborted years ago. And she knew Ms. Holier Than Thou Catholic of the Year would never be able to understand that.

Zuma never told Pat about her plans either. She tried never to bring up the subject of kids around Pat. In fact, clients weren't even allowed to bring their kids to the shop with them just because Pat couldn't take seeing and being around children without bursting into tears. Pat wouldn't be able to handle Zuma's artificial insemination. And she could never tell Pat about her abortion either. It would probably hurt Pat more than it hurt Zuma to know that Zuma had killed a child for no reason, when Pat had longed for one with such a passion. So, Zuma kept her plans of mother-hood a secret from her best friends. She knew she'd have to let them in on it soon. But that day would not be today.

"And speaking of men," Zuma said as she plugged in her hot curlers and brushed hair off her client's back. "When are you going to start dating again, Miss Faye?"

Oh no, Faye thought as she began sewing in the first track on her client's head. How many times did she have this discussion before? She knew exactly what was going to be said. "You're still young. You gotta get out there and start dating again." Faye had heard it all before. She knew Zuma was right, but she still felt it was too soon. She had already had the love of her life in Antoine, and now that he was gone, Faye couldn't imagine ever finding that kind of love again.

"You know what you should do?" Zuma said as she dabbed her finger against her hot comb to see if it was hot. "You should join one of those dating services."

"Oh please, Zuma. It's not that serious," Faye said and rolled her eyes.

"Oh yes it is. You need a man in your life, Faye. You can't be single forever."

"I'm not single, I'm widowed," Faye corrected as she shook out another string of fake hair.

The tone of Faye's voice kept Zuma quiet for a while. She knew she'd hit a nerve and it was time to change the subject. But Faye wasn't upset. She just knew the conversation was of no use. Even if she felt it was time for her to start dating again, she knew no man would ever want her. She was a hefty frump and had two kids to take care of. What man in his right mind would want to step into a situation like that? Faye had too much baggage, too many responsibilities — and too much flab and cellulite and wrinkles . . . and the list goes on. But Faye's life wasn't totally devoid of men. Not really. Faye had long since come up with a way to keep a constant flow of male companionship. She could have any man she wanted, at any time and any place. Oh yes, Faye thought, and smiled slyly to herself. Fantasy was a wonderful thing. In the real world, Faye couldn't snag a man with a sixty-foot-wide net, but in her fantasies, in her mind, she could have a different man every night. And it didn't have be just any old man either. Oh no! The men Faye created to satisfy her were hunks. Big, muscular, agile men with faces like exquisite jewels, bodies like boulders. And if Faye felt like living the high life, she'd just close her eyes and envision Denzel or Wesley or her ultimate fantasy king — Michael Jordan.

Oh, Faye moaned beneath her breath, and closed her eyes, remembering the way Michael had come home late last night from his basketball game. He was still in his red and white uniform, his bald head glistening, muscles firm and taut, his butt a mysterious yet seemingly hard mound of flesh bulging beneath his shorts. He had walked right over to Faye and positioned himself directly on top of her on the sofa bed. His eyes gazed on her with sultry delight as he picked up the bag of Oreos that lay beside her, took one out, and carefully twisted it apart. Slowly, he stuck out his tongue and licked the white, creamy center. "Mmm," he purred. "I like that," he said as he turned the cookie around and moved it to Faye's mouth. "Lick it, baby," he said as Faye stuck out her tongue. Then he took the other half of the cookie and put it between his front teeth. He moved closer to Faye's mouth and gently she bit down on the other end. Their lips touched as they chewed and after Michael swallowed, he looked deeply into Faye's eyes. "Who's the man, baby?"

"You are, Michael," Faye cooed. "Ooo, Michael. You the man."

"Faye . . . Faye . . . *Faye*," Zuma shouted.

Faye popped back to the real world and shyly looked around the room, making sure no one knew the love dungeon she had just visited in her mind. "What is it, Zuma?"

"I'm telling you, you need to get out more. You can't go through life alone. I'm sure there's a man out there for you somewhere."

"You know, Zuma," Faye said as she smiled in the direction of Pat. "If I could find myself a man like the boss lady's I wouldn't mind dating again."

"I know that's right," Zuma said and cast an envious smile at Pat. "Some people have all the luck," she said, and winked. "Now if I had a man like Pat's you would never hear me complaining."

"I heard that," Faye said and sighed. "Now Mark is a good man. He's got his head on straight. . . ."

"He's got money," Zuma added.

"He's romantic. . . ."

"Fine as fuck."

"Sensitive . . ."

"He's got money."

"You said that already, Zuma."

"Oh."

"Mark is the kind of man every woman wants," Faye said with a twinkle and a smile. "You have got to be the luckiest woman in the world, Pat," she said as she looked over toward the shampoo bowl and paused.

Faye and Zuma had been going on so, that they hadn't realized Pat had started crying. But when Faye finally saw the tears in Pat's eyes, she motioned to Zuma and mouthed, *What did we say?*

"*Pat?*" Zuma questioned as she turned to her. "You all right?"

"I'm fine," Pat said as she tapped her client on the back. "You can go sit under the dryer now," she told her, then tried to busy herself with straightening up the bottles of shampoo behind her. But Zuma and Faye were not so easily fooled.

"Come on, Pat," Faye said as she walked over to her with caution. "What's going on here?"

"Nothing."

"Nothing, huh?" Zuma said, joining the two. "You're standing over here crying and you tell us nothing's wrong?"

"I'm fine," Pat said, and tried to crack a smile. But the tears in her eyes told another story.

"Come on," Zuma said, and grabbed Pat by the arm.

"It's conference time," Faye said as she grabbed her other arm and led her to the front door of the shop.

As they walked out the rest of the women in the shop gasped. Some had seen the tears in Pat's eyes too, but others were just concerned about the time. There were a half dozen ladies still waiting to get their hair done as well as the three clients they left behind. "What are they doing?" one lady whispered. "I know they're not about to take a break," another scolded, only not so quietly.

"We'll be right back," Zuma announced as she stuck her head back through the door, then darted out to join Pat and Faye in front of the shop's window.

"This is ridiculous," Pat said as she wiped tears from her eyes. "I'm fine, really. We should get back to the customers."

"They can wait," Faye said and grabbed one of Pat's hands. "Now tell me," she said, looking deeply into Pat's eyes. "What's the matter?"

"Mark and I had a fight."

"Is that all?" Zuma said and put her hand on her hip. "Everybody has an occasional argument, Pat. My goodness. Get over it."

"It wasn't just an argument. I . . . I . . ."

"What?" Faye asked, and squeezed Pat's hand.

"I told him I wanted a divorce."

"What!" Faye asked, and dropped Pat's hand.

"Excuse me?" Zuma said and stepped back to take a look at Pat. "What the hell has gotten into you?"

"I don't know," Pat said, and looked back and forth between her friends. "I don't know what got into me. I . . . I don't know," she said as she put her hands to her face and shook her head.

"Well, you don't really want a divorce, do you?" Faye asked, staring at Pat like she was a freak. "I mean you just said that in the heat of the moment, right?"

"I don't know."

"You don't know?" Faye said, and squinted her eyes. She could swear she was talking to some kind of fool because there was no way in the world she'd ever think about divorcing a man like Mark—*if* she had a man like Mark.

"Wait a minute," Zuma said, and frowned. "Where is all this divorce talk coming from? I thought you were happy with Mark. I mean, who wouldn't be happy with Mark?"

"I know that's right," Faye said with authority. "You two have one of the best marriages I know."

"*I know*," Pat said and wiped her eyes for the umpteenth time.

"You know?" Faye repeated.

"Yes," Pat said again. "I know. Mark is a good man. He's a provider, he's caring, he's, he's . . . *everything*."

"Then what the fuck you talking about divorce for?" Zuma huffed, tiring of all the double talk.

"Because I'm not happy."

"You're not happy?" Faye said with a sarcasm that wasn't usual for her. "If Mark is such a good man then how can you be unhappy?"

"I don't know. I just am."

"Are you sure about this?" Zuma asked, and curled the corner of her lip.

"Yes, I'm sure," Pat said and burst out crying again. "I want a divorce. I do . . . I think."

Faye and Zuma gave each other the eye, both knowing that there was something Pat was not telling them. There was definitely more to the story and Faye knew exactly what it was.

"All this divorce talk isn't about you being unhappily married, Pat," Faye said and took her hand. "I think it's about your not being able to have children."

Pat sniffled and looked away out into the street.

"You don't want a divorce, Pat," Zuma said as she reached out for Pat's chin and turned her head to face her. "You want a baby."

Pat's lips quivered as she stared at Zuma. Her eyes glistened with tears that wanted so badly to fall.

"I know how you feel," Zuma said as her own eyes began to water. "I truly know how you feel." Faye squeezed Pat's hand again. "I don't know what was said between you and Mark last night, but I do know this. You don't want a divorce. I can see it in your eyes."

Pat turned away from Zuma and Faye and stared down the street in the opposite direction. She wondered just how stupid she looked to them. Here she was complaining about wanting a divorce from a man who had been to hell with her and back, a man who loved her, a man who would give her the world if it was his to give. She wondered how stupid she'd sounded to Mark last night when she told him she wanted a divorce. Had he believed her? Would it be enough for her to call him up and say that she was just kidding? No, she thought, and turned around to face her friends again. There was only one way she could fix things with Mark and that was by doing something she rarely did — she'd have to talk to him. "I gotta go," Pat said as she reached out for them and took them both in her arms. "I gotta go fix things with my husband."

"That's what I'm talking about," Zuma said, as the three headed back into the shop in a straight line headed by Pat. But just before she stepped through the door she stopped abruptly and Faye and Zuma crammed together at her back. "I've got a finger wave, two relaxers, and a press and curl," she said, putting her hand to her face. "I can't leave right now."

"No, girl," Faye said and moved around Pat and held the door open for her. "Zuma and I can manage around here."

"That's right," Zuma said, thinking of all the extra cash she would pull in off Pat's clients. "You go on home, girl. You've got more important things to fix than hair."

"Are you guys sure?" Pat asked hesitantly. "You all probably won't get out of here until after midnight."

"So what else is new?" Faye and Zuma said in unison.

In a hot second, Pat had her purse and keys and was headed out the door. She whispered a few apologies to her clients as she breezed through the shop, assuring them that they were being left in the best of hands with Zuma and Faye. But just as she was about to walk out the door, she was stopped once again.

"Hi Pat. Sorry I'm late," Sandy said, blocking Pat's way. "I know you told me you wanted me to be here early, but I had to—"

"You're hired, honey," Pat told Sandy and moved her out of her path. "Faye, Zuma," Pat said as she put her hand on the front door. "We've got a new coworker, ladies," she said, then leaned forward and whispered, "What's your name again, honey?"

"Sandy," she said, too astonished to fully accept the fact that she had just been given a new job.

Zuma stopped what she was doing and stared at Pat with wickedness.

"You can start right over here," Pat told Sandy, pointing to a ponytailed woman on the sofa. "She needs to be washed and conditioned, and when you're done with her just ask Faye to show you who's next. In a couple days I'll have you start on manicuring, but today I need you to help out Faye and Zuma. You can wash and condition, right?"

All Sandy was trained to do were nails, but it seemed easy enough. "Sure."

Faye gave Zuma the eye as she watched her standing at her hair station with her mouth hanging wide open. Zuma couldn't believe that Pat just hired a complete stranger off the street. But no one had time to ask questions. Pat said her piece, then exited the salon at the speed of light. Faye and Zuma stood staring at the pale vision before them. Zuma was stonefaced, but at least Faye tried to fake a smile.

Sandy stood in the middle of the room, yet again the center of attention. But Sandy didn't care who was watching her. All she knew was that she had just been given a job. A chance to make a few extra dollars, and a chance to get away from her kids and live among adults. *Oh yeah*, Sandy thought as she looked around the room, returning all stares with a big Colgate smile. Until, that is, her eyes landed upon Zuma.

Never once did Zuma take her eyes off Sandy, and if looks could talk, Zuma would be screaming BITCH.

But that was okay with Sandy. She could hear every syllable Zuma's mouth didn't say. And her response? She looked Zuma dead in the eyes and slowly and methodically scratched her nose—with her middle finger.

As soon as Pat walked through the door she began calling his name. She called him all the way through the living room to the dining room, the kitchen to the den. She opened the French doors that led to the backyard pool and called him once more, but there was no answer. The only sound that responded to her was her cat's purr. She turned around and walked back in the house past Kunta and tried to remember if he'd told her his plans for the day. But of course he hadn't. She hadn't asked. She hadn't even waited for him to wake up this morning before she quickly took a shower, dressed, and sneaked out of the house. Where could he be, she wondered, as she spun around and headed toward the staircase. She ran up, calling his name. "Mark, Mark," she called as she ran through the upstairs office, then back out and to the bedroom. She stopped abruptly when she walked through the door and saw the opened suitcase on the bed. Slowly she walked toward it, trembling, knowing for sure that Mark had taken her threat of divorce seriously. She picked up one of his shirts off the floor and held it close to her chest. "No," she whispered as she sat down on the bed and stared at the suitcase full of clothes. "I didn't mean it, Mark," she said as tears filled her eyes. How could she have said those things to the one man who'd stood by her side through thick and thin? And how could he have taken her seriously? She hadn't fooled Faye and Zuma. They knew she didn't want a divorce. But they weren't Mark. They weren't married to her. They weren't the ones she'd shut out of her life. They weren't the ones she'd ignored, barely talked to, and refused to have sex with for the past four months. But Mark was. He was the one who had been putting up with a wife who acted like she didn't love him. Of course he believed her when she said she wanted a divorce. Her actions and nonactions had been telling him that for months.

Pat stood up, still holding Mark's shirt against her chest. "I can't let it happen this way," she said to herself as she walked over to the closet and grabbed a hanger and wrapped Mark's shirt around it. "I can't let you leave this way," she said as she hung up the shirt, then grabbed a handful of hangers. She dropped them on the bed and began taking Mark's clothes out of the suitcase. Piece by piece she placed his clothes on hangers and walked them back to the closet. "No, no, no, no, no. You are not going anywhere, Mark," she said, shaking her head and closing the closet door. Pat was angry. Angry at herself. Angry for being so stupid and so selfish. Many women would give their last dollar to have a man like she had and she wasn't going to lose him. Not this way.

She closed the suitcase and carried it to the storage room in the hallway. She walked down the staircase and into the living room, where she took a seat on the sofa facing the front door. Whatever she had to do to convince her man to stay with her she was going to do. When he walked through that door, she was going to tell him all the things she hadn't said in months. The I love yous, the I'm so happy to have yous, the I can't take life without yous—she would tell her man everything her heart truly felt. It had been too long, but she was going to make things right. She had to. She couldn't let her husband walk out of her life because she was a fool. She wouldn't let that happen.

She sat on the sofa for hours, waiting, thinking, hoping Mark would at least give her a chance to explain. Kunta jumped on the sofa and lay beside her and as she waited, Pat stroked a mindless hand over her cat's fur, hoping it wasn't too late, that Mark was not gone for good. It was dark outside when she heard his car pull into the driveway. Her heart raced as she straightened herself up and waited for him to come through the doorway.

The door came open slowly, and at last Mark walked in. The room was dark and it wasn't until Pat leaned over and turned on the light that Mark saw her face. "Hi," Pat said as Mark jumped and dropped the folder he was holding in his hand to the floor. An almost frightened look crossed his face as he stared at Pat, then down at the folder he'd dropped.

"Where have you been?" Pat asked as she got up from the sofa and approached her husband.

"Out," he answered in a voice so full of bass that it scared Kunta and the cat jumped off the sofa and ran away.

"Out?" Pat repeated as she stood in front of him, wondering where she should begin. Should she apologize? Beg? Tell him she loved him? She didn't know what her next move should be, but as she stood before him, her eyes fell down to the floor and onto the folder Mark had dropped. She squinted as she tried to read the upside-down words on the cover. It took her a moment to see it clearly. It was a name. John Peters, Attorney at Law. "You've seen a lawyer?" she asked as her eyes slowly looked up at Mark.

Mark didn't say a word. He didn't have to.

Pat took a step backward and turned her back to Mark. She didn't want him to see the tears that were in her eyes. Maybe it was too late to save their marriage, she thought as she glanced around the room, wondering what she could possibly say to make things right. She hadn't had a real conversation with Mark in so long that she'd forgotten how to talk to him. Everything she wanted to say seemed so silly. She'd pushed him away for months and now she was going to tell him she was sorry? She couldn't tell him that. Sorry seemed such a small word. Too weak to define what she was really feeling inside. She turned back to Mark and stared into his eyes. There was so much she wanted to say, but instead of opening her mouth to speak she placed her lips on Mark's face. She pulled his body to her and swept her arms around his neck. She kissed his forehead, his ears, his nose, but as she pulled back to kiss his lips, Mark turned his head.

"What are you doing?" he asked, grabbing her arms from around his neck and holding them in front of him.

"I want you," Pat whispered and leaned forward, trying once again to kiss his mouth.

But Mark wasn't having it. He turned away again and stepped back. "This is crazy," he said, and shook his head.

"Mark," Pat said as she stared at her husband, realizing for the first time in months how deeply she felt for him. She wanted to tell him she loved him, that she didn't want a divorce, but for some reason the words wouldn't come out. Instead she lifted her dress above her head and took it off. Mark watched as the dress fell on the floor, but he made no moves toward his wife.

"Pat, don't," he said as she reached for him and pulled him to her. Again she kissed his face. Then his lips.

"Don't you want me?" she asked as she unbuttoned his shirt and placed kisses across his chest.

"Not like this, Pat," he said as his eyes rolled back in his head. "We need to talk," he said as Pat continued kissing him down his chest. She tugged at his belt and unbuttoned his pants. "Stop, Pat," he said as he felt himself growing. "I said stop it," he said, and backed away from her. "What do you think you're doing?" he yelled. "Is this some kind of game to you? Do you think you can just tell me you want a divorce one day, then try to seduce me the next? This is crazy."

"I don't want a divorce, Mark," Pat said, standing up in nothing but her underwear. "I love you."

"You love me?" Mark asked, wanting so badly to believe her. "You love me?"

"Yes."

"You don't talk to me, you don't touch me, you avoid me every chance you get. And now you stand here and tell me you love me?"

"I know I haven't been acting like a wife, but it has nothing to do with the way I feel for you. It's just . . . It's . . ."

"What?"

"It's . . ."

"What, dammit. Talk to me."

Pat looked at her husband, then turned away. "You wouldn't understand."

"Understand what?"

"You wouldn't understand how I *feel*," Pat screamed, and turned to face him. "Do you know what I've been through? Do you know how it feels to want something so bad and be denied time and time again?" she said as she put her hands on her stomach. "I feel so empty inside, Mark. I don't even feel like a woman."

"I *know* how you feel," Mark said, and watched as Pat rubbed her stomach.

"No, you don't," Pat yelled. "This is about me feeling inadequate as a woman. Why can't you understand that?"

"How can you say I don't understand?" he yelled back at her. "How do you think I felt when I found out we couldn't have kids? When the adoption fell through, do you think I didn't feel pain? I *understand*, Pat," he said, placing a hand on his chest. "I feel it too. But I didn't shut you out of my life. I didn't ignore you and I didn't tell you I wanted a divorce."

"No," Pat said as she bent over and picked up the folder off the floor that Mark had dropped earlier. "But you sure didn't waste any time going to see an attorney, did you?" She held the folder up for Mark to see.

"That's not what you think it is," Mark said as his eyes fell to the floor.

"Oh it's not," Pat said and turned the folder around. "John Peters, Attorney at Law," she read aloud, then stared at Mark.

"It's not what you think it is," he said again and shook his head.

"Then what is it?"

"Why don't you open it up and see for yourself?"

"What?" Pat said as she fumbled around with the folder. "You want me to see the terms of divorce? What? What?" she said as she opened the folder and glanced over the top page. She read for a moment, then slowly looked up at Mark. "What is this?" she asked as her eyes fell back down to the page.

"John Peters is an adoption attorney," Mark said, still looking down at the floor.

"An adoption attorney?" Pat whispered.

"Yes," Mark said as he walked closer to Pat. He stood for a moment without saying a word, then took the folder from Pat and looked her dead in the eyes. "This morning I was going to leave," he said firmly, then paused. "I told myself that I couldn't take it anymore. That I didn't want to stay if you didn't want me here. But then I thought about it. I thought about you. I know you, Pat. I know you love me and I know that I love you. There has only been one glitch in our relationship. And that's children," he said as he took Pat's hand. "I want to give you everything you want, Pat. I want us to have children."

"We've been through this before," Pat said, closing her eyes, not wanting to consider what her husband was suggesting, yet wanting so much to believe.

"But this time we're going to do it right."

"No," Pat said and looked at Mark. But though her mouth was saying no, the rest of her wanted to hear more.

"I was going to tell you about this last night over dinner," he said as Pat's mind traveled back to the candlelight dinner she'd seen set up in the dining room. "I have been meeting with this attorney for months now. I didn't want to tell you about it because I didn't want to get your hopes up before I knew for sure that I could make this happen."

"Make what happen?"

"John Peters has helped me find a foster family who has—"

"No," Pat whispered and shook her head, but Mark kept talking.

"A foster family who has a wonderful little girl who wants to be adopted."

"No," Pat said again, then paused, realizing her mouth was saying one thing, but that her mind and her heart longed to hear more.

"She's not an infant. She's four years old. She's been living with the same foster family since she was born."

Pat's eyes begged to hear more.

"The adoption process has already been started. A social worker has even checked out our background and last month she came out to inspect our home," he said, then paused, noticing the curiosity growing on his wife's face. "There's nothing left for us to do but meet the little girl. Her name is Tracy."

"Tracy?" Pat said as her eyes widened. "Tracy?"

"Yes," Mark said, and stroked his wife's face. "Our first visit with her is scheduled for Monday."

Pat threw her hands over her face, then slowly slid them down. She couldn't believe what Mark was telling her. She couldn't believe he'd done all this by himself. And at the moment she didn't know how she felt. The only thing she knew was that he'd done it again. All the while she had been avoiding him, pushing him out of her life, he had been thinking about her, trying to find a way to make her happy. Trying to find a way to bring joy back into her life, to give her the one thing she wanted most in this world — a child.

"Tracy," Pat whispered and watched as Mark nodded his head. "We can meet her on Monday?"

"Yes."

"Tracy," she whispered again, and looked curiously around the room. "Are you sure about this?"

"I'm sure," he said, and held out his hand.

Pat's lips began to quiver as she placed her hand in his. "I'm so sorry, Mark," she cried. "I'm so sorry. You're so good to me and I —"

"Ssh," he said, and pulled her to his chest.

"But I've been such a —"

"Ssh," he said again, and held her tightly.

"I don't deserve you," she said, and looked into his face.

"You deserve much more," he said, and held her face in his hand. "You deserve a family. And I'm gonna give it to you."

Pat sighed and moved forward until her forehead rested against his. "I love you, Mark," she said as she took one of his hands away from her face and moved it slowly down to her breast. "I love you so much," she whispered, then slipped her bra strap from her shoulder.

In less than a minute they were both completely undressed and as they sank down to the floor, moaning sounds of sheer ecstasy, Kunta rejoined the room and sauntered ever so easily toward her owners' naked bodies. There she stayed until Pat and Mark had proven their love to one another for the first time in months. And almost as if to say it was about time, Kunta purred and cushioned her furry body against them. And there the three rested until it was time to do it all over again.

7

Zuma could barely get through the front door of Blessings on Monday morning before she started bitching. "The Barbie doll has got to go," she said to Faye, who simply rolled her eyes and continued preparing her hair station for her first client. She had listened to Zuma's mouth all day on Saturday as she complained about Sandy. Every chance she got she was in Faye's ear whispering and pointing. "Look at her. She don't know what the hell she's doing. She better stay out of my way. Is she getting paid for this shit?" Faye was tired of hearing it. She herself had thought Sandy did an excellent job. She took care of all the washing and conditioning and even helped her out with sorting through her ever-jumbled stacks of fake hair. But Zuma had barely spoken a word to Sandy and the one time Sandy had asked her if she needed some help, all Zuma did was stare her down. Zuma's dislike of the new girl was too apparent, but for the life of her Faye couldn't figure out where Zuma's hatred was coming from.

"And where is Pat?" Zuma asked as she made it to her hair station and began unpacking her bag.

"I don't know," Faye said. "I opened the shop this morning. I wanted to call her on Sunday and ask what time she'd be in, but I didn't want to disturb her."

"Well, I'm gonna disturb her as soon as I see her 'cause this white chick ain't cutting it."

"Sandy did a fine job on Saturday, Zuma," Faye said, and stopped sorting through her fake hair. She walked over to Zuma's hair station and stood behind her chair. "You haven't even given the girl a chance."

"I don't need to give her a chance. She just needs to find herself another job."

"Why?"

"Because."

"Because why?"

Zuma sighed as she looked at Faye. The sigh was more a delay tactic than anything else. She thought about Faye's question, but she couldn't come up with an answer. Not one that made complete sense anyway.

"Why, Zuma? Why don't you like Sandy? What's she done to you?"

"You see the way she be looking at me?"

"Yeah, and I see the way you look at her. Both of you act like you're in elementary school."

"Well, she started it."

"Listen to you. How old are you? *She started it?* Come on, Zuma. You're more mature than that. You can't just not like somebody without a reason. That's so childish."

"Oh, I'm being childish?"

"Yes, you're being childish."

"Childish, huh?"

"With a capital C."

"If you see somebody childish then slap somebody childish."

"Good Lord, Zuma. That's from way back," Faye said and reminisced about all the schoolyard fights she'd seen as a child that started off that way.

"No, better yet," Zuma said, and foolishly picked up a comb from her counter and placed it on her shoulder. "If I'm so childish then knock that off my shoulder."

Faye laughed so hard she got a cramp in her stomach. "You used to do that too?"

"Yes, girl," Zuma said and took away the comb. "That's how we used to start fights in school. You were a bad motherfucker if you could knock a rock off somebody's shoulder."

"Oh, what about this one?" Faye said as she got up in Zuma's face and nudged her shoulder against Zuma's. "Did you guys do this too?"

"Yeah," Zuma said as they began walking around in a circle. "We'd walk around like this until we got dizzy," Zuma said and laughed. "Nobody really wanted to fight in those days. It was all about putting on a show for everyone else who gathered around to watch."

"And even when we did fight we used our hands," Faye said as she tapped Zuma on the back and stood still. "Today kids just pull out a knife and get to cutting."

"A knife, honey? You mean a three fifty-seven."

"I know, child. It's crazy these days. I don't know what I'm going to do when Christopher gets older. Maybe I'll put him in private school or something."

"Chris is a good kid. He wouldn't get himself involved in a gang or anything like that."

"I know he is," Faye said as she went back to her hair station. "But peer pressure is something else these days," she said as she glanced up at the picture of Chris she had stuck on her mirror. "You should be glad you don't have children, Zuma."

Glad, Zuma thought, and busied herself with arranging her hair products on her counter. Zuma didn't care about the worries of being a mother. She'd teach him right from wrong and keep a watchful eye on him. Whether she had a girl or a boy, she'd raise them right. With or without a father.

"Hey," Zuma said, pausing as she thought back to a previous evening. "What happened that night you called home, then ran out here like lightning?"

"Oh," Faye said, and smiled with embarrassment. "Antoinette had done it again," she said as she and Zuma both sighed. "She ran off and left Chris at home by himself."

"What?"

"She didn't even bother to walk in the house until after one o'clock in the morning."

"No she didn't." Zuma gasped. "She's only sixteen."

"I don't know what I'm gonna do with that girl," Faye said as she walked back to her hair station and sat down.

"So what did you do?"

"I took her phone away."

"Took her phone away?" Zuma mimicked. "You should have beaten her ass."

"And what would that have solved?"

"It would have shown her who was the boss."

Faye rolled her eyes and shook her head. She didn't believe in beating her children. She never had and she never would. Children are people, not animals, and Faye couldn't imagine raising her hand to a stray dog, let alone her own flesh and blood.

"You better stop letting those kids run over you, Faye," Zuma warned.

"Once a child knows they can run over you they lose all respect for you. Next thing you know Chris will be trying to step up in your face," she said, raising an eyebrow. "You need to nip that shit in the bud."

"I don't have to worry about Chris," Faye said, smiling as she thought of him.

"Is he still doing good in school?"

"At the top of his class."

"Excellent," Zuma said, and reached in her purse and pulled out a dollar. "Give that to him. Tell him it's from Auntie Zu."

"Okay," Pat said and slid the dollar into her right bosom so she wouldn't forget about it.

"They aren't trying to start none of that Ebonics shit down at his school, are they?" Zuma asked cautiously.

"Not that I know of," Faye answered as she checked out the grimace on Zuma's face. "But I don't see anything wrong with it."

"You don't see anything wrong with it?" Zuma said, turning toward Faye so quickly that she knocked over two cans of hair spray on her counter. "It's just the most stupid, racist, idiotic bullshit that has ever been suggested in the history of history. And to think a group of black people came up with the idea turns my stomach."

"What?" Faye questioned, and shrugged her shoulders. "If teaching Ebonics would help these minority children learn better, then what's the problem? You can't deny that minorities have a different way of talking," she said, faking her hardest ghetto stance. "I *be* chillin'. Whatchoo want that *fo?*"

"Ghetto kids don't talk like that because they have some kind of genetic malfunction, Faye. They pick it up from their environment. Just because they use slang doesn't mean they have a harder time learning than any other child. If that same ghetto child had grown up in Bel-Air, he'd be talking *Grey Poupon,*" she said, stressing an air of aristocracy.

"Then why are ghetto kids so far behind?"

"Because they don't take their asses to school, or when they do, they have too many other problems on their minds like the fact that they didn't eat breakfast or had to sleep in a cold house because the electricity got shut off. Shit, you got other things on your mind when you're poor. Who gives a damn if it's I'm going to the store or I be goin' to da sto?" Zuma huffed.

"Well, the way I understood it, Ebonics was supposed to help out white people. So that the teachers could understand the way their students talk."

"Fuck that, Faye," Zuma whipped out. "I could come in here and say,

Top of the morning to you, or I could say, Yo, what up? You still know what the fuck I'm talking about. Teachers aren't dumb. They understand. Ebonics was just a fucked-up idea. Shit, when a white redneck living down in the Louisiana swamp starts talking about, "I'm fi'na chop down dem der trees," nobody puts any labels on that. Nobody starts talking about poor-white-trash-onics," she said, and rolled her eyes so tight she had to work hard to refocus them. "And another thing," she huffed on. "All those educated black folks should have been using all that time they spent thinking up Ebonics on trying to think up a surefire way to stop gangs and teen pregnancy and drugs from taking over this country. That's what the hell they should have been doing."

"Okay, okay," Faye said, realizing that their conversation as usual had gotten too heated.

"Well, don't get me started on a subject if you don't wanna hear what I've got to say."

"I didn't start this, you did."

"Well, fine."

"Fine."

"Good."

"Hey," Pat said as she breezed through the front door wearing a peach silk pantsuit and a glowing smile.

Zuma and Faye stopped their bickering and gave each other a cautious eye. "So," Faye said hesitantly. "I take it things went well between you and Mark?"

Pat smiled, but didn't say a word.

"I mean, you didn't do anything stupid, did you?"

Still Pat smiled, with no words.

"Do you still have a marriage or what?" Zuma said, bluntly.

"Yes I most certainly do," Pat said, and broke out giggling.

"Oh Pat," Faye said as she walked over to her and put her arms around her neck. "I knew you would work things out with Mark. You two belong together."

"Thank you," Pat said as she let Faye go.

"So what happened?" Zuma asked as she walked over to Pat.

"Well, it was touchy there for a minute," Pat said, and set her purse down on the reception desk and sighed. "He had his things packed and ready to leave."

"Mmm." Faye moaned and sucked her teeth. "But you worked everything out, right."

"Yes we did," Pat said showing all of her teeth. "It was just like you said. Our problems have nothing to do with our love for one another. It was all about . . . you know . . ." Pat still had trouble admitting she was infertile. But the girls understood where she was going.

"Well, I don't mean to sound cynical," Zuma said. "But you still can't have no babies. So how are things supposed to get better?"

"*Zuma*," Faye said and hit her on the arm.

"Well, I'm just asking," she said, and hit her back. "I mean, if the problem was your inability to have kids, then how is it going to get better?"

Pat smiled again and looked Zuma dead in the eyes. She put both her hands in the air and braced herself. "We're going to adopt."

"Oh Pat," Faye said and gave her another hug. "That's wonderful."

"I know," Pat said. "I'm so excited."

Zuma cleared her throat and held up a finger. "Excuse me," she said, and raised her eyebrows. "Didn't you try that already too? And if I'm not mistaken, it didn't work out."

"*Zuma*," Faye said and frowned. "Is that any of your business? Can't you just be happy that things are working out?"

"Actually," Pat said and stroked the side of Zuma's face, "you're right. We tried adoption before, but we didn't handle it right. This time Mark has gotten an adoption attorney to work with us."

"You need an attorney to adopt a baby?" Faye asked.

"If you want to make sure everything goes smoothly you do," Pat said as she walked around the reception desk and browsed through the appointment book. "The last girl we were adopting from didn't want us to use an attorney, which is why we got screwed. But this time," she said, and looked back and forth between her friends, "this time I know it's gonna work."

"Well, I wish you all the best," Faye said, and gave Zuma the eye.

"What?" Zuma said and smirked. "I wish her all the best too," she said, trying not to notice Faye's dissatisfaction. "No, seriously," Zuma said, and walked around the reception desk to join Pat. "I'm happy for you," she said, putting her arms around her. "Just don't get your hopes up too high."

"*Zuma*."

"What? I'm just kidding," she said, and gave Pat a kiss on the cheek.

"Thank you, Miss Zuma," Pat said, and watched her walk away. "Now, let's see," Pat said as she skimmed through her appointment book. "Good," she said as she slid her finger down the Monday column under her name. Mondays were always slow for her and she was glad this Monday was no exception. "All I've got is a twelve o'clock press and curl and our first ever manicure appointment is at three," she announced, then closed the book. "Sandy can take care of that."

Zuma's neck almost snapped as she swung around to look at Pat.

"So how was Sandy?" she asked as she came around the reception desk.

"Terrible," Zuma shouted.

"Wonderful," Faye shouted back.

Pat paused and frowned. "Well, which one was it, ladies?" she asked as her eyes shot back and forth between the two.

Faye spoke up quickly. "She was just fine. She handled the phones and helped me out tremendously."

"She was in the way," Zuma said and stuck out her lips. "I don't see why we need her. We've been doing just fine without her."

"Don't listen to Zuma," Faye said. "That girl is a big help. As a matter of fact, we got out of here before nine o'clock that night."

"Nine o'clock on a Saturday?" Pat said and gasped. "My goodness. This place was packed when I left."

"I know," Faye said. "But Sandy was a total help. She knows what she's doing, and what she doesn't know, she can learn."

"She don't know shit," Zuma said, and slammed down a bottle of hair spray. "This is a black hair shop. Can't no white girl be sashaying all up and through here."

Faye huffed and put her hands on her hips. "We're back to the black, white thing."

Zuma slyly raised her eyebrows.

"Look, you guys," Pat interrupted. "I hired her to help out with phones and manicuring. I don't see what the color of her skin has got to do with that."

"Fire her," Zuma said definitively.

"No you don't," Faye said.

"Yes you do."

"No, you—"

"Hold it!" Pat said and held up her hands. "I've got a joke for you," Pat said, and clapped her hands together.

"Ah shit," Zuma said, and plopped herself down in her chair. "If you don't want us to argue just tell us."

"Quiet," Pat said. "This is a good one . . . Okay. Why did the lady get a tattoo of a turkey on her right thigh and a tattoo of Santa Claus on her left thigh?"

Zuma and Faye looked at each other and shook their heads.

"You give up?"

"Yes, we give up."

"Because her husband kept complaining that there was nothing good to eat between Thanksgiving and Christmas."

"Oh, Pat," Faye said, and blushed.

Zuma cracked a half smile. "That one was okay," she said, then went stonefaced. "But the white girl has still got to go."

"Well, she can't go today," Pat said as she wiped a piece of lint off her peach suit. "I have to leave early again."

"Oh yeah?" Faye said and gave Pat the once-over. "I was wondering why you were so dressed up. What? You and Mark going out to celebrate?"

"Sorta," she said, and clapped her hands together again. "We're going to a foster home this morning. The attorney Mark hired has a little girl he wants us to meet."

"Great," Zuma said sarcastically.

Faye gave her the eye, then turned to Pat. "That's wonderful," she said, and folded her arms across her chest. "So how old is she?"

"Four," Pat said, unable to hold back her enthusiasm. "I always thought I wanted an infant, but now I don't care how old the child is. I just want to have a little one in my life. I swear, you guys," she said, and spun around, "I feel it. I know it's gonna work out this time."

"Oh Pat," Faye said, and closed her eyes. "I am gonna pray for you every step of the way," she said, trying to hold back the tears of joy she felt for her friend. "Anything you want, the Lord will provide."

"Yes, Allah will," Zuma added.

"I hope so," Pat said, and took in a deep breath. "I really hope so."

"So what you're trying to say is that the white girl stays," Zuma said impatiently.

"Give it a rest," Faye barked.

"All I'm saying is this," Zuma continued. "If you're gonna hire some help around here, why can't you hire someone black? I mean, damn. I know it's some sisters out there who need a job."

"Well, I didn't see none of those sisters coming in here asking for a job," Faye retaliated.

"That help wanted sign hung on that door for weeks. The *sisters* weren't interested."

"Well, you should have taken out an ad in the paper. Not all blacks live in Inglewood and have a chance to walk by this shop. They probably didn't know you were hiring."

"Did you know Pat was hiring when you walked in here and asked for a job? No," Faye said and pointed a finger at herself. "And neither did I. But we saw what we wanted and we went after it. We walked our black behinds in here and gave it a shot. That's what's wrong with folks today. They sit around waiting for things to be handed to them on a silver platter instead of going out and getting what they want."

"So now black people not only have to be qualified. They have to be psychic too. Somehow they have to just know where all the jobs are?"

"They don't have to be psychic, they have to be hungry. They have to pound the pavement just like you and I did."

"Whatever, Faye. All I know is that if Pat had run an ad in the paper, there would have been plenty of sisters coming through here looking for a job," she said, and got up from her chair to walk over to Faye's station. "How do we expect white folks to be for affirmative action when we don't even practice it ourselves?"

"This ain't about affirmative action."

"This is exactly about affirmative action. It's about black people giving black people an opportunity."

"Are you saying Pat doesn't give black people an opportunity?"

"Okay, ladies," Pat broke in. "I've got another joke."

But Zuma and Faye were too busy with their debate for jokes.

"She didn't this time."

"Now you're taking it too far, Zuma. If you're so concerned about affirmative action then march your behind down to City Hall and picket."

"Ladies," Pat said again. "I've got a joke for you," she said as Faye and Zuma both looked in her direction.

"The joke is standing right behind you," Zuma said as she stared past Pat.

Sandy walked through the door and paused. She could feel the negative vibe almost immediately. Pat turned around with surprise. "Sandy," she said, and chuckled. "We were just talking about you."

Sandy smiled at Faye, but didn't give Zuma a second thought. "I didn't know what time I should come in today," she said to Pat.

"You're right on time," Pat said as she walked over to the reception area and picked up her purse. "I hear you did a good job on Saturday."

"Thanks," Sandy said as she stood in the middle of the floor not knowing what to do. She tried not to notice the curious eye Pat was giving her chosen attire for the day. Sandy had been an exotic dancer for so long that the only outfits that hung in her closet were too gaudy for casual, everyday wear. Today all she could find suitable was a pair of leopardskin Lycra stretch pants. She put on one of Cerwin's oversized T-shirts to downplay the look, but that had been negated by the strappy four-inch sandals she wore on her feet.

Zuma groaned and rolled her eyes as she passed Sandy and went back to her station.

Faye cut her eyes at Zuma as she walked past Sandy. "I just want to thank you for all the help," she told Sandy. "We'd gotten so busy in the afternoon that I never had a chance to tell you that," she said, and smiled as Sandy gave her a nod and a wink.

"Well, keep up the good work," Pat said as she headed for the front door.

"You're not staying?" Sandy asked as she turned around to face Pat.

"Nope. I've got some important business to attend to today," she said, and put her hand on Sandy's shoulder. "But you'll be fine. Mondays are pretty slow around here. All you'll need to do today is answer phones and make appointments. I've got a nail appointment for you at three," she said, then looked over at Zuma. "You can handle my press and curl at twelve, can't you?"

"Mmm-hmm," Zuma moaned.

"Well," Pat said with her hand on the door, "if you have any questions Faye can answer them for you."

Faye smiled at Sandy and nodded her head.

"Otherwise, ladies, I'll see you tomorrow," Pat said as she walked out the door.

"Good luck," Faye called behind her.

There was an uneasy silence that filled the room as the three ladies swapped glances at each other. Sandy was grateful when the phone rang out, giving her something to do. As she picked it up, Faye walked over to Zuma and whispered. "You be nice," she threatened, then jumped when Sandy called her name.

"It's for you," Sandy said, and put her hand over the receiver.

"An appointment?" Faye asked as she walked over to take the phone.

"No," Sandy said, and held it out to her. "It's your son's school."

Faye frowned as she took the phone from Sandy and put it to her ear.

Sandy walked away to give Faye some privacy and decided to pick up a cloth and do a little dusting. She could feel Zuma watching her every move and although she wasn't one to back down from a confrontation, she wished Zuma would just give her a break. Though Sandy had only worked at the shop one full day, she knew this job was something that she wanted to keep. And if she was going to keep it, she knew she'd eventually have to get over whatever it was that was going on between her and Zuma. As she dusted off the reception desk, she snuck a peek at her foe. Maybe I should go over and formally introduce myself, she thought. Shake her hand, smile, try to break down the wall? But she could tell by the look on Zuma's face that she didn't want to be bothered. Now was not the right time.

Faye hung up the phone and put her hand over her mouth. Flustered, she looked around the room as if she had no clue what to do next. "I gotta go," she said finally as she raced over to her hair station.

"What's up?" Zuma asked with concern.

"Christopher's been hurt."

"Hurt? What happened? Is he all right?"

"I don't know, girl," she said, shaking her head and grabbing her purse. "They want me to come down to the nurse's office," she said as she searched through her purse for her keys. "I'm gonna need you to call up my appointments and cancel them," she said to Sandy. "Their numbers are in the book."

"No problem," Sandy said and stood back as Faye came rushing her way toward the door.

"You're gonna be gone the whole day?" Zuma asked as she followed behind her.

"Yeah. I gotta go see what happened to my baby," Faye said as she opened the door and ran to her car.

Damn, Zuma thought, as she watched her from the window jumping into her car and speeding out of the parking lot. Please don't get in an accident, she thought to herself as she watched her zoom down the street. As she turned away from the window, Zuma paused abruptly. Wait a minute, she thought to herself. No Pat. No Faye . . . just . . . She slowly turned to Sandy just as Sandy was slowly turning to her. Both of them stared at each other, realizing it was just the two of them.

Zuma's head fell backward as she looked up to the ceiling. "Oh God," she said, and closed her eyes. "It's going to be a long day."

Faye's car bumped the fender of the car in front of her as she squeezed into the only parking space she could find in front of her son's school. She hurried out of the car and ran all 210 pounds of herself up the school steps and into the administration building. That's as far as she could go with the running. She slowed down as she walked through the halls, checking every door label for the nurse's office. Panting, she waddled down the hall until she found an opened door. She peeped in and saw the nurse.

"Excuse me," she said, and put her hand over her chest and caught her breath. "I'm Mrs. Cruz, Christopher's mom," she said, and looked around the room for her son. "Where is he? Is he okay?"

"Mrs. Cruz," the nurse said as she turned around and saw Faye sweating and panting. "Oh, Mrs. Cruz. Do you need to sit down?" she asked as she came over and put her hand on Faye's back. "Would you like some water? You look terrible."

"No," she said, and waved her off. "I just need to see my son. Is he all right?"

"Yes, Mrs. Cruz. Christopher is fine now. He was a little shaken up, but he'll be okay."

"Well, where is he?"

"Come on, ma'am," she said, and led her back out into the hallway. She pointed three doors down. "He's in the principal's office."

"The principal's office? I thought he was hurt."

"You ought to see the other boy," the nurse said, and patted Faye on the back. "Are you sure you're all right?"

"I'm fine," Faye said as she took in another deep breath and headed down the hall.

She walked into the room and stood behind the wooden banister until one of the secretaries came to greet her. "I'm Christopher Cruz's mother," she told the secretary. "Where is he?"

The secretary pulled back the swinging half door and held out her hand. "Right this way, Mrs. Cruz," she said as she waited for her to squeeze through the opening, then walked her down a short path to another office.

"Mrs. Cruz is here," the secretary said as she opened the door and stuck her head in.

As Faye walked into the room she was greeted again. "Good morning, I'm Alice Washington, the school's principal," a prestigious-looking black woman said as she stood up behind her desk. Faye smiled and held out her hand, but then she caught a glimpse of her son sitting in the corner of the room.

"Christopher," she said, and gasped. She rushed over to him and lifted his face up by the chin. "Oh hijo," she said, wincing at the scratches and bruises on his face. His forehead was patched with a white bandage and dried-up blood still traced the rim of his nostrils. "What happened to you?" she said as she bent over and placed kisses on the parts of his face that looked like they weren't hurt.

"Ow, Mami," Christopher said, and squinted his eyes.

"Oh, my baby," Faye whimpered as tears began to fall from her eyes. "How did this happen?"

Christopher shrugged his shoulders and snuck a peek at Mrs. Washington. "I don't know."

"Come, come, Christopher," Mrs. Washington said as she sat back down in her seat. "Tell your mother what happened."

"I don't know," Christopher insisted, and hung his head.

"Well," Mrs. Washington began, and sighed. "It seems your son has been fighting," she said as Faye took a seat next to her son. "His teacher, Mrs. Brooks, broke it up—"

"My son's been fighting? Fighting who? Who did this to my baby?"

"Jason Jackson," Christopher huffed. "He always messing with me, Mami. Calling me names and stuff."

"Jason Jackson," Faye said, and tightened her lips. "Where is this boy?"

"Jason is down the hall with the assistant principal and his mother."

"Well, I want to talk to that little boy," Faye said, and stood up. "I send my son to school to learn, not to be picked on by bullies."

"Just a second," Mrs. Washington said, and held up her hand.

"No," Faye shouted. "Look at my boy," she said, and pointed to her son. "How could you let this happen? I want to talk to that boy and his mother. She ought to be ashamed of the way she raised her son. Sending him to school to start fights—"

"Mrs. Cruz," the principal insisted. "Christopher is the one who started the fight. According to Mrs. Brooks, it was your son who threw the first punch."

Slowly, Faye turned to Christopher. "Is this true?"

Christopher shrugged.

Faye sat back down.

"I've been trying to get Christopher to tell me exactly what happened, but it seems the cat's got his tongue."

Faye scratched her neck and looked at Christopher. "Why did you hit that boy?"

"I don't know."

"Yes you do know, Christopher. Now tell me."

" 'Cause he always picking on me, Mami. He be laughing at me and pointing and stuff, so I cracked him in his mouth."

"*Christopher.*"

"Well, he oughtta leave me alone, shoot."

"Christopher," Mrs. Washington said. "What are we supposed to do when someone is making fun of us?"

"Tell the teacher," Christopher said grudgingly.

"What are we not supposed to do?"

"Use our hands," he said as if he were speaking in unison with some invisible group.

"I am so sorry about this, Mrs. Washington," Faye said, embarrassed. "I thought I taught Christopher better than this."

"I'm sure. But I am going to have to suspend Christopher."

"For how long?"

"A week."

"A week? Isn't that a bit long?"

"Mrs. Cruz, your son strangled Jason Jackson."

"*Strangled?*"

"Yes. The only reason I'm not kicking Christopher out of this school for good is because he is obviously a very smart young man. His teacher tells me he is at the top of his class. But that doesn't excuse what he's done. Not only am I suspending him for a week, I am recommending a series of counseling sessions for him with the school's psychiatrist."

"Psychiatrist? Are you suggesting my son is crazy?"

"No, Mrs. Cruz. But normal children don't go around strangling other kids. I've been trying to talk to Christopher to get to the root of where all this anger is coming from, but he refuses to talk to me. The only other viable solution is to have him talk with the school's psychiatrist. Of course you will have to be present at all the sessions since Christopher is so young."

Oh Dios mios, Faye thought as she sat listening to Mrs. Washington. She felt like she herself had done something wrong. Like she was somehow responsible for all this. Well, she *was* the mother. And as such she *was* responsible for everything her child did. As she continued listening to Mrs. Washington she looked over at her son. How could her precious little boy strangle anybody? He was just a baby.

"Oh good, you're here," Mrs. Washington said as she looked toward the door of her office. "This is Mrs. Cruz," she said, and pointed to Faye. "And this is Mr. Watson, the school's psychiatrist."

Mr. Watson extended his hand to Faye and flashed an unforgettable row of teeth. He had thick eyebrows and a mustache to match, and for a second there, Faye could swear she was staring at James from *Good Times.* Suddenly Faye found herself picturing Mr. Watson in a plaid shirt with a bright yellow construction hat. "Baby, I'm home," he said as he walked through the front room toward Faye. "Give me some sugar, Sugar."

"Mrs. Cruz?" he called and waved his hand in her face. "Are you all right?"

"I'm sorry," Faye said, shaking off her fantasy and extending her hand. "I guess I'm still in shock over what's happened."

"No problem," he said, and turned to Christopher. He kneeled down in front of him and patted his leg. "You all right, fella?" he asked, and flashed that smile once again.

Christopher slowly nodded his head, then turned to his mom. "Can we go now?"

"Yes you may," Mrs. Washington said as she stood up again.

"I'll walk you out to your car," Mr. Watson said. He stood up and took Christopher by the hand and led him to the door. "Mrs. Cruz?" he called over his shoulder as Faye still sat in her seat.

"Oh, I'm right behind you," she said as she struggled to get up and followed them out.

Faye walked a few steps behind Chris and Mr. Watson as they exited the building. Mr. Watson held Chris's hand and talked to him all the way out and as Faye watched the two of them together she realized this counseling thing wasn't going to be as bad as it sounded. She felt an immediate sense of trust for Mr. Watson and she could tell that her son was taking a liking to him too.

"My car's the burgundy one right in front," she called to them as they walked down the front steps of the school. As they reached the passenger side of the car, Faye took out her keys. "Excuse me," she said as she tried to squeeze by to open the door.

"I'll do that," Mr. Watson said, and took the keys from her. He opened the door and stood back while Chris climbed inside. "I can't wait until we have more time to talk," he told Chris. "I'm your friend. Remember that," he said, and held up his hand to Chris. Chris slapped him a high five and giggled just a little as Mr. Watson closed the door and turned to Faye. He smiled innocently at her, which for some reason made Faye a bit nervous. She ran a hand over the top of her braided ponytail, then down the front of the cotton sweatsuit she'd bought out of the men's department at Kmart.

Her face was still moist from all the sweating she'd done earlier when she ran and as she stood there looking at the husky Mr. Watson the only thing on her mind was that he must think she's a fat, sweaty pig.

"So Mrs. Cruz . . . uh, what is your first name?"

"Faye."

"Faye," he said and smiled. "That's a pretty name."

"Oh, ah, oh."

"Well, Faye, I think it's important that we be on a first-name basis. I don't want you to think of me as some old stuffy man in a suit. I want us to be friends. That's very important. For all of us to be friends."

"Oh, no, no problem."

"Good," he said, and pulled out a pink paper from his pocket. "I've gone ahead and scheduled a meeting for the three of us tomorrow afternoon. Is that okay with you?"

"That's fine."

"Good," he said, and handed Faye the paper. "Now, I've got a home-work assignment for you."

"Homework?"

"Yes ma'am," he said, strictly. "Your homework assignment is to talk to your son."

"Oh, but I do talk to my son," Faye said, and put her hand over her chest. "Please believe me, Mr. Watson. I'm not a bad mother. I don't know what got into Chris today, but he's not a bad boy either."

"I believe you, Faye. But from now on when you talk to your son, I want you to spend thirty minutes alone with him. No TV, no distractions. Just you, him, in a room alone, talking for thirty minutes. This will not only get him prepared for his sessions with me, but hopefully you can begin to crack the surface and find out what's really bugging your son. You know, fits of anger like the one your son showed today don't just happen for no reason. Chris is holding something inside and it's our job to find out what that is."

"Our job?"

"That's right. It's you and me together."

"Oh, ah, oh," Faye said as she ran her hand over her head and decided it was time for her to get going. She walked to the front of the car, but she'd parked so close to the car in front of her that she couldn't fit through. She walked to the back of the car and saw the same was true. Faye sighed and glanced shyly at Mr. Watson and walked down three car lengths until she found a space big enough for her to pass through. When she got to the driver's side of her car, she opened the door, then paused before she got in.

"I didn't get your first name, Mr. Watson," she said as he slowly began to backtrack up the front of the school steps.

He shouted something out that Faye could not hear. "What?" she asked, straining.

"James, you know, like on *Good Times*."

"Oh, ah, oh," Faye said as she watched him wave, then turn around and run back inside the school. "James," she whispered to herself as she sat down and closed her door.

"Mami," Christopher said, and turned his bandaged head to face her. "I'm sorry I got in trouble."

"I know, baby," she said, and smiled at her son. "Everything's gonna be all right."

Since McDonald's was Chris's favorite, Faye decided to resist her craving for a Big Mac. She didn't want Chris to think that he could be rewarded for getting suspended from school with a meal at his favorite restaurant. Instead, Faye went to the drive-through at El Pollo Loco and ordered an eight-piece meal plus a side of beans and rice. Christopher hated El Pollo Loco. There were no clowns, no happy meals, and no free toys with the order. But that was too bad. Chris had been a bad boy and he had to be punished.

By the time they got home it was noon. And before they even got out of the car, Faye warned her son that there would be no television, no radio, no nothing. "I want you to go straight to your room and think about what you've done. Do you hear me?" she said as she opened the front door and backed up for him to go inside. But when Faye stepped through the door, she could tell something was wrong. The house was quiet, but she could feel something was out of whack. "Go to your room, Chris," she said as she put her plastic bag from El Pollo Loco down on the coffee table in front of the sofa.

"Okay," he said as he hung his head and obeyed his mother.

Faye went to the kitchen and stood in silence. Something was not right here. She was sure she'd cleaned up this kitchen before she went to work, yet there were dirty dishes on the table. She frowned as she walked back to the front room and paused. Slowly she walked to the hallway and stood outside her daughter's room. She almost turned around to go get her chicken, until she heard what she thought was a groan. Puzzled, she opened the door to her daughter's room and almost fell out.

"*Antoinette*," she screamed as she saw the back of her naked daughter straddled atop her boyfriend. "Oh my Lord!"

"Mama," Antoinette screamed as she scrambled on the bed and pulled the covers over her. Her boyfriend jumped to the floor where he stood hanging out for all the world to see.

"Get out my house!" she screamed as the boy hurried around the room, picking up his clothes, trying to hide his body and get dressed at the same time.

"Is this what goes on when I'm not here?" Faye screamed so loud that Christopher came to the doorway to see what was going on. "You best get gone," Faye screamed at Antoinette's boyfriend as he rushed past her, hopping on one leg and only half dressed. "Oh Dios," Faye screamed as she stood staring at her daughter, barely able to breathe. She was so flustered that she couldn't think of anything to say to her, except, "Oh Lord . . . Oh Dios . . . Oh my God!"

"Mami," Christopher said as he ran to her side.

"Get in your room, boy," she yelled as he quickly turned around and ran. "And you," she said to Antoinette as she sat on her bed gripping her sheets in front of her. "You . . . you . . ." She shook her head and grabbed her chest. Her blood pressure was boiling and she could barely breathe. "I can't believe you," she said as she walked out of the room and slammed the door behind her. She stood outside the door and clasped her hands in front of her. "For the love of God," she said and looked up at the ceiling. "For the love of God!"

8

Pat gripped Mark's hand tightly as they walked to the front door of the house. Their attorney, John Peters, had tagged along just to make sure things went smoothly and the overseeing social worker assigned to their case would meet up with them later on at the park. Pat had asked Mr. Peters at least three times to explain what would be going on today and though Mr. Peters insisted this was just a routine preadoption visit, he broke everything down to Pat as many times as she wanted. Mark had told him about the disaster their first attempt at adoption had been, and Mr. Peters did everything he could to ease Pat's anxiety.

Still Pat was on edge. Her sweaty palms were proof of that, and although she'd been in a similar situation before, this adoption process was quite different from the one before. This time their child to be was four years old and living with a foster family. Her name was Tracy Evans and she had been abandoned by her mother at birth. Her mother was a prostitute and Tracy became a ward of the state when she had a drug-induced nervous breakdown during birth and was sent to a mental institution. Pat had asked Mr. Peters over and over again if Tracy's mother could ever come back and claim her parental rights over her daughter, but Mr. Peters assured her that was impossible. Tracy's mother had legally given up all rights to her daughter six months after she entered the institution, and he even showed Pat the court documents that made this so.

As the three of them reached the front porch of Tracy's foster home, Pat looked around with admiration. She hadn't expected the foster home to look so pleasant and cozy. When she thought of foster homes, she conjured the image of a small building with hundreds of children running around with no guidance. But this was a normal house, almost looked like a layout from the pages of *Better Homes and Gardens*. The street was quiet, the lawn well kept, and the house itself was modeled to perfection. Beside them on the porch was a swinging chair and as Mr. Peters knocked on the door, Pat could imagine Tracy sitting there. She had no idea how the girl looked, but intuitively Pat felt the girl was beautiful. Not only beautiful but somehow well adjusted. From the looks of things around here she was sure that Tracy had been given the best life she could imagine. And now, if all went smoothly, she would be given the parents she so desperately needed.

"Just relax," Mark whispered to Pat as he felt her hand trembling inside his.

Pat looked at him and took a deep breath as the door to the house slowly opened. In the doorway stood a tall white man, with hair so gray it was practically white. He looked at Mr. Peters and seemed to force a smile. "Afternoon," he said, and nodded as his eyes swept across all three people. Mr. Peters introduced himself, then turned around and introduced Pat and Mark as the Browns.

The gray-haired white man nodded, then stepped back and invited in his visitors. Pat was glad she wore pants so that no one could see her knees knocking as she stepped through the door and stood in the foyer. She wished she had worn cotton instead of silk, though, because the sweat from her armpits was soaking straight through. She hoped the gray-haired man wouldn't notice. She wanted to present herself in the best light possible. She knew the man was just one of Tracy's foster parents and had no authority over whether the adoption went through or not, still she wanted him to see her at her best. She wanted everything to go smoothly. She didn't know what she would do if this adoption fell through.

"My name is Henry Oppenheimer," the gray-haired man said in an effort to break the ice.

"I'm Mark and this is my wife, Pat," Mark said as he gripped Pat around her waist. "I can't tell you how excited we are to meet Tracy. My wife and I have been trying to adopt for years."

"This is a nice home you've got here," Pat said, and peeped over her shoulder to get a glimpse at the rest of the place.

"Yes," Henry said, and awkwardly stuffed his hands in his pockets. "My wife and I have lived here for twenty years."

"Where is she . . . your wife?" Pat asked, and looked around again.

"Upstairs getting Tracy ready," Henry said as he removed his hands from his pockets and walked over to the bottom of the staircase. "Elizabeth," he called, and put one foot on the bottom step. "The uh . . . the Browns are here."

There was a brief silence as everyone waited for a response, but none came. Mr. Peters cleared his throat as he opened his briefcase and pulled out a file. "I take it Tracy's social worker has kept you informed of all the procedures?" he asked in a professional tone so deliberate that it seemed to make Henry even more uneasy.

"Yes," Henry said as he looked up the staircase. "She sent over a stack of documents for us to sign yesterday."

"And I take it you'll be diligent with your cooperation?"

Henry turned to Mr. Peters and stared. "Of course."

"Good," Mr. Peters said and closed his file. "We would like this process to move forward with no delays."

"Yes," Henry said, somewhat agitated. "Of course."

Pat blew out a mouthful of air as she looked at Mark with anticipation. She was slowly going insane as she waited and waited for some sign of movement from upstairs, and just when she thought she was going to scream with frustration, she heard the tiny clamor of little feet. Her eyes floated up to the top of the staircase and onto the face of a shy little girl. Her eyes were big and brown, her skin the color of toffee. Her hair was pulled into a small ponytail puff at the top of her head. She was dressed in a pretty white dress with a blue border and on her feet were shiny white patent shoes with bobby socks laced in blue ruffles. "She's beautiful," Pat whispered to Mark, without taking her eyes off the wonderful little girl.

"Don't you look nice," Henry said as he broke out in a whimsical smile only a proud papa could muster.

Tracy giggled and put her hand over her mouth.

"Come on down, honey. There are some people here who want to meet you."

Tracy took her eyes off Henry and stared at Pat and Mark. Pat raised her hand and wiggled her fingers toward Tracy, but Tracy did not move. She stood at the top of the stairs, shut her eyes tightly, and licked her tongue out.

Pat's heart was broken. She gasped and turned to Mark. "Relax, baby. She doesn't know who we are yet," he whispered, and rubbed his hand up and down Pat's back.

"Now, now, Tracy. That wasn't nice, was it?" Henry asked sternly. "These are good people. Why don't you come on down and meet them."

Tracy pouted, then looked over her shoulder. Pat followed the direction of her stare and for the first time saw the woman who must have been Tracy's foster mom. She was a petite woman with obviously dyed red hair and green eyes. She was pretty and dainty although the look on her face was not very complimentary. It appeared she'd been crying, and when Tracy turned to look at her the woman fell to her knees and spread out her arms. Tracy immediately ran to her and flung her arms around her neck.

Henry became embarrassed. "Uh, I'm sorry about this," he said as he turned to Pat and Mark. "It's just that we've been the only family Tracy's known. It's going to be hard to let go."

"We understand," Mark said as Pat nodded her head in agreement. "It's gonna take awhile for Tracy to get used to a new family."

"It's gonna take awhile for us to get used to."

Mr. Peters sighed and checked his watch, then glared at Henry. Henry quickly got the message and turned back toward the stairs. "Elizabeth, honey. The Browns are waiting."

Reluctantly, Elizabeth let Tracy go, then wiped her eyes with the back of her hands. "Go ahead, honey," she said as she turned the girl around. "It's okay. Those are nice people. You'll be just fine."

"That's right, sweetener," Henry coaxed. "The Browns are going to take you out for the day. You're going to have lots and lots of fun."

Tracy returned to the top of the steps and slowly began walking down. She held on tightly to the rail, taking one step at a time, looking ever so accusingly in the direction of Pat and Mark. She wasn't sure what they wanted, but since her parents had said it was all right, she decided to go along.

When she reached the bottom of the stairs, Henry swept her up in his arms. "You're gonna be a big girl today, aren't you?" he asked her and tickled her middle as she giggled with delight. He walked close to Pat and Mark and spoke directly into Tracy's ear. "This is Pat," he said pointing, "and Mark. Don't they look nice?"

Tracy stuck out her bottom lip as she studied the two strangers. She concluded they were goofy as they stood smiling at her like a couple of clowns, so she decided to be a good little girl. "Hi," she said, and raised her little hand. "My name is Tracy. I'm four," she said, and held up one too many fingers.

Pat sighed with relief and almost started to cry. "Hi," she said, forcing a smile to keep the tears away. "You wanna go to the park?"

" 'Kay," Tracy said, and wiggled her body to let Henry know it was time to put her down.

"Bye-bye, sweetener," he said as he placed her on the floor and kissed her head. "Did you say bye-bye to Beth?"

"Bye-bye," she said, and tilted her neck to look upstairs.

Elizabeth wiped her eyes and mouthed the word 'bye, then turned around and walked away.

"Okay," Mr. Peters said and opened the front door. "We'll have Tracy back by the end of the day."

As the door opened, Tracy suddenly got a burst of energy and began yelling bye-bye to everyone as she skipped out the front door and down the steps.

"Take care of her," Henry said as he walked over to Pat and Mark.

"We will," they said in unison and walked out the door.

On the drive over to the park, Mark sat up front with Mr. Peters and Pat and Tracy sat together in the back. Pat's apprehension was erased once she began to see how comfortable Tracy was with her. As they drove Tracy engaged in a song of Knick-Knack Patty Whack as she bounced up and down in her seat. With every verse she got louder and louder as she clapped her hands and jumped around. She was a hyper little something, but Pat loved it. She was a little girl doing little girl things, and even when she started the song over for the fifth time, Pat didn't mind. This was the kind of noise she had longed to hear for some time. The blissful noise of singing and laughter that only a child could produce. She sat back and smiled as she watched Tracy, knowing for the first time that she was definitely going to be a mother.

Up front, Mr. Peters got on his cell phone and called Mrs. Truman, Tracy's social worker. Since it was their first meeting with Tracy, Mrs. Truman had to be present. He told her they were headed for Doo Little park and asked her to meet them there in the picnic area.

Once they arrived, Tracy jumped out of the car and ran toward the play area and Pat ran right behind her. Mark grabbed the picnic basket out of the trunk and he and Mr. Peters walked over the grass and set up lunch.

"Swing me," Tracy ordered Pat as she climbed up on the swing and dangled her feet. Pat obliged with glee. She pushed Tracy into the air over and over again as Tracy made more demands. "Higher," Tracy screamed and of course Pat did as she was told. When the swing had gotten old, Tracy headed for the slide, then the monkey bars, then the seesaw, and after about an hour Pat was exhausted. But Tracy was still going strong. She headed for the sandbox next, and Pat followed, and as they sat in the sand, Tracy stopped long enough to really examine Pat. She squinted from the sun and looked sideways. "What's your name again?" she asked as she swished her hands through the sand.

"Pat," she answered as she picked up a stick and drew lines in the sand.

"I like you, Pat," she said and picked up a stick to trace her own lines.

Pat paused and took in a deep breath. "I like you too," she said gratefully, then crossed her legs Indian style and marveled at the beautiful child who sat across from her. "Are you hungry yet?"

"Nope."

Okay, Pat thought, and smiled as she watched Tracy spell out her name in the sand. "Very good," she said as Tracy put down her stick and squinted her eyes at her again. She looked Pat over from head to toe, then dropped her head suddenly. "Are you all right?" Pat asked, and scanned Tracy's face.

"I already have a mommy, you know," she said matter-of-factly.

Instantly Pat's body tightened. "I know," Pat said, thinking about the horrific story Mr. Peters had told her about Tracy's birth mother.

"Do you miss your mommy?"

Tracy's face flushed with confusion. "No."

"Oh, of course not," Pat said, feeling silly. Tracy was taken away from her mother at birth. There's no way she could miss what she never had. "I guess you've never even seen your mommy, huh?" she said apologetically.

Tracy frowned her face and poked out her lip with even more confusion. "I see my mommy all the time," she said, looking at Pat with caution. "Elizabeth is my mommy."

Elizabeth, Pat thought to herself and looked down at the sand. "Elizabeth is your foster parent."

"She my mommy."

"Well, actually —"

"She my mommy," Tracy insisted. "She don't look like me," she said, as if repeating a story she'd been told over and over again. She stared down at the brown skin on her hands. "But she still my mommy."

Pat didn't know what to say. Trying to explain the reality of the situation would only confuse the child more, she thought, as she tried to think of the right thing to do. "Wouldn't you like a new mommy?" she asked and held out her hand for Tracy to see. "A mommy that looks like you?"

Tracy looked at Pat and squinted her eyes harder. "I already have a mommy."

Okay, Pat thought to herself, and bit her bottom lip. She knew this was going to take awhile for Tracy to understand. It was only their first meeting and she couldn't expect the child to comprehend exactly what was going on. But that was okay. Pat knew she was making headway and soon Tracy would come to love her and want her as her mother. She knew it. That was a fact. She could feel it.

Pat looked over to the picnic area and saw Mark waving.

"Ooo, look," she said, and pointed. "Wouldn't you like a sandwich now? We've got chips and soda and cookies and —"

"Cookies," Tracy said and jumped to her feet. "What kind?"

"Sugar."

Tracy curled her lip and frowned.

"And chocolate chip."

"Ooo," she said, and reached out for Pat's hand. "Come on, Pat," she said, and pulled and pulled until Pat was on her feet. She ran up the hill and straight to Mark. "What's your name again?" she asked as she sat down on the blanket and crossed her legs.

"Mark," he said, unable to do anything else but gawk at her and smile.

"Can I have a cookie?"

Mark hesitated. "How about a sandwich first?" he asked, realizing he was making his first compromise as a parent.

"Mmm . . . okay," Tracy said and looked over her shoulder for Pat, who was so pooped that she could barely make it up the hill. "Wanna share my sandwich?" Tracy asked as Pat sat down beside her.

Pat glanced over at Mark with fresh tears in her eyes, then turned to Tracy. "Sure, honey. I'd like to share with you."

That Zuma was unbreakable. Once she made it up in her mind that she didn't like someone she made it a point to be as bitchy and irritating as possible, which for her came quite easily. Sandy, on the other hand, had vowed to try to be as nice as she could today. She promised herself that she would at least try to form some kind of working relationship with Zuma for the sake of her job, but she wasn't going to be no pushover. Still, after the other girls had left, Sandy decided it was time to break the ice between her and Zuma. They had gotten off on the wrong foot and she was going to correct that, but she knew Zuma wasn't going to be easy.

Sandy stood behind the reception desk and tried to make like she was busy, all the while sneaking peeks at Zuma, trying to figure out what she could possibly say to her. She figured the best way to strike up a conversation would be to ask questions about the shop. How could Zuma refuse to talk to her about that?

Sandy cleared her throat and took a deep breath. "Uh, hey," she said as she looked over to Zuma, who sat silently at her hair station. "I was wondering . . . do you guys take checks?" Good question, Sandy thought. That was important stuff. She tapped her finger on the counter, waiting for Zuma's answer, but all she did was stare at her, then stare past her as if Sandy were retarded. "Well," Sandy said, and held her hands in the air.

Zuma let out a sigh and continued staring past Sandy so hard that Sandy turned around to see what she was looking at. On the wall above her head was a sign that read: Sorry. No checks. "Oh," Sandy said as she turned back around. "I didn't see that."

Dumb bitch, Zuma thought to herself, then spun around in her chair. She hoped that would be the end of the questions, but she was wrong.

"So," Sandy said, walking over to Zuma, "is there anything you need me to do?" she said as pleasantly as she could muster.

Zuma looked at her out the corner of her eye, thinking there was indeed something Sandy could do for her. Like get out of her face, shut up, drink a bottle of dye, *leave*. But all Zuma did was shake her head and spin around in her chair.

Sandy stood looking at the back of Zuma's head. Well, fuck you too, bitch, she thought as she walked away. Sandy hated to be ignored, but if that's how Zuma wanted it, then fine. She wasn't going to beg, but she did want to know one thing. As she walked back to the reception desk, she stopped dead in her tracks and turned around to face Zuma. "I've got just one question for you," she said, and stood her ground.

Zuma rolled her eyes to the back of her head and decided to speak for the first time. "What?"

"What the hell is your problem with me?"

Zuma chuckled and shook her head. "Who says I've got a problem with you?"

"Well, you obviously do or you wouldn't be acting like this."

"Acting like what?"

"A bitch."

Oh, Zuma thought as she stood up from her seat. So the white girl is trying to jump bad? She walked over to Sandy and folded her arms across her chest. "First of all," she said, taking her time. "You best watch who you calling a bitch if you want to continue having the use of your arms and legs."

Sandy hesitated a second, but stood her ground.

"Secondly, just because you work here does not mean that we have to be buddies, okay. I'ma tell you straight out—I don't like you. Period. I don't like your attitude, I don't like your look, I don't even like your name."

"Talk about ignorant."

Ooo. She was pushing it, and for a split second Zuma thought about knocking the shit out of her. But she didn't. Sandy wasn't worth it.

"Why don't you just come out and say it so we can get it over with?" Sandy said and threw her hands up.

"Say what?"

"Just say it!"

"What do you want me to say?"

"That you don't like me because I'm white."

"I didn't say that."

"But it's the truth. You took one look at me, saw my skin color, and decided you didn't want to have nothing to do with me. You people are all alike."

"You people?"

"Black people. You're all the time marching around talking about race discrimination and prejudice and you guys are some of the most racist, prejudiced people on this earth."

Zuma's eyes fluttered with anger. "We have a right to be. What goes around comes around, baby. We learned all our tricks from you—Devil."

"So now I'm the devil?"

"That's right."

"And I guess I'm responsible for slavery and the whole nine yards?"

"You and the rest of your Klan."

Sandy rolled her eyes. "I've done nothing to you," she screamed. "I can't help what happened four hundred years ago. That's not my fault."

Zuma shook her head. She'd heard this rationalization before. "Let me ask you this," she said, and raised a brow. "If your father dies and leaves behind a debt of fifty thousand dollars, who's responsible for paying that debt?"

"His next of kin."

"I rest my case," Zuma said and turned to walk back to her hair station.

"That's not fair," Sandy said, following behind her. "I grew up around black people all my life. I have no problem with you. I can't understand why we can't be friends."

"There will never come a time when black people and white people can truly be friends. To be a friend you have to understand where I'm coming from. You have to have something in common with me. We're just too different to ever be friends."

"How do you know? Have you ever tried being friends with a white woman?"

"Hell no."

"Then why don't you give it a shot?" Sandy prodded.

"Please."

"What are you scared of?" she teased.

"I ain't scared of shit, least of all you."

Sandy snickered with an air of superiority. "Then let's give it a shot. Let's be friends."

"You just can't say you're going to be friends and expect it to happen just like that."

"I think you're scared."

"Scared of what?"

"That you might like me," Sandy said sternly. "That I might shatter your whole theory about white people and you'd have to stop holding on to all your anger. Or, you might be scared because deep in the back of your mind you've been convinced that you're not worthy to be friends with a white person. You're scared that I'm not going to like *you*."

"*Paleeze*," Zuma said, and laughed it up.

Sandy stood back and folded her arms across her chest. She was daring Zuma in the worst way and Zuma was not one to back down from a challenge.

"Okay," Zuma said. "You wanna be friends? Let's be friends. Fuck it."

"Baby, I'm from the hood," Sandy informed Zuma. "I don't take verbal promises," she said, reaching into her tight push-up bra and retrieving a twenty-dollar bill. "Let's put some money on it."

"I don't have a problem with that," Zuma said, and snatched up her hair bag. She pulled out her own twenty, took Sandy's hand, and placed the bill inside her palm. "I'll even let you hold the kitty."

"Cool," Sandy said, satisfied.

"So now what?"

"Well," Sandy said, and looked up at the ceiling. "Since we are friends now, we have to act like friends," she said, lifting an eyebrow. Zuma lifted her own in agreement. "Friends tell each other their deepest thoughts and secrets, right?" she continued. "So let's start out our friendship by telling each other a secret."

"I ain't telling you shit," Zuma said, blowing Sandy off.

"See, you're not playing fair already."

Zuma had to laugh. This was just too ridiculous. A minute ago, she couldn't stand Sandy, and now she was supposed to be her ace boon coon? "Okay, I'll tell you my secret, but you go first."

Sandy paused and threw her hair out of her face as she thought quietly. "Okay," she said, as she leaned against Zuma's hair station. Zuma shifted in her seat, crossed her legs, and tried to look interested. "Well," Sandy began, "this isn't really a secret. It's a story, okay?"

"Whatever."

"Okay, let me see," Sandy said as her blue eyes roamed around the room. "I must have been about fifteen years old, and me and my mom used to live in Compton."

"Compton?"

"Yeah. I told you I grew up around black people all my life."

"Okay, go 'head."

"Anyway, it was my first day of high school, and I didn't really know anyone there."

"You didn't have any friends from junior high?"

"A few, but I mostly kept to myself anyway."

"Hmm. Too good to hang with the black folks?"

"No, *Zuma*," Sandy stressed. "Actually, I had dyslexia, but I didn't know it at the time. So I was pretty stupid and everybody would make fun of me."

"Oops. Sorry."

"Anyway. It was my first day of high school and over the summer I had gotten a little cute," she said and smiled. "I got hips, my face cleared up, I'd given myself one of those home perms — I was looking pretty good. So anyway, I go to my first-period class, I'm minding my own business, just trying to make it through my first day of high school, right."

"Right."

"And as the bell for first period rings, this guy comes up to me and puts his arm around my neck. He was a smooth talker, girl. I think his name was . . . Oh forget it. I can't even think of his name. Anyway, he does his little Mack daddy routine and gives me his number on a piece of paper."

"Oh, I bet you loved that."

"Yes I did, but it's not what you think."

"And what am I thinking?"

"You think I only liked it because he was black."

Zuma raised her eyebrow.

"Well, that wasn't it. I liked him because he was the first guy to ever approach me. In junior high, everybody made fun of me because I was slow and then for the first time someone actually thought I was cute. Of course I loved it."

"Okay, okay. Go 'head."

"Anyway, he gives me his number and that's that. I don't even think I would have called him. I would have been too scared. But anyway, as I'm walking out the class this girl pulls me by the arm," she said, and yanked her hand through the air. She straightened her back and put her hand on her hip and started rolling her neck, trying to mimic the girl's voice. " 'I know you wasn't talking to my man, bitch.' "

"Uh-oh," Zuma said and shifted in her seat. "So Mr. Suave was *her* man."

Sandy nodded, then went back to mimicking the girl. " 'You just wait till after school.' "

"Oh shit. Did you leave?"

"No," Sandy said, and rested against the counter. "If I had had any sense I would have run home right then and there. But stupid me. I stayed in school and when the bell rang to go home, I thought I'd be slick and duck out through the back gate. But guess who was waiting for me?"

"Ah shit. What did you do?"

"I booked," Sandy said, and started swinging her arms beside her like an Olympic medalist. "Girl, it was five of them and when they saw me run off, they came running right behind me. I thought I'd be slick by running to the front of the school. You know, maybe there were some teachers up there or something. But that's when they caught me."

"Oh my goodness. Did she beat the shit out of you?"

"*They* beat the shit out of me."

"All five of them?"

"Plus whoever else was standing around and felt like jumping in."

"Damn," Zuma said as she imagined how it must have been.

Sandy looked down at the ground as she replayed the incident over in her mind. "I swear I thought I was going to die. All I could hear was cheering, and an occasional 'white bitch.' All I could see were these black and brown fists and palms and arms swinging at me. And then I saw the scissors."

"Scissors?"

"I thought for sure they were gonna stab me. All I could do was ball myself up on the sidewalk and shut my eyes," Sandy said, pausing for a moment to get a grip on herself. "Then I felt this tug on my hair and somebody screamed, 'Yeah, cut all that shit off.' And as I laid there on the ground they passed the scissors around and each one of them cut off a clump of my hair," she said, and turned to Zuma with a slight hint of water in her eyes. "I tell you," she said, trying to hide her rising emotions. "I never got near another black man since."

Zuma looked away and didn't speak for a moment. For some reason she felt embarrassed. It was the same feeling she got when she listened to a crime report on the news and found out that the culprit was black. It was a feeling of shame for her race. Though Zuma would never say this out loud, sometimes she could really understand why white people thought blacks were savages. "You know," Zuma said, and lifted a finger, "you can't blame all black people because a group of stupid teenagers beat you up."

"Who pays the debt our fathers leave behind?"

Zuma nodded. Point well taken, she thought, and sighed as she looked at Sandy. Though she wasn't promising anything, at that very moment, she sorta felt that maybe she and Sandy could be friends. But that was a big maybe. Zuma did have to admit it would be nice to have someone to talk to. There was one secret she'd been holding on to that she was dying to get out, and of everyone in the shop, Sandy seemed to be the only one who wouldn't pass judgment on her. Or, so she thought.

"Okay," Sandy said as she bounced back from her storytelling adventure. "Now it's your turn."

"Hey Zu-Zu," a voice called from the doorway, interrupting the conversation.

Zuma looked over Sandy's shoulder and saw her first appointment of the day. "Come on in, Mrs. Tatum. You can have a seat at my station." Zuma stood up and began to walk away. "Sorry," she said to Sandy. "Duty calls."

"That's not fair, Zuma. Come on quick. Tell me a secret."

"Sorry."

"You're not playing fair."

"All right," Zuma said, and turned around. "I'll tell you a secret."

"Yeah what?" Sandy said, full of interest.

"You *might* be all right."

"Why thank you," Sandy said and sucked her teeth.

"You're quite welcome."

9

Faye sat on the sofa in the front room for hours trying to figure out how she was going to deal with her daughter. But after five pieces of El Pollo Loco, six tortillas, and half a carton of beans, she still couldn't find a solution. It was still hard for her to believe that she'd walked in on her sixteen-year-old daughter having sex, but her eyes had not lied. Images of her naked daughter played over in her mind like a porno flick until they finally disgusted her so much that she couldn't eat another bite. She put her sixth piece of chicken on a napkin and slid it out of her way as her stomach swirled and swished around. She paused for a second, put her fist to her mouth, then let out a polite burp only she could hear. She lay back on the sofa and stared up at the ceiling still trying to decide what she should do. What punishment do you give a child for having sex in your home? What do you do? Shake your finger and say, "You're grounded"? Like that would do a bit of good. If Zuma were there she'd tell Faye to go get herself an extension cord and wear that child's behind out. But that wasn't the answer for Faye. She'd never struck her kids before and she wasn't going to start now. Besides, what good would a spanking do for a sixteen-year-old? Was a spanking really going to stop her daughter from having sex? Doubt it. Antoinette's problem was that she didn't have any respect, and there was no way beating her could change that.

Faye sighed and sat back up on the sofa. She wondered if she should go back to her daughter's room and try to talk to her. But what would she say? How would she get through to her this time when so many times before she had spoken to her daughter only to be disobeyed? She sank back into the cushions of the sofa and put her hands over her face. "Antoine," she mumbled as her voice quivered and a vision of her husband's face came into view. "I need you so much." Tears of frustration and loss filled her eyes as she searched her mind for answers. She wished she'd had a parenting manual. Some sort of book to tell her what to do in these types of situations. But most of all, she wished she had a husband. Someone to share the load of responsibility with. Her pain grew deeper as she remembered her husband and all the grand plans they'd made for their family. How they spoke of raising the world's most perfect children and how they vowed to stay close. But nothing they had discussed had come true.

Faye quickly wiped her face when she heard her son's tiny voice calling out to her.

"Mami," he said cautiously as he slowly walked over to the sofa. "Mami, what's wrong?"

Faye wiped her eyes and cleared her throat. "Nothing," she said, and sat up straight so that her lie would seem convincing. But her son was not so easily fooled.

"Then why are you crying?" he asked, and put his hand on his mother's thigh.

"I wasn't crying."

"Uh-huh," he insisted. "Your eyelashes are still wet," he said, and kneeled down before her. "Did Antoinette make you cry?"

"No," Faye barked so loud that her son jumped. She didn't want to explain her tears and she didn't want him to see her so defeated.

"Did I make you cry?"

"No," she said, and frowned. "Now get back to your room. Don't think I've forgotten about what you did today."

Christopher stood up and began to walk away with his head hung low and as she watched him, Faye knew she'd overreacted. There he was just being concerned and she had hollered at him. That wasn't the answer. "Christopher," she said, stopping him in his tracks. He turned around to look at her and she motioned for him to come back. Though her problems with Antoinette were enormous, she couldn't pretend that her son didn't have problems of his own. She remembered what the school psychiatrist, Mr. Watson, had suggested earlier and figured now was as good a time as any for them to have their one-on-one talk. Something was bothering her son and it was something Faye wanted to get to the bottom of before it got out of hand.

She pulled Christopher up onto the sofa and turned his little body around so that he was completely facing her. She smiled and stroked the side of his cheek so that he would know she was not mad at him. "We're gonna have a little talk," she said as she looked into his eyes, seeing all sorts of remnants of his father.

"Okay," he said like a grown man. "Is Antoinette in trouble?"

"We're not going to talk about Antoinette. We're going to talk about you," she said, and tapped the end of his nose. Christopher tensed up, knowing that his mom was not going to let him off the hook. "Now tell me what happened at school today. Why were you fighting?"

Christopher looked down at the sofa and began tracing the flower pattern with his finger.

"Did you hear me, Christopher?"

"Yes," he whined.

"Why did you hit that boy?"

"I told you. 'Cause he be picking on me, calling me names and stuff."

"What did I tell you about sticks and stones?" Faye said, waiting for him to complete the tired old lines. But Christopher wasn't having nursery rhymes today. He poked out his lips and flung his arms across his chest.

"I'm tired of that boy. He always meddling me, Mami."

"Then you go tell the teacher. You don't hit him."

"The teacher ain't gon' do nothing. That's why I knocked that fool in his mouth."

"*Christopher*," Faye said and tightened her lips. "What you did today was not right."

"Then he oughta stop calling me names."

"What names?"

Christopher bowed his head and began tracing the flower pattern on the sofa again. Faye placed her finger under his chin and lifted his head.

"I said what names?"

"Sissy Chrissy."

"Sissy Chrissy," Faye said, and almost chuckled, but when she looked into her son's face she was glad she hadn't made light of the situation. His hazel eyes were turning watery and his breathing grew deeper as he tried not to cry. "He was only teasing you, Christopher."

"I don't care. I'm tired of him. Always be calling me a girl and talking about me 'cause I'm littler than everybody else," he said and bowed his head. "They don't be letting me play ball with them or nothing. Always talking about I play like a girl and stuff. Shoot, I can't help it 'cause I'm small," he said, suddenly looking up with rage in his eyes. "He be picking on me 'cause he think he can whip me 'cause I'm little. That's why I kicked his ass today, Mami. I ain't no punk. I ain't no girl."

Today was the first time Faye had seen her son act and talk this way. Around the house he was such a good little boy. Always the helper, always happy. This side of him was new to her, but she had an idea where it came from. Antoine had always had a temper. He'd take everything in until he couldn't hold anymore, then all of a sudden he'd pop. Faye didn't know if bad tempers were hereditary, but in this case it sure seemed to be true.

Christopher raised his hands to his head and untied his ponytail. Long, black curls surrounded his face and as he looked up at Faye, all she could see was her husband. "Mami," Chris said as he looked her in the eye. "Do I look like a girl?"

Faye smiled and ran her hand through his hair. "No," she said softly. She got up from the sofa and walked over to the television. She picked up the frame that sat upon it and brought it back to the sofa with her. She sat down and turned the picture around for Christopher to see. "You look just like your daddy."

Christopher took the picture from Faye and looked at it for a long time. Then he looked back at his mother and threw the picture to the floor. "I don't want to look like him," he screamed.

"*Christopher,*" Faye said, reaching out for him as he jumped up from the sofa.

"He's dead," he shouted at the top of his lungs. "I don't wanna look like him."

"*Christopher,*" Faye shouted again, as she rose up from the sofa and ran to him. She tried to take him in her arms, but Christopher wouldn't allow it.

"He's not my father. I hate him. I don't wanna look like him," he screamed as he ran off to his room and slammed the door shut.

Faye bit her lip and looked around the room, stunned. She didn't understand her son's reaction. Even though he never knew his father, she always taught him to love him. There were many nights she'd sit alone in the living room with Christopher on her lap, going through old picture albums, showing him his father, telling him what a good man he'd been, how she hoped he'd one day turn out to be just like him. She wanted

Christopher to feel close to his dad, to feel love for him, to know that his dad loved him. Hearing Christopher say those awful words broke Faye's heart. She bent over and picked her husband's picture up from the floor and held it to her chest. "He didn't mean it," she whispered, and closed her eyes. "He's just upset." She pulled the picture from her chest and looked over it, as her mind swept back to the last time she'd seen Antoine alive. "Make sure my kids remember me," he'd said. *Make sure my kids remember me.* She ran her hand over the cold frame and for a moment she could actually feel Antoine. Not with her hand, but with her heart.

"You won't be forgotten, sweetheart," she whispered as a tear fell from her eyes and splashed on the frame. Briskly, she turned around and went to Christopher's bedroom. Whatever pain her son was going through was not enough to excuse the disrespect he'd shown his father. If there was only one thing Faye would ever do, it was keep her promise to her husband. She would not allow her son to forget his dad.

Faye opened the door to her son's room, took one step inside, and gasped. Christopher sat on the edge of the bed, trembling. In his hand was a small pink shaver, the same shaver Faye had used that morning to take away the straggly pieces of hair from beneath her arms. And all around Christopher on the bed and on the floor were strands of hair. His hair. Gone was the ponytail that reminded Faye so much of Antoine, and in its place, all over Chris's head were patches of uneven hair that stuck straight up like prickly pine needles. "What did you do?" Faye screamed, rushing to her son and removing the shaver from his hand. Christopher sat motionless and in silence. His eyes focused straight ahead as if he were mesmerized. Faye eyed him in unsettled awe, as she picked up pieces of his hair in her hand. "Christopher," Faye said, kneeling down in front of him. She put her hands on his arms and shook him hard. "Why did you do this?"

Christopher didn't so much as blink. He continued staring straight ahead as if something before him was holding his attention. "Look at me," Faye shouted, and shook him once again, this time jarring him so that his eyes slowly moved to meet hers. "Your father loved you," she said as her body began to shiver. She held up the picture of her husband and put it directly in Chris's face. "He loved you," she said as the picture shifted under the grip of her unsteady hand. "I don't ever want to hear you say you hate your father again. Ever. Do you hear me?" She waited for a response. A yes, a nod, an "Okay, Mami." But Christopher said nothing. His silence frightened Faye. She had no clue what was going on inside that tiny head of his, but as she stared at her son she began to realize that he hadn't meant the words he'd said. Sitting before her was not a child who hated his father. This was a child who needed his father. An angry child who knew no other way of expressing his pain than to lash out.

Faye sat the picture of Antoine next to Christopher amid the severed locks of hair and stood up. She backed her way to the door, watching him all the way and wondering if he had heard a word she'd said. As she stood watch, she saw the first sign of movement from her son. He picked up the picture of his father and laid in on his lap. Faye wanted to say something, but she kept her silence and eased her way out the door. Christopher needed to be alone with his dad.

Faye stood behind her son's closed door and took a deep breath, hoping Christopher would be all right. Then as she walked back toward the front, she paused as she heard the door to her daughter's room fly open. Antoinette stepped out in her pink terry cloth bathrobe and stopped. She stared at her mother for a split second, rolled her eyes like she was the diva most diva, then walked off to the bathroom. The sight of her surprised Faye so that she couldn't speak. She hadn't made any decisions about how she was going to deal with Antoinette yet, but she knew she had to do something. She wasn't going to get out of this one with just a slap on the hand.

Faye stood in the hallway listening as the medicine cabinet opened, then slammed shut. Next it was a cabinet door opening, then slamming, and in a hot second Antoinette reappeared carrying a tube of lipstick, mascara, and a bottle of Jergens. She paused, gave Faye another look, then went into her bedroom and slammed the door.

Faye stood in the hallway feeling like she had done something wrong. Like she was the one who'd been caught in the act and Antoinette was the mother, biding her time until she was good and ready to deliver her punishment. She stood outside the door, knowing it was now or never. She had to go in there and show her daughter who was the boss of this family. She put her hand on the doorknob, wondering what she'd say. But this was no time for contemplation. It was time for her to put her foot down.

She threw open the door and stepped in as it banged against the wall. Antoinette sat at her vanity table and paused when she heard the noise, but never bothered to turn around. Faye watched her from behind as she sat at the mirror applying huge black strokes of eyeliner to her brows. I know she doesn't think she's going anywhere, Faye thought to herself as she moved in closer. I know this girl is not that crazy. "What are you doing?" she asked as she stood behind her daughter watching her primp.

"What does it look like I'm doing?" Antoinette quipped as she sat with one made-up eyebrow.

Faye took in a deep breath and tried to remain calm. "It looks like you *think* you're going somewhere."

"I don't think, I know."

"Oh really?" Faye said, and moved in even closer. "And where do you think you're going?" she asked, hoping the answer would be into the kitchen or living room because anywhere else would be out of the question.

"Out."

Out? Is she crazy? "Oh no, young lady," Faye said as she grabbed Antoinette's hand and snatched away the eyeliner. "You are not going anywhere."

Antoinette jerked her hand away from her mother and rolled her eyes. "We'll see about that," she mumbled as she got up from the vanity and stomped over to the closet.

"Don't you walk away from me when I'm talking to you," Faye said. But Antoinette kept on about her business. She opened her closet and took out a jogging suit and pair of sneakers. As she turned around she bumped smack dab into Faye. Faye snatched the clothes and shoes from her hand and threw them to the floor. "You are not leaving this house," she screamed, and grabbed her stomach as it began to turn and knot up.

"You don't tell me what to do," Antoinette screamed directly into her mother's face. "I'm grown. I can do whatever I want."

"Not in this house, you can't. This is my house, little girl. And I'm telling you right now you and your little funky attitude have got to change. I'm sick of it. You are not grown. You are sixteen years old and as long as you're living under my roof, eating my food, begging for my money, wearing my clothes, and burning up my electricity, you will follow my rules."

Antoinette mumbled something under her breath and turned her head.

"What did you say?" Faye asked, and turned her daughter's face back around to meet hers. Faye looked into her daughter's face and noticed how ugly she'd become. Her skin was as youthful and radiant as a newborn baby's, her eyes bright and glowing. She could be a model if she wanted to be. It wasn't her features that made her ugly. It was her attitude, her spirit. No amount of exterior glamour could hide the hatefulness that had taken over her soul. Antoinette gritted her teeth like a dog as Faye asked the question again. "What did you say?"

"I said fuck your rules," Antoinette hollered. "I ain't no prisoner. You can't keep me locked up here. If I wanna go out, I'm going out."

"You will not talk to me like that," Faye stressed.

"I'll talk to you however I feel like. Fuck you."

"I will —"

"You will what?" Antoinette said boldly, and lifted her chin.

Faye raised her hand in the air and stopped. She began to shiver as she fought with all her might to keep from hitting her daughter out of anger.

"Go ahead," Antoinette prodded. "Hit me, Mama. Go ahead," she said standing there, just waiting. "If you hit me, I'll call the child abuse hotline on you so fast you won't know what happened."

Slowly Faye took her hand out of the air and put it over her stomach. She trembled with fear. Not of her daughter, but of what she was thinking about doing. She wanted so badly to hit her that she couldn't stand it. But she didn't do it. She couldn't.

"*Good girl,*" Antoinette said as she bent over to pick her clothes up off the floor.

"You are not leaving this house," Faye said, and snatched the jogging suit out of her hand. "You are going to sit down and we are going to talk."

"I ain't got nothing to say about nothing."

"Antoinette, please!" Faye screamed, and shut her eyes. "What is happening to you?"

"Ain't nothing happening to me. I just wanna go out."

"If you leave this house tonight you will never come back," Faye said, hoping Antoinette would take her seriously.

"What you saying? You kicking me out?"

No, Faye wasn't kicking her out. She was just trying to get through to her. But she couldn't back down now. "I'm saying if you go, leave your keys behind."

"Fine," Antoinette said, once again picking up her outfit. "I ain't gotta stay here. I don't need you or this run-over house."

"Oh you don't?"

"No, I don't," she said, as she pulled the sleeve of her robe down to reveal her tattoo. "I got a man."

Faye huffed. "And I guess he's gonna take care of you, huh?"

"Damn right," Antoinette said as she pulled on her robe and fastened it tightly. She went to her closet and got on her knees. She reached far into the back and pulled out a duffel bag and began to stuff clothes inside it.

Faye knew this was just a ploy. There was nowhere for her daughter to go. That boy she was so in love with would freak out the minute he saw her coming up the street with a bag full of clothes in tow. "You know what?" Faye said as she walked to the closet. "Let me help you," she said as she began pulling shirts off hangers and throwing them into the duffel bag. Out of the corner of her eye, she could see the amazement on her daughter's face. She couldn't believe her mother was helping her prepare to leave. Antoinette stopped what she was doing and stood up. "Come on," Faye said as she walked over to the vanity table and scooped up Antoinette's makeup. "Let's be quick about this," she said as she tossed the makeup into the bag. Faye took Antoinette by the hand and led her over to her dresser. She opened the top drawer and grabbed a handful of underwear. "You get the socks," she said as she took her handful back to the bag.

Antoinette stood in awe as she watched her mother swarm around her room, grabbing everything she had and tossing it into the bag.

"You wanna take this jewelry?" Faye asked, and held up a box, then jammed it into the bag. Faye turned to her daughter and paused. "What's wrong with you? Why aren't you helping? Don't you wanna get out of this prison? Isn't your man out there somewhere waiting to take care of you? I'm sure you'll have much more fun living with him than in this old run-over house."

Antoinette gritted her teeth and kept silent.

"Come on," Faye demanded as she walked over to her and pulled her by the arm.

"Don't touch me," Antoinette said, and yanked away.

"Look, I'm not going to do all this packing by myself. Now, come on," she said and grabbed at Antoinette's arm. When Antoinette tried to yank away again, Faye caught hold of the sleeve of her robe. She pulled it so hard that the robe fell off her daughter's shoulders and came swinging open.

Antoinette tried to cover herself up quickly, but she wasn't fast enough. Faye squinted her eyes as she looked at her daughter's naked body head-on. And, as Antoinette tried to cover herself, Faye moved in and pulled back the robe. "Stop it," Antoinette said, swinging around.

"Open this up," Faye said, gripping the edge of the robe in her hand. She yanked it back and pulled it clean off her daughter's body. Faye could barely keep her mouth closed as she scanned her daughter with horror. On her sides were new-forming stretch marks that swept around to her bloated belly. Faye reached out and felt her daughter's stomach. It was as hard as a rock. Just as hers had been the two times she had gotten pregnant. "Are you . . . are you . . ."

Antoinette rolled her eyes and yanked her robe out of her mother's hand. The fury in her eyes could not be denied. She gritted her teeth as she wrapped her robe around her and fastened it loosely. There was no need to make sure it was tight. Her secret was already out.

"Are you . . . *pregnant?*"

With every ounce of sixteen-year-old rage she could muster, Antoinette said, "Yes, I am."

"Dear God," Faye whispered and put her hands to her temples. She turned around in circles, not wanting to face the truth.

"And so what if I am?" Antoinette said, and folded her arms across her chest. "It ain't none of your business. You ain't got nothing to do with it."

Faye nearly choked on her tongue. "Nothing to do with it? You can't take care of no baby. You're just a baby yourself."

"Me and my man can take care of our baby. We don't need you."

"You and your man? Take care . . . Baby? What?" Faye screamed. "You can't even buy yourself a can of soda. How are you gonna take care of a baby?"

"Don't worry about it."

Faye stopped and took a deep breath. Her head was in so many places that she couldn't think straight. Her sixteen-year-old daughter was pregnant? No. This couldn't be real. Part of Faye was so mad that she wanted to scream, just holler and yell until she lost her voice. But the other part of her felt remorse. This was all her fault. Everything Antoinette was going through was somehow tied to Faye's failure as a parent. Maybe there was something she should have done differently. Maybe this, maybe that. "Oh God," Faye said as she looked at her daughter. "Where did I go wrong?"

"When you gave birth to me," her daughter spit out with so much fire that Faye gasped. "But don't worry, Mama. I ain't gonna go wrong. That's why I got pregnant in the first place. So I could have my own baby and treat her right."

Faye shook her head. "You mean you planned this? You got pregnant on purpose?"

"Yes I did and ain't nothing you can do about it."

"But why? Why would you want to get pregnant?"

"So I could have someone to love me. Someone who paid attention to me. Someone who was all my own. Not some afterthought. Not just somebody I had to deal with because they just happened to be here."

"What are you saying? That I don't pay any attention to you? That I don't love you?"

"Don't nobody love me, but my baby and my man."

Faye raised her hand to her head. "How can you say that? I love you with all my heart. You're my only daughter. I love you more than I love myself. More than that so-called boyfriend of yours will ever love you."

"Shut up," Antoinette yelled, and pointed her finger at her mother. "You don't know nothing about him. My man does love me. He tells me all the time. And you hate him for it. You hate it because don't nobody love you. Look at you," she said, gawking at Faye. "All fat and out of shape. Ain't no man gonna want your fat ass. And now that somebody loves me, you're just jealous. Well, too bad. I know my man loves me and he's gonna take care of me and my baby so just stay out of it," she said, and walked closer to her mother. "And while you're at it, why don't you get a life. Stop walking around here fantasizing about a dead man and find you a real man."

Faye slapped her daughter so hard that her hand stung. Then she slapped her again. And again. And again. As she raised her hand for the last time she caught herself. She saw her hand floating in the air as if it weren't even a part of her body. She crumbled her fingers together and dropped her hand. Slowly she turned away from her daughter and headed for the door. But before she could step out, Antoinette was at her back. She slung her hands against the back of Faye's head and neck as if she were swatting insects out of the sky. Faye turned around to catch her daughter's hand but she wasn't quick enough. Antoinette punched at her face and scratched at her arms so fast and furious that Faye could barely see. All she could do was put up her arms to protect herself. "Wait," Faye screamed as she fell down to one knee.

But there was no stopping Antoinette. "I hate you," she said over and over as she continued firing blows.

"Wait . . . Antoinette . . . Please . . ." Faye pleaded. As she knelt there shielding herself, she couldn't believe this was happening. She thought the attack would go on forever. She didn't know what stopped her, but soon Antoinette was gone. When she looked up she noticed she was in the hallway and Antoinette was staring at her from her bedroom door. She slammed the door, leaving Faye slumped behind it. She tried to scramble up from the floor but her head hurt so much that all she could do was grab it and try to take off the pressure. Long strands of hair covered her face and rose and fell with every breath Faye took. The collar of her shirt hung halfway off, exposing deep red scars across her chest. The blood from her forehead trickled down her face to the corner of her eye, causing Faye to blink uncontrollably until the red line moved onward to her cheek. She sat there on the floor against the wall, wondering what the hell had just happened. "I never should have slapped her," she mumbled to herself as tears welled up in her eyes.

Minutes later the door to her daughter's room came flying open. Antoinette was fully dressed and on her arm was the overstuffed duffel bag. She said nothing as she walked past Faye and into the front room.

"Antoinette," Faye said as she scrambled up from the floor. "Wait a minute," she said as she chased behind her to the front door.

Antoinette paused for a moment and stuffed her hand inside her pocket. She pulled out a set of keys with a red heart on the chain. She threw the keys on the sofa, opened the door, and stormed out.

"Wait a minute," Faye screamed as she ran behind her. But as she reached the door she fell against the wall. She grabbed her head and tried to shake off the pain. "*Antoinette*," she screamed as she regained enough strength to run out the door. But as she ran across the lawn she couldn't see her. "Antoinette," she screamed into the night air as she held her head. She winced as she walked to the edge of the grass and dropped to her knees. The pain in her head was overwhelming, and when she tried to get up, she fell right back down. "Antoinette," she cried as she groveled around on the ground. "Antoinette!"

She couldn't remember how long she stayed out in the cold air, but once she had the strength to get up she knew one thing. Her daughter was gone. As she turned to go back in the house, she saw Christopher standing in the doorway. He looked at her like he didn't even know her name. In his hand was the picture of his father and as he turned to walk away, the picture fell to the floor. He didn't bother picking it up. He just walked on.

Faye moved to the door and picked up the picture before closing the door behind her. As she walked over to the sofa, she set the picture down on the coffee table, grabbed her rosary from the end table, then sat on the edge of the cushion, bowed her head, and interlocked her fingers. She began to pray. What other solution was there?

10

Zuma pulled her car into the barren parking structure at seven-fifteen in the morning. She knew the place didn't open up for another forty-five minutes, but she was anxious to get there early anyway. Nervous would be a more appropriate adjective to describe the way she was feeling, but Zuma was not the nervous type. Nothing in the world could shake her. But this morning was a different story. She turned off the engine and cracked the window so she could get some air. As she sat behind the steering wheel she drummed her hands against it, then on her legs. "I am *not* nervous," she told herself as she continued to pat her hands. "Nope, not me," she said, then realized how much noise she was making and stopped herself. She folded her hands in her lap and blew out a stream of air from her mouth. "Just relax," she said as she rested her head against the car seat. "There's nothing to be afraid of."

Zuma tried to calm herself by doing some controlled breathing exercises, but it wasn't working. No matter how hard she tried she couldn't get her breathing to move down into her stomach. It stayed in her chest, which according to one of the books she'd picked up at the library was not a good sign. She finally gave up and tried another relaxing technique called positive imagery, but every time she closed her eyes and tried to focus on something positive like flowers or the beach, her mind kept floating back to the reason she had come here in the first place. She looked through the cement partitions in the parking structure toward the front of the gray and white brick building she would soon be entering and concluded the place looked too plain, considering the wonderful things that went on inside it. Here is where life began, where seeds were planted. Here was the beginning, Zuma thought to herself as she closed her eyes, feeling her anxiety rise. "Okay, dammit," she said to herself, and checked her watch, finding that only two minutes had passed. "I'm nervous. I admit it. So what?"

Yes, Zuma was human after all. She was antsy and the simple admittance of that was enough to calm her down — just a bit. But who wouldn't be nervous? Today was the big day. The day she'd been planning for the past five years. The day she'd kept a secret from everybody — Well . . . almost everybody. Of course Taj knew, but Zuma had never expected Sandy would be the next to become hip to her secret. But once Sandy had decided the two were going to be friends, she wouldn't let up. She wanted to know everything about Zuma and she wouldn't take mind your own fucking business for an answer.

Sandy waited patiently while Zuma finished up with Mrs. Tatum, the client who had come into the shop and interrupted their conversation. Sandy had already checked the book and found that Zuma didn't have another appointment for two hours and when Zuma walked her client to the door and bid her farewell, Sandy was right there to pick up their conversation where they had left off.

"So, *friend,*" Sandy said as she followed Zuma back to her station. "It's your turn to share."

"Share what?" Zuma said as she grabbed a broom and swept up a pile of curly clipped hair.

"Come on, Zuma. We're supposed to be friends now. I told you a secret, now you've got to tell me one."

"I don't have any secrets, Sandy. I'm an open book. What you see is what you get," Zuma said as she scooped up the hair with the dustpan and dumped it in the trash. "And by the way, I wouldn't exactly call us friends yet."

"That's because you don't trust me yet. But you can't trust me until you open up to me."

"Are you my therapist now?"

"No," Sandy said as she sat down in Zuma's chair. "I just want to prove to you that black and white people can be friends."

Zuma leaned the broom against the counter and stood next to it. "This is so fake. Real friends don't have to work this hard."

"Are you saying you're giving up?" Sandy asked and patted her chest where she held the twenty dollars Zuma had placed on their friendly wager. " 'Cause if you are I can find a zillion ways to spend this money."

"Okay," Zuma said, not willing to give in. "But you go first."

"I went first last time."

"Well, go first again. I gotta get used to this friendship stuff."

Sandy sighed, trying to think of something more personal to tell Zuma. "Okay," she said, and put a finger to her chin as she thought. "What else can I tell you about myself? Oh, okay," she said as the lightbulb flashed on in her head. "I hate kids."

"What's so deep about that?" Zuma asked and frowned. "So you hate kids — don't have any."

"Too late. I've already got two."

Zuma looked at her and waited for the punch line, but none came. "Let me get this straight. You don't like kids — "

"I *hate* kids."

"Okay, you *hate* kids, but you've got two of them?" she said and held up a couple of fingers. "Why did you have them then?"

"They were mistakes."

"No," Zuma said, flatly. "Children are never mistakes. The only mistakes are parents who don't plan properly. If you don't want children there are many ways to keep yourself from getting pregnant. You know, like birth control pills, condoms . . . *Hello.*"

"Well, I guess I screwed up. Twice."

"So where are your kids now?"

"At home with their *baby-sitter*," Sandy said, and rolled her eyes.

"Problems?"

"No. It's just that I took this job so that I could get away from the kids, but now I've got a whole new set of problems." Sandy bit her lip as she thought about her children's baby-sitter, and if it hadn't been for the phone ringing out she would have told Zuma the whole story. Instead, she got up and ran to the reception desk. "Blessings," she said as she held the receiver to her ear. "It's for you," she said to Zuma.

"Another appointment?" Zuma asked as she walked over to get the phone.

"No," Sandy said, and held out the receiver. "It's some guy named Taj."

Zuma stopped and backed away from the phone like it was contagious. "Tell him I'm not here," she whispered, waving her hands through the air furiously.

"But I already told him—"

"Just tell him anything," she said, flagging her arms. "Tell him I'm in the rest room."

Sandy put the receiver back to her ear and began to stutter. "Uh . . . um, Zuma had to . . . to . . . go to the rest room," she said, and bit her lip. "I know, but, um, she's uh, she's got the runs. Yeah, and uh, oh, it's terrible. She could be in there for a while."

The runs. Zuma gagged and shook her head, but she did tell her to say anything.

"Sure you can leave a message," Sandy said, looking around for the pad and a pen. "Uh-huh . . . Yeah . . . Okay . . . Got it," she said, and hung up the phone.

"I've got the runs?"

"It's the only thing I could think of." Sandy tore the message off the pad.

"So what did he say?"

"He said don't do anything until you talk to him," she said, reading from the paper. "You're not Superwoman. You can't do everything by yourself."

"He said that?"

"Yep."

"Forget him," Zuma said, and frowned.

Sandy put the piece of paper in the trash and folded her arms across her chest. "Let's hear it."

"Hear what?"

"The story." She walked back over to Zuma's station. "It's your turn now. Tell me what's going on. Who's this Taj?"

"Nobody."

"Come on now, Zuma. I know better than that."

Zuma bided her time. She wasn't sure just how much she wanted Sandy to know. This friend thing seemed silly to her. Sandy was an okay girl, Zuma was coming to realize, but she had never been one to open up and tell her business. But Sandy was persistent.

"Who's Taj?"

"An old boyfriend."

"Ooo," Sandy said and made herself comfortable in her seat. "And?"

"And nothing. He wants to get back with me, but I'm not having it."

"Is he cute?"

"Yeah."

"Working?"

"Uh-huh."

"Any bad habits?"

"Not really."

"So what's the problem?"

"The problem is Taj had his chance and he blew it a long time ago. And I'm not too keen on offering second chances. You get one opportunity with me. You screw up and it's see ya."

"Well, check you out. You must be one of those women who thinks she doesn't need a man in her life."

"No, I'm one of those women who doesn't want just any old man in my life. I don't believe in settling."

"So there's no chance for this Taj guy?"

"Nope."

"Why? What did he do that was so wrong?"

Zuma sighed and shook her head. "I don't want to get into that."

"Did he cheat on you?"

"Not really."

Sandy raised an eyebrow.

"We were never actually a *couple* couple."

"Oh, I get it. Just bed buddies, huh?"

Zuma shrugged.

"Well, did he ever abuse you?"

Zuma gave Sandy a look that said you must be kidding.

"Are you seeing someone else right now?"

"No."

"So what's up? What could he have done that was so bad?"

Zuma turned away from Sandy and walked over to the shampoo area. It wasn't what Taj had done, it was what *she* had done. That's what was so bad. She sat down at the shampoo bowl and tried not to think about the abortion. She knew Sandy was waiting for an explanation, so she made one up. She told her she and Taj had broken up because he'd gotten engaged to another woman. It wasn't a very imaginative lie but it did the trick. There was no way Zuma would ever admit to anyone that she'd had an abortion.

"Why that lousy bastard," Sandy said. "Is he still married?"

"Uh, no," Zuma said finishing off her lie. "They never even got married."

"That serves him right. Now he's trying to run back to you, huh. Who does he think he is?"

"Yeah, who does he think he is?" Zuma mumbled as she got up from her chair. She desperately wanted to change the subject but there was no way Sandy was going for that.

"So do you ever think about settling down and having kids?"

"I used to, but now I don't even think about it."

"Smart girl. Marriage is a prison and children ain't nothing but headaches. No, migraines . . . No . . . tumors."

"Wait a minute," Zuma said quickly. "Marriage may be out of the question, but children? I still want children. At least one."

Sandy smirked. "You can have mine."

"Well, if it's all the same to you, I'll have my own."

"But how? You need a man first, honey."

"I don't need anything or anybody but myself."

"Okay," Sandy said and lifted a finger. "Now I know I ain't no brain surgeon, but I ain't retarded either. And as far as I know, ain't no way you can have a baby without having a man. At least for a night."

Zuma didn't say a word. She knew exactly how to have a baby without a man, but that was her own little secret. Zuma excused herself and walked over to the soda machine. As she searched her pockets for some change she couldn't help but smile. The next day she was going to get herself artificially inseminated and she couldn't wait. Everything was set. The plan was in motion. All there was left to do was do it. By tomorrow, Zuma could be pregnant. *Pregnant*, she thought to herself, and cracked a smile. But after getting her soda and turning back around her smile faded.

Standing in the middle of the doorway was Taj. Sandy walked over to him and offered her help, but all Taj did was look at her, then dismiss her with a hardened sigh. He turned back to Zuma and folded his arms across his chest. "You shouldn't have any carbonated drinks if your stomach's upset," he said sarcastically. "Might give you the runs."

Sandy knew the man must have been Taj. She gave a hesitant look to Zuma, then backed her way to the rest room. "I'll give you two a chance to talk," she said as she opened the door.

"Wait a minute," Taj called to Sandy. "Maybe you ought to let Zuma go first."

Sandy grinned nervously and gave Zuma a look that said, We're busted, then slowly eased back and closed the rest room door.

Zuma sipped her Pepsi slowly as if she didn't have a care in the world, while Taj stood staring at her like a betrayed ex-lover — which he was, but Zuma didn't feel one ounce of guilt. To Zuma, Taj looked pathetic. She knew the only reason he was here was to nag her again. As if there was anything he could say to stop her from doing what she wanted to do. Didn't he know by now that she was her own woman? That she was going to do what she wanted to do regardless of what he had to say about it? Zuma walked over to her hair station, ignoring Taj as if he weren't even present. As he walked over to join her she let out a deep sigh and set her Pepsi down and waited for him to start in on her, which he did quite promptly.

"You ought to know by now that you can't dodge me."

"I'm not dodging you, Taj. It's just that I don't wanna hear none of your shit."

Taj lifted his finger in preparation to go off, then stopped himself. "I didn't come here to argue with you Zuma. I just want to know how you're doing."

"Just fine, thank you."

"You know, I've been doing a lot of thinking and—"

Zuma stared up at the ceiling, knowing exactly where this conversation was going and wishing she didn't have to hear it all over again.

"I thought about what you said the other morning," he said, and stared at Zuma with a question in his eyes. "Were you really serious? Are you really planning on getting artificially inseminated?"

"I don't say things I don't mean."

Taj looked down at the floor, then slowly lifted his face to Zuma. "Don't do this," he said, shaking his head slowly. "Let me be a part of your life."

Zuma bowed her head and breathed in slowly, then looked back into Taj's eyes. The eyes that had once ruled her when she was younger, the eyes that she would have done anything to please. But that was then. Now Zuma realized again that she was irrevocably over Taj, and as she stood watching him plea for another chance to get back into her life she felt so deeply sorry for him. She knew too well how he felt. She understood the aggravation and pain he must be going through. It was the same type of aggravation and pain that he'd put her through when they were younger. Still, there was a limit to the sympathy she allowed herself to feel for him, and at that moment, she had reached her limit. "I don't want to talk about this," she said, turning away as her emotions began to catch her off guard. For no apparent reason, Zuma suddenly felt a pang in her heart. It was so unexpected that she didn't know how to react. She had felt the pang many times before, but never had it hit her during the day. Usually it crept up on her in her quiet hours, when she was at home alone, resting, or in the middle of the night while she was sleeping. But today it had come out of the blue and Zuma, not wanting Taj to see her like this, ordered him to leave. "Just go," she said, grabbing her throat as her voice rattled.

"I can't," Taj said as he put his hand on Zuma's shoulder and turned her around to face him. But Zuma yanked away, turned her back to him, and placed her order again.

"Leave," she demanded, but Taj didn't budge an inch.

Taj was there on a mission. He hadn't come there just to talk, he'd come to show and prove. His hand shook as he stuffed it into his pocket and retrieved its tiny contents. Meticulously, he examined the precious prize in his hand as he stood behind Zuma, realizing it was now or never. He reached his hand over Zuma's shoulder, displaying for her the thing he knew would let her know once and for all that the words he spoke to her were on the real.

"A ring?" Zuma questioned, the surprise of the revelation adding even more angst to the pang that gripped her heart.

"Yes," Taj said softly. "I want you to marry me, Zuma," he said, putting his mouth to her ear. "Let's get married and start our own family."

Zuma grabbed her chest as her emotions began to run over. Oh, how she had wanted to hear him say those words to her. How many times had she dreamt of hearing those words? How many times had she wished this day would come? The day that the man she longed for for so many years would do right by her. She bowed her head and put both hands over her face.

Taj smiled as he clutched the ring in his palm and wrapped his arms around Zuma's body. She understood, he thought to himself, and kissed the back of her neck. But as he held on to her, he could sense something odd. "Zuma," he whispered in her ear. "Are you crying?"

Zuma stood stiffly, saying nothing.

"Zuma," Taj started, then walked around to face her head-on. He looked into her eyes and found no tears. But what he did find was a peculiar thing, a mixture of disgust, shame, and hysteria. "What is it?" he pleaded, eyeing Zuma closely as she bowed her head and shut her eyes. "Tell me what's wrong."

Slowly Zuma opened her eyes and revealed the dampness that now filled them. She looked at Taj as if he were transparent and slowly began to speak. "What's wrong with me?" she asked as the words seemed to float from her lips. "The same thing that has been wrong with me for the past nine years. The same thing that won't ever let me take you back into my heart."

The defiance in Zuma's eyes caused Taj to back away.

"What did you do when I told you I was pregnant nine years ago?"

"That was so long ago —"

"What did you do?" Zuma shouted so loudly that Taj jumped. She wanted him to say the words. She couldn't let the subject go. She wanted to hear him admit what kind of man he was. "When I told you I was pregnant, what did you do?"

Taj opened his mouth to speak, but no words came out. He put his head in his hands as Zuma stood stoically before him waiting for an answer.

"Say it!"

Cautiously, Taj looked up and into her eyes. "I told you to get an abortion."

"Yes you did," Zuma replied with satisfaction. "You told me to get an abortion. And I did, Taj. I did just like you told me. I followed your instructions."

"I'm sorry, Zuma. I mean, what do you want me to say? I made a mistake. But you know I wasn't ready back then."

Zuma put her hand to her cheek as if she were in deep thought. "I wonder if it was a boy or a girl, Taj. What do you think? Huh?"

"Stop," he said, and shook his head.

"Wonder if it would have looked like you?" she asked too seriously. "If it was a boy we could have name him Taj, Jr. Nice name, huh?"

"Stop it."

"Let me see," she said, thinking hard. "If it was a girl we could have named her . . . Tajeeta. No, too ghetto. How 'bout Taj Mahal?"

"Stop it, Zuma," he shouted, and pounded one fist on top of the other. "What? Do you wanna blame the whole situation on me?" he said, then slammed his hands against his chest. "Okay, fine, Zuma. I'll take the blame if it makes you happy. But you were in this too. I may have suggested the abortion, but you are the one who went down to the clinic and had it done."

Zuma's veins popped out on her forehead as she winced at the vibration of every word Taj spoke.

"Silently you've been holding this whole abortion madness against me for years. But remember, Zuma. You had a part in this. You had a choice. I didn't physically force you to do anything. You are the one who —"

Zuma couldn't take it anymore. She lunged out at Taj and grabbed him by his shirt. "I know what I did!" she grunted through tight lips as she held on to Taj's shirt with trembling hands. "I have to live with that knowledge every day," she said, and shook him. "Do you know what it's like to wake up screaming in the middle of the night because you think you hear your baby calling you? Huh? Do you know how it feels to go sit in a mosque all by yourself, begging Allah to forgive you for killing your own child and wondering what will happen to you? Huh? I walk the streets looking over my shoulder, Taj, because I know one day I'm going to reap what I've sown. I'm going to have to pay for what I've done, Taj, and I'm scared. There is nothing I can do in this lifetime that will make up for what I did nine years ago. It was bad. It was wrong, and I'm scared."

Zuma didn't even know she was crying until a salty tear rolled over her lips. Taj wrapped Zuma in his arms as he too began to weep and the two held on to each other as if it were the end of their lives. Then, almost as if possessed, Zuma pushed Taj away. She picked up a white towel from her countertop and blotted her eyes, trying to regain her composure. Taj wiped his eyes with the sleeve of his shirt and by the time he had pulled himself together Zuma was moving toward the door. "It's time for you to leave," she said, too seriously. "Take your cheap-ass ring, your proposal, and get out."

"No," he said adamantly. "It's time for you to listen. I want to make this right, Zuma. I know we've made mistakes in the past, but now I'm ready to correct them. I want to marry you, Zuma. I want us to try to get things back together."

"It's too late."

"No, it's not," he said as he walked over to her and grabbed her by the arm. "We can still do the right thing. We can make another baby. It's not too late."

Zuma shook her head fiercely. "I told you what I was going to do and I'm going to do it."

Taj turned halfway around and bowed his head. "Are you still talking about that artificial insemination shit? That's crazy."

"It's not crazy. It's exactly what I'm going to do."

"What? Is this your way of trying to punish me?" he said, turning back to her. "You wanna have a baby and raise it all alone just to spite me?"

"This has nothing to do with you. I'm doing what is right for me."

"Artificial insemination is not right for you. A baby needs a father. You're going to need someone to help you."

"No I don't."

"A baby deserves a father, Zuma. Can't you see that? What if it's a boy?

Don't you think he's gonna need the guidance of a man? And what if it's a girl for that matter? Isn't she gonna need the strength of a father? Someone to teach her what a good man is all about? You can't do this by yourself."

"I will teach my child all it needs to know. I've been planning for this for the past five years. I know what I have to do."

"You act like planning for a child is like planning to build a house."

"It is," she said, firmly. "You decide what you want and what you don't want and you build accordingly. I want a child, I don't want you, and tomorrow I'm going to make it happen."

"Wait a minute. Tomorrow? You're going through with this tomorrow?"

"Yes I am."

"Hold on, Zuma. You can't be serious. This is ridiculous. Absolutely ridiculous."

"What's ridiculous is the fact that you are still here. I don't want your advice, Taj. I don't need it. In fact, the only thing I need from you is to be left alone."

Taj stared at her, looking for some sign of resignation. But Zuma was adamant. "You're making a big mistake."

She lifted a stiff finger and breathed deeply. "The only big mistake I made was nine years ago. Tomorrow I take one step toward making it right."

"I can't believe you," Taj said in a tone so low it was barely audible. "I can't . . ." He started, then paused to stop his lip from shaking. "I just can't believe you."

Zuma watched Taj as he slowly walked out the door and got in his car. He sat for a minute, then banged his hand against the steering wheel before starting up his car and speeding away. Zuma closed her eyes and breathed in slowly. "I know what I'm doing," she whispered to herself as a defying tingle of uncertainty crept into her head. She shook it off and turned around and headed for her hair station. But when she looked up she stopped completely.

Sandy stood next to the rest room, eyeing Zuma like a hawk. Zuma hesitated for a moment, then continued on her way.

"You lied to me," Sandy said softly.

Zuma turned around and gave her a defensive look. She didn't need this right now. "What are you talking about?"

"I heard everything, Zuma. You and Taj didn't break up over an engagement. You broke up because of the abortion."

Zuma gritted her teeth and turned away. "That's none of your business."
"Why did you lie?"

"Look," Zuma snapped. "I don't owe you anything, okay. There are some things that I keep to myself and that's all there is to it."

"Friends don't lie. They tell the truth. I would have understood."

Zuma spun around and faced Sandy head-on. "We aren't friends, baby," she spat out in a whirl of frustration. "Fuck friends," she said, and put her finger to Sandy's chest. "Keep the money," she said. "You win."

The alarm on Zuma's wrist watch beeped and shook her back into the present. It was eight o'clock on the dot. She grabbed her purse off the passenger seat and quickly got out of the car. In seconds she was inside the Century City Medical Center on her way up to the third floor. The elevator let her out right in front of the reception desk, and as she walked off the lightly tanned woman standing behind it called out to her. "Miss Price," she quipped like a bird. "Today's the day, huh?"

Zuma cracked a nervous smile as the receptionist buzzed the door and Zuma walked in.

"How are you this morning?"

"Just fine," Zuma said. "And you?"

"Oh, don't worry about me. Today's your day," she said as she took Zuma by the hand and ushered her down the hall to an open door. "I want you to get undressed, make a trip to the rest room, and I'll be back with the doctor in about fifteen minutes."

"Wait a minute," Zuma said, and put her hand to her chest. "Aren't we moving a bit fast? I mean isn't there something else I have to do first?"

"No, Miss Price. That's why we had you go through all that paperwork on your first two visits. All we want you to do is relax. There is nothing to this procedure. The hard part is over. You've signed all the paperwork, had your counseling sessions and your physical, and we've picked out a donor for you. This is the easy part. All you've got to do is undress, pee, and relax."

"Undress, pee, and relax?" Zuma said as she looked around the room. "Okay, I can do that."

"Good," the nurse said as she walked out the door. "I'll be back with the doctor in fifteen."

Zuma sighed as she began unbuttoning her blouse. She tried to do her deep breathing exercises again, but by the time she had undressed and put on her green robe she was practically hyperventilating. She rushed into the bathroom and splashed cold water over her face, then drank some of it out of her hand. She couldn't find a towel to dry off with so she grabbed the toilet tissue and rolled off a gigantic blob and blotted her face. That made her feel better — just a bit. She quickly used the toilet, then came out and took a seat next to the examining table. She tried to relax while she waited for the doctor and nurse to come in, but just as she was about to close her eyes and try some positive imagery, the door opened up. That was the fastest fifteen minutes of Zuma's life.

The doctor walked in and right behind him was the nurse wheeling a silver cart topped with bowls and all kinds of funny-looking instruments. The doctor smiled briefly, said hello, then turned around and started fiddling with the tray. The nurse stood next to the examining table and patted it. "It's time," she said, and waved Zuma up from her chair. "I need you to lie down and put your feet in the stirrups. Just as if you were getting a pap smear."

Zuma hopped up onto the table as the nurse walked down to the end of it. "Slide down," she told Zuma as she turned on a light and pulled over a chair. She flashed the light between Zuma's legs, then reached for a pair of gloves and a box of cotton swabs. "You've got a bit of discharge this morning," she said, slipping on the gloves. She wiped the swabs across Zuma's vagina. Zuma flinched and grabbed the sides of the table. "Relax, Miss Price. I'm just cleaning the surface."

"What's he doing?" Zuma asked, and motioned toward the doctor, who immediately turned around.

He smiled and lifted up a long syringe that was big enough to baste a turkey. "I'm filling this with the donor sperm."

"That big old thing?"

"Big?" he said and turned around to finish his business. "I hope you've had bigger?"

So the doctor's got jokes, huh? Zuma thought as both the doctor and nurse giggled. When the nurse saw that Zuma wasn't joining them she placed her hand on Zuma's stomach and rubbed it. "Relax," she said again. "Trust me, this is no big deal."

"Okay," the doctor said as he turned around and carried over the syringe. "I'm ready."

The nurse stood up and the doctor took her place at the foot of the table. He stuck his glove-covered finger inside Zuma and pushed it so far that Zuma screamed. "What are you doing?"

"Just searching for your cervix," he said, then took his hand away. "Now I'm going to insert the sperm."

"Wait," Zuma said and squeezed her knees together. "How do I know you got the right donor sperm?"

The nurse grabbed Zuma's hand. "We've done this thousands of times, Miss Price. We don't make mistakes."

"But I'm just saying. Are you one hundred percent sure? I mean I don't want to wait nine months and find out I gave birth to an Asian baby. I've got enough problems as it is."

"Ssh," the nurse said, and squeezed her hand. "Just relax."

"Are you ready?" the doctor asked.

Zuma nodded her head, then screamed out again.

"What now?" the nurse questioned.

"Nothing," Zuma said, then shut her eyes. "Go ahead."

The doctor inserted the syringe deep inside Zuma. She could feel it as it bumped against her walls. Then she felt a cool squish, then nothing. She slowly opened her eyes and saw that the doctor was standing erect. He placed the syringe back on the silver tray, then peeled out of his gloves.

"What?" Zuma said when he turned around to look at her.

"All done," he said and grinned.

"All done?"

"All done," the nurse said.

"So I'm pregnant now?"

"Hopefully," the doctor said. "We'll know for sure in about three days."

"And that's it?"

"That's it."

"So what do I do now?"

"You lay there and be still," he said, and shook his finger at Zuma. "We want to make sure that all those little guys stay in there. If you move they could spill out, and we definitely don't want that."

"Okay," Zuma said, freezing almost as if she were a kid playing Red Light, Green Light. The only thing she would allow herself to move were her eyes. She tried to look over to the nurse but her peripheral vision didn't reach that far. "How long do I have to stay like this?" she asked like she was engulfed in a full body cast.

"One hour."

"One hour?"

"Yes, Miss Price," the nurse said as she walked over to the door. She opened it for the doctor and as they walked out they both waved like little happy campers.

Zuma lay stiff as a stick with her legs open as wide as the sky. She hadn't come this far to mess it all up by moving. As she lay there she began to think. Girl or boy? Boy or girl? She didn't care, though. Whatever Allah blessed her with would be fine with her. But then she had another thought. In her mind she pictured Taj. She was by his side and in her arms was a baby. Their baby. For a second there, Zuma smiled. But just as soon as it came it disappeared. That was an old dream, Zuma thought as she lay staring straight up at the ceiling. Today was the beginning of a new one. Zuma was making her own dreams come true. And she was doing it all by herself. She was a Superwoman, dammit. And in nine months, she was going to be Supermom.

11

Sandy sat up in bed all night long while Cerwin twisted, turned, and snored like a sweathog. She watched his beer belly pump in and out as he lay with his mouth wide open as if he hadn't a care in the world. Sandy, on the other hand, didn't sleep a wink. She was too frustrated, too agitated, and too through with that woman Cerwin had hired to watch her kids. *Bronze*, Sandy thought, as she angrily kicked the covers off and pulled her knees up to her chest. She had had it up to here with that woman and every time she tried to talk to Cerwin about her he acted like he was too busy or too tired to talk. But Sandy knew better. He had always had time to talk to her before, but now when she mentioned the name *Bronze*, Cerwin would suddenly remember something he had to do or yawn and stretch out his arms like he was *so* exhausted. Yeah, right, Sandy thought, and squinted her eyes. She didn't know exactly what was going on, but she was going to make it a point to find out.

There was one thing Sandy was certain about and that was that Bronze had more on her mind than mere baby-sitting. The first time Bronze watched her kids, Sandy came home to a sparkling clean house. She walked through the front door, looked around, and found the place in immaculate condition. The front room was neat, no pieces of mail cluttering the coffee table, no Power Rangers or empty baby bottles on the sofa, and the floor actually looked like it had been vacuumed, not just swept. Sandy raised her eyebrow suspiciously as she crept into the kitchen and flipped on the light. She had planned on grabbing a soda out of the refrigerator, but when she saw how tidy the room was she froze. No dishes in the sink, no pots on the stove, no dirty plates on the table. Strange. Too strange, Sandy thought as she turned off the light and headed for the bathroom. She knew this was all the work of Bronze, and if it were anyone else, Sandy would have felt grateful. But all she was supposed to do was watch the kids. Didn't nobody tell her to go cleaning up shit. There was something about a stranger's cleaning up her house that embarrassed Sandy. Was this Bronze's way of telling Sandy she thought she was a slob? Was that why she took it upon herself to clean up? Was this her way of saying she was better than me? Sandy thought.

When she entered the bathroom she found it sparkling too. Even smelled like potpourri in there, which only pissed Sandy off even more. Who said she liked air freshener? Maybe she was allergic or something. I mean what's going on around here? Sandy thought, then paused as another thought entered her mind. Sandy stormed out of the bathroom and headed down the hall to her bedroom. "I swear if that bitch has been in here going through my personal things, I'll . . ." Sandy's train of thought was broken up when she flicked on the lights in her bedroom and found it just as rummaged through and stuffy as it had been when she left that morning. The bed was still tossed up, the panties she'd worn the day before still lay in the corner, and Cerwin's socks, which never ever seemed to make it to the hamper, were still laying at the foot of the bed.

Sandy was relieved Bronze hadn't gone traipsing through her private room, but as she closed the door to her bedroom she still felt a twinge of uneasiness about the woman. She stopped in the middle of the hallway in shock. For the first time Sandy noticed it was quiet in the house. Where were the children? Where the hell was Bronze? For a second there, Sandy panicked. She thought about picking up the phone and calling down to the club to see if Cerwin knew where everyone had gone. But then she thought again. She wasn't calling nobody. This had been the first time in years that she had had her house all to herself and she was going to enjoy her time alone. She threw her hands in the air and danced her way back to the kitchen. She flicked on the light again and spun around in circles until she reached the refrigerator. As she opened the door she kicked her leg backward, then rolled her stomach like a wave on the ocean, just like she used to do when she danced down at the club. "I miss those days," she mumbled to herself as she took out a soda and popped the top. She closed the refrigerator and put the soda to her mouth, shimmying backward like a sultry cat.

"Oh hi, Sandy."

"What the—" Sandy said as she spun around, spilling half her soda onto her shirt. Startled, she looked up and found Bronze standing in the kitchen. "Shit," Sandy huffed and tugged on her dripping wet shirt.

"Oh, I'm so sorry," Bronze said as she quickly grabbed a paper towel and rushed to Sandy's rescue. "I didn't mean to scare you," she said as she dabbed at the wet spots on Sandy's shirt. "I didn't even hear you come in."

Sandy snatched the paper towel from Bronze's hand and stepped back. Hmm, she thought to herself as she wiped her own shirt and studied the woman before her. Where had she been hiding? Was she stalking her now? This girl is sneaky, Sandy concluded. And that wasn't her jealousy talking. That was the truth. "What bush have you been hiding behind?" Sandy asked as she continued to eye Bronze.

She laughed and flashed a goofy smile. "I've been in the children's room, putting them to sleep."

Children's room? Like this was some kind of mansion. "Oh, is that right?" Sandy said and balled the paper towel up in her hand.

"Yes, your children are delightful."

"My children?"

"Yes. They're beautiful. We had a wonderful time today. Oh, and Dalila —what a doll," she said, almost boiling over with giddiness. "And David. He's so smart. He even helped me clean up today."

"Wait a minute," Sandy said, and cocked her head to the side. "You're talking about *my* kids? Those kids are demons. The both of them."

"Oh no," Bronze said and shook her head. "We had a ball together. They were so well behaved."

Sandy raised an eyebrow, knowing for sure this woman was running a game. There was no way in the world her kids could be described as wonderful. Not those brats. Whiny, spoiled, hardheaded, yes. But well behaved? Please. She walked over to the sink and poured out the rest of her soda, then sat down at the kitchen table as Bronze went on and on about how *delightful* it was taking care of her children.

"I hope I didn't put them to bed too late," she said as she walked over to the sink and ran the water to wash down all traces of the soda Sandy had just poured out. "We were having such a good time together that I completely lost track of time. I bet you like to get them to bed around eight, huh?"

"Eight? Those bad asses usually stay up until midnight," Sandy said.

"Oh no," Bronze said as she turned around. "They shouldn't be staying up that late. Children their age need a lot of rest. Early to bed, early to rise," she said, and politely folded her arms across her chest and smiled at Sandy. "Oh, there was one thing," she said and held up a finger. "I noticed there wasn't any baby food for Dalila."

"She drinks milk."

Bronze paused for a second to weigh her words. "Well she's really at that age when she can begin taking in food. But don't worry, I ran out to the store and bought her a few jars of Gerber's."

"Well, I know she's at that age, but when she's not drinking milk I usually give her what I eat."

"What you eat?"

"Yeah. If I'm having chicken and rice, she's having chicken and rice too. I just mash it up and stick it in her mouth."

This information did not sit well with Bronze. She took a deep breath before she spoke. "Well, just to be on the safe side, you should give her baby food. Even if you smash up regular food it can get lodged in a baby's throat. There have been cases of babies Dalila's age choking on peas, you know."

No, I didn't know, Sandy thought to herself, and rolled her eyes. Who died and made her a baby expert?

"How you know so much about kids, anyway?"

Bronze smiled as if she'd just been complimented. "I come from a huge family. My mom had twelve kids. I was number seven." Bronze looked away from Sandy and leaned against the cabinet. "There were five kids under me and Mom always taught us to take care of our younger brothers and sisters," she said as a look of longing crept onto her face. "There's a lot of love in my family," she said and smiled. "I have a brother David's age as a matter of fact."

Sandy rolled her eyes, wondering when she had asked for all these details.

"I used to baby-sit him every day," Bronze continued. "We'd go for walks, to the mall, out for — "

"So why aren't you at home watching him right now?"

"I've gotta make some money. Somebody's gotta help my mom feed all those faces."

Well, aren't you the Charity Queen, Sandy thought and sighed out of boredom. She didn't like this conversation, and after all, she was home now. Bronze's job was over. Time to go. Bye-bye. "Well, I'm sure you had a long day. Bet you're ready to get back to your own place now," Sandy said, faking a smile.

"You know," Bronze said, shaking her finger in the air as if she hadn't heard a word Sandy had just said. "David's a very bright boy. We sat down together and watched *Sesame Street*," she said, smiling as she replayed the event in her mind. "He knew his ABC's like the back of his hand and he even counted to one hundred by tens," she said, amazed. "You must practice with him a lot."

"That's what the television is for. I'm no teacher."

"Well," Bronze said hesitantly. "There's no teacher like a mother, you know."

Whatever.

"Actually, I looked in his room for some educational-type toys, but I couldn't find any."

'Cause he don't have any, Sandy thought.

"He's at that hungry stage, you know. He wants to learn everything he can. He asked me so many questions today that my brain almost shut down."

"You should have told him to leave you alone."

"Oh no. When children want to learn we have to teach. I mean, that's what parents are here for."

"But you ain't his parent."

Bronze giggled and threw her head back. "Oh, you know what I mean."

Yeah.

"Anyway," Bronze said as she pulled out a chair and made herself at home. "How was your day?"

Sandy grimaced and leaned back in her seat. "Fine," she answered, wondering what business it was of hers.

"Great," she exclaimed with glee. "You must be so excited about having a new job," she said, and rested her hand underneath her chin as if they were about to have some deep conversation.

But for Sandy it was time to cut the bullshit. It was time for the nosy baby expert to get gone. "Look, I'm sure you must be tired," Sandy said, and rose from her seat. "And since I'm home now there's no need for you to hang around," she said as she slowly walked toward the kitchen door, expecting Bronze to get up and follow behind her. "It's been nice chatting with you, but you can go now."

"Actually, I can't," she said, as Sandy stopped in her tracks and turned around with a look of "huh" written all over her face. "I don't have a car. I've got to wait for Cerwin to get off so he can give me a ride home."

"You too good for the bus?"

"No, it's just that I live so far, and besides, Cerwin said he was going to pay me tonight. I really need that money."

"But Cerwin doesn't get home from the club till after three in the morning."

"I know," Bronze said gleefully. "I guess it's just me and you till then."

"How nice," Sandy said, forcing herself to smile.

Being alone with that woman was the last thing Sandy wanted to do, and as soon as Cerwin got home she was going to have a little talk with him about Bronze's working arrangements. There was no way Sandy was going to spend all her evenings with that woman. She'd rather be stuck with the kids if that was going to be the case.

Sandy sat down on the sofa and turned on the television and in no time Bronze was right beside her. Sandy flipped the remote till she found an old black-and-white movie and as she tried to relax and get into it, Bronze began running her mouth.

"Do you ever take the kids to the park?"

"No," Sandy said, trying to focus in on her movie.

"No?" Bronze said and tsked her teeth. "Oh well, maybe I'll take them sometime next week. You know children love the outdoors. They need to get out more. Play with the earth."

Sandy sneered at Bronze out of the corner of her mouth, then turned her attention back to the television.

"You know, when I was a child I loved going to the park. I remember when—"

"Do you mind?" Sandy interrupted and pointed toward the television.

Bronze winced, then grinned. "I guess I'm talking too much, huh?"

Damn right.

"Sorry," she said as she sat back and hushed. But only a minute passed before she tapped Sandy on the arm. "Just one more thing," she said meekly.

"What?"

"When I was helping David change into his pajamas I noticed some bruises on his legs and back," she said and frowned. "Did he run into something?"

"Yeah," Sandy snapped. "My belt. I whipped his little ass good. Maybe next time he'll do like I tell him."

Bronze stared at Sandy, then shook her head. "But he's only three years old. What could he have done that was so bad to deserve a beating? I mean couldn't you have just talked to him? Given him a time-out?"

"Talking don't work with that bad-ass boy."

"It worked for me and my brothers and sisters."

Sandy slowly turned to Bronze. "Are you trying to tell me how to raise my children?"

Bronze seemed stunned. "No. I'm just saying—"

"Do you have kids of your own?"

Bronze began to reply, but Sandy cut her off.

"No, you don't! So what right do you have to judge how I rear my kids?"

"Well, I—"

"Look, Bronze. I don't know who you think you are, but I am the mother around this house and I will discipline my kids any way I want. If you want to talk and give time-outs to your kids, then fine. When you have some you can do that. But until you are a mother you will never know what I go through. So don't sit there and tell me I'm a bad mother. I do the best I can."

"I never said you were a bad mother. I'm just saying—"

"You ain't saying shit," Sandy said, and rose up off the sofa. "I suggest you remember who you're working for. Cerwin may be paying you, but I'm the boss. Don't forget that," she said, and stomped off to her room.

That night Cerwin had come home at his usual time and had taken Bronze to wherever the hell she lived and when he came back Sandy made her first attempt to try to talk to him. But all Cerwin was interested in was a little nookie, and since it had been so long since their last encounter, a whole two days, Sandy dropped her complaining and gave in. The next day she tried to bring the subject of Bronze up again, but Cerwin had to rush down to the club so he could be there when his new vinyl bar seats arrived. Cerwin had put Sandy off long enough. This morning she was going to have her say because Bronze had gone too far. It was bad enough that she was telling her how to raise her kids, but last night she took it to another level. A level that almost got her slapped.

When Sandy came home last night, the house was quiet and spotless, and except for Bronze's puttering in the kitchen everything was peaceful. Sandy wasn't in a very good mood to start with. Her mind was still lingering over the argument she had had with Zuma earlier that day at the shop. Just when Sandy thought she had found a new friend, she'd lost her, and she wondered if Zuma would ever speak to her again. All Sandy wanted to do was go to her bedroom, rest, and try to think how she could make amends with Zuma. But before she could even get through the front room, Bronze's happy ass was in her face.

"Hey," she greeted Sandy from the kitchen. "You're just in time for some of my famous meat loaf and potatoes."

"No thank you," Sandy said politely. She still wasn't too pleased with Bronze telling her how to raise her kids, but she wasn't in the mood for bickering. "I'm not very hungry."

"Oh no. Please," Bronze said and grabbed her by the arm. "You've got to try this. I want your opinion on it," she said as she guided Sandy into the kitchen and over to a chair. "I'll just fix you a small helping," she said, and turned around to grab a plate.

Sandy watched her navigating through the kitchen like it was her own, and as she moved around opening cabinets and drawers, Sandy noticed that everything had been rearranged. She held her tongue for a minute because she didn't want to get into it with Bronze that night. But when she brought over her plate, Sandy couldn't keep silent anymore. "I see you've moved a few things around," Sandy said as Bronze placed her food in front of her.

"Oh yes," she said, quite pleased with herself. "See, you had all the chemicals down in the bottom cabinet where the children could get them. I just moved them up. Wouldn't want the kids getting their hands on a bottle of bleach, you know." She pulled open a cabinet and pointed. "Then I put all the plates on one shelf, the cups on another, and the glasses over here. You can find what you want a little easier now. You like?"

"I knew where everything was before."

"Oh," Bronze said, and slowly shut the cabinet. "I can change it back if you —"

"Forget it," Sandy said, and turned her attention to the plate of food in front of her. "So let me get this straight. Not only are you a baby-sitter, but a maid and a cook?"

Bronze smiled humbly, then pulled out a chair and sat across from Sandy. "So how is it?"

Sandy took a bite of meat loaf and sat back in her seat. It was delicious, she thought, wanting to take another bite but not wanting to feed into Bronze's ego.

"Well?" Bronze asked impatiently.

"It's all right."

"Oh," Bronze said, her feelings stomped flat. "I must have added too much oregano."

Sandy shrugged and took another bite.

"Well, I guess I messed up," Bronze said as if it were the end of the world. She stood up and went back to the counter and wrapped foil over the rest of her meat loaf.

Sandy quickly took two more delectable bites, then pushed her plate away. "Maybe you'll get it right next time."

"Oh, but I wanted it to be right this time." Bronze turned around slapping her palms against her thighs.

"Damn," Sandy said, trying to swallow down her food. "What's so important about meat loaf?"

"It's just that Cerwin asked me to make it for him. He's been so good to me, giving me this job and all. And I wanted to do something nice for him."

Sandy swallowed hard. "Cerwin asked you to make this for him?"

"Yeah. He said he hadn't had a decent home-cooked meal in a while and . . . Oh," Bronze said and put her hand over her mouth as she saw the ghastly look on Sandy's face.

"He said what?"

"Nothing," Bronze recanted quickly.

Sandy sat quietly and stared down at the table. What's going on here, she thought, feeling her face turn hot. The more she thought the more she came to the conclusion that this woman was trying to take her place. First it was the kids, now it was Cerwin. Bronze was taking care of them all. She felt like an outsider in her own home.

Bronze eased herself into the chair across from Sandy and folded her hands in front of her. "I wanna talk to you," Bronze said softly. Sandy looked up at her and squinted. "I just want you to know that I heard what you said to me the other night. I know I'm not the boss around here. You are. You had every right to go off on me. It's not my place to tell you how to raise your children. I'm just here to help, not take over." Bronze paused and waited for Sandy's reaction, but Sandy didn't budge. "I also want you to know that there's absolutely nothing between me and Cerwin. It's just like he told you. I came down to the club for a job, but I was too young. And Cerwin being the sweet guy he is offered to let me watch your kids for some extra cash. That's all there is to it," she said, pausing to measure her words. "You know, Cerwin told me that you could be a little jealous at times, but I just want you to know you have no reason to be jealous of me. I'm actually a little jealous of you."

Sandy put on a sly grin. "Why is that?"

"You have it all. A nice job, lovable children, and a wonderful man. I wish I had all those things."

"I bet you do," Sandy said, smugly.

"Well, that's all I wanted to say," she said as she got up from the table. "I'll leave you alone now," she said, and walked out of the kitchen.

"Hmm," Sandy moaned as she got up from the table. Good try. Bronze had said all the right words, but Sandy wasn't buying her song and dance. No matter what Bronze said, Sandy still believed she had something up her sleeve. Call it jealousy, an overactive imagination — call it what you will, but Sandy knew an out-and-out lie when she heard one. She wasn't fooled.

Sandy began pacing the floor, trying to figure out this woman's game. There was something about her that just didn't sit right with Sandy. She couldn't put her finger on it, but she knew something was up. She turned out the light in the kitchen and decided it was time to go to bed. She had to be at the shop early the next morning for a manicure appointment and figured she should get some rest. There would be more time to figure out Bronze later, she thought to herself as she walked down the hall to her bedroom. But just as she opened the door, Bronze came out of the bathroom.

She heard Bronze say, "good night," and as she turned around her mouth nearly dropped to the floor. Bronze was dressed in a large white T-shirt with a huge yellow happy face printed on the front. The T-shirt was sorta cute and would have looked very casual over a pair of shorts, only Bronze wasn't wearing any shorts. The T-shirt was the only piece of clothing on her body, and the sight of her perky seventeen-year-old breasts popping out underneath the eyes of the happy face made Sandy's jealous nature rise. Sandy looked her up and down and tried to catch her breath. "What do you have on?"

"It's my nightshirt," Bronze said, innocently.

"Nightshirt? Excuse me? What are you doing in a nightshirt?"

"Cerwin said it was okay for me to camp out on your sofa tonight. He said it doesn't make any sense for him to drive me home at three in the morning when I have to be right back here at nine before you go to work."

"Cerwin said it was okay?"

"Yeah," Bronze said as if she didn't have a care in the world. "You don't mind, do you?"

Sandy stared at Bronze like a hungry tiger. She stepped inside her bedroom and slammed the door. She was on fire. She snatched off her clothes and threw them piece by piece across the room as she mumbled through clenched jaws. "Cerwin said it was okay? Bastard. What? She's moving in now? Huh. Fuck that. I'm not having this shit. This is my house, damn it. My house!"

She slipped on an old T-shirt and threw herself across the bed. Sandy was so much in rage that she could barely think. All she knew was that when Cerwin walked through the door she would be waiting on him. He had some explaining to do and this time she wasn't going to let him off the hook.

Five hours passed before Sandy heard Cerwin's car pull up in the driveway, but her rage had not dissipated one ounce. She heard the front door creep open, then the sound of footsteps heading toward the bedroom door. She jumped up from the bed, stood in the middle of the room, and as the door came open her mouth began spitting fire. "What the fuck did you tell that woman she could stay here for?"

Cerwin glanced at Sandy briefly, shook his head, and began undressing.

"Did you hear me?" she said, walking up behind him. "How dare you tell her she could stay here. This is my home. You could have at least asked me."

Cerwin passed Sandy and headed to the dresser and without even bothering to look at her he asked, "Who pays the bills in this house?"

"That is not the point," Sandy said, following behind him. "The point is—"

"And who decided she had to get a job?" he asked as he pulled out a flannel pair of pajama pants and slid them over his long legs.

"I did," she said, moving backward out of his way as he turned around and headed for the bed. "But that's not the point either."

"The point is," he said as he pulled back the covers and got in bed, "I need someone to take care of this house and my children. That's why I hired Bronze. And the reason why I told her she could stay the night is because I work all day long and I ain't about to drive nobody home at three in the morning, then turn around six hours later and go pick her up again. I need my rest. If she stays here during the week I can get my sleep," he said, and turned over. "Now turn out the lights and shut up."

"I will not turn out the lights, and I will not shut up," she said, climbing onto the bed and resting on her knees right beside Cerwin.

"Look," Cerwin said, totally fed up. "All I'm trying to do is cut the girl a break. She's just a kid. She ain't got nobody, no money, no nothing. She's only seventeen and until she's eighteen, I can't let her dance down at the club or I'll lose my license. So what the hell?" he said and shrugged his shoulders. "I decided to let her take care of the kids for some extra dough. That's all there is to it."

"So this is your charity contribution for the year," she huffed, sarcastically.

"I'm just helping the girl out, just like I helped you out, remember?"

Yes, Sandy remembered, and that's what she was afraid of. She remembered how she'd left home and come back to L.A. without a dollar to her name. She remembered how Cerwin had given her a job, how he saved her from life on the streets. She also remembered how he fell in love with her and moved her into his house and knocked her up with two kids. Just how similar was Bronze's story going to be to hers? "I know what you're trying to do, Big C," she said, leaning over into his face. "You're trying to piss me off and it's working. I'm telling you right now, she ain't staying here another night. I don't want her traipsing around my house half naked. Did you see what she had on?"

"No," Cerwin said, and sat up. "But now that you mention it, I should go see," he said, and lifted his body halfway off the bed.

Sandy socked him in the arm. "Stop playing. This is not funny."

"Well, if there's a half naked woman in my house I think I should know about this," he said, and giggled.

"This is not funny," she said, hitting him on the arm again.

"Hey," he said, and gave her a serious look. "Watch who you're hitting." Sandy folded her hands in her lap.

"Say you're sorry."

"I'm sorry," she said as he lay back down. "I'm not going to have this, Cerwin. I'm not."

"Okay," he said, and yawned. "Whatever you say."

"I'm serious," she said, almost whining.

Cerwin yawned and closed his eyes. "Shut up and turn out the light, please."

Sandy sat stoically, refusing. Cerwin wasn't taking her seriously at all and it really pissed her off.

He opened one of his eyes and repeated himself. "Turn out the light," he said, and eyed her until she moved.

Sandy did like she was told. She got out of bed and flicked the switch on the wall. As she got back into bed, Cerwin pulled the covers over his head and in no time, he was snoring. Sandy fluffed her pillows against the headboard and sat back. If he thinks this conversation is over he's got another think coming, she thought to herself, seething. She barely moved the whole night, except for when she got up to go to the kitchen. She got what she needed, then came right back and sat next to Cerwin as he slumbered peacefully.

At around seven o'clock, the sun came seeping through the windows of the room. Though Sandy hadn't had a second's worth of rest, she knew she would have to get up for work in a few minutes. But first there was something she had to take care of.

She pulled the covers off of Cerwin's body and climbed on top of him. Slowly, she moved his hands above his head and clasped them between one of her hands by the wrists. Then, with the other hand, she reached for the object she had gotten from the kitchen in the middle of the night. "Cerwin," she cooed into his ear. "It's time to get up, honey," she said as he wiggled beneath her, trying to hold on to his sleep. "Cerwin," she cooed again. "Get up, baby. I need to talk to you." Cerwin kept his eyes shut as he frowned uncomfortably and sank his head deeper into his pillow. "Cerwin," Sandy snapped. "Get up!" she said as he slowly opened his eyes.

"What the hell do you want?" he said, then froze. Cerwin's eyes widened as he looked up at Sandy. "Oh shit," he said as he gradually became more and more alert. "What the fuck are you doing?"

Sandy smiled as she straddled him and tightened the grip she had around his wrists. In her other hand she gripped a knife, which she held just below his chin.

"Sandy," he said, cautiously. "I don't know what you're thinking about doing, but I'm telling you now, if you cut me you better kill me or I'm going to —"

"Shut up," Sandy said nicely. What she was doing was not out of anger, it was out of frustration. She knew Cerwin wouldn't listen to her under normal circumstances, but this way he had no choice. But make no mistake about it, Sandy would use the knife if she had to. It wouldn't have been the craziest thing she'd ever done. Knocking him over the head with a skillet — now that was crazy. But the knife — that was nothing.

Cerwin closed his mouth and swallowed hard. He knew what Sandy was capable of and he didn't want to agitate her. She traced the curve of his neck with the tip of the knife and sighed slowly. "Now," she said, and placed the knife back under his chin. "You're going to tell me exactly what is going on with you and the bitch on the sofa."

"What are you talking about?"

"Shut up," she said, and placed the knife closer to his neck. "Here's how it works. I ask a direct question and you give me a direct answer. Now, what is going on with you and Bronze?"

"Nothing," he said sincerely, eyeing Sandy's hand on the knife.

"Do you like her?"

"No."

"Then why the fuck did you give her this job?"

"Who the hell else is going to take care of the kids?"

"Nicely," Sandy said, and stared into Cerwin's eyes.

"Because we needed someone to take care of the kids," he said, calmly.

"And?"

"And nothing."

Sandy pushed the knife against Cerwin's neck, almost drawing blood. "And?"

"Look, Sandy . . . darling . . . The girl came down to the club asking for a job. She wasn't old enough so I had to turn her away. But she started begging, talking about how much she needed to make some money and that's when I realized she could work for us as a baby-sitter. That's all there is to it. I swear."

"I don't believe you."

"What do you want me to say, Sandy? It's the truth."

"You're lying," Sandy said, and bit her bottom lip. "There's more. Tell me the truth. There's more."

"Sandy," Cerwin pleaded. "Sandy, you're going through one of your jealous spells again, honey. Why don't you put the knife down? Okay? Please, baby. Put the knife down and we can talk."

Sandy shook her head vigorously. "You never listen to me. That's why I have to do things like this, Cerwin. I have to get your attention."

"Okay. You've got my attention. I promise I'll listen to whatever you have to say. Just, please, put down the knife."

Sandy slackened her grip on the knife for a second, then gripped it tighter. "No," she said, and shook her head. "Hear me, Cerwin. I want that woman gone. And I want her gone now," she said furiously.

"Okay, Sandy. What do you want me to do?"

"Call her."

"Wha —"

"Call her. Now."

"Bronze," Cerwin creaked out, feeling the knife rubbing against his Adam's apple. "Bronze," he screamed this time at the top of his lungs. He called for her three more times before Sandy could hear the approach of footsteps outside the bedroom door.

"Tell her to get in here."

"Bronze? Could you come in here please?"

Sandy waited as the door slowly crept open. "Yes," she heard Bronze say, then all she heard was silence.

"Oh my God," she gasped. "What's going on?"

"Shut up," Sandy called over her shoulder, not taking her eyes off Cerwin. "Tell her she's fired."

Cerwin hesitated a second too long, which got him a firm poke with the tip of the knife. "Now," Sandy screamed.

"I'm gonna have to let you go," Cerwin said, looking beyond Sandy to Bronze. "It's just not working out. I'm sorry."

Bronze couldn't even listen to Cerwin's words. She was too concerned with Sandy and the knife she held to his throat. "What are you doing, Sandy? My God!"

"Are your ears working?" Sandy shouted. "You are fired. Now get the hell out of my house."

"Just go, Bronze," Cerwin warned. "Just get out of here."

"But," Bronze started until she heard a sound behind her. It was David. He ran to Bronze's side and grabbed her around the waist. "What's going on?" he said softly, then looked into his parents' bedroom. "Daddy," he screamed, and ran to the side of the bed. "Daddy!"

Bronze ran behind him and pulled him back. "Come with me, sweetheart," she said as David began to cry. "It's all right," she said as she picked him up. "Everything's all right."

"Go get dressed, Bronze," Cerwin said, and watched her disappear with his son. He turned his attention back to Sandy and began to plead. "Okay, baby. It's all taken care of. You can put down the knife now."

Sandy pressed her fingers against the knife's handle. "Tell me you love me."

"I love you, Sandy. With all my heart."

Sandy smiled and loosened her grip. "I love you too," she said, and bent down to kiss Cerwin on the mouth.

Instantly Cerwin shook his hands out of her grip and grabbed the knife. He pushed her off of him and rolled over on top of her and held the knife blade down above her face. "What the fuck is wrong with you, huh? Pulling a knife on me?" he screamed. "I ought to slice your ass into a million pieces. What the hell is wrong with you?"

"I'm sorry, Cerwin," Sandy said as her eyes nearly bulged out her head. "No, please don't," she said as she eyed the knife hovering above her face. She screamed as Cerwin came down with the knife and stabbed it into the pillow beside her head. He grabbed her by the throat with both hands, threatening to kill her.

"Cerwin," Bronze shouted, appearing in the doorway now fully dressed. She ran over to the side of the bed. "Stop it, Cerwin," she said as she watched Sandy's face turn red. "Stop it, Cerwin. She can't breathe. You're killing her," she said, and placed her hands over his, trying as best she could to loosen his grip. "Cerwin," she shouted over and over again, until he finally let go of Sandy's neck. He pushed Bronze out of his way and got up from the bed as Sandy lay there grabbing her neck and gagging.

"I'm tired of this bullshit," he shouted as he rummaged around the room picking up the clothes he'd worn the day before and putting them on. "You are one crazy bitch," he said, and turned back to Sandy as she sat up in bed, still holding her throat. "Every time you get jealous you pull one of these stunts. Well, this is the last time. I'm not putting up with this bullshit no more. I'm out of here," he said as he stomped out of the room.

Bronze ran after him, leaving Sandy gagging on the edge of the bed. "Wait," she screamed as she got up and stumbled across the room. "Wait, Cerwin. Please." She ran to the front of the house as Cerwin and Bronze walked out the door. In Bronze's arms was Dalila and following closely behind was David.

Sandy panicked, but kept control. She ran to the front porch and caught David by the back of his shirt. She yanked him back so hard that he fell. "Get your ass back in the house," she said as she ran behind Bronze and caught her just as Cerwin had gotten into the car and leaned over to unlock the passenger side door. Sandy slapped Bronze's face and pushed her against the car. She snatched her baby girl out of Bronze's arm and screamed. "You aren't taking my kids. They're mine."

"You're not stable right now, Sandy," Bronze tried to reason. "Just let me take the kids until you're feeling better."

"No," she screamed, then rushed around the car as David ran to his father's door.

"I wanna go with you and Bronze, Daddy," he cried, until Sandy cut him off.

"Get in the house," she screamed to him, stopping him dead in his tracks. She turned around and gripped Dalila in one arm. With the other, she pointed at Cerwin. "You ain't taking my kids," she screamed as Cerwin opened his car door and put one foot on the ground. He started to stand up, then changed his mind. He closed the door of the car, then called to Bronze.

"It's okay," he said as she opened the door. "She won't hurt the kids."

"But she's not stable, Cerwin. The kids should come with us."

"Just get in," he said, and sighed, then started the car.

Sandy gripped her baby against her hip as she leaned over Cerwin's window. "Just like I thought. Where are you taking your new girlfriend? A hotel?" she screamed as the car began backing out of the driveway. She walked beside it as she continued to talk. "So you're leaving me for her?"

"No," he said as he reached the curb. "I'm leaving you because you're crazy. I'm taking Bronze home, then I'm going to find me a new place to stay. You are one mixed-up chick. You messed up on a good thing, baby."

"Fuck you." Sandy screamed so loud, the neighbors began poking their heads out of their windows. "Fuck you and fuck her. You'll be back, Cerwin. You always come back," she said as the car backed into the street and turned. Sandy walked across the front yard still screaming. "You'll be back, Big C. You my man. You ain't going nowhere," she said as the car sped off down the street and bent the corner.

She stood on the lawn, breathing so hard you'd think she'd just run a marathon. The neighbors had begun to congregate on their own lawns and when Sandy noticed all eyes were on her, she stuck her middle finger in the air and waved it around. She turned back to her house and walked up the front steps. David stood there sniffling and heaving his shoulders up and down. Sandy smacked him dead in the mouth. "I said get your ass back in the house," she screamed. David let out a piercing yelp and ran through the screen door.

She looked at little Dalila and frowned. The baby was gurgling and smiling at Sandy as if the whole world was a circus. "What the fuck are you smiling about?" Sandy said, and bounced the baby against her hip. "Stupid kid," she said, and walked through the door. "Ain't a damn thing funny."

12

Pat **walked** through the house with her hands wrapped around a huge cup of coffee and smiled so naturally and unconsciously that if one were to see her for the first time they'd swear she'd been born with that expression. She couldn't remember the last time she had been so happy, and if she had any reserve about going through another adoption it had been erased yesterday when she met Tracy for the first time. If it was possible to fall in love at first sight, she had done it. Tracy was an angel and Pat knew that she would make a wonderful daughter. It had taken Tracy only a moment to get used to Pat and Mark and on the ride back to Tracy's house from the park, she sat in Pat's lap, laid her head against her chest, and fell fast asleep. Pat had never felt more comfortable or relaxed as she did when Tracy was in her arms. She had tried to hold back her feelings, knowing that nothing was certain in the adoption process, but she couldn't help herself. She smoothed her hand over Tracy's face and rocked her gently. Mark looked over his shoulder at the both of them and smiled. "She's beautiful," he said, turning around in the front seat and reaching out his hand. Pat grabbed it and looked at him with glistening eyes. She was too choked up to speak, but her eyes said everything her mouth could not. We're going to be a family, Pat thought as they drove in silence, gazing down at the girl who would soon be all theirs.

When they reached Tracy's home, Mark got out and opened the back door. He took Tracy from Pat's lap and placed her sleepy head on his shoulder. That was a moment Pat would never forget. The sight of Mark with Tracy in his arms made Pat feel so proud. She had never seen him in the father role before, but she always knew he'd make a good one. Pat got out of the backseat and grabbed Mark's hand as the three of them headed for Tracy's door. It wasn't until they rang the door bell that Tracy woke up. She rubbed her tiny fists against her eyes then wrapped her arms around Mark's neck. "You're back home," Pat said, smoothing out her hair. "Did you have a good time?"

Tracy was too groggy to speak, but she nodded her head.

"Would you like to go out with us again?" Mark asked.

Tracy turned her face to his and cracked a shy smile, then hid her face against Mark's neck.

"Is that a yes?" Mark said as he tickled her sides, sending Tracy into an hysterical fit of laughter.

The three stood in front of the door giggling for the longest time until Pat realized no one had come to answer the door yet. She rang the bell once again and waited as Mark put Tracy down and began chasing her across the front yard. Still there was no answer at the door and Pat began to knock. She thought this was strange, but deep inside her she hoped no one would ever answer the door. She hoped the Oppenheimers had somehow vanished from existence and she could take Tracy home with her tonight and keep her forever. She turned around and walked back to the car and leaned down to the window to talk to the attorney. "No one's home," she told Mr. Peters, hoping he'd say it was okay for them to take Tracy back to their own home. But just as she spoke, a gray station wagon came honking down the street. She stood up and saw the Oppenheimers as they pulled into the driveway and turned off their engine. They got out of the car and walked onto the lawn. Mrs. Oppenheimer held out her arms for Tracy, but Tracy was having too much fun playing with Mark to give her foster mother a hug.

Elizabeth dropped her hands and walked to the door as Henry approached Pat. "Sorry we're late, but we didn't know the exact time you'd be bringing Tracy back home," he said, and patted the side of the briefcase he held in his hand. "We had a bit of business to take care of," he said as he looked past Pat to Mark and Tracy.

Mark scooped Tracy up and carried her over to Pat and Henry. When he reached them, he put her down and reached out to shake Henry's hand. "So," Mark huffed, trying to catch his breath. "You're back."

"Yes," Henry said. "I was just telling your wife we had some business to take care of," he said, and patted his briefcase once again.

"Oh no problem," Mark said and glanced down at Tracy. "We had a good time today, didn't we?"

"Uh-huh," Tracy said, and nodded her head.

He patted the top of her head, then put his arm around Pat. "Well, I guess we'll be going," he said, and smiled past Henry to his wife. Elizabeth didn't even try to fake a smile.

Mark leaned over and tickled Tracy's stomach. "Bye-bye, kiddo."

Tracy looked up at him with wide eyes, then dropped her head. "You gotta go," she said, staring down at the ground.

"Yes," Pat said as she kneeled down in front of her and held out her arms. Tracy walked into them and held Pat around the neck. It felt so good that Pat didn't want to let go.

"When am I gonna see you again?" she asked, and stared smack dab into Pat's eyes. Pat's heart felt so full. She looked into Tracy's eyes, wishing this day would never end. But Pat stayed strong. She knew it was only a matter of time before she'd be able to spend every day with Tracy and though that day could never come fast enough for Pat she was willing to wait.

"Maybe we could go to the zoo tomorrow," she said as she saw the light pump back into Tracy's face.

"For real?" she said as if she were about to burst. But before Pat could answer Elizabeth spoke up.

"No," she said as she walked from the front door to Tracy. Tracy turned around with questioning eyes. "Remember you have piano lessons tomorrow," she said, and took her place directly behind Tracy.

"Oh yeah," Tracy said, turning back to Pat. "I can't go tomorrow," she said and dropped her head.

"Well maybe you could skip practice tomorrow," Pat said, speaking more to Elizabeth than to Tracy.

"I don't think so," Elizabeth said, and grabbed Tracy by the hand.

"Well, what about the next day?" Pat said firmly, and stood up to face Elizabeth.

Elizabeth stared at Pat without answering, then gave Tracy a tug. "Say good-bye to the nice people," she said as she pulled Tracy toward the house.

Tracy waved vigorously over her shoulder as Elizabeth walked her to the door and Henry followed behind.

"We'll see you the day after tomorrow," Pat called to Tracy just before she walked in the door.

" 'Kay," she yelled as she stood in the doorway, still waving. She would have stood there forever, if Elizabeth hadn't come up behind her and pulled her away.

Pat immediately turned to Mark with blazing eyes. "How rude," she said, and frowned.

"I know," he said, and turned her around to walk back to the car. "But you gotta see it from their perspective. They've raised Tracy since she was a newborn. This has got to be painful for them."

"Yes, but they should know as the foster parents that someday they would have to give Tracy up," she said as she reached the car. "And I tell you another thing, they better not try to play games."

"They won't," Mr. Peters said, leaning across the front seat to talk out the window. "All foster parents are a little apprehensive in the beginning, but they always come around. They want what's best for Tracy as much as you do."

"That's right," Mark said as he opened the back door for Pat. As she leaned down to get in, he grabbed her by the arm and pulled her close to him. "I think she likes us," he said, grinning like a Cheshire cat.

Pat grinned back and let go of her anger. "I know," she said, and giggled. "It's gonna happen this time, Mark. I can feel it."

"I feel it too," he said, and gave her a kiss that sent her mind back to the first time they met.

Pat got into the car knowing everything was going to be fine. Her marriage was back on track and stronger than ever and soon, very soon, she and Mark would have what they always wanted — a complete family.

Pat put two hands around her cup and sipped as she walked up the staircase and into one of the spare bedrooms. There were two upstairs and one down and of the three Pat had chosen the one closest to hers and Mark's to set up for Tracy. She set her coffee cup on the floor and held out her hands before her like a director scoping out a movie scene. The room was filled with gym equipment that neither she nor Mark ever used. It was supposed to be a home gym, but looked more like a cluttered storage room. Besides the gym equipment, there were boxes of old records, clothes that were supposed to be taken down to the Salvation Army but never made it, stacks of books, and anything else that Pat didn't quite know what to do with. As she turned around the room looking through her imaginary lens, Pat could perfectly see how the room would look once cleared out and replaced with the beautiful canopy bed she and Mark had seen yesterday.

After Mr. Peters had dropped them back at his office to pick up their car, Pat and Mark had decided to go get an early dinner. But they never quite made it to the restaurant. On the way, they passed by a Levitz furniture store and Pat insisted they stop in. Mark thought it was too soon to be picking out furniture for a child that wasn't theirs yet, but he went along anyway, seeing how excited Pat was. As they walked in the store they promised each other they were just there to look, but that looking lasted over three hours. Once inside they both became excited as they strolled from bed to bed, sizing up their options, adding up the pros and cons, and slowly driving themselves insane trying to figure out which bedroom suite Tracy would like most. They'd been there so long that other customers were coming up to them asking questions as if they worked there. Finally they were able to narrow their choices down to two. One was a pink double bed with a headboard in the shape of a house with a window and fake curtains in the middle. The other was a white canopy bed that sat high off the ground. There were daisies painted on the headboard and on the posts, plus a matching white dresser and two nightstands. It took another hour for them to decide on the canopy bed, but after making their decision another dilemma came into view.

"Are we gonna buy it?" Pat asked as she sat on the edge of the bed next to Mark.

Mark sighed and rubbed his chin as he looked over at Pat and shrugged his shoulders.

"Do you think we're getting ahead of ourselves?" Pat asked and fell back onto the bed. "I mean we just met Tracy for the first time today. We don't even know if this thing is gonna go through."

"Hey," Mark said, and lay down next to Pat as they both stared up at the ceiling. "The adoption is going to go through. Don't you worry about that."

"I'm not worried. I'm just being realistic. We really don't know what's going to happen."

"We know that we are doing everything by the books. Mr. Peters is a damn good attorney. He's been doing adoptions for the past twenty years and he says everything is moving smoothly. Nothing's going to go wrong."

Pat closed her eyes and breathed deeply. "I thought nothing would go wrong last time and look what happened."

"This is not last time. Don't even think about last time," Mark said as he moved closer to Pat and put his arm across her chest.

"But I can't help it."

"Ssh," Mark said as he rolled on top of Pat and looked down on her. "I don't want you worrying," he said seriously. "Let me do that. All you have to do is be patient. Do you understand me?" Mark had always been best at putting Pat at ease and this time he'd done it again. "You're going to be a great mom," he told her, and kissed her lips gently. But what started out as a simple kiss turned into more, as they rolled around on the canopy bed as if they were in the privacy of their own home. They didn't even notice the passersby who stared and pointed, but they did hear the menacing coughing that sounded above their heads. Mark slowly looked up and saw a sales associate peering down at the two of them. He coughed loudly one more time and Mark hurriedly slid off Pat and they both sat up.

"This is a family store, guys," the sales associate said as he shifted his tie and smiled at the onlookers.

Mark stood up from the bed as Pat straightened out her shirt and pressed down her pants. He put his arms around the sales associate and grinned. "We'll take this one," he said, and gave the man a firm slap on the back.

Pat put her hand over her mouth and snickered. "Are you serious?" she said, and bounced up and down on the bed.

"Our daughter's got to have somewhere to sleep," he said as Pat jumped up from the bed and leaped into his arms.

"I love you," she said as she hugged him as tightly as she could. "Aaahhh!"

They picked up Chinese on the way home for dinner and since it was such a beautiful day they changed into their bathing suits and ate outside on the lanai. Mark took a quick dip in the pool as Pat unpacked the food and grabbed a bottle of wine and two glasses from the kitchen. He turned on the Jacuzzi before he sat down and tossed a whole wonton into his mouth. Pat pulled her hair to the top of her head and fastened the bun with the chopsticks, then picked up a fork and ate the Kung Pao chicken right out of the container.

"Mmm," she crooned as she took another forkful and held it out for Mark. "You've got to taste this," she said as he opened his mouth and leaned across the table. "Isn't that good?"

"Mm-hmm," he said, then opened the bottle of wine and filled the glasses. "It's time for a toast." Pat held her glass in the air and waited for Mark to begin. "Here's to you, me, and Tracy," he said as he clinked his glass against Pat's.

Pat sipped her wine, then raised her glass again and cleared her throat. "Here's to you," she said, and looked at Mark longingly.

"To me?" he said and sipped his wine.

"Yes," she said, and set her glass down. "You are so good to me, Mark. I know I've been hard to live with lately, but you stuck in there with me. You never gave up on me. Even when I turned my back on you, you held on. And I just want to say thank you."

"You don't have to thank—"

"Yes I do," she said, and stood up. She walked around the table and sat on his lap. "Thank you for loving me when I didn't deserve it. I promise I will never shut you out again. Ever," she said, and wrapped her arms around his neck. She put her forehead against his and they sat there holding each other, knowing they had gotten through the roughest spot of their relationship and had remained together, still in love, still happy, and still whole. They were a team no man could put asunder and if there was ever a doubt that they'd be together forever, it had been clearly erased.

"You know what?" Pat said as she kissed Mark on the nose and stood up. "I don't think you truly understand how thankful and grateful I am to you."

"I'm your husband," he said, and turned around to watch as Pat walked toward the pool. "You don't have to thank me for sticking by you. I took vows, remember. For better or worse," he said, feeling quite uncomfortable with his wife's apology.

"But I just don't feel right," she said as she stood next to the pool and put her finger to her forehead. "I just feel like there's more I could do to prove to you how much you mean to me."

"Honey, please," Mark said, and stood up frowning and waving his hands in front of him. But when he took a closer look, he dropped his hands and his frown turned into a devilish smirk. "What are you doing?" he asked as Pat reached behind her and unsnapped the top of her bathing suit.

"I've got to come up with a way to really show you how much I appreciate you," she said as she tossed the top of her bikini into the air. It landed on Mark's head, but he didn't bother snatching it down. He just stood there frozen and awestruck. He watched with anticipation as his wife's hands hovered around the top of her bikini bottom. "Maybe I should buy you a present," she said as she slowly eased the bottoms off. "What do you think about that?" she asked as her bottoms fell around her ankles. She stepped out of them with one foot, then used the other to kick them in the air. The bottom landed against Mark's chest. He fumbled them around, but couldn't keep hold of them. He was mesmerized by Pat and she knew it. She had held out on him for so long that seeing her like this made him nervous. In a way he thought the love they'd made last night was just a fluke and that Pat had only allowed it because she felt she owed it to him for arranging the adoption. But now he was sure. He had his wife back. All the way back. And she hadn't lost a bit of her spontaneity or passion.

Pat curled her finger at Mark and watched as he walked toward her. Halfway there, he remembered the bikini top and snatched it off his head. Pat giggled at Mark's awkwardness, knowing she was the cause of it and as he reached her and began to touch her shoulders she pushed him off her and frowned. Mark nearly freaked, wondering what he had done wrong, until he saw a hint of a smile cross Pat's lips. She threw her hands above her head and fell straight back into the pool. Mark wasted no time coming to the edge of the pool and leaning over, preparing to dive in. But Pat stopped him. "You're overdressed for this party," she said as she waded in the water. Mark looked like an anxious undersexed school boy as he hurried out of his trunks and dove in headfirst. He swam toward Pat as she backstroked and caught up with her in the center of the pool. Slowly, they waded into the water, wrapped tantalizingly around each other until they were connected. And as Pat floated aimlessly with her husband inside her, she wondered why in the world she had ever stopped wanting to be with him this way. I must have been crazy, she thought, as she tightened her thighs around his waist and he buried his head between her breasts. This is like candy, Pat thought as her eyes rolled in her head. Just like candy.

Pat smiled as she remembered the night before and walked down the hall to check on Mark. He was still sleeping so she decided to go back downstairs and fix him breakfast. As she headed back to the kitchen, she passed the French doors and looked out at the pool. But this time her thoughts were not on last night. She thought about Tracy and all the wonderful days they would spend together in the backyard and knew that she would have to get a fence installed around the pool for safety. She'd read somewhere that drowning was the number one cause of death for children in the home and figured she'd better get right on the case of finding someone to childproof the pool. But first, there was breakfast. Pat had never been much of a cook. That was Mark's territory. Still, she did the best she could. She pulled out a box of grits, a pack of turkey bacon, and a couple of eggs. Though she sucked as a gourmet, she could read instructions. She scoped out the back of the grits box and did exactly what it said. Then she read the bacon package and decided she'd use the microwave to heat them up. Next she pulled out a skillet and started on the eggs and in no time the kitchen was filled with delicious smells. Pat felt proud of herself as she checked on all her preparations, feeling like a black Julia Child sans the accent. She walked around the center island and decided to use her good china plates that she kept in the curio cabinet in the dining room. But as she headed to get them, her attention was swept away. She looked into the living room and thought about Tracy again. In the corner between the love seat and window where Kunta lay playing with a ball of yarn was a huge space that Pat had planned on filling with a grandfather clock and an array of plants. But as she held up her imaginary lens with her hands and looked through, she thought of a better decoration. "A piano," Pat said as she walked through the living room checking it out from every angle. A piano would make the perfect addition to the home and since Tracy was taking lessons she'd have somewhere to practice all the time. "Yes," Pat said, and clapped her hands. She could just imagine the scene. Christmastime, the piano, Tracy's little body sitting there playing "Jingle Bells." How beautiful it would be. The lights, the tree, the . . . "Oh shit," Pat said as she sniffed the air and spun around. "My eggs," she screamed and ran back to the kitchen and into a cloud of smoke. She turned off the fire underneath the eggs and grabbed a dish towel. Then she saw the grits as they boiled over in their pot and spilled all over the stove. She cut them off, then waved her hands around the room, trying to rid the air of smoke. "Fuck," she huffed as she opened the window and shooed the smoke away. Then she stopped and put her hands on her hips. I'm going to have to watch my language from now on, she thought. There was no way she was going to let Tracy hear her speak that way. Besides, Pat was a Christian and should know better. And furthermore, she thought as she coughed and covered her nose, I'm gonna have to learn how to cook. She and Mark had survived on take-out and his occasional surprise dinners, but that wouldn't do for a child. Pat leaned against the center island and waited for all the smoke to clear out of the room. All the while, she thought of nothing but Tracy. She could picture Tracy running through the house, playing on the grass, in the pool with Mark as he dunked her head under the water for the first time. She could see it all so clearly and the more she could see it, the more she believed it.

Pat sighed as she pushed off the island and looked over at the stove. Everything was a disaster. Since when are eggs supposed to be black, she thought as she picked up the skillet and put it into the sink. She thought she could maybe salvage some of the grits, but what hadn't spilled over onto the stove was stuck to the bottom of the pot. Then Pat remembered the bacon and popped open the microwave. At least it had come out right, she thought as she took out the plate. She decided to make Mark a bowl of cereal to go with the bacon and even though it was an awkward combination, she knew Mark wouldn't complain. It's the effort that counts, right? She pulled out a breakfast tray and set the bowl of cereal and bacon on it with a cup of coffee and headed upstairs. Halfway up, she heard the phone ring out and paused. But there was nothing she could do. Her hands were tied up and by the time she got back down to the kitchen it would probably stop ringing. So she continued up the stairs and when she got to the bedroom she saw that Mark had picked up the phone anyway.

She stood outside the door waiting for him to get off so she could go in and present him with her surprise. But as she stood at the door listening to Mark speak she realized something was wrong. The tone of his voice was too serious. Pat figured it was one of the tenants from Mark's apartment buildings calling to complain about some defect or other. The power breaker went out, the toilet system is backed up — Pat had heard them all. She peeped into the room and caught a glance of Mark leaning over the bed and rubbing his head with the phone clamped between his ear and shoulder. Must be a serious problem, Pat thought as she heard Mark say good-bye and hang up the phone. She waited, giving him a minute to gather himself, then she kicked open the door and stepped in. "Ta-da," she said as she stood in the middle of the floor holding the tray of food. "Breakfast in bed for my wonderful man," she said, smiling from ear to ear. But Mark didn't share in her enthusiasm. She saw the worried look on his face and sucked her teeth. "Problems with one of the apartments?" she said and sighed. "Which one is it this time?"

Mark slowly stood up from the bed and faced Pat. He clasped his hands over his face, then drew them down.

"Oh shit — I mean shucks," Pat said briefly thinking of Tracy and correcting herself. "Is it the building on Termino? I swear, every week those folks have a different electrical problem. It's probably from all those satellite dishes they have on the roof. I'm telling you, Mark. You ought to make those people take those satellites down. If the cable company ever finds out they're gonna come after you."

Mark shut his eyes and waved his hand in front of him. "It's not the apartments," he said and dropped his head.

"Then what is it?" she asked with growing concern.

"It's Tracy."

Pat's eyes fixed on Mark like a hawk's.

"That was John Peters on the phone. He just received word that the Oppenheimers have hired an attorney of their own." Mark paused to steady his trembling voice. "They filed for custody on Monday," he said. He shook his head slowly and ran a hand over his face. "They want to keep Tracy."

Pat didn't know the breakfast tray had slipped out of her hand until she heard it crash to the floor. She couldn't bring herself to speak. She just stood there in shock, shaking her head.

Mark rushed to Pat and grabbed her just as her legs gave out. She fell into his arms, trembling and murmuring, "No."

"It's okay, Pat," Mark said over and over. "We'll get through this. We've got rights," he said as he sat her down on the bed. "But you can't lose it, Pat. If we're gonna fight this thing you've got to stay strong," he stressed. "Pat? Do you hear me?"

She looked at him with watered eyes, but said nothing.

Mark balled his fists as he saw his wife slipping away right before his eyes. He swung his fists in the air and grunted. "Pat," he yelled, and pushed her hard on the shoulders. "You better toughen up, do you hear me?" he said, and pushed her again even harder. "If we have a chance to get Tracy we are gonna have to fight. You can't break down, Pat. Do you hear me?"

Pat bit down hard on her lip and nodded her head. "I hear you," she said, trying to suck back tears. "We've got to fight," she said, and breathed in deeply. "I'm okay. I'm okay . . . I'm okay."

Mark sat down next to her and took her hand in his, hoping that Pat would make it through this ordeal. That was the same hope Pat had as she squeezed his hand. But Pat was confident. She could handle whatever came her way as long as she had her husband beside her. I'm okay, she kept telling herself. I'm okay . . . okay . . . okay.

13

It *was business as usual* at Blessings with just a couple of twists. Zuma had not come in yet, and the usual free-flowing conversations that normally livened the place up were limited to mere pleasantries. Pat, Faye, and Sandy worked quietly at their stations, bothering only to speak with their clients, and even then, it was only to ask pertinent questions like "Do you want a trim today?" or "What color polish would you like?"

The other twist was that the shop was filled with children. Sandy and Faye had no other choice but to bring their children to work with them today. Faye's son sat quietly on the sofa, his hair still an uneven crop of spikes even though Faye had gotten him up early this morning and taken a pair of shears to his head in an effort to try to correct the damage he'd done with her shaver. Sandy's son sat on the floor beside her at the manicure station next to his sister's car seat, which Sandy had used to carry the girl to the shop. The two boys occasionally passed curious glances at one another but neither had the courage to formally introduce himself. Christopher sat with his hands folded neatly in his lap, his mind still lingering over the trauma he'd experienced the day before, and David was too scared to speak. Sandy had smacked him on the back of the head three times as they walked to the shop this morning, warning him that he had better not make a sound or cause any type of disruption — or else.

There were no words spoken between the women except for their initial greetings. Pat hadn't even questioned the fact that both Faye and Sandy had come in with their children. Her mind was too full with the unexpected telephone call that Mark had intercepted this morning. She had wanted to stay home so badly, but Mark insisted that she go to work. He didn't want her loafing around the house, thinking negative thoughts and slipping back into the depression that had plagued her after the last adoption had been fouled up. And Pat didn't want that either. Besides, it wasn't over yet. Mark was going over to John Peters's office this morning to find out exactly what was going on and to plot out their next course of defense. Just because Tracy's foster parents had filed for custody didn't mean a thing, Mark had told her this morning. This was just one little bump in the road, a small hurdle that they would have to climb over. The Oppenheimers had no legal right to Tracy, and just because they filed for custody did not automatically mean that they would get preference over Mark and Pat. Mark had started the adoption process weeks ago, the social worker had given them four stars, and most importantly, Tracy liked them. What it came down to now was which family would be the best family to raise Tracy. And even though the Oppenheimers had done a fantastic job with Tracy so far, Pat knew that she and Mark would make the best parents for her. First of all, they were younger than the Oppenheimers. They had more money than the Oppenheimers. But most important, they were black and the Oppenheimers were not. There was no way Henry and Elizabeth could give Tracy the well-rounded life she deserved. They couldn't teach Tracy about her heritage or her culture or prepare her for the challenges she would face as a black woman growing up in a country that still, after four hundred years, refused to embrace her as one of its own. No, Pat insisted. There was no way a white family had any business raising a black child. Tracy belongs with us, Pat thought to herself as she put the finishing touches on her client's hair and handed her a mirror. She walked to the front of the shop and waited for her client to join her so she could pay the bill, and as she waited she looked out the window hoping to get a glance of Mark. He'd promised her he'd stop by the shop as soon as he finished his meeting with John Peters. She couldn't wait to see Mark. She wanted to let him know that she was not giving up. She'd told him as much this morning before she left, but now that she had more time to think over the situation, she'd felt even more resolved to be strong and fight the good fight. If it was a battle the Oppenheimers wanted, Pat thought as she looked out the window and gritted her teeth, then it was a battle they were going to get.

Faye bent over and rubbed her knee after sewing the last row of hair onto her client's head. She had taken a couple of Tylenols this morning to ward off the aches and pains her body still felt after her knock-down drag-out with her daughter last night. She stood up and began fluffing out her client's shoulder-length weave and caught a glimpse of herself in the mirror. No one had questioned the fact that she was wearing makeup this morning even though she never wore it before. But she had to today. It was the only way she could cover up the bruise on her forehead and save herself from having to explain how it had gotten there. The makeup also did a good job of fading the dark circles that had formed under her eyes from having stayed up all night, hoping Antoinette would come home. The waiting had been hell on Faye. There was nothing she could do. She didn't have the numbers of any of Antoinette's friends so she couldn't even call around to find out where she was. But she knew whom she was with. That damn boy, Shock G, or whatever the heck his name was. But there was no way to find him or her daughter. All Faye could do was wait and hope that her daughter would have enough sense to come back home, but she knew that was a far-off hope. Antoinette did what Antoinette wanted to do and she had made it perfectly clear that what she wanted was to get away from her mother.

Faye glanced over at Christopher and noticed that he hadn't moved an inch since she sat him on the sofa when they came in. She wondered what he was thinking and if he knew exactly what was going on. He hadn't asked any questions about Antoinette, but she knew he was curious. The first thing he did after she woke him up this morning was go to her room. He looked inside, then came right back out and stood in the front room. He didn't say a word until Faye told him he was spending the day at the shop with her until the afternoon when she would take him to see his counselor. And even then all he said was "Okay," then went back to his room to get dressed before Faye started in on his patchy hair. Faye knew it was foolish to think that Christopher wasn't aware of what was going on. Children hear and see everything. But she didn't want him worrying about his sister. He had problems of his own and today she hoped Mr. Watson would be able to get to the bottom of Chris's anger problem, or at least get him to start talking again.

Faye took the money her client offered her plus a ten-dollar tip and said her good-byes as Sandy looked up from the manicure station. Her eyes briefly connected with Faye's but she quickly looked away. Sandy was in no mood to be social. She could barely focus on her client's fingers for thinking about Cerwin and Bronze. Where had they gone? Were they together right now? Would Cerwin come home tonight?

She knew the answer to that last question, which is why even though the situation seemed grave now, she hadn't become frantic. She was certain Cerwin would come home tonight. He always came home. Even after the time she washed all his clothes in bleach because she thought she had found a lipstick smear on his shirt collar. It was the story of their lives. Break up to make up, that's all they did. No matter how bad the fight, Cerwin always came back to her. She was the love of his life and the mother of his children. He wasn't going nowhere, Sandy reassured herself as she swished a final coat of clear polish over her client's hands and tightened the cap back onto the bottle. She directed her client to pay at the front desk and accepted a one-dollar tip, which she stuck into her bra. As she cleaned off the top of her counter, her thoughts naturally crept back to Cerwin and that bitch, Bronze. Sandy's face turned red as she thought about that woman and all the trouble she'd caused in her household. If it hadn't been for her none of this mess would have gotten started in the first place, she told herself as she sat back in her chair and gazed out the window. She wished she could see that tramp again if for no other reason than to spit in her face. Sandy would love to catch Bronze in a dark alley one night. She could just imagine how it would feel to punch her in the face, slam her against the wall, kick her in the stomach, knock her teeth down her throat, beat her . . ."What?" Sandy huffed and turned around to David. "Didn't I tell you not to bother me today?" she whispered as she leaned over him and pointed her finger against his nose.

"But I'm hungry, Mama," David whined, looking up from the floor. "When we gonna eat?"

Sandy spoke softly through clenched jaws, making sure no one could hear her except David. "Didn't I give you a banana before we left home?"

"It was rotten, Mama."

"Shut up," she said, and grabbed the tail of his shirt. "Wasn't nothing wrong with that fruit, boy. You shoulda ate it. Now I don't give a damn if your little ass starves. Just sit there and shut the hell up."

David bowed his head and crossed his legs together tightly as Sandy glared at him until she was completely satisfied that he would not be bothering her again. But just as she turned around, Dalila's voice took flight. Sandy immediately picked her up and shushed her, not wanting her cries to disturb anyone. The clients had all gone, but Sandy was terrified of upsetting Pat and Faye. She hadn't even asked if it was all right to bring her kids to the shop and she didn't want to be a burden to anyone. She bounced Dalila on her knee, then rocked her in her arms. When none of that worked she looked around the car seat for her pacifier. She found it on the floor, picked it up, and slammed it into Dalila's mouth. Her baby quieted down for a while but Sandy knew it was just a matter of time before she began hollering again. It wasn't a pacifier the child needed, it was food. Sandy hadn't had time to prepare her a bottle before she left home and now it was twelve o'clock and the baby had yet to eat. Sandy put Dalila back in her seat and grabbed her purse from beneath the station to see how much money she had to splurge on lunch. Inside the zipper compartment were the two twenty-dollar bills she and Zuma had put up for their friendship bet, but Sandy was not going to touch that money just yet, even though Zuma had conceded defeat. Something inside Sandy told her that she and Zuma could still be friends one day, and by keeping that forty dollars intact she felt she was somehow ensuring that possibility. As for her two hungry kids? Well, they'd just have to make do with the other change Sandy could find in the bottom of her purse. She searched around and found she had only sixty-five cents plus the dollar tip her client had just given her to spend on lunch. She looked toward the back of the shop at the vending machines and figured she could get Dalila an orange soda with seventy-five cents and then she'd have . . . sixty-five, seventy-five, eighty-five . . . ninety cents left. With that she'd buy herself a Snickers bar, she concluded, then she thought about David and knew he'd have his hand out begging once he saw her and Dalila eating. So, she decided she'd split her Snickers with him and let him drink half the soda with Dalila.

When Sandy stood up to go to the vending machine, both Faye and Pat looked her way. There had been no movement in the shop since the customers left and still none of the ladies had said a word to one another. By this time the three were wondering what they'd each done wrong. Is she mad at me? What did I do to her? But still they said nothing. They were all too consumed with their own thoughts and problems, so much so that they didn't even notice Zuma as she stood in the doorway carrying four bags underneath her arms and sporting a smile so bright she could make a blind man squint.

"What's up y'all," she said as everyone turned toward her. She stepped through the door and looked around the place astonished. "Don't tell me you guys have finished with all your morning clients already. It's only twelve o'clock," she said as she bopped over to the reception desk and sat down her aroma-filled bags. "Well, I guess you guys must have been working your asses off," she said as she opened up a bag and pulled out a bucket of chicken. "I tell you one thing. I am star-ving," she said, pulling out another bucket, plus an array of side orders. She hummed a bubbly tune as she finished unpacking the food, then she breezed to the back of the shop and picked up a stack of paper plates and a cup of plastic utensils. "Y'all dig in now. I bought enough for everybody," she said as she returned to the reception desk. She piled her plate high, then paused. "Damn. I forgot the drinks." She snapped her fingers. "Oh well," she said, and reached into her pocket for some change. She counted out three quarters, then turned to walk back to the soda machine. But halfway there she paused. Something was strange here, she thought, and looked around at the ladies. Zuma was all aglow, having just come from her visit at the insemination clinic and knowing that there was a good chance that a little baby was growing inside her. She couldn't have felt better, but her positive energy was not catching on to the other women. No one had uttered a word since she'd come in. She glanced over at Faye and saw her sitting in her chair pretending to read a magazine. She turned to Pat, who sat behind the reception desk, flipping through the appointment book like there was something really interesting in there. Then she briefly looked at Sandy, but she figured she would have an attitude especially after the little argument they'd had the day before. Still, the silence in the room didn't sit well with Zuma. Something was going on here and she just had to find out what it was. "*Hello,*" she said and waved her hands above her head. "Is anybody home?"

Just then Sandy's daughter screamed out and Zuma turned to see the little girl for the first time. She also caught a glimpse of David. She figured the two belonged to Sandy since they were sitting right next to her, but she didn't ask any questions. She watched as Sandy quickly quieted Dalila, then turned around to the other ladies. "Did I miss something?" she said, and spun around, this time catching a glimpse of Christopher as he sat calmly on the sofa. Is this a beauty shop or a preschool, she thought to herself as she smiled at Christopher.

"Pat," Zuma called and walked back to the reception desk. "Is everything all right?"

"Yeah," Pat answered, still flipping through the appointment book. "I thought you were taking the morning off. Your first appointment's not until two."

"I know, but I got finished with my business early so I decided to pick up lunch for everybody," she said and looked over her shoulder. "Faye? I got chicken over here," she said, knowing how Faye could never resist a meal.

"I'm not hungry," she said, not even bothering to lift her head from the magazine.

Now Zuma *knew* something was up. "What about you?" she said as Sandy looked up surprised. "You hungry?"

Sandy shook her head with enough attitude to break it, but Zuma wasn't fazed. She was in too good a mood to let Sandy spoil things for her.

"I am," David shouted and stood to his feet. Sandy gave him such a look that it would have scared him shitless had he been paying her any attention.

"Well, come on over here," she said, jerking her neck. "And who are you?" she asked as she prepared him a plate.

"My name is David," he said, too innocent to hide the fact that he was starving. He licked his lips and bounced up and down until Zuma handed him his plate. "Thank you," he said, grabbing the plate with two hands and eyeing it like it was a prized possession.

"Be careful now," Zuma said, turning him toward the sofa. "You can eat right over here," she said, and helped him to his seat. David wasted no time digging in and all Zuma could think was when was the last time this boy had eaten. She glanced over to Sandy and shook her head, but she didn't say a word. It was none of her business. "Hey Christopher," she said to Faye's son and gave him a noogie on his forehead. "Why you over here being so quiet?"

Christopher shrugged his shoulders and barely looked up at Zuma.

"And what happened to all your hair?" she said, frowning and looking at Faye. But Faye acted like she didn't hear a word. That's none of my business either, Zuma thought, and turned back to Christopher. "Are you hungry?" she asked, but got no response. "Christopher," she said, creeping toward him like a phantom. "Are you hungry?" she said and began to tickle him until he giggled.

Faye looked up when she heard the sound of her son's voice and watched as Zuma fixed him a plate and bought it back to the sofa for him. Faye kept watch of her son as he bit into his chicken and it wasn't long before he had turned to David and gave him a playful sneer. Faye sighed with relief behind her magazine, hoping that his silent spell had faded forever. That was one less problem she had to deal with she thought as she felt her stomach growl under the pressure of the chicken aroma. She wanted so badly to go fix herself a plate but she didn't dare. If she got too close someone might see the bruise on her forehead and start in with the questions. She figured she'd just wait. She had a one o'clock braid wash and after that she would take Chris to see the school psychiatrist.

She could eat then, she figured, wondering if she'd be able to last that long.

After seeing to the kids, Zuma walked back to the reception desk and stood in front of it as she took a bite of her crunchy chicken breast. "So what's up?" she said, eyeing Pat and smacking as she talked. "What's wrong with y'all?"

"Nothing," Pat said innocently.

"Uh-huh," Zuma said, and bit into her chicken again. "I mean look at y'all," she said waving her chicken around. "Did Denzel stand y'all up? I mean, damn. No music's playing, no TV, ain't nobody talking—I mean what's up? Where the party at?"

"We're grown women, Zuma," Pat said, and stood up. "Just because we happen to all want to sit around and be quiet doesn't mean something's wrong with us. We aren't from the hip-hop generation like you. We don't need a lot of loud music in order to *chill.*"

"Ouch," Zuma said sarcastically. "You really hurt my feelings just now. But for your information I will be thirty years old next week."

"Whoopee," Pat said, and turned to look out the window for Mark. She saw no sign of his car and turned back around. "So what do you want for your birthday?"

"Ain't nothing you can get me, girl. I've already given myself the best present I could ever hope to receive."

"And what's that?"

"Damn, I need a soda," Zuma said, clearing her throat and doing an excellent job of dodging the question. "This chicken is really spicy," she said, and headed for the machine. As she passed Sandy she saw a look in her eye that made her heart skip a beat. Sandy knew the present Zuma had given herself, and Zuma prayed she'd keep her mouth shut. Zuma was happy about what she'd done, but she still wasn't ready to tell everybody and she hoped Sandy had enough sense to respect that.

Faye was Zuma's next target and as she walked back to the front she eyed her from head to toe. Who does she think she's fooling, Zuma thought. Since when did Faye pick a boring magazine over chicken. Is the sky orange? Do turtles fly? She set her soda down on the desk and continued eyeing Faye. It took her a while to pick up on it, but she finally noticed she was wearing makeup. "Uh-oh," Zuma said, and grinned. "Do we have a date, Faye?"

Faye peered over her magazine. "What are you talking about?"

"What's with the eye shadow and lipstick, Miss Au Natural?"

Damn, Faye thought as everyone turned to look at her. This had been the very thing she was trying to avoid, but thanks to Zuma . . . "I had a few extra minutes this morning, so I put on a little blush. No big deal," she said, hoping Zuma would drop the subject.

"Looks good, girl," she said, smacking. Just as she was about to grab another piece of chicken she remembered what had happened yesterday. "Oh," Zuma said, and wiped her hands off. "What happened at the school yesterday?" she said, slyly jerking her head toward Christopher.

"Suspended," Faye answered in a whisper.

That perked up Pat. "Suspended?" she said, and put her hand against her chest. "Not little Christopher."

Faye sighed and nodded her head.

"Yeah," Zuma butted in. "He got caught fighting," she said over her shoulder to Pat.

"Well, how long is he out for?" Pat asked with concern.

"A *week*," Faye whispered, checking to see if Christopher knew they were talking about him. But Chris was too busy with his newfound friend David to be in the midst of grown-folk conversation.

"A week," Pat mouthed. "My goodness."

"I know," Faye said, waving a hand like she didn't want to discuss it anymore. "Anyway, I'll be leaving for the next few days around three-thirty so I can take him to see his school's psychiatrist." She saw the ghastly look on everyone's face and waved her hand again. They all knew that meant not to ask any more questions and they didn't. "So if anyone calls for an appointment in the afternoon check with me first."

"Okay," Pat said, the concern she felt still written all over her face.

"Guess I don't have to ask what's bugging Faye anymore," Zuma said, and turned to Pat. "So what's your story?"

"I don't have one," Pat said, and turned her back to Zuma to look out the window.

It was at that moment when Zuma remembered Pat's good news from the day before. "Pat," she screamed so loud Pat jumped and bumped into her chair.

"What?"

"How'd it go yesterday? Did you meet her? Was she cute?"

"Oh yeah," Faye said, livening up for the first time. She put her maga-zine down and leaned forward in her seat. "The adoption. Is everything all right?"

Even Sandy gave a heads up and waited for Pat's response.

Pat swallowed hard and told the absolute truth. "She was beautiful," she said and smiled.

"Oh," Faye said, and put her hand over her mouth. "What's her name?"

"Tracy," Pat said, remembering the exact contour of the little girl's face. "We spent the day together. We had a picnic at the park and . . . and . . ." she said, at a loss for words. "It was just beautiful. What can I say?"

"Bless you," Faye said and clasped her hands together. "Why didn't you say anything earlier?"

Pat fidgeted with her hands and looked down to the floor.

"Uh-oh," Zuma said, now biting into a stem of corn on the cob.

"We ran into a little problem," she said, then paused.

"*Pat?*" Faye questioned and stood up from her seat.

"Spit it out," Zuma said, and dropped her corn.

"The, uh . . . The foster parents filed for custody of Tracy yesterday. They want Tracy to stay with them."

"What!" Zuma hollered as a kernel of corn slipped out of her mouth.

"Oh no," Faye said, and slumped her shoulders.

Pat held a cautionary hand in the air. "Hey," she said abruptly. "It's not over yet. Mark and I are going to fight."

"How?" Zuma asked. "I mean hasn't the girl been living with them for most of her life already?"

"Yes, but foster parents don't get any preferential treatment over adoptive families. It's all gonna come down to which family would make a better home for Tracy."

"Well, who would make better parents than you and Mark?" Faye contended. "You guys are perfect."

"Yeah," Zuma added. Then she saw the uneasy look on Pat's face. "Oh, please don't tell me. It's some rich black doctor and his even richer wife, huh?" she said, sucking her teeth. "I mean, you and Mark do well, but I don't know if you could compete against the Huxtables."

"*Zuma,*" Faye warned.

Pat threw her head back and clenched her teeth. "They aren't even black," she said, and pressed her lips together.

"Oh, hell naw," Zuma said, frowning. "Case closed. A white family can't give that girl what you and Mark can. Shit," she said, then gave a look to the children, hoping they hadn't heard her curse.

"I agree," Pat said, definitively. "That's why we aren't giving up. Tracy belongs to us."

Faye looked at Sandy, hoping she wasn't offended, before she continued. "What does the girl think about all this?"

"I don't know. I don't see her again until tomorrow. This all happened so suddenly."

"She'll want to go with you and Mark," Zuma said picking up her corn again. "I don't care how long she's been living with those white folks, once she's around you and Mark for a while she'll know what time it is."

"I hope so," Pat said, and smiled with confidence as tears began to form in her eyes. They weren't tears of defeat because she knew she and Mark would prevail. They were tears that indicated that she needed the support of her friends.

Faye rushed over to Pat and put her arms around her as Zuma wiped off her hands and reached out to touch her shoulder. Sandy stood up, hesitating.

"I wish you luck," Sandy said from across the room.

"Thank you," Pat said, and as Faye let her go she wiped her eyes and returned to her confident stance. "Thank you all," she said, and nodded. "But I just know every thing is gonna work out fine."

"I'll pray on it," Faye said, grabbing Pat by the shoulders. "God didn't bring you this far to lose."

Zuma added an "Amen" to that, then took a closer look at Faye. "What's that?" she asked, and touched Faye's forehead.

Faye winced and shut her eyes tightly.

"You okay?" Pat asked, eyeing the spot Zuma pointed out. "Goodness, Faye," she said, checking her out more closely. "What happened to you?"

Faye giggled and took a step backward. "Silly me," she said, and fidgeted with her blouse. I was opening the medicine cabinet and wham! I smacked myself right in the face."

"Uh-huh," Zuma said, not believing the hype. "I guess that medicine cabinet must have some long fingernails too," she said, raising an eyebrow.

"What?" Faye asked, and chuckled.

"Your neck is all scratched up," Zuma said, touching the red lines that marred Faye. She traced the marks all the way behind Faye's neck and pulled down her shirt just a tad. "How do you explain this bruise on your back?" she asked like her name was Columbo.

"Get off of me," Faye huffed, and jerked away from Zuma. "This is none of you guys' business," she said, waving a finger between the both of them.

"This is too our business," Pat said, and pulled Faye by the arm. "You're our friend," she said, then let go of her as Faye winced in pain.

Faye grabbed her arm as Pat and Zuma looked on in amazement.

"You tell us what happened right now," Pat ordered, the mother in her coming to the surface. "Were you mugged? Robbed?"

"Raped?" Zuma added.

"No," Faye screamed then quickly lowered her voice. "I, I, uh, I fell. That's all. I just—"

"Do we look like Scooby-Doo and Shaggy to you?" Zuma demanded. "What the fuck happened, Faye? The *truth*."

Faye stuttered around for a few seconds, then knew she had to come clean. Lying was not her forte, and besides, someone must have died recently and named Zuma detective of the decade. "I had a fight."

"A fight?" Pat repeated. "What do you mean you had a fight? With whom?"

"Antoinette."

Pat and Zuma looked at each other and shook their heads.

"You've got to be kidding," Pat said, flustered.

"You let that girl hit you?"

"No Zuma. I didn't let her do anything. It just happened. Things got out of control. . . . I got out of control . . . and—"

"What do you mean you got out of control?" Pat asked.

"I struck her first," she said, and dropped her head. "I slapped her."

"Hallelujah," Zuma said. "It's about time you put your foot down and stopped letting that girl run wild."

"No, Zuma. I was wrong. I should have never hit her. I had no right. She's my daughter, not some punching bag."

"Sometimes you've just got to smack a kid," Zuma said.

Sandy listened from afar and gave a mental thumbs up to that comment. She knew she and Zuma were on the same wavelength.

"You've got to put some kind of fear in them. Let them know who's boss."

"I don't know about all that," Pat said, and shook her head.

"Look," Zuma said, and raised her hands in front of her. "I am in no way talking about child abuse. In fact, after around five or six years old, I don't even think whipping works anymore. All I'm saying is that you've got to discipline your children from the beginning."

"I can get with that," Pat said. "It starts the day you give birth. You have to let them know who's the boss. You can't run to a baby every time she cries. That's when they first learn they can control you. Sometimes you've got to put your foot down and let the child know that they can't have everything they want every time they ask for it. But I don't think you teach that by hitting them, Zuma."

"I ain't talking about hitting no baby, Pat. All I'm saying is this — if you have a crystal bowl on the table and your three-year-old is constantly moving it, even though you've told him fifty million times to leave it alone, then I say it's time to pop him on his little hands. Then if he does it again — you pop him on his butt," she said, and held her hand in the air. "What's wrong with that?"

"Seems to me that if you have a three-year-old you shouldn't have any expensive things lying around where he can get to them. You don't have to hit the child, just move the freaking bowl off the table. What's the problem?" Pat asked sternly.

"The problem is the child needs to be taught to *listen*. I wouldn't be rearranging my whole house for no child."

"You don't have any expensive crystal bowls, Zuma."

"Ha-ha," she said, and gave Pat a wink. "Shut up." She waved her hand in the air. "All I'm trying to say is that a little bit of discipline never hurt nobody."

"If you hit a child you teach that child to hit others. Then before you know it you've got this angry, violent stranger on your hands with no respect for anything or anybody."

"Oh please," Zuma shouted. "Do you think these little bad-ass teenagers just wake up one day during puberty and decide, 'Hey, I'm gonna be a fuck up from now on'?" she asked. "No. They've been fucking up since they were little snot-nosed brats and no one ever took the time to discipline their little asses, and by the time they reach puberty they're straight out of control. I say you've got to smack a child's behind early on. Let 'em know that there are consequences to their actions."

Pat huffed and stuck out her lips. "Beating and discipline are not the same things, Zuma. You don't have to smack a child around to teach them right from wrong. There are other ways to — "

"If you say 'time-out,' I'm going to scream."

That's exactly what Pat was going to suggest, but since she'd been forewarned she decided to pass on the opportunity to rave about the wonders of giving kids time-outs. "I'm surprised at you, Zuma," she said rationally. "Don't you know the whole ritual of black people beating their kids is rooted in slavery?" she asked, and pointed at Zuma. "Black people learned whipping as a form of discipline because the slave owners used to beat them. If they did something wrong, here came Massah with his whip. But Massah didn't beat his own children. No, he considered his kids part of himself, they were *human beings*. But slaves? Slaves were beasts, *creatures*, and deserved to be slapped and whipped. That's where the whole dynamic began," Pat said. "If you beat your kids you're only perpetuating that slave mentality. Your kids are part of you. They aren't animals."

Zuma sucked her teeth, pretending not to care about the knowledge Pat had just dropped on her. But as she stood there thinking, she realized Pat had a point. A damn good point.

"Anyway," Pat continued. "Faye's daughter is fifteen. She ought to know right and wrong by now." Pat turned to Faye.

"Hmm," Zuma huffed, and rolled her eyes. "Have you heard the mouth on that girl? Ooo, child! She called here once for Faye talking about 'Put my mama on the phone,' " she said, faking teenaged rebellion. "Honey, I could tell that girl needed an ass whipping right then and there. She is entirely too damn grown. Whatever happened to 'Hello, how ya doing, may I please speak with my mother?' Whatever happened to *respect?*"

"Faye," Pat said softly, and grabbed her hand. "What did you two fight about?"

"She stayed out too late? Didn't do the dishes? What?" Zuma quipped.

"It doesn't matter," Faye said, and closed her eyes. "The point is that I can't reach that girl anymore. She doesn't listen to a word I say, she just does what she wants to do, goes where she wants to go. . . . I just don't know what to do."

"Send her over to my house for a week," Zuma said. "I'll whip her into shape for you."

"Maybe that's not such a bad idea," Pat said, thinking out loud. "Zuma is young—"

"I'm thirty," she corrected.

"You *act* young, you're hip—she could probably relate to you," she said, and turned to Faye. "Why don't you bring her into the shop and let Zuma talk to her tomorrow? You know, maybe she'll be more apt to open up to someone who's not her mother."

"Yeah," Zuma said, practicing her jab. "Bring her on in here. I'll scare her straight."

"That's not what I mean, Zuma," Pat said. "I mean you should *talk* to her. Be a friend, a confidante."

"I know," she said, and stopped clowning. "Bring her to see me, Faye.

I'll try to talk to her for you. Maybe there's something bothering her that she can't tell you about."

Faye rubbed her hands together and shook her head. "I can't."

"Ah, girl, please. I ain't gonna hurt the child. I was just kidding."

"*I can't.*"

"Why not?" Zuma said, offended. "You don't think I can do it? What? You think I can't handle the responsibility? I mean, what?"

"She's gone," Faye said, unable to hold back the tears. "She ran away last night."

"She what?"

"My goodness," Pat said, and wrapped her arm around Faye as Faye cried. "Do you know where she went? Did she contact you?"

Faye shook her head and grabbed the napkin Zuma held out for her. "I don't know anything except that she's gone. I don't even have any of her friends' numbers. I don't know where to turn."

"What about the police?" Pat asked.

"Gotta be gone forty-eight hours before they get involved," Zuma interrupted. "I learned that from TV."

"Are you sure?"

"She's right," Sandy said as she walked up behind them.

Everyone was shocked to hear her voice.

"And how do you know?" Zuma asked sarcastically.

"I ran away a couple of times before when I was a kid," she said as she stared at Faye. "I'm so sorry," she said, feeling out of place. "What you can do for starters is call her school and see if she attended any of her classes."

"Good idea," Pat said, and sat down behind the reception desk and picked up the white pages from the floor. "She goes to Dorsey, right?"

"Yeah." Faye nodded, then turned back to Sandy when she heard her speaking again.

"Do you know where she hangs out?"

Faye shook her head.

"What about the last names of some of her friends, or her boyfriend."

"Nope. All I know is that her boyfriend's name is Shock G. She never told me anything else about him."

"Damn, Faye," Zuma said. "This is your daughter. You should know this stuff."

"Just shut up, Zuma, all right," she said, trembling. "I know I should know this. I feel like a fool right now. But I don't need you adding to —"

"Ssh," Zuma said, and took her in her arms. "I'm sorry, Faye. I'm sorry.

I was out of line," she said as she rubbed her hand up and down Faye's back. "Don't worry. Everything's gonna be all right."

Pat hung up the phone and sighed. "She didn't show up to school today," she said, and stood up.

"Damn," Zuma said, letting go of Faye.

"So what else can we do?"

"Aside from actually going out in the streets and looking for her," Sandy said, "you can't do nothing. It's a waiting game now."

A silence fell between them as they stood looking at one another, no one knowing exactly what to do. Then, almost as if possessed, Faye spoke. "She's pregnant."

Pat gasped, Sandy lowered her head, and Zuma shut her eyes.

"My baby's having a baby and I don't even know where she is," Faye said, and looked longingly out the window as tears rolled down her cheeks.

"Everything will work out," Sandy said, and gave Faye a hug. For the first time she knew the pain her mother had gone through when she had run away so long ago. She also knew the pain Faye's daughter must have felt. Running away from home wasn't a trivial thing. She knew firsthand that it wasn't something kids did just for the hell of it. Faye's daughter must have been hurting real bad, Sandy thought, and gave Faye a pat on the back. But just as she was about to pull away, Pat joined the embrace, and in another second Zuma had placed her arms around the huddle.

Faye felt a tingle in her stomach as she stood in the arms of all these ladies. And for the first time since her daughter left home, she knew that there would be a calm after the storm.

A tingle also swept across the pit of Sandy's stomach, and though she didn't let on, for the first time she actually felt like one of the crew. She knew she'd probably been included in the huddle just as a courtesy, but still — it felt so good to be in the company of women.

14

At three-thirty, Faye said her good-byes, then grabbed Christopher's hand. As she headed to her car to take her son to his counseling session, she ran into Mark. She threw up her hand as she got in her car and watched Mark go into the shop.

Mark stepped through the door and walked straight over to Pat, who was busy dusting off countertops. When she saw him, she threw down her dust rag and rushed to his side. "Let's talk outside," he said, and waved at Zuma and Sandy as he guided his wife back toward the door.

"Hmmm," Zuma moaned as she watched them walk out, straining her neck to catch a glimpse of their conversation and wishing she had super-sonic hearing. When she finally realized that she was being a bit too nosy she checked herself and sat back in her seat. She looked at the clock on the wall, wondering if her three-thirty appointment was going to show. She hoped she wouldn't since the woman wanted her hair dyed blond, which was one of Zuma's biggest pet peeves. She couldn't understand why black women adored blond hair. Everybody knows it's not natural, she thought, shaking her head. But even black women get caught up trying to chase that white ideal of perfection. She hoped she'd be able to convince the woman to get golden highlights instead, but she knew that was a far-off wish. Once a woman made up her mind on a particular hairstyle it was hard to get her to change it, even when a seasoned hair specialist like Zuma recommended against it. The clients always think they know best, Zuma thought as she sat waiting. But what did she really care anyway. She was getting paid regardless.

Zuma crossed her hand over her stomach, remembering the procedure she'd just gone through hours before. Could it be that she was pregnant right now? Could it be that the baby she'd promised herself by her thirtieth birthday was growing inside her at that very moment? She smiled as she stroked her belly with sweet anticipation, and as she looked up with bubbling eyes, she caught a glimpse of Sandy. She wondered if she should say something to her. She'd been thinking about her all day long, and though she'd blown up at her the day before, she wanted to at least salvage some sort of working relationship with her. Sandy had been nice enough to make the first move, Zuma thought as she watched her sitting at the manicure station with her two children in tow. Maybe it was her turn to make the first move now. She could at least say hello, couldn't she? Nothing's wrong with a little small talk.

Sandy tried to look busy by rearranging the nail polish display. She too was thinking about Zuma and their last conversation, but she wasn't about to say anything to her. She didn't know if Zuma was still tripping off the fact that Sandy had found out about her plan to get artificially inseminated and she didn't want to embarrass herself by talking to her, only to get blown off.

Instead, Sandy looked at her kids and thought about the conversation she'd had with Faye before she left and wondered if Faye had been right.

Sandy remembered the look in Faye's eyes as she walked over and sat down in front of her. She had the most sincere eyes Sandy had ever seen and when she reached out to touch her on the hand Sandy could feel there was something unique about her. She felt a strength from Faye that could not be explained. On the outside Faye looked like an old insecure frump, but when she touched Sandy, she felt a spark. A spark that let her know that Faye was a survivor, and although she appeared timid on the outside, inside she was a warrior. It showed in her eyes, and as Faye spoke Sandy felt a calm that she had never experienced before.

"Thank you for trying to help," Faye had said softly. "I know we haven't had a lot of time to get to know one another, but I hope we get the chance real soon."

"Me too," Sandy said. "I hope your daughter comes back home. The streets are not a safe place for a child to be."

Faye paused for a second, wondering if she should ask the question that was on the tip of her tongue, and when she saw the hopelessness in Sandy's eyes, she knew she had to. "You said you'd run away when you were a child?" she asked. Sandy nodded her head. "Did you ever go back home?"

"I did the first time," Sandy said, and looked down, wondering just how much of her guts she should spill. "I was sixteen when I left for the first time."

"Sixteen?" Faye asked, astonished. "Why, Sandy?" she asked in an almost scolding tone. "What in the world could have been so bad that a sixteen-year-old girl would want to leave home?"

Faye's naïveté amused Sandy. She locked onto Faye's eyes and chuckled. "I got tired of my mom's boyfriend," she said.

The trivial words seemed to arouse anger in Faye. "What kind of excuse is that?" she asked. "You shouldn't have just up and left home because you didn't like some man your mother was seeing."

Sandy chuckled again and leaned closer to Faye with her eyes locked so tightly on her that it made Faye draw back. "It wasn't that I didn't like him," she said almost whimsically. "It was just that I got tired of him creeping into my room at night and sticking his dick in my mouth."

A lump lodged in Faye's throat so quickly that she thought she'd lost her voice. Sandy realized how uncomfortable she was making Faye and sat back in her seat and looked away.

"I didn't stay away long the first time, though," she said, regretfully. "One night sleeping on a bus bench was all I could stand."

"I'm sorry," Faye finally said as her voice came back to her, but Sandy wasn't in the mood for sympathy.

"Don't cry for me, Argentina," she said, and held up a finger as she grinned. She paused before going on and bit down on her lip. "I came back home and stayed until I was seventeen," she said shamefully. "I tried to tell my mother why I'd left, but she'd never hear me out completely. Every time I got to the point about her boyfriend sneaking into my room she'd stop me. 'You're exaggerating. You're making this up,' she'd say. So I stayed until I was seventeen and that was when I left for good. I guess you can't call that running away," she said, and looked back at Faye. "I was grown by then. I could take care of myself."

"So you never went back home? You never saw your mother again?"

"Nope," Sandy said without shame. "My mother probably didn't even miss me," she said with a dollop of raw anger. "I wasn't one of those planned babies, you know. My mother never knew what to do with me, so she did nothing at all. I practically raised myself and there just came a time when I said fuck it. I can't take this no more."

"You don't speak to your mother?" Faye asked, then saw the blank stare form on Sandy's face negating that question. Faye shook her head slowly. "Whatever your mother did or didn't do, I'm sure she loved you, still loves you."

"Yeah," Sandy said, still amused by Faye's naïveté.

They sat together quietly for so long that it became uncomfortable. Sandy wondered if she should have told Faye her story. She wondered what she thought of her now. "Hey," Sandy said, trying to liven things up. "I'm sure you're nothing like my mother. Your daughter will realize soon enough that she needs you. She'll be back."

"I hope so," Faye said, and sighed. "I just don't understand. I do all I can for that girl and she just *refuses* . . ." Faye stopped herself from getting too excited. She took a deep breath and shook her head.

"I know," Sandy said, she too shaking her head. "Kids can get on your nerves," she said, and glanced down at her own two kids. "I swear sometimes I wish I'd never had them."

Faye frowned for a moment, then looked at Sandy with confusion. "What do you mean?"

"I mean I can't stand these damn kids sometimes," she said matter-of-factly. "Girl, I tell you, if I had it my way I woulda had my tubes tied. I know you know what I mean."

"You shouldn't say that, Sandy," Faye said, sounding just like a mother. "Children are the most precious things on earth. When you really think about it, that's what women were put on earth to do — give life."

"Well, I don't know about you, but I know my only purpose in life was not making babies. What about career? What about having time to yourself? What about doing what you love to do? Children take all that away from you."

"See, you're thinking like a nineties woman," Faye said. "I'm thinking like a child of God. Now think, really *think*. There is only one thing that sets women apart from men — our ability to re-create. Why else do you think we have a uterus, Fallopian tubes, and all the rest. God made us to give life. To carry on the generations. That's why we are here. A child is a present to God. It's a gift that says thank you for creating me. What greater gift can you give to Him than a child to carry on His kingdom?"

"Whatever," Sandy said, and glanced at her kids again. She wasn't buying Faye's sermon, but if that theory worked for her who was she to disagree?

"I don't mean to preach," Faye said, and chuckled as she touched Sandy's hand again. "All I know is that no matter what my daughter puts me through, I will always love her. I just hope she knows that," she said, and sighed. "I just hope she comes home."

Sandy leaned forward and rubbed Faye's shoulder. "If I'd had a mother like you I would have never left home."

Faye put her hand on top of Sandy's and smiled. Then she looked at the clock and realized it was time for her and Christopher to go. "We'll talk again soon," she said, and rose up. And as she walked away Sandy watched her, thinking Faye was the wisest woman she'd ever encountered. She wondered if one day she too would be that wise, then shuddered at the thought. To be wise one must go through pain and come out a winner. Sandy didn't see herself as a winner. All she was was an unwed mother of two trying to hold on to her sanity. And with every day that passed she was losing it, one drop at a time.

Zuma checked the clock once again and realized that her three-thirty appointment had stood her up and thought, oh well. Usually when clients pulled a no-show Zuma would get upset. But this time she just leaned back into her seat and put her hand over her stomach. She giggled with the knowledge that mysterious things were going on inside her and sighed delightfully. She thought about all the plans she had to make before her little one's arrival, and that she had only a short time in which to finish up with her business correspondence class, which she approximated would only take her another three months at the most. Then she could dip into the rest of her savings funds and go out scouting for a beauty salon of her own. Her master plan wouldn't be complete until she was fully established and had everything in position to guarantee that she and her baby would have flourishing futures. But all Zuma's contemplation didn't mean she was worried. The only cloud of doubt hanging over her plans was the fact that Zuma knew she would one day have to leave her friends at Blessings behind. Once she opened her own shop, she was sure her clientele would follow, leaving Pat's shop on the brink of bankruptcy, just as it had been before she'd come to work for her. She hated the fact that her growth would hurt Pat, but hey — a girl's gotta do what a girl's gotta do. Zuma's master plan was not constructed out of selfishness. Everything she intended to do was for the good of her baby. She knew Pat would understand that. Zuma had everything under control, and by the time her baby arrived she would be in business for herself and have enough money left over to see her and the baby through for at least three more years. By then her business would have taken off and she and her baby would be living the life. Zuma loved the fact that she could see her future so clearly and positively. She knew exactly where she was going and she wasn't afraid to walk on. But what she loved even more was the fact that she had done it all by herself, and whether she had a girl or a boy, one day she would tell her child about her master plan. She'd teach her child how to make it in the world alone, how to be self-sufficient and make life obey their expectations. She'd teach her child not to depend on anyone but herself, because in the end you is all you really have anyway, she thought as she stroked her belly. She looked into the mirror and wondered how she would look pregnant. She spun her chair to the side and peered at her profile. Gaining weight was of no concern to Zuma. All she hoped was that her nose didn't swell up like a lot of pregnant ladies' she'd seen and that she'd be fortunate enough to keep the stretch marks down to a minimum. She couldn't wait for her breasts to get bigger. The two little sacks that sat on her chest now were of no consequence. But soon, Zuma thought, as she checked out her other profile. Soon I'll have enough boobs to actually fill up a man's mouth. She chuckled to herself, then stopped abruptly as her mind drifted into thoughts of Taj. She hadn't heard from him since he left the shop the day before. She had thought he would try to talk her out of her plans again that night, but her phone hadn't rung once. But that was just like Taj. He talked a big game, but when it came down to it, he really didn't care. Not that she minded. It would have made no difference if Taj had called her, come by her house, or sent a telegram. There was no way she would have let him talk her out of getting artificially inseminated. This was her life, her master plan, and soon she would have the baby she always wanted.

With a rush of what could only be described as nervous exhilaration, Zuma jumped up from her seat. She took a sneak peek outside to Pat and Mark, then headed for the radio. She turned it on and blasted the smooth grooves of Maxwell throughout the shop. "Shouldn't I realize," she sang and pranced about. "You're the highest of the high." She did a little dip and spun around, catching a brief glimpse of Sandy, and when she saw Sandy snapping her fingers and gyrating in her seat, she did a double take. So the girl's got a little funk in her, she thought as Sandy raised her arms into the air and did a move that looked like it came straight off of Soul Train.

Zuma watched for a minute, then decided it was time she said something to Sandy. She was about to be a mother and it was high time she started acting like an adult. Fussing and fighting and holding grudges were the MO of the young. She needed to be more mature now. Not that she had any inklings of turning into an old mother hound like Faye. No, Zuma was going to be a hip and cool mom. One of those moms her child's friends would look up to and say, "You so pretty." Still, Zuma knew she needed to be more mature and for starters she let go of her grudge with Sandy and called a truce. She sidestepped over to Sandy's station and stood next to her, sashaying her hips. "So," she said, popping her fingers. "I see you've got some rhythm."

Sandy looked up at her, pushed her seat back, and stood up with a stone face. She moved to an open space and began turning it out. Zuma watched as she cut moves like she'd never seen before. Sandy had a slinky way of dancing that fascinated Zuma, and as she moved Zuma tried to catch on to what she was doing, but even a soul sister number nine like Zuma was no match for Sandy.

Sandy performed for a good minute until Maxwell's song completed and when she'd had enough she came to a halt and returned to her stone face. She looked at Zuma, rolled her eyes, and sat back down in her chair and looked out the window.

Attitude, Zuma thought and sat down across from Sandy. She couldn't expect Sandy to be nice to her considering the way she'd spoken to her the day before, but she was adamant about making amends. Be mature, Zuma thought, and smiled. *Be mature.* "So," she said, and patted her hands on her knees, "where'd you learn to dance like that?" She cheesed, waiting for an answer, but Sandy played like she didn't even hear her. "Sandy," Zuma called, and snapped her fingers in the air. "Sandy!"

"Oh, are you talking to me?" she said, faking surprise.

Zuma chuckled and nodded her head.

"But I thought you said we weren't friends," Sandy said politely. "That is what you said, isn't it?"

"Let's forget about yesterday," Zuma said quickly. "Today is a new day. How about we start over?"

Sandy raised her eyebrows and shrugged her shoulders.

"So," Zuma started afresh. "Where'd you get the moves?"

"I used to be a dancer," she said abruptly, knowing Zuma was just making small talk. She wasn't the least bit concerned about her dancing.

"That's interesting," Zuma said. "Where did you dance?"

"In L.A."

"Where you a part of a dance troupe?"

"No."

"A theater company?"

"No."

"A music group? Did you dance in videos?" she asked and looked closely at Sandy. "Yeah," she said and squinted. "You do look sort of familiar. Where you in one of Prince's videos?"

"No, Zuma," she huffed. "I was a stripper, okay. You know Big C's on Imperial and Century? That's where I worked, okay. Damn."

"Oh," Zuma said, and gawked.

"And what's that supposed to mean?" she said, taken aback by the look on Zuma's face. "There's nothing wrong with being a stripper, you know. I danced for a living, I didn't sell my body," she said, raising her voice. "And I was damn good at it," she said, and pointed her finger. "Damn good."

"All right," Zuma said, and held up her hands. "Don't get so touchy," she said, and waited for Sandy to calm down a taste. "I can see you were good at it."

"Damn good," Sandy said again.

"What did your man think about you stripping?"

"He owned the place," Sandy said as thoughts of Cerwin slipped into her mind. "Still does."

"So why did you stop?"

"Because of these fucking kids," Sandy said, and looked down at the floor. David was curled up in a ball snoring and Dalila was resting quietly and playing with her toes.

Zuma frowned at the way Sandy referred to her children. When she had told her that she hated her kids she'd thought she was overstating the fact. But the growl on Sandy's face dispelled that assumption. Zuma leaned over to get a better look at the children and snickered. "They're so cute," she cooed as Sandy gave her a look that said, whatever. "So why did you bring them to work with you? Didn't you say you had a baby-sitter?"

Sandy sighed and looked out the window. "I fired her."

"Oh shit," Zuma said. "Was she mistreating the kids?"

"No."

"So why did you fire her?"

"Because I wanted to, all right."

Zuma shrugged her shoulders and decided not to pursue that line of questioning. She remembered how difficult it had been for her to open up about what was going on in her own life, and figured she'd allow Sandy to hold on to her privacy. But as she tried to come up with something else to talk about, she noticed a sign of deep distress on Sandy's face. She wondered if it had to do with the reason why her kids were with her today, but she didn't pry. Still, seeing as how she was turning over a new mature leaf and all, she thought she should at least extend a courtesy. "I'm here if you want to talk about it," she said as sincerely as she could muster.

Sandy sucked her teeth and leaned her head to the side. "Excuse me?"

"I'm just saying," Zuma said, realizing Sandy wasn't taking her seriously. "You've been sitting here all quiet all day long. There must be something bothering you . . . and if you want to talk about it, I'm here."

"Oh sure. Like you really give a damn."

Well, actually, I really don't give a damn, Zuma thought to herself. *I'm just trying to be nice bitch, so don't push it.*

Sandy could tell Zuma was just toying with her and that pissed her off. "Why don't you just leave me alone?"

"What?" Zuma said, and threw her hands in the air. "I'm just trying to be nice. Damn. Can a sister get some credit for trying to be mature?"

Sandy leaned forward abruptly and clenched her teeth as she spoke softly. "The only reason you're in my face trying to be nice is so that I won't slip up and spill your little secret to Pat and Faye. I know where you were this morning. I heard your conversation with Taj yesterday, remember? Well, don't worry honey. I won't tell your business. See, unlike you, I know how to be a true friend."

Zuma leaned forward and whispered, "I'm trying to be nice to you, *girl.*"

"Why?"

"Because I'm trying to make up for the way I acted yesterday. I didn't mean to hurt your feelings or anything. I just got a little pissed and now I'm trying to make up for it."

Sandy paused and looked into Zuma's eyes for a sign of authenticity. She saw many things, but true concern was definitely not one of them. "I don't believe you," she said, and moved backward.

"Then don't believe me," Zuma said, and sat back.

They stared at each other like two stubborn sisters playing I Can Make You Blink First. It annoyed Zuma that Sandy was being so tough. Didn't she know this was my way of apologizing, she thought. It wasn't every day that Zuma put herself on the line like this, but that didn't make Sandy any different. Sandy didn't think Zuma cared about anything, least of all her feelings, and she hadn't the slightest idea why Zuma was putting on this charade. But since she obviously wanted to know so badly she decided to go ahead and tell her.

"I had an argument with my baby's daddy. Okay," she said, and smirked at Zuma. "He walked out on me this morning. Are you happy now? Is that what you wanted to know?"

"So that's the reason you've been sitting over here looking worried all day?"

"I'm not worried about a damn thing. He'll be back," she said confidently. "He always comes back."

Zuma raised her eyebrows as she watched Sandy like a hawk. She could tell that Sandy's confidence was just a put-on. This was much more serious than she was willing to say. "You wanna tell me what you two argued about?"

"No."

"It may help to talk about it, you know."

"What difference does it make?" she said, and jumped when her baby began to cry. "Ssh," Sandy said, leaning over her daughter. She rocked her baby seat with her foot and frowned. "Would you shut up?" she said, overtaken with frustration.

Zuma was no baby expert, but she was sure Sandy's mothering tactics were not right. "Why don't you pick her up?" she asked, and leaned over to get a glimpse of the baby. "Maybe she's hungry or something."

"No she's not," Sandy said as Zuma got up from her seat and walked around to Dalila. Sandy watched as Zuma picked up her child and cradled her in her arms.

"Hey, sweetie," Zuma cooed and began walking around in circles. "Whatsa matter, huh? You hungry? Is the baby hungry?" she said, and cuddled Dalila against her chest until she calmed down. "Where's her milk?" Zuma asked and turned to Sandy.

"Uh, she drank it all."

"Did you drink all the milk, pookie?" she whispered to the baby, and puckered her lips. "Well, where's her food?" she said to Sandy.

Sandy lied again and said she'd eaten it up before Zuma came in, but that didn't go over too well with Zuma.

"So what's she supposed to eat for the rest of the day? It's only four o'clock."

Sandy couldn't come up with a lie to get out of that one, so she said nothing. Zuma stared at her for an instant, then decided to take matters into her own hands. "You wanna walk down to the market with me, pookie? Auntie Zuma will get you something to eat. Yes she will," she said, and rubbed her hand over the baby's stomach. Zuma walked to her hair station and took out her wallet. She didn't say anything to Sandy until she paused for a second and inhaled. "Uh-oh. Somebody's stinky-winky," she said, and crunched her face together. Then she turned to Sandy. "When was the last time you changed her diaper?" she asked, thinking back to when she first walked in the shop at about twelve. It was now four and Zuma could not remember Sandy ever changing the baby. "Sandy?" she questioned as she walked back to her. "When was the last time you changed her diaper?"

"I don't remember," she said, annoyed.

"You don't remember?"

"No, damn it. I don't remember."

Zuma could see Sandy was embarrassed, as she rightly should be. There was no food, no milk, and as she leaned down with Dalila in one arm to check her baby bag, she realized there were no diapers either. She didn't even ask Sandy to explain this, but she couldn't let it go completely. "You know, Sandy," she said as she stood back up. "Just because you are going through tough times with your man does not mean that you can shirk your responsibilities to your children."

Sandy looked at Zuma with eyes that could cut glass. "Who in the hell do you think you are?" she said, trembling with anger. "How dare you talk to me like that. I'm not shirking any of my responsibilities. I take care of my kids, damn it. I am a good mother. I'm just having a bad day."

"So why didn't you ask any of us for help? We look out for one another around here."

"I just forgot, okay. I've got a lot on my mind."

"You never forget your children, Sandy. They always come first. I'm not even a mother and I know that."

"The kids, the kids, the kids," Sandy shouted so loud that David jumped up from the floor where he'd been napping. "What about me? What about what I'm going through?" she said, and balled her fists by her side. "Sometimes I need to come first, damn it."

"Then you never should have had kids," she said definitively. Zuma could see there was no use arguing with Sandy because if this is what she called being a good mother she obviously was mixed up. Even though Sandy was enraged, Zuma felt sorry for her. For the first time she felt that she really did want to be friends with Sandy. Aside from the rage, Sandy was a woman in need and Zuma felt a responsibility to reach out to her. She always believed in the old adage that when you see someone with a hand out you fill it. And although Sandy didn't know it, her hands were out. She was on her knees. She was begging. "I'm gonna run down to the store and pick up some diapers, some milk, and some baby food," she said as she carried Dalila to the door of the shop. "Is there anything else you need?" she asked as Sandy glared at her like a stubborn child. "Sandy," Zuma said softly and directly. "I wanna help."

Sandy glared at her, again searching for a sign of sincerity. But all she could find was blame, accusation, and pity. "No," she said trying to hold on to some semblance of dignity. Not knowing that she had lost all traces of it a long time ago. She bent over abruptly and dug into her purse. "Here," she said as she held out the forty dollars from her bet with Zuma. "I won't be needing this."

Zuma turned away from the door and watched Sandy with eyes that, though not fully knowing, understood her pain. "You keep that," she said, and bounced Dalila. "This one's on me . . . friend." She stared at Sandy for an extra second, then turned towards the door and ran smack into Pat. "I'm going down to the—"

"I heard," Pat said as she gave Zuma a knowing look and moved out of her way. She had heard the last part of the conversation, but she hadn't wanted to butt in.

"Everything go all right with you and Mark?" Zuma asked as she stepped onto the sidewalk.

"I'll tell you about it later," she said and turned her attention to Sandy, who had no idea that Pat was watching her. She watched as Sandy's son rose up from the floor and rubbed his eyes. "Mama," he called as Sandy sat back down at the manicure station trying her best to ignore him. "Mama," he said again and patted her leg. But Sandy didn't respond. Her mind was off in another world. A world where there were no children, where she was the center of attraction and danced around without a care. A world where she had friends, true friends, and a man who adored her. Sandy often drifted into this world. A world where she could not be disturbed, a world where . . . Sandy lifted her hand straight in the air as she heard David calling her name and felt him patting her leg. "Leave me alone," she screamed, preparing to come down on him with a force so hard he'd never forget it. But just as she was about to make contact . . .

"Sandy!" Pat called and stopped her hand in midair.

Sandy slowly turned to face Pat, her hand still hovering above her son's face. What she saw in Pat's eyes shamed her, and slowly, very slowly, she brought her hand down.

15

Faye and Christopher arrived just a tad late to their first appointment with Mr. Watson. They would have been on time, but Faye decided to make a quick stop by her house. Before she walked in the door she stood outside and said a quick prayer, hoping that Antoinette would be inside, but when she opened the door she was sadly disappointed. All was quiet, just the way she'd left it this morning. She walked into Antoinette's room and found it was still a mess. Left-behind clothes still strewn everywhere and a spot of blood on the rug from when they tussled. Faye stood in the room for a while wondering where her daughter could be, imagining her in all sorts of predicaments that sent chills up her legs just to think of them. She thought of her daughter's pregnancy and wondered if she had even been to see a doctor, and with that thought came Faye's first conscious realization that she would soon be a grandmother. A *grandmother*, she thought as a pang ripped her stomach. A thirty-three-year-old grandmother? Faye had once thought she wouldn't reach grandma status until her mid-forties, but Antoinette had rushed her promotion. Antoinette had rushed many things, Faye thought, and as she stood in the room staring at her daughter's things an unsettling thought popped into her mind. Would it be so bad if Antoinette never came home? she thought. It was only too obvious that she could not control her daughter, and even if she did come back home how long would it take for her to revert back into her old sly, sneaky, disrespectful ways? Just how much is a parent supposed to take from their kids? When is enough enough?

Faye put her hands to her face and spun around quickly. She walked out of the room and said three Hail Marys for repentance. She was ashamed of her thoughts and vowed never to let them creep up on her again. No matter what, Antoinette was still her daughter, and until she was a legal full-fledged adult it was her responsibility to do all she could to help that child.

Faye stood in the middle of the hall at a loss until she remembered what she had initially come home to do. She gathered herself, then rushed into the front-room closet and picked out a floppy orange hat to put on her head. It didn't quite match with her sweat pants and shirt, but she had to wear something to cover up the bruise on her forehead. The makeup obviously wasn't enough to fool anybody and she didn't want Mr. Watson asking any probing questions about how the bruise had gotten there. While she was in the house she also put on another coat of lipstick and grabbed a pair of colorful earrings from her rarely used jewelry box. For some reason the thought of seeing Mr. Watson made her want to fix herself up. She didn't know why. She wasn't interested in the man and she was sure he'd never be interested in her, not with an extra hundred pounds riding on her plus two kids she could barely control. Still, she primped and primed and even put on a dabble of baby oil behind her ears and on her wrists. Faye wasn't into expensive perfumes. In fact, the highest-priced perfume she'd ever bought was for $12.95 from Kmart and she ended up giving that to Antoinette, who ended up throwing the cheap shit in the trash. But Faye did love the clean, soft scent of baby oil and often dabbed herself with it on special occasions. She couldn't really consider this occasion special, though. Taking her son to see a psychiatrist was nothing to brag about, she thought as she walked back out of the house and over the lawn to her car, which she had left running.

Faye and Chris were fifteen minutes late to their appointment and as they walked hand in hand up the front steps to the administration building, Faye caught a glimpse of herself in a window and came to a halt. She snatched off the earrings and put them into her purse. "Too gaudy," she mumbled, and resituated her hat on her head. When she was good to go, she and Chris proceeded through the building and the first person they saw was Mr. Watson. He was standing outside his office and watched them as they approached.

"I thought you weren't going to show," he said, and shook Faye's hand. He leaned over in Christopher's face and held up his hand for a high five, which Chris gladly granted. "You all right, little man?" he asked, and in return was given a shy smile.

"Sorry we're late," Faye said, making sure she only gave Mr. Watson a profile look just in case her hat didn't do its trick. "I got tied up at the shop."

"Shop?" he said, and stuck his hands into his pockets. He looked at Faye directly in the face, which made her nervous. She had his full attention, something she rarely got from a man, and she couldn't handle it.

"Yes," she said, and looked down at the floor. "I work at Blessings. The beauty shop over on Centinela."

"I've passed by there a couple times," he said, and nodded. "What do you do?"

"I braid hair mostly. Weaves and such."

"Yeah, the sisters gotta have the weaves," he said, and chuckled.

"Yeah," Faye said, briefly looking at him, then away. She fiddled around with the brim of her hat, then pulled on her sweat shirt. "So, um . . . are we . . ."

"Oh yes," Mr. Watson said, and stood back so Faye and Chris could walk into his office. "I need to have a brief chat with you in the other room," he said just as Faye squatted down above a chair in the corner. She almost lost her balance straightening up and Mr. Watson held out a hand for her. She took it and steadied herself, but Mr. Watson didn't let go. He held her hand and turned to Christopher. "You have a seat right there, little man, and your mother and I will be back in a second."

Mr. Watson walked Faye over to another door and let her hand go to open it. There was a desk with two chairs in front of it and a sofa along the far wall. "Have a seat," he said, and pointed to the sofa, then walked to his desk, grabbed a pad of paper and a pen, and returned to the sofa sitting down right next to Faye in the middle of it. He was very quiet for a while as he scribbled down notes on his pad. Faye watched him out of the corner of her eye feeling so nervous that she didn't know what to do. It was almost as if she were on a date. She couldn't remember the last time she was this close to a man, except for that time she was in the grocery store and bumped into the produce man as she tried to squeeze by him down the aisle to get one of those clear plastic bags. Her nervousness made her feel dumb, though. Why was she getting all riled up by this man she didn't even know? To him, she was probably just another stupid mother who had no idea how to raise her children correctly. A guy like him needed a young girl. Somebody who had a degree in something and a career where she could move up and make lots of money. Mr. Watson needed a cute girl, she thought as she stared at him and pictured him with some model-actress-doctor-lawyer kind of woman. And since she was definitely not that woman she looked away and tried to relax.

"Okay," Mr. Watson said, and stopped writing. He turned to Faye and propped his leg on the sofa. "Did you do your homework assignment?"

Faye looked at him strangely until she remembered what he was talking about. "Oh yes. I had a serious one-on-one talk with Christopher."

"And what did you find out?" he asked, and moved his pen into the ready position.

"He told me about the fight he had yesterday," she said, as Mr. Watson seemed to write down every word she spoke. "It was really silly. The other boy called him some names and Christopher just lost it. I guess the boy had been picking on him awhile because Chris is so small compared to all the rest of the boys in his class, and they just got into it. Actually, I don't think it's very serious," she said, and shrugged her shoulders. "It was just one of those things."

Mr. Watson stopped writing and looked at Faye. "Calling names is not serious, but strangling a kid because of it — now that's serious."

Faye felt a little foolish. She didn't mean to downplay her son's reaction at all. She just meant . . . oh, she didn't know what she meant. She was nervous. All this talking and being alone and sitting so close was getting to her.

"Anyway," she said, trying to seem more concerned. "He did reveal something to me that I wasn't prepared for," she said, looking down at her hands in her lap. "He told me he hated his father."

Mr. Watson swept a straight line across his pad, then stared at Faye while tapping his pen against the side of his face. "Was his father abusive?" he asked as Faye shook her head. "Is he still in the home?"

Faye looked away, still shaking her head. Mr. Watson placed his hand on Faye's hand. "It's okay. You can talk to me."

Faye turned around and looked down at his hand and Mr. Watson, getting the feeling he'd overstepped his bounds, slowly removed it. "Christopher's father is dead," she said calmly and dignified. "He died before Chris was born."

Mr. Watson frowned and scribbled on his pad with fury. When he finished he nodded his head and looked at Faye. "I'll talk to him about that," he said, and flipped his pad shut.

"Oh?" Faye said as Mr. Watson stood up. She wondered if she should get up too and when she saw him walking to the door she did.

"I want to meet with Chris for about thirty minutes alone and then I'll talk to you after the session's over."

"Okay," Faye replied, worried. Although she trusted Mr. Watson, she didn't know if Chris would take to them meeting alone. But when he opened the door and called Chris in she could tell everything was going to be fine. Chris skipped right on in and took a seat and as Faye walked out he waved bye-bye.

"Don't worry. I won't hurt him," Mr. Watson said with a sly grin. He patted Faye on the shoulder, then closed the door.

Faye let out a big sigh as she stood in the middle of the room, confident in the knowledge that her son would be just fine with Mr. Watson. He had a way with people, she thought. She put her hand to her chest and smiled as she thought of him. She felt proud of him. Like he was her son or brother. She hadn't known many men who did what he did — devoted their lives to the betterment of children. She was sure there was some other job he could be performing. He could probably have his own private therapy office somewhere, but instead he chose to work in the school system. How nice, Faye thought, and smiled even bigger. It wasn't until her stomach growled that she recognized how goofy she looked. There she was in an empty room, grinning about the accomplishments of some man she barely knew. "This is ridiculous," she said to herself, and turned around wondering what to do with the next thirty minutes. She decided she had enough time to go out and get a bite to eat and walked out of the office and back to her car.

Food was the only thing that could get Faye's mind off Mr. Watson. When she wasn't fantasizing about men she often thought of food, especially at night when she lay in bed. She'd wonder what she would eat the next day, imagining herself biting into it and experiencing the pleasure a smidgen of salt, a drip of grease, or a sweet nip of sugar would give her. Faye couldn't help thinking about food, the thoughts came automatically. But sometimes when she'd finish a meal she'd catch herself planning ahead to what her next one would be. She hated that. Her food wouldn't even be digested and already she'd be wanting more. When she'd catch herself doing that she'd feel so weak. She hated to admit it but food controlled her. It was her only vice. She used to pride herself on the fact that food was her only crutch. It wasn't destructive like alcohol, cigarettes, and cocaine. But now she had to admit that food wreaked as much havoc on her life as any of those other things, and if there was such a thing as a food addict she was it. But there was nothing she could do about it, except turn in to the Jack-in-the-Box drive-through and feed her habit.

The line was four cars long and as Faye waited she looked ahead to the menu and tried to figure out what she wanted. The grilled sourdough burger was her favorite, but the double fried chicken patty with bacon was pretty good too. She decided to try something new and looked at the advertisement on the store's tinted window, which showed two new items. One was some sort of patty melt thingamajig and the other was a low-calorie chicken pita sandwich, but of course Faye didn't want to have anything to do with that. The line was cut down to three cars and as Faye pulled forward she thought it best she get her money ready. She had thrown her purse over the seat when she got in the car, so she reached her right hand back to get it. Only she couldn't get to it. Faye's body took up every available space on the driver's side of the front seat and she simply had no room to maneuver. She took a deep breath and held in her stomach as she reached for her purse again, but she still couldn't get to it. Finally Faye had to get out of the car, walk all the way around to the back passenger side door, and pick her purse up off the floor. "This is ridiculous," she mumbled in disgust as she walked back to the driver's side. She caught a glimpse of the chicken pita sandwich in the window again and decided right then and there that she would skip the extra calories and fat and opt for the pita. She sat back down and closed the door, disgusted with her big, fat ass . . . and arms, and legs, and neck, and toes, and . . . "There has got to be a better way," she said and looked at the chicken pita sandwich again. As the line was cut down to two cars, Faye moved up and when she turned back to look at the window the sunlight reflected off its tint, brightening the inside of the restaurant just enough for her to see . . . "Oh my Dios," Faye said, adjusting her eyes, trying to make out the figure in the tinted window. "Is that . . . ? Oh my God!" she screamed and turned off her car engine right in the midst of the drive-through. "Thank you, Father," she said as she scrambled out of the car, dragging her purse. She ran as fast as she could to the side door, but it was locked. So she ran on to the front of the restaurant and flung open the door. "Antoinette," she said as she rushed down the aisle. "Oh honey," she said as she reached the order counter and wrapped her arms around the girl.

"Get the fuck off of me," the young hip-hop-influenced girl said as she grabbed her bag of fries and gave a look to her group of friends. "I know she didn't just run up in here grabbing all over me. What the fuck is wrong witchoo?"

This was definitely not her daughter. She had her daughter's nasty disrespectful mouth, but this was certainly not Antoinette. "I'm sorry. I thought you —"

"Yeah, well, you thought wrong. Dumb bitch. Your big ass coulda squashed me to death," she said as her friends rang out in laughter. "Come on, y'all," she said as she eyed Faye and walked over to her friends. "I'm glad we got our food now, 'cause you know it ain't gonna be nothing left after fat-ass gets through in here."

Faye couldn't hide her disappointment, though she tried. Jack in the Box was not the place to break down and cry, but there was no way she could stop the flood. Her tears only brought her more snickers and giggles from the other patrons who sat in the restaurant. Faye walked to the counter and grabbed a napkin out of the dispenser and wiped her eyes. She needed a cup of water to help calm her down and asked the cashier if she would please give her one.

"We can only give out water if you order something," the net-haired girl said with the enthusiasm of a snail.

Faye finished wiping her eyes and decided to go ahead and place her order. She needed food right now more than ever. Whatever mood Faye was going through, whether it be sadness, depression, or even joy, she couldn't get through it without food. This time was no different. And as far as a chicken pita sandwich? *Please.* "Let me have the grilled sourdough bacon burger, a small order of onion rings, a small order of fries, and a strawberry shake," she said, balling up her napkin.

"Okay," the cashier said, pushing buttons on her register. "That will be —"

"Oh yeah," Faye said raising a finger. "And the cup of water . . . and an apple pie."

The cashier blew out hot air and pressed some more buttons. "Your total —"

"And a taco."

The cashier gave Faye a look that equaled that verbalized equivalent of "oink-oink," then punched another button.

"Can I have all this supersized?"

"Supersize is McDonald's. We jumbo size around here."

"Whatever," Faye snapped, completely fed up with this whole experience. She felt like hollering right then and there, but somehow kept her cool.

The cashier paused for a second, making sure the coast was clear, then gave Faye her grand total. Faye dropped a ten on the counter and in no time her food was all set to go. She grabbed her bag quickly, forgetting to even wait for her change or the all-important cup of water. All she wanted to do was get out of that place. Only when she got outside she was destined to catch more hell. Faye had totally forgotten that her car was blocking the drive-through lane and as she walked out the driver of the car behind her got out of his car.

"What the fuck is wrong with you? How you gonna straight block the fucking drive-through?"

"Sorry, sorry," Faye said opening her car door, so flustered that she dropped her keys. "Sorry," she said, and bent over to pick them up, seemingly turning the stomach of the driver behind her, who looked on disgusted by the view he was getting of her butt. She saw the look on his face as she stood up and turned to apologize one more time. But the look in his eyes embarrassed her so much that she just got in her car and closed the door.

Faye sipped on her strawberry shake to no avail as she drove the block and a half back to the school. The darn thing was so thick that when she sucked, the straw thinned out and it took her about fifteen sucks to get her first swallow. The smoothness of the shake calmed her and comforted her, and by the time she parked her car in front of the school she was feeling a bit better. She took out her burger, onion rings, fries, taco, and apple pie and set them on the passenger seat. She always ate all of her fries first no matter what because she hated the way they tasted cold. She sipped on her shake in untimely intervals, then started in on her burger and onion rings. She was completely content as she filled her mouth with the familiar flavors, not even once considering the amount of calories, fat, cholesterol, and all-around bad stuff that she was gorging her body with and she didn't care. All she knew is that the food was serving its purpose. It was keeping her company, soothing her nerves, and making her happy.

Faye coughed a little as a small piece of meat went down the wrong pipe in her throat. When she'd coughed it up she spit it onto a napkin, then leaned out her window and looked into the side view mirror and wiped her mouth. "Oh no," Faye said as she saw Mr. Watson and Chris walking out the school's gate. "No, no, no," she said as she bundled up her burger and threw it back into the bag. She tossed in the apple pie, taco, shake, and onion rings and balled it up. She did not want Mr. Watson to see her stuffing her face, or to know that she had an order of fries *and* onion rings? Oh no! She tossed the bag to the backseat, wiped her face once more, and put on a smile as Mr. Watson and her son approached looking like a duo from one of those sentimental Big Brother commercials.

Christopher waved at Faye as he got in the passenger door and Mr.

Watson walked around the car to her window. He squatted down beside her door and peered inside her window, directly at Faye, as if he was her long-lost lover seeing her for the first time in years. Or at least that was Faye's off-the-wall impression of what was going on. He rubbed his nose and sniffed the air. "You smell McDonald's?"

"No," Faye said, not lying one bit since it really wasn't McDonald's. "So how was the session?" she asked, trying to move as far away from the subject of food as she could.

"Perfect," he said, and pointed across Faye to Chris. "Are we cool, Chris?"

"Sho you right," he responded like a prepubescent Barry White.

Faye watched them laughing together, then laughed herself. It was wonderful seeing her son connect with a man, she thought. Mr. Watson would make an excellent role model for Chris, at least for the next few years that Chris was in elementary school.

"So listen, Faye," Mr. Watson said and when Faye turned to look at him her face landed only inches from his. If a strong gust of wind happened to blow along they'd be kissing. Faye moved back, but not too far, and as Mr. Watson spoke, she focused on his lips. "I want to ask you a question."

She froze when she caught his eye, noticing how frazzled he seemed all of a sudden. There was something major on his mind and all Faye could think about at the moment was that he must have found out something terribly bad about Christopher. "What is it?" she asked, and breathed deeply, waiting for the bad news. *Her son was crazy, had multiple personalities,* she expected him to say—but he said nothing. He looked down at the ground with the most nervous look on his face that Faye had ever seen. "Tell me," she said, full of worry and anticipation.

When Mr. Watson stole his glance from the ground he realized the torture he was putting Faye through. "It doesn't have anything to do with Christopher," he said, but Faye wasn't convinced. She eyed him with curiosity, her eyes begging him to speak on. "Do you . . ." He hesitated and breathed deeply. "Do you think I should cut all my hair off?"

Huh? Faye raised her eyebrows, waiting for him to explain what this had to do with Christopher being nuts. "Do I think you should cut your hair off?"

"Yeah," he said, innocently. "You're a beautician, right?"

"Yes."

"Well, I figured you should know best," he said, then slowly lowered his head before Faye and patted the top of it. "I'm going bald," he said, then looked up. "You think I should just go ahead and cut it all off?"

"Oh Mr. Watson," Faye snickered, and rubbed her chest. "No one can even see that," she said, surprised by his self-consciousness.

"But it really bothers me though, you know?" he said, and winced. "I feel like everybody's always looking at it."

"Well, I never even noticed," she admitted, her words seeming to ease Mr. Watson's anxiety.

"You sure?"

"Yes, I'm sure," she said and giggled.

"So no haircut?"

"No haircut."

Mr. Watson sighed, then chuckled a bit himself, realizing how goofy he must have appeared.

"I'm sorry for laughing," Faye said, and covered her mouth.

"No problem," he replied, then looked at Faye head-on, saying nothing for so long that Faye almost thought he'd gotten a glimpse of the bruise on her face.

"What's the matter?" she asked, fearing the worst.

"Pretty."

"What?"

"You're pretty."

Faye nearly gagged as she felt the blood rush to her brain. "Oh . . . ah . . . oh," she said, and looked away. "I guess I'd better be going," she said, and looked at her son.

"I guess I'll see you tomorrow," he said, smiling from ear to ear.

"Yes," Faye said, and stupidly waved even though Mr. Watson was still right in her face.

He stood up and patted the top of the car and waited for Faye to pull off before he walked back onto the curb. Faye watched him in her rearview mirror as she rolled down to the end of the street.

"Watch out, Mami," Chris shouted, jolting Faye to instantly step on the brakes and throw her right arm across Chris even though he was snug in his seat belt.

"Whoa!" he said as his head tilted forward, then fell back against the seat.

"Oh Dios mio," she said, and looked in her rearview again and found Mr. Watson still standing on the sidewalk. She wondered what he was waiting for as the car in front of her turned right and she rolled into its place. Was he seeing her off? Making sure she started out on her journey safely?

"Mami," Chris said, and patted her on the arm. "You can go now," he said, pointing ahead to the clear street.

"I'm going," she said as she turned on her blinker and rolled ahead slowly. She took one last look in the rearview mirror and saw Mr. Watson waving. He *was* seeing me off, she thought, as she turned into the street. What a gentleman, she thought, and smiled. But as she drove down the street her smile turned into a smirk. He probably does that to all the mothers, she thought, and picked up speed. But even as she dismissed him from her mind, she couldn't help feeling a tingle of joy over the fact that he'd called her pretty. She couldn't remember the last time someone had said something so nice to her. Thank you, Mr. Watson, she said silently to herself and wondered if he had a steady woman in his life. It wasn't that Faye even remotely thought that she had a chance with Mr. Watson or even that she wanted a chance. She knew no man like him would ever go for an overgrown whale such as herself and she was okay with that. She had resolved to be alone for the rest of her life years ago. It was just that Mr. Watson was such a good-looking man that she couldn't help but fantasize about him. She knew they'd never have a relationship, but she also knew that about Denzel, Michael, Wesley, and Prince, but that didn't stop her from fantasizing about them.

It was a game to Faye. A wonderful, harmless game that didn't hurt any-body. She could invite any man she wanted into her life with the simple use of her imagination. She could create any kind of circumstance she wanted. Even give herself a smaller body, which she often did with Denzel and Wesley, but she'd heard Prince liked it kinky so she stayed her normal big self with his fantasies. And now there was another man entering her fantasy world. Mr. Watson, she thought as a smile swept over her face.

"What you laughing 'bout, Ma?" Christopher asked, and looked at her.

Faye just snickered and looked straight ahead. You're too young to know, she thought, and smiled even wider as Prince laid on the hood of the car, gyrating his pelvis. Denzel stood behind him flexing his muscles and Wesley . . .

"Mami," Chris cried out again and Faye slammed on the brakes, com-ing *this* close to running a red light.

"Sorry," she said, and stroked the side of Chris's alarmed face.

"You should pay better attention, Mami," he said like a full-fledged adult.

"Yes sir," she said, and saluted her son. . . . Now if Wesley would only put back on his underwear . . .

"Mami," Chris called to her with a weak voice.

She looked over at him and smiled when his hazel eyes found hers. "I'm sorry I said all that stuff about Papi," he said, softly.

Faye turned and looked straight forward, remembering her son's words, remembering how it hurt her so to hear him say he hated his father.

"Mr. Watson asked me about Papi today," Chris said, looking downward. "I told him I get mad at Papi a lot 'cause he died and now I don't have no papi like the kids be having on TV."

Faye swallowed hard, trying to relieve the lump in her throat.

"But Mr. Watson said that Papi couldn't help it 'cause he had to die. He said he didn't do it on purpose."

"Mr. Watson is right," Faye said, still staring straight ahead.

"I know," he said, and looked out the window. "It still make me mad though 'cause sometimes I really wish I had a papi."

"I know, hijo," Faye said, and reached out for the side of her son's face. "I know."

The light turned green and Faye took off again down the street, still stroking the side of her son's face.

"Mami," he said, and turned to her. "Is Antoinette coming back home?"

Faye looked at him out of the corner of her eye and wondered what to say. She wanted to tell him the truth, but that was something she hadn't found yet. "I don't know, mijo," she said softly. "I hope she does."

"I don't wanna lose Antoinette too," Chris said, then looked away.

"Neither do I," Faye said and gripped the steering wheel tightly. "Neither do I."

16

Pat and Kunta followed behind the deliverymen as they plowed through her home, scraping and scratching everything valuable they got within two feet of. "Watch the . . . lamp," she screamed, but it was too late. The men had already bumped into it and it was on its way to the floor until Mighty Mark stepped in and caught it just before it crashed. Pat let go of her breath as the men apologized and continued on their rampage. She decided to just move out of the way and let them take over. Whatever they broke she'd just have to fix or replace once they were gone.

Mark whipped past Pat, giving her a quick kiss on the cheek as he headed back to the kitchen with his tool belt. He was putting child safety locks on all the cabinets and drawers, and outside in the backyard, there were more workmen setting up a five-foot gate all around the pool. She could hear the sound of their drills and hammers all the way from the living room where she stood quietly with Kunta purring at her heels, and hoped everyone would get through with their projects quickly and get the hell out of her house.

"All done upstairs," one of the deliverymen said as he and his partner came down and passed Pat on their way out. "We're outta here," he said as they walked away, leaving the front double doors wide open.

"Thanks," Pat called to them as she went to the door. She looked down at the dirt they had tracked all over her carpet and slammed both the doors shut. She walked to the closet to get the vacuum, then decided to leave the clean-up work for later. All she wanted to do now was get upstairs and see the finished product. She ran up the staircase and into the spare bedroom and gasped. It was beautiful. The canopy bed set fit the room perfectly, but there was one thing missing. Pat ran out of that room and into her own where she grabbed a huge bag from Macy's, then headed back. She turned the bag upside down and let the packages fall to the floor. She picked up the new pink-and-white sheet set, ripped it open, and put them on the bed. Next was a matching comforter and bed skirt, and last but not least were the matching covered pillows. When she was done she kicked all the plastic coverings out of her way and stood in the doorway for an overall look. "Perfect," she said, and clasped her hands in front of her face. "Tracy is going to love this," she said, and snickered as she looked around the room with dreamy eyes.

She walked over to the bed and sat down with her back against the pillows, fantasizing about the many nights she planned to sit in that exact spot reading Tracy bedtime stories. She couldn't wait to be a full-fledged mother, to have her own daughter to love and cherish and teach. She couldn't imagine anyone not loving the whole experience — except, Pat thought, and frowned as she crossed her legs, Sandy.

Pat hadn't spent much time with Sandy since she'd hired her, and while she seemed to be a great addition to the staff, what Pat experienced with her yesterday was enough to make her wish she'd never hired her. Pat's heart nearly dropped to her stomach when she interrupted Sandy just as she was about to hit her child. All the boy was doing was calling for his mother and for that Sandy was prepared to smack him. That didn't make much sense to Pat. She herself had planned on instilling enough discipline in her child that she would never have to use physical force, which she concluded was nothing more than child abuse pure and simple. But regardless of her views, she could respect the rights of other parents who occasionally spanked their kids in order to get their points across. And Pat was never one to say never. Who knew, there might come a time when the only way for her to reach her child would be with a stiff hand across the butt. Still, there was no excuse for Sandy to hit her son yesterday and Pat had stepped up to let her know that.

"What are you doing?" she screamed as Sandy put her hand down and her little boy backed away from her. Pat rushed over to David as Sandy sat frozen, and placed her hand against his back. "What is it that you want, honey?" she asked the frightened boy.

"I just wanna know where the bafroom is?" he whispered in the tiniest of voices.

"Oh, sweetie," she said, and took him by the hand. "It's right over here," she said, and guided him into the bathroom and closed the door behind him. She then turned to Sandy and waited for an explanation, but Sandy acted as if there was nothing wrong. "Do you always smack him when he wants to ask a question?" Pat asked as she walked over to Sandy.

But Sandy was tired of explaining herself. She'd already been through it with Zuma and Faye and she didn't feel like going through it again. "Look, Pat," she said, and turned around in her seat. "I know you're the boss around here and I respect you for that. But please," she said, and raised a hand. "Please don't tell me how to raise my kids. I've had enough of you guys butting into my business for one day."

"Well, excuse me," Pat said. "I know these are your children, but I will not sit by and watch you abuse them."

"If you think you can do a better job, then you take 'em," Sandy said, fed up to the fullest. She pushed her chair back, stood up, and walked right out of the shop.

Pat stood in the middle of the room in shock. No, she didn't just talk to me like that, she said to herself, and took a deep breath to calm her nerves. Pat felt like firing Sandy right then and there, and if it hadn't been for the conversation she'd heard between Sandy and Zuma just minutes earlier she probably would have done so. But from what she'd heard, Sandy was going through a hard time, so she decided to let that little attitude attack slide.

She walked over to the reception desk and sat down just as Sandy came back through the door.

"I'm sorry," she said, standing in front of the desk and running a hurried hand through her hair. "I didn't mean to blow up like that. It's just that I've got a lot of things on my mind."

Pat leaned back in her chair and smiled at Sandy, hoping to let her know she was not upset with her. Still, she had a point to make. "I don't know if you know this, but the reason I'm trying to adopt is because I've been unable to have children. I'm infertile."

Sandy stared at her with surprise. Not because of the infertility, she couldn't see what was so bad about that. But because of Pat's frankness. She was sure that was something most women wouldn't open up about. Especially not to her.

"I've never been able to have my own kids so I can't say how I would react in certain situations. But I know this," she said, and paused to smile once again so that Sandy would know her words were coming out of concern, not hostility. "You should never hit a child out of anger or frustration."

"I don't abuse my kids!" Sandy said, pleading with her hands.

"Sandy, Sandy," Pat said, and stood up. "Wait a minute. I didn't say that you did, darling."

Sandy huffed and folded her arms across her chest. "Why is everyone attacking me today?"

"Sandy," Pat said, and reached across the desk and placed her hand on her shoulder. "I'm not attacking you. No. I'm not attacking you at all," she said, trying to soothe Sandy, who obviously had been taken through the wringer that day. "Listen to me. I know it's hard being a mother. You have to sacrifice a lot of things, but whatever you do, don't sacrifice your children."

"I don't!"

"Okay," Pat said, and held up her hands. She sat down in her seat and shook her head. What had been meant to be good solid advice was being taken as a putdown, and no matter how nicely Pat spoke her words, Sandy never heard them right.

"I'm sorry," Sandy said again. "I didn't mean to—"

"No, I'm sorry," Pat said softly. "Why don't we forget about this whole conversation."

"Yeah," Sandy said, and looked away. She turned to Pat and opened her mouth once again to apologize, but Pat stopped her.

"Forget about it," Pat said, and watched as Sandy walked back to her manicure station. She kept watch over her out of the corner of her eye and it was plain to see that Sandy was going through something—big time. She could barely keep still in her seat and the look on her face was absolute danger. Her whole body language read Caution: Don't fuck with me. Pat wanted to go over and talk to her some more, but she figured she'd better leave well enough alone. Whatever Sandy was going through was intense and Pat got the overwhelming feeling that she should just mind her own business.

When David came out of the bathroom Pat motioned for him to join her at the reception desk. She didn't want him going over to his mother and risk catching her wrath once again. When David reached her she pulled him up onto her lap. She pulled out a pencil and a scratch piece of paper and slid it in front of him. "Why don't you draw me a picture," she said as his face lit up and a smile filled it.

" 'Kay," he said as he grabbed the pencil and got straight to work.

She looked over his shoulder as he sketched out what could be a mountain, or a ship . . . or a house . . . or something, and she chuckled to herself as he stuck out his tongue and got really caught up in his work.

How cute, Pat thought, and stroked the side of his face. How could anyone be mean to a beautiful child like you, she thought. To Pat, Sandy acted as if she didn't even want kids, and that was a hard one for Pat to comprehend. She couldn't understand the way the world worked. How people like Sandy could be blessed with two lovely children, while people like her, women who would die for the chance to be a mother, were left childless.

But soon Pat wouldn't have to worry about that anymore, because soon she would have a child and she would love her unconditionally forever, she thought, and leaned back into the cushiony softness of Tracy's new pillows. She popped out of her dream state when she heard Mark calling her name. She rushed out of the bedroom to the top of the stairs and looked down at him. "We got a little problem."

That was not what Pat wanted to hear. She had only two hours before she and Mark were to go pick up Tracy for their second day together and she wanted everything to be finished in the house so she could bring Tracy by for a visit and show her her new home. "What, Mr. Fix It?" she asked as she sloughed down the stairs slowly. "I knew we should have had those safety locks installed professionally."

"For your information I'm almost through with my job in the kitchen," he said, tugging at his tool belt with pride. "Actually the problem is with the fence installers."

Pat stopped halfway down the stairs and took a listen. She didn't hear any banging or drills coming from outside. "What happened?"

"They didn't bring enough material to fit all the way around the pool so they had to go back to the warehouse and get more."

Pat sucked her teeth and came all the way down. She walked past Mark and through the kitchen and looked out the window. "Look at my backyard," she said. "The grass is all torn up. Look at this, Mark."

"They'll be back. They're gonna finish everything up today. I told them I'd wait for them."

"But we have to pick up Tracy in a couple hours."

Mark snapped his fingers and slapped his forehead. "What was I thinking?" he said, and paused for a moment. "All right. We'll do this. You go pick up Tracy and take her to the zoo, I'll wait here for the installers to finish and I'll meet you two at Chuck E Cheese afterwards."

"But we were supposed to go *together*."

"Well, what do you want to do?" Mark asked, at a loss.

Pat thought about it for a minute and knew there was no other way. She definitely wanted everything to be perfect when she brought Tracy by later on and Mark's plan was the only way to accomplish that goal. The only thing that worried Pat was having to go pick up Tracy by herself. She didn't know how the Oppenheimers would react. They must have heard the bad news by now and she knew they'd be none too thrilled to see her today. "What about the Oppenheimers?" she said as Mark pulled a screwdriver out of his tool belt and opened the drawer next to the stove.

"What about them?" he said nonchalantly, then looked at Pat. He saw the distress on her face, then put his screwdriver down and walked to her. "Just remember what I told you yesterday," he said, putting his hands on her shoulders. "It's too late. They can't stop us now. The judge held an emergency meeting with the lawyers yesterday evening and he made his ruling. The Oppenheimers waited too late to file for custody. He threw their case out."

"I know, I know," Pat said, and smiled. "Tracy will be able to come live with us next week," she said, astonished. She dropped her head and began giggling like a schoolgirl. She did it for so long that Mark caught the giggle bug too and joined in with her. "Can you believe it?"

"Yes I can," Mark said definitively. "We have a daughter," he said, and pulled Pat to his chest. "We're gonna be parents."

They rocked from side to side in each other's arms until the tears came again. They'd cried all night long, once Pat got home and Mark told her about the judge's ruling. When he had stopped by the shop earlier in the day all he'd said was that the attorneys were meeting with the judge. But she had never thought that his decision would be so quick and in their favor. The wait was over. The years of depression and faking it were over. Their prayers had been answered. All she could do was hold on to Mark last night and cry, and now, they had started up again.

"Okay, okay, okay," Pat said as she pulled away from Mark and wiped her eyes. "We've got to stop all this crying."

Mark chuckled as he snatched a paper towel off its roll and held it over his face. But when the two had wiped their faces and turned to look at each other again — the tears came right back.

∞

Pat's hands trembled on the steering wheel as she made her way to Tracy's house. She'd thought she'd be able to calm her nerves by turning on the radio to 92.3, The Beat, and listening to the hilarious comedy acts of John London and the House Party, but when she tuned in she realized she was too late. The House Party had gone off and the only voice she heard was the deep croon of Theo. She sat and tried to let the smoothness of his voice mellow her out, but just as she began to relax, Theo introduced some song by some new rap group and all at once bass filled the speakers so obnoxiously that she quickly turned the radio off. So much for that, she thought as she gripped the steering wheel and blew out a breath full of anxiety. She was even more nervous today than she had been the first time she'd gone to meet Tracy, because this time she knew that the girl was practically hers. By this time next week Tracy would be living with her, eating with her, sleeping just feet from her. She wished she could take Tracy home forever today, but there were still papers to sign and legalities to get past and, most important, a bond to be made between her and her new daughter.

As she parked in front of the Oppenheimers' house and got out of the car, Pat braced herself. She walked up to the door, took a deep breath, and rang the doorbell. Within a second Mr. Oppenheimer swung the door open and without expression told Pat to come in. She hadn't expected a warm reception, but the chill that Mr. Oppenheimer gave off was almost enough to send Pat running. She stepped through the door and stood beside it as Mr. Oppenheimer closed it and immediately walked away, leaving her alone and wondering what to do. She wrapped her arms across her chest and began pacing the floor until she heard the sound of little feet running from above.

"Hi, Pat," Tracy said as she came to the top of the stairs in a pair of panties with ruffles on the backside and nothing else.

"Hey," Pat said, and waved as Elizabeth came running behind Tracy and grabbed her by the arm.

"You're not finished dressing yet," she told her, and guided her back to her room. "Put on the outfit we picked out and don't forget your shoes," she said, closing the bedroom door. Slowly, she turned around and walked to the top of the staircase. Pat looked up at her and watched her as she walked down, feeling like a lost camper about to be eaten by a bear.

When Elizabeth reached the bottom of the staircase, she held out a hand. "Why don't we go sit down," she said, pointing to a small sitting room to her left.

Pat hesitantly moved toward the dark-colored room with paneling on all four walls. She watched Elizabeth ever so carefully, feeling every ounce of negativity she was giving off. Pat sat in the first chair she saw and Elizabeth followed behind her and took a seat directly across from her. There was a long silence between them as they sat looking in different directions. Pat wished that the woman would say whatever she wanted to say and be done with it. In the end, there was still nothing Elizabeth could do. Her petition for custody had been thrown out. She'd lost. There was nothing she could say that could change that.

Elizabeth slowly turned to look at Pat and Pat, feeling her intensity, looked back at her. Elizabeth scooted to the end of her seat and leaned forward slightly before she spoke. "If you have any decency at all you will back away from this adoption," she said, fighting to keep her lips from trembling.

Pat was stunned. She hadn't expected Elizabeth to say that and it caught her so off guard that she couldn't speak a word.

"Tracy is at home here. She is stable. We love her and she loves us. Why do you want to ruin that? Why do you want to remove her from the environment and the people she has grown to love? The only home she's ever known?"

Pat shifted around in her seat, her shock turning to anger as Elizabeth stared at her with accusing eyes as if she were some thief. "It's time for you to let go," Pat said calmly. "I am not trying to ruin Tracy's life. My husband and I are trying to make it better for her. We love Tracy and —"

"You don't even know Tracy," Elizabeth said, speaking in a low grunt. "You've seen her one time," she said, raising a finger. "One time," she said, pausing to regain her cool. "Henry and I have raised that girl for four years. We've watched her grow, we've been there for her, we've —"

Pat raised her hand and cut Elizabeth off. "Look, I'm not here to argue with you. I won't deny you've done a great job raising Tracy, but you are her foster parents. You knew from day one that you'd never be able to keep Tracy forever. The state says your job is to provide a home for Tracy until a suitable adoptive family can take over. Now I know it's hard for you. Tracy is a beautiful child and I know you've become attached to her. But it's time for you to let go. Mark and I will be her new parents and," Pat said with growing confidence, "we can provide a much better life for Tracy than you and Henry ever could."

"How dare you," Elizabeth said as a look of sheer horror passed over her face. "What exactly is that supposed to mean?"

Pat was getting irritated. She hadn't come here for this and she really didn't want to get into it with the lady. But since she was insisting, she decided to break it down for her. "Tracy needs — no," she said, and shook her head, "she *deserves* to be brought up in a black home. She deserves the right to know her culture, to know who she is and where she came from and to be proud of it all. You can't give her that knowledge, Elizabeth. No matter what, you could never give her that."

"But I can give her love," Elizabeth said, her face turning beet red. "That's the most important thing she needs," she said, and shook her fist. "You talk about her deserving the right to know who she is and where she came from? Well, I know who she is. I know where she came from. When Henry and I first brought Tracy into our home she was a three-month-old premature baby addicted to crack. When she would scream ten hours straight because her body was going through withdrawal, it was me who sat with her through the night," she said, and pounded her fist to her chest. "It was me who stroked her head and her belly and her arms when she laid in her crib starving for another human's touch. At six months she was still too small to be picked up, but I stroked her, I rubbed her, I let her know that she wasn't in this world alone. And when she made it through the hell of her first year and a half on this earth, I was the one who was there to teach her how to crawl, how to walk, how to eat with a spoon. It was my heart that stopped whenever she'd trip or fall or poke herself in the eye, and I was the one who kissed her boo-boos and told her everything would be all right. And when she said Mama for the first time, who do you think she was talking to?" She paused. "She was talking to *me*," she said, and pointed a trembling finger against her chest. "I know who Tracy is," she said as tears piled up in her eyes. "I know what she's been through, not you. And just because you are black does not mean you are a better parent for her. It just means that you are black."

Elizabeth sat back in her seat and put her hands over her face as Pat stared across at her, wondering what to say. She felt for the woman, she really did. But Pat still did not believe Henry and Elizabeth were the best parents for Tracy. She knew in her heart that Tracy belonged with her and there was nothing Elizabeth could say that would change her mind. And Pat knew that there was nothing she could say to take away the pain Elizabeth felt knowing she would soon have to give Tracy up. Pat decided to just drop the subject. There was no sense in going around and around with this. But Elizabeth wasn't quite finished.

She jumped out of her seat and walked over to the bookcase against the window. She snatched down five or six books, then managed them in her hand as she walked back to her seat. "You think just because I'm white, I can't teach Tracy about her culture?" She held up the first two thick books in her hand, then dropped them to the floor and grabbed the next two off her lap. Pat couldn't read the entire titles of the books because Elizabeth moved them too fast. But from what she could tell they were all about black history and culture. "I can teach Tracy everything she needs to know," Elizabeth said, and held up the last two books.

"Look at these books," Pat said, and scoffed. "They're thick as dictionaries. Tracy's too young to read those."

"They aren't for Tracy," she said, and leaned forward. "They're for me. I know that I don't know all there is to know about what it means to be black, but I'm willing to learn. When Tracy gets old enough to start asking questions I want to be prepared. These are the sacrifices I'm willing to make. I want Tracy to know about her culture and I want to be the one to teach her her beautiful background."

"There are some things you can't learn from a book. You've got to live them."

"You think you know so much." Elizabeth grinned. "Well, tell me this. Where were you when King marched on Washington?" she said with intensity. "Well, I was there. Marching with him. I was there holding my banner, marching with the man. Oh, I've lived the life, honey," she said with pride. "What about you?"

Pat squirmed around in her chair feeling as if she were being attacked by a pack of wild dogs. She had obviously underestimated Elizabeth, but she wasn't giving up. She had waited too long to find Tracy, had suffered too much, and she wasn't going to let this woman kill her dream. "If you wanted Tracy so badly, why didn't you file for custody of her a long time ago?"

"Because I didn't know I had to," she said, shaking her hands. "When Henry and I filed to be foster parents we were retired. We didn't know all the legalities of the situation. All we knew is that we had extra time on our hands and we wanted to do something useful with it. Then Tracy was sent to us and all our attention was focused on helping her to survive. They gave us Tracy because they didn't expect her to live. And when she did live through her first couple of years, nobody was interested in adopting her because of all the health problems she was going through because she was born addicted to crack. Then after she passed three nobody wanted her because she was too old. We just thought . . . it just never crossed our minds that someone like you would ever come along and try to take her away from us."

"I'm not—" Pat started to raise her voice, but stopped when she heard the rumblings on the stairs.

"Hi, Pat," Tracy said as she ran in the room and jumped on her lap. "Where are we going today?"

"To the zoo," she said, and gave Tracy a huge hug. Funny, Pat thought. If Tracy loved Elizabeth so much, why didn't she run to her first?

"Let's go, let's go," she said, jumping down and pulling Pat by the hand.

Pat stood up and as Tracy led her out of the room she looked over her shoulder at Elizabeth. She smirked with pride at the way Tracy took to her, and all Elizabeth could do was sit and stare.

Elizabeth followed them to the door and watched as Tracy and Pat walked hand in hand to the car. But suddenly, Tracy stopped. She shook her hand free from Pat and left her standing on the sidewalk as she ran back to the door and balanced herself on tiptoes. "Give me a kiss, Mama," she said, and puckered her lips.

Elizabeth briefly looked over to Pat, then bent over and gave Tracy a kiss.

"Love you, Mama," Tracy said as she turned around and ran to Pat's car.

"I love you too, Tracy," Elizabeth said as she waved.

Pat took one more look at Elizabeth before she closed her front door. Someday, Tracy will say that to me, she thought as she unlocked the car door for Tracy and helped her inside. Someday, Pat thought as she walked around to the driver's side. Someday.

The zoo was . . . eventful to say the least. Pat had never run so much in her entire life. She and Tracy saw absolutely every single solitary animal there was to be seen, and Pat could prove it by the corns she felt growing on her swelling toes. But while it may have been exhausting for her, it was a wondrous time for Tracy. She was amazed at all the animals and the flowers and pretty green grass and when it came time for the park to close it was hard getting her out of there. She kept running back to get one last look at the polar bears, then it was the elephants, then it was the zebra. But once Pat finally got Tracy out of there and back to the car, all the energy she'd exerted throughout the day caught up to her and she passed out practically as soon as she hit the seat.

As they left the park, Pat wondered if she should skip taking Tracy to Chuck E Cheese, but she knew Mark would be there waiting for her. They'd planned to meet up at six o'clock and it was a quarter till already.

So Pat kept her promise and drove to the pizza parlor and as soon as she woke Tracy up, the little tike was ready to roll. She jumped out of the car and ran across the parking lot, nearly scaring Pat to death. Luckily there were no moving cars around, but Pat made a note right then and there always to grab Tracy's hand until they were safely inside wherever they were going.

Mark was standing at the front entrance and when Tracy ran up, she stopped and bugged her eyes. She wasn't sure if it was the man she'd met two days ago until Mark spoke out. "Tracy," he said and held out his arms.

"Mark," she shouted and ran to him. "Hi, Mark," she said as he kissed her cheek.

"Where's Pat?" he asked just as Pat walked through the door.

"She got away from me," she said, smiling, and gave Mark a hug. Then she bent over and turned Tracy around to face her. "Remember to always wait for me, okay," she said and wiggled Tracy's hips from side to side. "Always grab my hand, okay. I don't want you to get hit by a car or anything like that. Can you remember that?"

Tracy nodded her head, looking like she was really trying to remember what Pat had just said. "Come on." Pat smiled as she stood back up. "It's pizza time!"

"Pizza time!" Tracy shouted, and jumped up and down.

They walked to the counter and as Pat ordered the pizza Tracy looked around and saw the balloon cave. She patted her tiny hand against Pat's behind and looked up at her. "Can I?" she said, and pointed in the direction of the balloons.

"Come on," Mark said, and took her hand. "I'll take you." He walked off with an ecstatic Tracy in tow.

Pat finished ordering, then went to pick out a table near the playpen where Mark and Tracy were. She sat down and slipped out of her shoes and rubbed her hot feet as she looked at the two of them having fun. Pat's feet hurt like hell, but she didn't care. It was a small price to pay for making Tracy happy.

By the time the pizza was served at their table Tracy and Mark had had enough of the balloon pit and came back to join Pat. But after only a slice and a half of pizza Tracy was begging to go play again. Mark took her over to the ball bounce area, which was right in front of their table, then came back to join Pat. He sat down next to her and gave her a kiss on the mouth. "So how did things go today?" he asked, wiping a bit of sauce off her cheek.

"The zoo was great," she said, and put her foot in her chair. "My foot may not agree," she said as Mark took it in his hand. "But it was great. Tracy had a ball."

Mark rubbed Pat's foot as she shook crushed peppers over her third slice of pizza. "How did it go with Elizabeth and Henry?"

"Just as I suspected," she said, and took a bite. "Elizabeth went on and on about how badly she wanted to keep Tracy and how evil we were for tearing their precious family apart," she said, and shook her head. "I tell you, I'll be so glad when this whole thing is over."

Mark tapped Pat on her other leg and motioned for her to give him her other foot. He took it and massaged it as Pat continued.

"I really feel for her, you know. She did raise Tracy and she did a hell of a job at it. She went through a lot of ups and downs with Tracy's health and all and we've got to give her credit for that. But we are adopting Tracy now. It's time for her to back off."

"She'll get used to the idea soon enough," he said, looking over his shoulder to make sure Tracy was still in her spot. "I'd probably have a rough time giving her up too if I was in their position."

"You're right," Pat said, and discarded the crust of her pizza slice.

"Well, the house is in perfect condition," Mark announced. "The fence is up, the safety locks are on all the cabinets and drawers, and I even cleaned up."

"Thank you, sweetie," she said, and leaned over for a kiss.

"But there's another thing I was thinking about today."

"What's that?"

"Well, Tracy is coming to live with us permanently next week, but we haven't worked out any of the loose ends."

"Like what?"

"Like are you going to continue working?"

Pat nearly gagged as she bit into another slice of pizza. Her eyes widened as she turned to Mark and dropped her slice. "I haven't even thought about that," she said, wiping her hands on a napkin and thinking in gasping silence until she came up with her answer. "Well, there's no question about it," she said, shaking her head having come to a quick and unquestionable conclusion. "I'll just quit."

"Quit?" Mark jerked his head. "But I thought you loved working there."

"I do, but nothing compares to Tracy," she said, straining her neck to check on her. "Besides, I've been missing a lot of work lately and nothing's gone wrong yet. The other ladies will just have to take up the slack until I can find a replacement."

"And who's gonna keep the books?"

"I can still do that," she said, nodding as she thought. "I can come in a couple times a week and keep track of the books. Besides, we're all friends. I can trust Zuma and Faye."

"Who's the new girl I saw in there the other day?"

"Oh, that's Sandy," she said, and paused. "I didn't tell you about her?" she asked. Mark shook his head. "Well, she came in and asked for a job and I gave it to her. And apparently she's been working out really well. But I'm still gonna have to keep my eye on her."

"Problems?"

"No, not with work anyway. It's just that she brought her kids to the shop, which I had no problem with," she said, and placed her hand over her chest. "But I don't know. I just get the feeling something's not right between her and her kids."

"Like what?"

"I don't know," she said, and waved her hand in the air to dismiss the subject. "I haven't even spent that much time with the woman yet. I'm probably just overreacting," she said, and gazed off into thoughts of Sandy and her kids until she heard the sweet sound of Tracy's voice.

She giggled as she ran back to the table and jumped up and down in front of it for no other apparent reason than because she was happy. Mark and Pat looked at each other and started laughing, then Mark stood up and made an announcement. "I've got a surprise for you," he said to Tracy, who immediately screamed out "Yay!"

"It's time to go home, ladies," he said, and picked Tracy up as Pat tried to squeeze her swollen feet back into her shoes.

Tracy squirmed out of Mark's arms and ran all the way to the exit and out the door, but this time she waited patiently on the steps until Mark and Pat caught up with her. She held out her hand for Pat and Mark took the other and walked them back to Pat's car. "I'll follow you guys," he said, and left to go get his own car.

In no time they were back at the house. Pat and Tracy walked to the front door as Mark pulled up and rolled down his window. "Wait," he yelled as he turned off his car and got out. "Let's go around back first."

Pat figured he wanted to show Tracy the pool and as they walked around the side of the house she ran up to the gate. "Water," she screamed, and looked up at Mark. "I wanna get in the water."

"It's too cold right now," he told her. "But one day real soon I'll take you for a swim. How about that?"

Pat looked around the yard, amazed. The grass was all cleaned up and the fence around the pool fit perfectly. "Well, I'm certainly surprised." She walked behind Mark to give him a hug.

"The surprise is not over," he said, and took both his ladies' hands and led them to the back door.

Pat looked at Mark suspiciously, trying to figure out what else he had in store for them. As they walked in through the kitchen, she checked the safety locks on the cabinets and drawers. But that wasn't the surprise Mark had in store either.

"Close your eyes," he said to Tracy and Pat as he grabbed their hands and pulled them along. He guided them to the living room, making sure their eyes were closed, then suddenly yelled out, "Surprise."

Pat opened her eyes and gasped. Tracy stood squeezing her eyes together and said, "Can I open 'em yet?"

"Yes you can," Mark said as she peeled her eyes apart.

"*Piano*," Tracy screamed and ran to it. She sat down on the black leather seat as Pat stood against the wall, still in shock.

"Oh, Mark," she said with tears in her eyes. She hadn't even told him that she wanted to get a piano for Tracy and couldn't believe that he'd gone and done this all by himself. "It's lovely," she said, eyeing the huge black instrument. "I love it," she said as he took her in his arms.

"I think our daughter does too," he said as they both looked at Tracy.

"I can play 'Twinkle, Twinkle, Little Star,' " she informed Pat and Mark as she placed her hands on the keys. They walked over to her as she began to play. She started off slowly, then started over again. It was the oddest rendition of "Twinkle, Twinkle" they'd ever heard, but as long as it was their daughter who was playing it, it sounded beautiful.

Pat and Mark sat on either side of Tracy as she banged out the off-key song with delight and when it was over, they both applauded, then wrapped their arms around Tracy.

Tears spilled out of Pat's eyes as she held her daughter and thought how absolutely perfect this all was. Once more she had been struck with the unbelievable knowledge that she was going to be a mother, and as Tracy placed her fingers on the keys to play the song again, she looked over at Mark, who was already looking at her. He leaned behind Tracy and wiped the tears off Pat's face. "I love you," she said, and pressed her lips together to keep from breaking down.

"I love the both of you."

17

Sandy sat on the sofa with the phone on her lap. It had been seven whole days since Cerwin had left. Seven whole nights she'd slept alone in their bed. For the first couple of days, she didn't even sweat it. She kept telling herself Cerwin would be home. But on the third day she received a letter in the mail. It was addressed to David and Dalila Sloan. Inside was a couple hundred dollars and a note that read: "For my children, Love Daddy." Sandy had flipped the note over, turned it upside down, even held it to the light. But there was no mention of her. No *I love you*, no *I miss you*, no *I'll be home soon* — no nothing. That note pissed Sandy off. She would have preferred never hearing from him again to being sent this note that totally ignored and disregarded her. To Sandy it seemed Cerwin didn't give a damn about her. All he cared about were his kids. But didn't he realize that she was the one who carried those kids for nine months? Didn't he understand that it was she who was taking care of the kids all by herself now that he was gone? "What about me?" she screamed as she tore the note up into tiny pieces. Didn't she count for anything?

She bundled the pieces of paper in her hand and picked up the phone and dialed the club. It was ten o'clock at night, but when the phone picked up and she said her name and asked for Cerwin she was told he wasn't in. "Bullshit," Sandy screamed. She was no fool. She knew Cerwin was there and she cursed and bitched and hollered until he came to the phone.

"What is it, Sandy?" he said in an irritated and rushed voice.

Sandy was silent for a second. She knew Cerwin was still upset with her and she with him, but the sound of his voice, the sound she hadn't heard in days, was like music to her ears and she paused for a second to enjoy it. But only for a second. "You trying to dodge me, Cerwin? You got people screening your calls now? What? You're too busy to talk to me? *Sandy?* The mother of your kids?"

"What do you want, Sandy?"

"Why haven't you called me?" she screamed.

"I don't have anything to say to you right now," he said with such coolness that Sandy was taken aback.

His calm only served to heighten Sandy's anger and anxiety. If he had raised his voice, or told her to fuck off or kiss his ass, she would have been satisfied. But the coolness with which he spoke gave Sandy the feeling that he cared so little about her that she wasn't even worth arguing with. Oh yes, Sandy was pissed and she let Cerwin know it. It was motherfucker this, motherfucker that, you're a loser, you're an asshole, fuck you, I don't give a fuck, bastard this, bastard that . . . until, that is, Sandy heard the click. "Cerwin?" she called into the dead phone. "Cerwin!"

She slammed the phone down, then picked it right back up. "Hang up on me? Hang up on me?" she said as she dialed the club again and as soon as the line picked up . . . "Don't you ever hang the fucking phone —" Click. "Hello . . . Hello . . . Motherfucker," she screamed, and slammed the phone down. Again she picked it up and dialed and again the line was answered, then immediately disconnected. She played this scene out three or four more times until she finally gave up. She slammed the phone down for the last time and began pacing the floor, calling Cerwin every name she could think of plus a couple that she made up like bastardbitchfuckerhead.

But all Sandy's ranting and raving did nothing to soothe the rising tension she felt creeping through every inch of her body. "I have to see him," she said to herself as she stopped pacing, then walked back to her bedroom and pulled out a jacket from the closet. She picked up her purse off the bed and searched it for money. Cerwin had taken the car and the only way she could get to him was by bus. When she saw she didn't have any change, she left her bedroom and went back to the front where she picked up one of the hundred-dollar bills Cerwin had sent with his note. And with that she was out the door.

She didn't stop for a second to think about her kids. They were the last and least things on her mind. She just walked out the door, locked it, and went on about her business. This wasn't the first time Sandy had left her kids home alone. Ever since the last time she'd taken them to work and everyone at the shop had taken it upon themselves to rake her over the coals about how she was such a bad mother, Sandy had been leaving her kids home during the day while she went off to her job. The girls at the shop had all asked her where her kids were, but she just told them that she'd paid one of the neighbors on her street to baby-sit them during the day. Pat was the only one to question her story, asking how she'd come up with the money to hire a sitter. But Sandy covered her lie well. She told her the lady watching them was an elderly woman who loved kids and only charged her ten dollars a week since she was already keeping a couple of her own grandchildren as well. That had been enough to shut Pat up, but Sandy would have conjured up any kind of lie to cover her tracks. She refused to bring her children to work with her anymore. She was tired of answering everyone's questions, hearing Faye talk about how children were gifts to God and hearing Zuma scold her because she didn't bring enough diapers or hearing Pat go off on her because she raised her hand to her child. They were all so concerned about her kids, so worried about how she was raising them. But what about her? What about what she was going through? What about the fact that she was doing it all by herself? The fact that she didn't have a man and was going crazy because she couldn't stand sleeping alone? Going crazy with worry because she didn't know who Cerwin was with or what he was doing or when — if ever — he'd be coming home. Someone was always interested in the kids, but never her, so Sandy just left them at home every day. She'd put a new diaper on Dalila before she left for work and put two bottles in her crib. One with water, one with milk. For David she'd leave a carton of milk and a box of cereal on the kitchen table and warn him over and over never to open the front door. And that was that. She'd go off to work and lock the kids in the house just like she did this night, the night she went down to the club to confront Cerwin.

She wrapped her arms around herself as she fought off the cold and headed to the bus stop. But first she stopped at the liquor store to break the hundred-dollar bill so she'd have change. She picked up a bag of chips, but put them down. She wasn't hungry, hadn't had an appetite since Cerwin had left her. She wasn't thirsty either, but she had to buy something to break the bill. So, she figured she'd go ahead and grab a box of cigarettes. She hadn't smoked since before her children were born — Cerwin wouldn't allow it. "Secondhand smoke kills," he'd say like some damn scientist. But she needed something to calm her nerves and a good drag on a cigarette would surely do that. She asked the guy behind the counter for a pack of Marlboros and handed him the hundred-dollar bill. When he said that he didn't have enough change to break it, she almost lost her cool, but somehow she was able to control herself. She batted her eyes and smiled as the man looked at her and ran a hand over his balding head. "Please," she cooed, and shook her long blond hair as the man licked his lips and grinned.

"Oh all right." He opened his register and gave her ninety-six dollars plus two dollars in change.

"Thank you, sweetie," she said, and blew him a kiss as she grabbed her money and headed for the door.

"You'll come back sometimes, won't ya?" His eyes followed behind her.

"Certainly," she said, and threw up her hand. "Dumb bastard," she said once she was finally out of earshot. Men were so easy, she thought as she opened up her pack of cigarettes and stood at the bus stop behind the bench. "Throw a little pussy their way and you can have anything," she mumbled with a cigarette flapping between her lips. She lit her stick, inhaled deeply, then took the cigarette out her mouth. She didn't even exhale that first time, just let the smoke roam through her mouth and down her throat, closing her eyes and feeling it as it made its way through her body. When she opened her eyes, she saw the bus coming from two blocks away. She took another puff on her cigarette, then stamped it out under her feet. As she reached in her purse for the change an idea popped into her head. She thought back to the liquor store and how she was able to defeat the old man with a whiff of femme fatale and decided that would be how she'd get Cerwin back. She wouldn't argue, she wouldn't scream, she'd simply do what she did best. She be the young girl Cerwin fell in love with all over again. The young girl who'd walked into his club so many years ago and swept him off his feet. Oh no, she thought as the bus reached her and its doors came flapping open. I will not be sleeping alone tonight.

The club was only about a mile and a half away, but it took two buses to get there because of the way the streets intertwined at the ending of LaBrea. But when Sandy stepped off the last bus the only thing she had on her mind was Cerwin. She walked down the extra block to the club and walked right inside. She knew what she was going to do. She had it all planned out.

The inside of the club looked very different with all the renovations

Cerwin had performed. The new carpet was a rich shade of mahogany and the walls a tad lighter. Still, it was a seedy place. No amount of remodeling could change that. A strip joint was a strip joint was a strip joint, she concluded as she gazed about the room of desperate, horny men. She took off her coat and laid it in a chair next to the entrance, then searched through the crowded club full of men and caught a glimpse of Cerwin behind the bar. He looked beautiful to her. His long curly hair swept down his back, his beard still full and furry, his stomach still hanging just over the rim of his pants. That's my man, Sandy thought to herself, almost unable to take her eyes off him. But there'd be time for gazing later. Right now she had to do what she had to do.

Sandy crept around the far end of the club behind the patrons and made her way to the side of the stage without being noticed. The deejay was blasting that old seventies jam "She Works Hard for the Money" by Donna Summer and onstage was a girl Sandy had never seen before. She was all decked out in see-through bell bottoms and stilettos and her bare breasts, what there was of them, jiggled up and down as she shook her shoulders and pranced around the stage. She was definitely working hard for her money, Sandy thought. Too bad she was about to be fired.

No one even noticed when Sandy climbed up on the stage. She stood outside the spotlight by the red velvet curtain, watching the bare-breasted dancer, and as the lady twirled over to where she stood, Sandy grabbed her by the arm, spun her around, and pushed her through the curtains to the backstage as the woman yelled out, "Hey . . . What the hell?"

Sandy quickly turned around as the spotlight illuminated her. She could hear the murmurs rushing through the crowd as she stood frozen for a moment on the stage where she had once felt most comfortable. But now Sandy felt awkward. It had been so long since she'd been in front of a crowd, so long since she had been the center of attention with all eyes on her. It wasn't until someone in the crowd recognized her and called out her name that she began to feel at ease.

"It's White Chocolate," the man in the front row shouted out and clapped his hands.

"She's back," another screamed and stood up to pump his fist in the air.

There were a few more murmurs as the audience caught on to what was happening and soon it was back to old times. Sandy recognized some of the faces of the regulars as they all stood to their feet, chanting her name. And even the faces that weren't familiar got caught in the whirlwind of excitement and began calling out for Sandy to put on a show. And she did.

She blew the audience a kiss, then turned her back to them and paused. Slowly, she looked over her shoulder, blew another kiss, threw up her arms, and kicked out her leg. She turned her back to them again, swirled her hips from side to side, then bent over and looked at them upside down through the part in her legs. The audience was going crazy. Sandy could feel their heat, their passion, their intensity, and she gave it right back to them. She tumbled down to the floor, rolled over, and crawled across the stage like a slithering snake. When she reached the edge of the stage, she stood to her feet, and as the music pumped and the crowd screamed for more, she remembered why she was here in the first place. She looked over to the bar area as she held out her arms and rolled her stomach. All of this was for Cerwin, and when she saw him looking at her she smiled, put her hands on her shirt, and ripped it clear off her body. Remember this, Cerwin? she thought as she spread her legs and gyrated her pelvis. *Remember this?*

She turned away from Cerwin and sashayed over to one of the men crowded around the stage. She bent over in his face as she unsnapped her bra and snatched it off, releasing her breast right in front of his nose. She wanted Cerwin to see this. She wanted him to know how it would feel to see her with another man. She hoped he was jealous. She hoped seeing her again, this way, would make him want her. Make him come back home. But just as she was preparing to slip out of her pants, the music shut off. Sandy looked over to the bar for Cerwin, but he wasn't there anymore. The crowd began hissing, shouting out, "What's wrong. Turn the fucking music back on." And Sandy, not knowing what was happening, searched through the crowd for Cerwin, barely able to see through the spotlight that shone directly in her face. She put back on her bra amid protests from the audience and snatched her shirt out of the hands of one of the men in the front row. As she threw her shirt over her shoulders and continued looking for a sign of Cerwin, she nearly jumped off balance when she felt a tap at her back. She turned around and had to search no longer. Cerwin was right behind her, staring her in the face.

"Hello, Sandy," he said politely. "May I speak to you in private?"

Sandy's initial shock was swept away when she saw the soft look in Cerwin's eyes. Got to you, didn't I, Sandy thought, and put on a sly grin. She had known Cerwin wouldn't be able to take seeing her again and now that he had he was begging to come back. *May I speak to you in private?* You mean, *Can I kiss your feet and come back home because I can't stand living without you,* Sandy thought as she nodded her head. Cerwin took her by the hand and led her backstage as the patrons booed and hissed. "We want White Chocolate," they screamed as Sandy waved over her head, then disappeared through the velvet curtains.

When the girls backstage saw Sandy they freaked. Her old dance buddies came running to her and engulfed her in a group hug. "Where've you been?" her old friend Silky Smooth asked. But just as Sandy was about to respond, Cerwin cleared his throat and spoke up.

"Cinderella," he said as a new girl Sandy had never seen before stood up in a see-through lace gown with a crown on her head. "You're on next," he said as the girl nodded and headed to the stage entrance.

Cute gimmick, Sandy thought as she watched the girl wait by the curtains until whispy fairy-tale-sounding music came on and she dashed onto the stage.

"Listen up," Cerwin said to the other girls. "I need you all to clear out of here for a few minutes. I need to talk to Sandy alone."

Her old friends groaned at Cerwin's announcement but they didn't protest. When Big C gave a command, his girls obeyed.

Sandy gave a few of her friends pecks on the cheek as they all walked out through the side exit, leaving Sandy and Cerwin alone. She was so glad to be alone with Cerwin, to have him all to herself for the first time in what seemed like months. And it was apparent that her little scheme to show Cerwin what he was missing had worked. Cerwin was calm and polite and when he looked at Sandy she could tell he was getting that old feeling again. He motioned for Sandy to sit down and she did. She figured Cerwin was going to give her some long-drawn-out speech about how wrong he was to have left her and how grateful he would be if she'd take him back. But Sandy didn't want to put Cerwin through all that. The truth was that she missed him just as much as he missed her. She hadn't come all the way down here by bus to beat around the bush. She wanted her man back, no apologies were needed.

"Don't say a word," Sandy said as Cerwin stood before her preparing to speak. "I know what you're going to say, honey. We've both been fools. But it's time to put all that behind us. I love you just as much as you love me, baby. There's no need to apologize, just come on home, Big C."

Cerwin stared at Sandy, then dropped his head. "I can't."

"I love you, the kids love . . ." Wait a minute, Sandy thought, and frowned. "What did you say?"

"I can't come home. I'm not coming home."

Sandy just knew she wasn't hearing what she was hearing. She almost felt like pinching herself or slapping herself to make sure this was all real.

But when she looked into Cerwin's eyes, she knew. He was serious. "What do you mean you're not coming home, Cerwin?" she said as her voice began to rise. "What about us? What about all the years we've been together? Everything we've gone through together?"

"It's because of all those years and everything that we've been through that I can't come home, Sandy. We're no good together. All we do is fight and I'm sick of it. I'm getting old, Sandy. I can't deal with all the games you play anymore."

"Games?" Sandy screamed, then quickly stopped herself. No, she couldn't get upset. Cerwin was tired of the fighting and she would prove to him that she could be different. "Okay," she said calmly. "I'll change. No more fighting and screaming and throwing things. I promise, Cerwin. Just come home. Everything will be different."

"That's what you said the last four or five times, Sandy. Nothing's changed. You can't change," he said, and turned his back on her for a moment. When he faced her again she could see that his eyes were watery and that was enough to convince her that he still loved her.

"Look at you, Cerwin," she cooed, and puckered her lips. "You don't mean what you're saying. You're still just a little upset with me." She stood up. She walked close to him and put her hands on his chest. "Please, baby. Come home, I'll make you forget all about this," she purred as she rubbed his chest, then locked her arms around his neck and squeezed him tightly. She kissed his cheek and swept her lips over his face to his mouth.

But as she pressed her lips to his, Cerwin reached behind his head and grabbed her wrists. He took them from his neck and held them in front of him. "It's over, Sandy," he said and stroked her hands. "It's over."

Sandy snatched her hands away and gritted her teeth. "That's it?" she snapped.

"That's it, Sandy."

"Well, fuck you, Cerwin," she yelled as he stood before her shaking his head, making her feel worthless. "Where is she?" she said, and looked around the room. "Where is that bitch?"

"Who?" Cerwin asked, and held out his hands.

"That damn Bronze. She's the reason you're leaving me. I know it."

"I haven't seen her in a week. I told you there was nothing going on between me and her."

"You're lying. I know you're seeing her."

"You see what I mean?" he said, and pointed his finger at her. "You're so jealous. You're always accusing me of being with other women, but it isn't about another woman. It never was."

Sandy couldn't believe that. There had to be someone else. Why else would he leave her?

"I can't take this anymore," he said, and sighed. "You're just going to have to accept the fact that we can't be together."

"No," Sandy screamed as she turned around and kicked over the chair she'd been sitting in. "You can't do this. What about me? What about the kids?"

"I will take care of my kids, always. And as soon as I get myself situated in a new place, we'll work out a schedule so they can come stay with me for a while."

"Hell no," Sandy yelled. "The only way you'll see your kids again is over my dead body," she said, hoping against all hope that this threat would frighten Cerwin so much that he'd reconsider. But it didn't work.

"I will see my children," he said boldly.

"No you won't. I'll move away," she said quickly. "I'll pack up the kids and we'll move so far you'll never find us."

"We will see about that," he said as if he could see straight through her threat. As if he wasn't the least bit worried about what Sandy claimed she'd do. "Now if you'll excuse me," he said with a politeness that only served to piss Sandy off. "I've got to get back to work."

That's it? Sandy thought as she stood watching him walk away. It's over, just like that? How could this be? How could he do this to her after all they'd been through? When she loved him and needed him so much? Suddenly Sandy realized that she meant nothing to Cerwin anymore, and as he disappeared from the room, leaving her all by herself, a rage took over Sandy unlike any other she'd ever experienced before. The knowledge that she was once again on her own, by herself, without anyone else to depend on was setting in and she couldn't handle it. She responded in the only way she knew how, the way that was most comfortable.

She ran out the backstage area into the club. She spotted Cerwin through the crowd as he was walking back to the bar and caught up with him. She grabbed him by the arm and spun him around. "You don't want me anymore?" She slapped his face. "You think you can just leave me like this?" She slapped him again, so hard that the sound turned the heads of the patrons at the bar. Cerwin cowered, trying to block her hands, but they just kept coming. Sandy knew he wouldn't strike her in front of all these people, and when he stepped back to get away from her, she lunged at him, swinging her arms at every part of his body. Cerwin yelled for help, but none of the drinkers at the bar stepped in, and Sandy's rage continued as she picked up a bottle of Courvoisier and slammed it against the bar, breaking it in two. She held the broken glass in her hand and swung toward Cerwin. But from out of nowhere Sandy was stopped. A hand so big and so forceful caught hold of her arm and forced the bottle out of it.

It was Tucker the bouncer who picked Sandy up as she kicked and screamed. He held her up as Cerwin swallowed hard and shouted, "Get her out of here."

Tucker carried the frantic Sandy out the front door and put her down on the ground. Still she was kicking and screaming, but when she lunged at Tucker he pushed her backward so hard that she fell to the ground. He looked at her to make sure she was all right, then opened the door to the club. "Go home, Sandy," he said, looking at her like she was a pitiful excuse for a human being. He walked back into the club leaving Sandy as she scrambled to get up from the ground.

She had been humiliated like never before, and although she wanted so badly to go back inside, she didn't. For minutes she stood solitary and motionless in front of the club's door, wondering what, where, when . . . how. Then, reluctantly, she walked down the block to the bus stop and sat down. Okay, Cerwin, she thought as she tried to regain her composure. "This means war."

Sandy lit a cigarette as she continued sitting on the sofa with the phone on her lap. She had been smoking constantly ever since that night she'd gone down to the club and it seemed smoking was her only salvation. She inhaled deeply and looked down at the phone. She checked the phone's plug to make sure it was connected, then picked up to listen to the dial tone. It was working all right, but it hadn't rung ever since she set it on her lap. She was waiting for a call from Cerwin and she knew sooner or later, the phone would ring. Since that night at the club she had been calling him incessantly, leaving messages for him that he never returned. But tonight was different. When she got home from work she'd had her son call down to the club. She dialed the phone for him and told him exactly what to say and for once the little silly boy had done a good job. She handed him the phone knowing Tucker would answer like always and when he did David did exactly as told.

"Can I speak to my daddy, please?" he'd asked in the precise tone Sandy had instructed him to use. Sandy huddled next to David so she could hear every word Tucker said.

"Is this little David?" he asked.

"Uh-huh."

"Hey, partner. How ya doing?"

For a second there David looked rattled, but Sandy helped him out by mouthing the word *fine*, and soon David recovered. "Fine," he squeaked out. "Can I speak to my daddy?"

"Sorry, partner, but your dad's not in right now. How about I have him call you back a little later?"

This pissed Sandy off. Tucker had been telling her the same thing for days, but this time she believed him. Tucker wouldn't lie to a kid. Sandy nodded her head at David and he said, "Okay. Can you . . . I mean, please tell my daddy to please call me please, okay."

"All right, little partner," Tucker said. "Bye-bye now."

"Bye-bye," David said as Sandy took the phone from him and hung it up. "Did I do it right, Mama?" he asked, jumping up and down.

"Yeah," Sandy said as she sat on the sofa and put the phone on her lap.

"*All right*," David said, and threw his fists in the air. He jumped on the sofa and sat right next to Sandy. He was so used to getting into trouble with his mom that he couldn't believe he had pleased her. He sat dangling his legs off the edge of the sofa as he watched his mom light up a cigarette. "What's that, Mama?" he asked, fascinated by the white smoke that blew from her mouth.

But Sandy didn't answer. Her mind was elsewhere. All she could think about was hearing Cerwin's voice on the other end of the phone when he called. Ever since the day she'd gotten booted from the club her mind had been ticking on a plan to get even with Cerwin and tonight when he called she'd put her plan into action. She figured her first tactic at getting back at him hadn't worked since she hadn't heard anything back from the state licensing department. A couple of days ago she had made an anonymous call to them and told them that Cerwin's club was operating under a suspended liquor license. They swore they'd check it out and shut down the club if they found any violations, but she guessed they saw through her little charade. She didn't know if Cerwin had renewed his liquor license or not. She was just hoping to cause trouble for him. But it obviously didn't work. Tonight, however, she was working on another plan. She didn't know exactly what she would say to him when he called, but all she needed was to get him to the house. Although he said he'd never come back, Sandy figured she could change his mind if she told him that one of his kids was sick. It seemed they were the only ones Cerwin cared about and if it took using them to get Cerwin back home then that's what she'd do. Sandy's only concern was getting even with Cerwin and she'd do whatever she had to do to achieve that end. "I'll get you, Big C," she whispered to herself as ugly thoughts of Cerwin danced around her brain. It wasn't until she heard her son coughing that she allowed herself to think of anything else. She looked over at David and almost lost her mind. There he was, nearly gagging to death with a lit cigarette in his hand.

"What the hell are you doing?" she screamed, snatching the cigarette from his hand and smacking him on the face. "You don't play with these," she said, picking up her pack of cigarettes and matches off the sofa and setting them on the coffee table. She stood up and yanked David up with her and pushed him toward the back of the house as he continued to cough and gag. "Take your ass to sleep," she screamed and watched him as he slowly walked off, holding his stomach. "I better not ever catch you messing with these cigarettes again," she yelled as he scurried off down the hallway.

"Stupid boy," she said and sat back down, replacing the phone on her lap. She couldn't take her eyes off him for a minute without him getting into something. There was no way Sandy was going to raise those two kids all on her own. No way. Cerwin had to come back, she thought as she checked to make sure the phone was still working again. "Come on, Cerwin. Call," she mumbled as she laid her head back on the cushions.

When the phone rang out her heart stopped. She stamped out her cigarette in the ashtray on the coffee table and took a deep breath. She lifted the phone to her ear, and . . . "Hello," she said smoothly.

"Hey, Sandy. It's Pat."

Fuck! "Hi, Pat," she said as she banged her fist on the arm of the sofa. "Is there a problem?"

"No," Pat said, and laughed. "I just needed to talk to you away from work."

Oh shit, Sandy thought as her mind began replaying the past week at work, trying to pinpoint if she'd done anything wrong. The last thing she needed was to lose her job right now. "What's wrong?" she asked timidly.

"Nothing," Pat said and laughed again. "I just wanted to tell you about the birthday party we're planning for Zuma at the shop this Sunday."

"Oh," Sandy said, and relaxed.

"I didn't want to say anything at work because Zuma hears everything. She must have supersonic reception or something," she said and chuckled. "Anyway, I figured we'd have it Sunday since the shop is closed. Faye's handling all the decorations and getting the cake, so all you have to do is show up with your party shoes on."

Sandy didn't know if she was in the mood to party, especially with all she'd been going through with Cerwin. But she did need a break, so she agreed to show up Sunday night.

"Oh yeah. You can bring your kids," Pat added at the last minute. "Faye's bringing her son and of course you know I'll have custody of my daughter by that time, so it's going to be one big family affair."

"Sure," Sandy said, and frowned, knowing there was no way in hell she was bringing her kids. Sure, she'd show up, but the kids would have to stay right here at home by themselves like they'd been doing all week long. This would be the first night in months, no, *years*, that Sandy had out and she wasn't going to spoil it for herself by dragging along her two brats.

"Okay," Pat said. "I'll see you at work tomorrow. And remember, not a word of this to Zuma. We want her to be surprised."

"See you tomorrow, Pat," Sandy said, then hung up the phone.

She thought about Zuma and her artificial insemination and wondered if she actually knew if she was pregnant or not. She hadn't said anything about it at work since the day she'd gone down and had the procedure. But knowing Zuma, Sandy thought, she was probably just waiting for the right time to spill her secret. As a matter of fact, she wouldn't be shocked if right after Zuma walked into her party and everyone yelled surprise, she'd yell surprise right back and tell everyone she was pregnant.

Sandy had never told Zuma this, but she didn't agree with her getting artificially inseminated. Not because it was morally wrong or anything, but because she knew how it was to be a mother and it was no joyride. Zuma was setting herself up for disaster, but Sandy knew that telling Zuma that wouldn't make a difference. She'd just have to find that out the hard way, Sandy thought as she reached for her pack of cigarettes and matches.

But just as she was about to light up, the phone rang out again. She could feel in her heart that it was Cerwin this time and when she picked up the phone she learned she was right.

"Put my son on," he said without so much as a hello.

Sandy inhaled deeply, preparing herself for the lie she was about to tell. "I can't."

"Damn it," he shouted. "I said put my son on the phone!"

"He's sick," she shouted back. "He can barely walk. I don't know what's wrong with him," she said, making her voice quiver.

"Oh shit," Cerwin said and paused. "Did you take him to the doctor?"

"How am I supposed to do that without a car, Cerwin?"

"Hold on," he said, and put the phone down. Sandy wondered if her little plan was working out. She knew Cerwin would run in an instant once he heard something was the matter with his precious children. He got back on the phone and said, "Tucker says David sounded just fine when he talked to him earlier."

"Fuck Tucker. This is your son. He's sick, Cerwin. He needs to go to the hospital."

"Okay, okay," he said, sounding worried. "I'll be right over," he said quickly. "But I swear, Sandy, this had better not be another one of your silly games."

"It's not," she said as sincerely as she could muster. "Just hurry. I'm really concerned about him."

"Okay," he said, and hung up the phone.

"Dumb fucker," Sandy mumbled as she put down the phone. She knew that would get him over here, but when he arrived she would make him sorry he ever messed with her.

She got up from the sofa and ran to the bathroom. She looked at herself in the full-length mirror and wondered what exactly she should do. Then she pulled up the sleeve on her shirt, braced herself, and ran straight backward into the wall. She clenched her teeth when she made contact, then slowly walked back to the mirror. She looked at her pale white arm and could see the bruising already beginning. Next she walked over to the door and grabbed hold of the knob and tugged it as hard as she could against her left thigh. She doubled over from the pain, but quickly recovered. She lifted up her mini skirt for a look and saw a huge red circle forming. Tears began to well up in her eyes from the pain, but she could take it. She looked into the mirror. "I'm gonna get you, Cerwin," she said as she looked at her face. The bruises on her body would probably be enough to convince the police that Cerwin attacked her, but she wanted more visible proof. Then again, she thought as she examined her face, she didn't want to do anything to it that would last too long. Giving herself a black eye would take too long to recover from. So instead she bit down on the side of her lip so hard that she could barely stand it and after about thirty seconds, she drew blood.

"Perfect," she said as the blood ran down her lips onto her face. There'd be no way Cerwin could talk himself out of this once the police got a good look at her. Finally she took the sleeve of her shirt and ripped it halfway off, then once again looked at herself in the full-length mirror. She rumpled her hair for a bit of added drama, then turned the light off in the bathroom and walked back to the front of the house.

She knelt down on the sofa and peered out the window, waiting for a glimpse of Cerwin's car. She pulled the phone next to her, just waiting to see his face, and when she did she would pick up the phone and call the police. "Leaving me is not so easy, Cerwin," she mumbled to herself as she waited. And when she heard the engine of a car pulling up outside her house, her heart began to race. She placed one hand on the phone and with the other she pulled the curtain back to get a glimpse of Cerwin's face. But the man she saw getting out of the car was not Cerwin. She frowned as she looked closer, recognizing the tall, muscular man, and shouted, "No!"

The man she saw walking across her grass was Tucker and as he reached the steps, she jumped off the sofa and ran to the door and flung it open. "Where is Cerwin?" she demanded, looking through the screen door past Tucker to see if Cerwin was out there hiding somewhere.

"He sent me," Tucker said as he opened the screen and stood face-to-face with Sandy. "I'm gonna pick up David and take him to the hospital. Cerwin's already on his way there."

"What?" Sandy screamed, realizing that her plan had been foiled and wondering how she was going to get out of all this. "Wait a minute," she said as Tucker barged past her and looked around the front room.

"Where's David?" he said, turning a critical eye on Sandy, then stopped abruptly. "What the hell happened to your mouth?" he said, and winced.

Sandy licked her lip and wiped the blood off her face. "Nothing," she said, fumbling around for an excuse.

Tucker shrugged and looked around the room again. "Where's David?" he said and began walking to the back of the house.

"Wait!" Sandy screamed running behind him, but she wasn't quick enough to stop him before he opened up the bedroom door and saw David sleeping peacefully in his twin bed next to his sister's crib.

Tucker gave Sandy a suspicious look, then walked over to the side of David's bed and shook him. "Hey little guy," he said as David opened his eyes. "You sick, partner?"

David sat up groggy from sleep and barely able to keep his head straight.

Sandy nodded her head furiously at David behind Tucker's back, hoping her son would catch her message and say the right thing. But this time she wasn't so lucky. David rubbed his eyes and looked directly at Tucker and said, "Unh-uh."

Shit.

"Go back to sleep, partner," Tucker told David as he smoothed the covers over him and patted him on the head.

Tucker turned around and walked right past Sandy and out of the room. She hoped he'd just leave, but when she followed him back to the front he stopped at the door. "Cerwin figured this was just another one of your games." He put his hand on the screen door. "I'll be sure to tell him he was right," he said, and walked out.

"Be sure to tell him to kiss my ass," Sandy screamed after him. "It's not over," she said, and kicked the screen door. "You tell Cerwin, it's not over."

Tucker paid Sandy no mind until he got halfway across the lawn. "By the way," he said, and turned around. "You wouldn't happen to have had anything to do with the state licensing department showing up at the club the other day, would you?"

Sandy glared at Tucker and winced as a bolt of pain struck her where she'd banged herself up earlier.

"Well, just so you know, that little scheme didn't work either. Cerwin keeps all his licenses up to date," he said, and headed for his car again. "Give it up, Sandy," he said as he opened his door and got inside.

"Fuck you," Sandy hollered as she watched him drive off. She slammed the door shut and threw herself on the sofa. "Damn you, Cerwin," she screamed, and snatched up another cigarette. "Damn you to hell."

18

Faye sat in the last row of St. Xavier's Cathedral, listening to the silence, trying to avoid the thoughts that bombarded her mind. She had come to the cathedral to pray and confess, but now that she was here all she wanted to do was rest. This had been the longest, most depressing week of Faye's life and the days to come could only get worse. She still hadn't heard a word from Antoinette and even after going to the police and filing a missing person's report she was still no closer to finding her daughter. Somehow, magically, she thought bringing the police in on the matter would help her locate Antoinette. But the circumstances remained the same. She couldn't tell the police who her daughter's friends were or even give them the full, real name of the boyfriend Faye was sure Antoinette had run away with. The only thing the police could do was contact Antoinette's school and put them on alert. Faye couldn't even find a phone book in Antoinette's room or any other clues that might help the police out. So after a week, Faye found herself in the same frustrating position she'd been in all along, and now all she could do was turn it over to the Father. There was nothing else for Faye to do but let go and let God. But somehow she still felt worthless. Like she had failed at the most important job in life — raising her children.

The only spot of relief she'd been given this week was that Christopher had been given a clean bill of mental health by Mr. Watson and given the okay to return to school. She had taken Chris to his last appointment with Mr. Watson yesterday afternoon and like always he talked to Christopher alone for almost an hour and afterward he called Faye into his office for a private chat.

Faye had been a bit nervous yesterday. She had first thought that Mr. Watson would tell her her son was mentally ill and needed to go to a psychiatric hospital, but those thoughts were just Faye's overly dramatic imagination going overboard. Mr. Watson could see that she was a bit anxious when she walked into his office, but Faye's anxiousness wasn't caused solely by her apprehension to what Mr. Watson would say about her son. It was also due to the fact that Faye had been constantly fantasizing about Mr. Watson, and being alone with him in his small office was one of the fantasies her mind often slipped to when she was at home thinking about him. Just last night, in fact, she had envisioned Mr. Watson inviting her into his office. He'd called to her from the sofa where he lay, staring across the room at her with delectable eyes of pure passion. His long legs ran the length of the sofa and twisted at the ankles. His head was propped lazily against the cushions, his body wrapped in a silk jacquard robe opened ever so slightly at the neck to reveal a solidly sculpted chest with a dash of curly hair just waiting for Faye's fingers to roam through. She sauntered across the room to him and stood over him, watching as his eyes moved upward to catch her gaze. Then, like a love bandit, he snatched her by the arm and pulled her down on top of him as his hungry lips ravished her body and naked emotions engulfed her soul. . . . But of course, that was just fantasy. Still, Faye couldn't help thinking about it as Mr. Watson sat down next to her on the sofa, crossing his thick, muscular thighs and looking over at her with such intensity that her hands began to sweat.

"Are you okay?" he asked, softly patting her hand. "You look a bit nervous."

Faye smiled shyly, hoping the lust she felt for Mr. Watson was not apparent. "I'm fine," she said, softly. "I'm just concerned about my son. He's going to be all right, isn't he?"

"Your son is fine, Faye," he told her, flashing a bright smile. "There's no need to worry."

"You mean he's not turning into some monster?"

"No," he said and chuckled. "The only thing Chris needs to do is turn off the TV."

"Excuse me?"

A sly grin crossed his lips. "Let me explain," he said, shifting his position on the sofa so that he was fully facing Faye. "Chris was recommended for counseling because he got into a fight and ended up strangling the little fellow he was tussling with. Now his teacher and the principal thought this was very odd behavior. They thought that Chris was harboring *issues*, that he had severe anger control problems, but that's not the case at all."

"But it's not normal for a little boy his age to strangle someone."

"Well, I agree with that," he said. "But Chris didn't strangle the other guy because he is mentally ill. He did it because he'd seen Arnold Schwarzenegger do it in a movie."

"Huh?" Faye said, and shook her head.

Mr. Watson smiled, then bowed his head. He tried to stop himself from laughing, but the more he tried the more he couldn't control himself. "I'm sorry," he said as he tried to settle back down. But as soon as it looked like he was in control, he burst out laughing again. Faye couldn't tell what was going on. She didn't know whether to join in on the fun or to be offended. This was her son Mr. Watson was laughing about. What was so darn funny?

"Please excuse me, Faye," he said, and finally stopped laughing. "I was just thinking back to when I was a kid. I thought Bruce Lee was the be-all and end-all. I would watch his movies over and over again, trying to memorize his moves," he said, chuckling just a bit. "Then one day I got into a little scuffle with one of the neighborhood boys and the only way I could think to protect myself was to pull out my Bruce Lee moves," he said, and stood up. He spread his arms out, then kicked out his leg, surprising Faye so that she let out a whimper. He started chuckling a bit as he flurried his fists in front of him, then kicked his long leg out again. Only this time he must have pulled something because he let out a gasp and grabbed hold of his knee. "I guess I'm a bit too old to be Bruce Lee again," he said as he sat back down, still chuckling.

Faye eyed him strangely, wondering where this whole demonstration was leading. Mr. Watson could see Faye needed more reassurance and decided he'd better give it to her straight.

"What I'm trying to say, Faye, is that Chris is not psycho. He was being picked on, he got into a little tussle, like all boys his age do every once in a while, and instead of just socking the boy, he copied what he'd seen his favorite action hero do. He strangled the guy. He didn't do it because he has some deep-seated violent tendencies. He was just emulating Arnold Schwarzenegger, just like I used to emulate Bruce Lee when I was a kid."

"So you're saying he's normal?"

"Yes, Faye," he said, and patted her on the hand. "Now please don't get me wrong. Chris still needs to learn that fighting is wrong and we covered that in our sessions. We even made a pact," he said, and flung his arm through the air like Bruce Lee again. "I told him I'd teach him some of my karate moves if he promises to never get into another fight at school."

"You're gonna teach him karate, then tell him not to fight?" Faye said, not getting the contradiction.

"The theory of karate is not based in violence, it's based in self-protection. Karate is about more than jump kicks. It's a metaphor for life. It's about mind control, turning the other cheek, balance," he said, clearly able to speak on the subject for hours on end, but stopping when he saw the blank look on Faye's face.

"I see you're really into the Bruce Lee thing," she said, watching Mr. Watson chuckle and loosen up.

"Bruce was a bad boy," he said, nodding his head. "I'm gonna show Chris just how bad when I give him his lessons," he said, swinging his arm in the air, then stopping abruptly and grabbing it. "Cramp," he said and winced a bit.

"That's awfully nice of you to give Chris karate lessons, but please, don't put yourself out on his account."

"Don't worry," he said, still soothing his arm. "I don't mind at all. Anyway, what's really important here is that Chris knows he should never resort to violence in any situation and we went over that very thoroughly. But as far as him having mental problems?" He shook his head. "That's simply not the case."

Faye felt so relieved. She had always known that Chris wasn't a violent boy. But hearing Mr. Watson say it made her feel better. She had been so frightened of what Mr. Watson would conclude about her son, but now that it was all over she felt as if this huge weight had been lifted off her shoulders. She had one less burden to bear now, she thought as her mind shifted from Chris to Antoinette. And although she felt happy in the knowledge her son was just fine, she couldn't help the feelings of sadness that lingered for her daughter. Her eyes began to water as she thought about Antoinette, and just like the outburst of laughter Mr. Watson experienced earlier, Faye was suddenly overtaken by an outburst herself — an outburst of tears.

Faye's tears did not come in silence. She moaned and blubbered so intensely that for a second there Mr. Watson thought it was all a put-on. At any second he expected her to suddenly stop and yell out, "Gotcha." But after a minute, Mr. Watson realized Faye was not putting him on. She was in pain, he thought, as he slid closer to her on the sofa and wrapped his arm over her shoulder. He pulled a handkerchief from his pocket and handed it to Faye and rubbed her back as she leaned her head on his shoulder.

It didn't take too long for Faye to realize the awkwardness of her position. For a moment, she had been so caught up in her tears and her thoughts of Antoinette that she couldn't focus on anything else. But when she felt Mr. Watson so close to her, rubbing her back, shushing her cries, she realized she was overstepping her bounds and moved away from him. "I'm so sorry," she said, trying to stifle her tears amid feelings of embarrassment. She quickly stood to her feet and clutched her purse under her arm. She wiped her eyes with the handkerchief as Mr. Watson stood up beside her.

"It's no problem, Faye," he said as he reached out for her shoulder.

Faye blew her nose with the handkerchief, then held it out for Mr. Watson. "Oh," she said, quickly pulling it back, realizing what she'd just done to it. "I'll have this cleaned," she said, and backed up toward the door. "I'm so sorry about this," she said as her purse fell out of her grasp and on to the floor. Mr. Watson reached for it, but Faye beat him to it. "Really, I must apologize. I didn't mean to . . ." She paused and tried to gather herself. "I've got to go," she said, and backed up again. "Thank you for all you've done for my son. I really appre —"

"Wait a minute," Mr. Watson said, and grabbed her arm. "You can't leave like this," he said, and pulled her back toward him. "Please, sit down. I think we need to talk."

"No," Faye pleaded. "You've already been kind enough. I should go. Really, I should go."

"I insist." He put his hand on her shoulder. "Please, sit down. I can't let you leave like this."

Faye sat back down feeling so silly. He must think I'm an idiot, she thought, knowing how crazy she must appear to him with the way she just broke out into tears and all.

"What's bothering you, Faye?" he asked as he sat down next to her and took her hand in his.

What a nice man, Faye thought, feeling the warmth Mr. Watson was offering her. She could see why he was such a good counselor. He had a way of soothing people, of making them feel close to him. Still she didn't want to burden him with her problems. She was grateful that he had helped her son, but she couldn't imagine what he could do for her now.

Antoinette was her problem, and there was nothing he or anyone could do to bring her daughter back home to her.

"Faye," he said, and tightened the grip on her hand. "You can talk to me. I want to help."

"But there's nothing you can do."

"I can be a friend," he said softly. "I can listen. Sometimes that's all we need to help us feel better."

Faye was still hesitant to speak. But the more he sat holding her hand the more secure she felt with him. "It's my daughter."

Mr. Watson raised an eyebrow. "I didn't know you had a daughter," he said, unable to believe he'd seen Faye every day for a whole week and the subject of her daughter had never come up.

Faye's lips quivered as she looked into his eyes. "I don't know if I have a daughter anymore either," she said as a sole tear slipped from her eye. "She ran away," she told him, then closed her eyes to take a deep breath. "She's been gone for a week and I don't know where she could be. I've called the police but they've been no help and I . . . I just feel . . . I just feel like it's my fault," she said as more tears began to fall. "The night she left home, I found out that she was pregnant. We got into a big fight, I hit her, she hit me, and . . . and now she's gone and I don't think she's ever coming back." Faye dabbed at her eyes with the handkerchief as Mr. Watson sat in silence, just listening. She liked the fact that he didn't say a word. He didn't butt in or cut her off, he just listened, giving Faye the courage she needed to voice what she was really feeling inside. "Sometimes, I feel so worthless," she continued through a raspy voice. "When my husband was killed, I vowed to be strong. To hang in there for my kids, to give them the life my husband and I always wanted them to have. I know I'm not the only single mother in the world. I know women raise kids alone all the time. Sometimes a single mom will come into the shop bragging about her kids, and how well they're doing, and I just wonder why I can't be like that. I never knew it would be this hard to raise children by myself," she said, and dabbed at her eyes again. "I feel like a failure. I don't know where I went wrong."

Faye blew her nose with the handkerchief, then balled it up in her hand. She sat silently in Mr. Watson's company, peacefully absorbing the kindness he offered her and reveling in the comfort of her hand in his. She almost felt embarrassed over the lewd fantasies she'd been having about him. Somehow her fantasies cheapened him, were disrespectful to him in a sense. And although her fantasies were her own, she could not help feeling wrong for having them now. Mr. Watson was a good man, a kind man, not some sex toy for her mind to fiddle with. Mr. Watson was the kind of man Faye would jump through hoops for a chance to be with. If, that is, she was younger, prettier, and a hundred pounds lighter. But she wasn't and the kind of warmth Mr. Watson showed her was not that of a lover, but of a friend. Suddenly Faye felt like she didn't want this time with him to end. Her son was finished with his counseling sessions and if she were to leave right now she would never have the opportunity to see Mr. Watson again. She would miss him, she thought to herself. He was the only male friend she had. Still, all good things must come to an end.

"Thank you," she said, and turned to face Mr. Watson. "Thanks for listening. You do it well," she said, smiling graciously. "Most people try to analyze and offer advice, but not you. You just listen and for that I thank you."

"It's my pleasure," he said as he got up from the sofa and walked to his desk. "I can only imagine the heartache you're going through over your daughter," he said as he sat down. "The not knowing must be driving you insane."

Faye nodded her head slightly. "I don't know if she's dead or alive," she said as if in a daze. "And it's all my fault."

"You can't think like that, Faye," he said firmly. "You've got to believe your daughter is all right."

"I know, I know. Everyone keeps telling me that, but I just feel I could have done more. I should have spent more time with her, I should have . . . I don't know . . . I should have . . ."

"Told her how much you love her?"

Faye looked at Mr. Watson as if he'd stolen those words off the tip of her tongue. "Yes," she said softly. "I should have told her how much I love her."

Mr. Watson leaned back in his chair and put his finger to his temple. "I take it you and your daughter weren't very close."

"I tried," Faye said honestly. "But it seemed the older she got the more she pulled away. She started getting herself in trouble, skipping school, backtalking, *boys*. I could never understand it. Chris and I have always been so close, but it was the complete opposite with Antoinette and me. She's always been so distant."

"Hmm," Mr. Watson said as an alarm seemed to go off inside his head. "I hear a lot of parents complain about their children being distant, aloof, spending more time closed up in their rooms than socializing with the rest of the family."

"That was Antoinette for you. She hardly ever came out of her room. It was as if she just didn't want to be bothered with me and Chris."

Mr. Watson looked as if he were in deep thought. He nodded his head, then spun around in his chair and searched the bookshelf behind him. "That's usually a sign that the child feels unwanted," he said as he pulled out a book and turned around to place it on his desk. "I was just reading something on the subject of aloof children," he said as he thumbed through the pages of the book, then stopped. "Here it is," he said, picking up the book and taking it over to Faye. "The second paragraph talks about the withdrawn child," he said, and handed the book to her. "It's not the child's withdrawal that comes first. Usually the child feels unwanted, like she doesn't fit in, and because of that she withdraws, thinking the rest of the family doesn't want anything to do with her. Not the other way around."

"But Antoinette wasn't an unwanted child," Faye said, not even bothering to look down at the book Mr. Watson had handed her. "I loved that girl just as much as I love my son."

"But did you show her in the same way you showed your son?"

Faye's eyes slanted as her mind scrambled.

Mr. Watson sat down next to Faye and crossed his legs. "It's not uncommon for mothers to have a preference for one child over the other," he said matter-of-factly.

"But I don't have a preference. I love both my kids the same."

"Are you sure?"

"What do you mean am I sure? Of course I'm sure, Mr. Watson," she snapped, and twisted her neck as if she'd just been offended.

Mr. Watson raised a hand. "I didn't mean to upset you, Faye. It's just that I've dealt with a lot of mothers who have children of both sexes and what I usually find is that mothers tend to *love* their sons and *raise* their daughters," he said, shifting around until he found the most comfortable position. "You see, the time mothers share with their sons is spent laughing, talking, cleaning up behind them—the things children equate with love. But when it comes to the girls, mother tend to *train* them, teaching them how to cook and clean, scolding them for unladylike behavior. Now," he said, and paused slightly, "the mother may have the same level of feelings for her children, but she just doesn't show it to them in the same way. Teachers do it too, you know," he said offhandedly as Faye eyed him with slow-growing contempt. She couldn't believe he was suggesting she didn't love her daughter as much as her son. What kind of mother did he think she was? What kind of woman did he think she was?

"There was a study out last year," he continued, oblivious to Faye's changing mood. "It surveyed teachers nationwide, showing how they seem to be more attentive to their male students than their female students," he said, reaching over Faye's arm to turn the pages of the book that sat on her lap. "See," he said, and tapped the page. "They spell it out right there, page three fifty-two."

Faye slammed the book shut so quickly that she caught Mr. Watson's finger in it. "I think it's time for me to go," she said, and rose up from the sofa. Faye didn't want to hear another word from Mr. Watson. She had just praised him on his ability to listen without analyzing and what did he do? Turn around and try to pick her apart.

"Did I say something wrong?" he asked as he stood up beside Faye, finally noticing the scowl that crossed her face.

"Yes, you did, Mr. Watson. You've insulted my motherhood," she huffed in a tone unusually high for her. "I know I'm not the best mother in the world. I make a lot of mistakes, I'll admit that. But I don't care what they say in that book, I have never made the mistake of not loving my daughter."

"Faye, listen," he said, taken aback by the anger in her voice. "I didn't mean to insult you. That's the last thing I wanted to do. I was just trying to help."

"Well, thank you for your help, Mr. Watson. But if you don't mind, I'll be leaving now."

"But Faye," he said as she walked to the door and opened it.

"Good-bye, Mr. Watson," she said, and walked out.

Their last conversation had been roaming through Faye's mind all night and now that she was here, alone in the cathedral, she had to admit for the first time that some of the things Mr. Watson was trying to tell her were right on point. She thought back to the days following her husband's death, remembering how upset Antoinette had been because she hadn't let her come along with them for dinner on the night he died. She remembered how her daughter cried and cried over the loss of her father. But Faye had been so swept up in her own grief that she could barely keep her own head straight, let alone console her confused, heartbroken child. Maybe Antoinette took that as a sign that her mother didn't care about her. Faye thought back on how she had pawned Antoinette off on her grandparents. At the time she thought she was doing the right thing for

Antoinette. She didn't want her to see her mother in such a state of disarray, but now she had to think twice. Was that where it all started? Is that where Antoinette got the idea that her mother didn't love her?

And even after Faye had gotten herself together, she still never quite had enough time to really sit down with Antoinette and explain her father's death to her. Then less than a month after he died, Christopher was born and all Faye could focus on was her new baby boy. She remembered how she'd sit on the sofa, holding Chris in her arms, while Antoinette would stand against the wall watching them with longing eyes. Was she feeling out of place? Faye thought now as she remembered how she had to call on Antoinette to keep the house clean while she spent her time fawning over her newborn son. Is this when she first began to feel unwanted, like she didn't matter?

Until now, Faye had never really considered how her daughter must have felt during that time. Within a month, she had lost her father, and the mother who had always been there for her was so distracted with her new son that she didn't have time for her. Could it be that Mr. Watson was right? Faye wondered as she leaned her head back onto the pew and stared up at the etched ceiling. Could it be that she didn't show her daughter enough love and attention? Could that be why Antoinette felt the need to go looking for love outside the house? Is that why she was pregnant right now? Because the only way she could find love was with some little boy?

"Oh God," Faye said softly, and closed her eyes tightly. "What kind of mother am I?" She wept. "Oh God," she said louder. "I promise. If you just return my daughter to me safely I will show her all the love I have for her. I'll be the mother I should have been. I'll hold her, I'll comfort her, I'll keep her. I promise, Lord," she said, and looked up at the intricate paintings that graced the ceiling of the cathedral. "Please, Lord. Give me one more chance."

Faye wept for so long that by the time her tears finally dried up, she had lost track of the time. She peered down at her watch and noticed it was ten forty-five. She jumped up from her seat, realizing her first braid appointment had been at nine-thirty. She grabbed her purse, wiped her eyes for the last time, and headed out of the cathedral.

Faye walked into the shop and as always since the girls found out that her daughter had run away, they stopped what they were doing, looked at her, and waited for her response. And as always, Faye shook her head, indicating that her daughter had not returned home.

Zuma and Pat looked at each other and sighed and Sandy went back to her manicure client.

Faye walked over to her hair station and found her seat empty, then looked over at Pat.

"She got tired of waiting," Pat said, and shrugged her shoulders as she walked over to Faye.

"Sorry I'm so late," Faye said as she dropped her purse onto the floor and sat down in her chair. "I had to take Chris to school this morning. His suspension is over."

"Great," Pat said. She stood behind Faye's chair, looking at her image in the mirror. "What did his psychiatrist say?"

"Chris is fine," Faye said with a halfhearted smile. "He's not some self-destructive lunatic."

"Well, that's good news, huh?" Pat said hesitantly.

"I guess," Faye said and closed her eyes.

"She'll come back," Pat whispered as she wrapped her arms around Faye's shoulders. "We've all been praying for you, girl."

Faye leaned her head back onto Pat's chest and as she sat with her eyes closed, she silently prayed that she was right.

"May I help you?" Pat asked as she raised her head and looked at the man standing in the doorway.

"Yes," he said as he walked into the middle of the room. "I'm looking for . . ." He paused and pointed his finger.

Pat looked down at Faye and shook her shoulder. "Someone's here to see you," she said as Faye opened her eyes, completely stunned by who she saw standing before her.

"Mr. Watson," she finally said. "What are you doing here?"

"I was hoping you'd have a minute to talk," he replied, smiling cautiously at the stir his presence seemed to cause. All heads turned to check out the male figure and all heads liked what they saw. "I'm on leave for lunch. Do you have a minute?"

"Sure," Faye said as she got up from her seat and walked toward him. "We can talk outside," she said as she walked past him and out the door.

Mr. Watson followed her and Zuma nearly stretched her neck out of its socket trying to see what was going on.

"Mind your business," Pat scolded as she went to the front door and closed it.

Zuma sucked her teeth, still trying to catch a glimpse of Faye and her friend through the window, but since she couldn't read lips she gave up her spying routine.

Outside, Mr. Watson and Faye stood face-to-face, each seeming more nervous than the other. There was a brief yet uneasy silence between them until both of them decided to speak at the same time. They stopped and chuckled to themselves, removing any tension that was in their way.

"Listen, Faye," Mr. Watson said.

"No, let me go first," Faye said and raised her hand.

"No, no," he said, and shook his head. "I should go first," he said. Faye gave up and put her hand down. Mr. Watson took a deep breath before he spoke. "I was way out of line yesterday," he said, looking Faye directly in the eyes. "You came to me as a friend and I turned it around and made you into one of my clients. I had no right to do that. It's just sometimes I have a hard time putting the counselor side of myself aside," he said, looking down at the ground in shame. "I'm sorry if I hurt your feelings, Faye," he said, and looked back into her eyes. "Can you forgive me?"

Faye put her hand over her chest. She was so taken aback by Mr. Watson's sincerity that she could barely speak. "You don't have anything to be sorry for."

"Yes I do."

"No, you don't," she said, and took a deep breath of her own. "The truth of the matter is that you were right," she said, and looked away from him. "I did a lot of thinking after I left your office. I put myself in my daughter's shoes, trying to imagine how she must have felt after her dad died, and I realized I made a lot of mistakes with her. After my husband passed, Antoinette took a backseat to everything. All my attention went to my new baby and trying to get myself on my feet and find a job. But I never took the time to really show her how much she meant to me. I was too busy trying to find a way to provide for my family that I neglected to give her what she really wanted — love."

"You were doing what you had to do to survive."

"But a child doesn't understand that. All Antoinette knew was that her mother was too busy for her."

"You can't beat yourself up over that, Faye."

"I know," she said, and sighed. "You know I used to pride myself on the fact that I never hit my kids. I thought that made me such a good mother. But now I see it takes more than that. All kids want is to be shown a little love and attention. I gave that to my son, but somehow I overlooked Antoinette."

Faye blinked her eyes really fast, trying to ward off the tears she felt welling up. Mr. Watson could see her turmoil as he reached out his hand to her and pulled her to his chest. Faye's eyes nearly popped out of her head. She stiffened like a rock as Mr. Watson held her in his arms. She hadn't expected him to hug her. A handshake maybe, but a hug? For a split second there, she allowed herself to imagine that the vibe she felt coming from Mr. Watson was love, but when he patted her back she knew she was letting her imagination get the best of her again. Lovers never pat your back when they hug you. They stroke it up and down and squeeze you tightly. Back patting is only done when you're hugging a relative or in this case, Faye thought as Mr. Watson let her go, a friend.

"Well," he said, and clasped his hands together. "I just wanted to stop by and apologize," he said, humbly. "I want you to know I consider you a friend, Faye. And even though I won't be seeing you at school anymore, I hope we can stay in touch," he said as he slowly began to walk away toward his car.

Friend, Faye thought, and smiled though she wanted to howl. He considered her just a *friend*. How nice. But Faye knew there'd never be anything more between her and Mr. Watson and when she caught a glimpse of herself in the shop's window, she could understand why. She sucked in her gut and waved good-bye as Mr. Watson got into his car and started his engine.

He waved back as he began to drive off and Faye watched as his car disappeared down the street. What a nice man, she thought as she headed back into the shop. And as soon as she walked through the door, Zuma was in her face.

"Ooo," she said so loud the whole shop could hear. "I saw y'all," she said, pointing her finger in Faye's face and stretching out a goofy grin. "You got a man? How come you didn't tell us?"

"Oh, *Zuma*," Faye said as she waved her off and walked over to her hair station. "That's Mr. Watson. The school's psychiatrist."

"Ooo," Zuma said following behind her. "You're dating your son's psychiatrist?"

Pat stood at the shampoo bowl, laughing and listening in on the conversation.

"I'm not dating him. We're just friends."

"Well, that hug he wrapped you in looked real serious, girl."

Faye turned to face Zuma head on. "He patted my back."

Zuma twisted her neck. "He patted your back?"

"Yes."

"Oh," Zuma said, and calmed down. "Only relatives and friends pat you on the back."

"I know," Faye said and sat down.

Zuma examined Faye as she walked back to her own hair station. "Friend or no friend," she said, still eyeing Faye, "you like him."

"I do not," Faye combated.

The rise in Faye's voice let Zuma know she wasn't telling the truth. "You do like him," she said, satisfied with her knowledge.

"No, I don't."

"Yes, you do."

"*Zuma.*"

"*Faaaayeeee.*"

"Zuma!" her client yelled out and turned around in her seat. "Can you please stop talking and do something with my hair? I've been here for two hours already."

Zuma put her hands on her hips and stepped back, looking at her client like she was crazy. No, she didn't just try to get loud with me, Zuma thought, turning up her lip in preparation for her response. If it hadn't been for Pat clearing her throat, Zuma would have given the woman a piece of her mind — a big piece — a hunk. But instead, Zuma smiled politely, pulled out her hair dryer, and got back to work.

Pat shook her head as she wrapped a towel around her client's head and helped her up from the shampoo bowl. She directed her client back to her hair station, then dried off her hands and walked over to Faye. She looked at her with questioning eyes as Faye stared at her right back.

"What?" Faye asked, finally.

Pat leaned over close to Faye's ear. "Have you gotten the decorations for Zuma's surprise party?"

"Of course," she said, and looked at Pat strangely. "You know I always take care of business."

"Good," Pat whispered, and leaned in even closer. "You know," she said, and put her hand on Faye's arm, "it would be perfectly okay with me if you invite Mr. Watson. You know Mark's coming and there's always room for one more."

"We're just *friends*," Faye whispered quickly.

"*Okay*," Pat said, and held up her hands. "I got it."

"Good," Faye said as she watched Pat walk away.

What is wrong with these people, Faye thought as she sat in a funk at her hair station. One man stops by to see me in all these years and everybody goes crazy. She shook her head as she thought about Mr. Watson, and the more she thought about him the more his words began to sink into her head. "I consider you a friend," he'd said. "I hope we can stay in touch."

Was he serious about that, she thought as she tapped her fingers on her thighs. "I mean if we're friends, what would be so wrong with inviting him to the party? Don't friends invite friends to parties?" she mumbled beneath her breath like a derelict. "Didn't he say he wanted to stay in touch?"

"Huh?" Zuma looked at Faye like she was out of her mind. "Are you talking to me?"

"No," Faye said loudly. "I was talking to myself."

"That man's got you sprung," Zuma said, and shook her head.

"We're just —"

"I know, I know," Zuma said and turned her back on Faye. "Friends."

"That's right."

"Good."

"Great."

"Perfect."

"*Fabulous!*"

19

Pat smiled from ear to ear and held on to Mark's arm as they sat side by side in their attorney's office waiting for the Oppenheimers. But their lateness didn't faze Pat. She expected them to lollygag today, especially since they had fought the adoption tooth and nail. But they'd have to show up sometime. Today was the day everything became official. The day the Oppenheimers were to sign the final adoption papers. The day Pat and Mark became Tracy's official parents.

When the door to Mr. Peters's office opened, Pat's heart skipped a beat. The Oppenheimers stepped in without saying a word and sat down at Mr. Peters's desk directly across from Pat and Mark. Pat squeezed Mark's arm as they all sat in silence while Mr. Peters fumbled around with papers and slid them over to the Oppenheimers. Pat only looked at Elizabeth Oppenheimer briefly. She could see the woman was in pain and oddly enough Pat felt sorry for her. She knew what the woman was feeling inside and she knew this procedure could not be easy for her. But Pat didn't let herself get too emotional. She had gone through enough pain herself over the last ten years and the only thing she wanted to focus on today was the joy she felt in her heart knowing that today she would have the daughter she always wanted.

Mr. Peters stood up and began explaining all the papers he'd pushed in front of the Oppenheimers, but Henry waved him off with his hand. "Just tell me where to sign," he said bitterly, and took a pen out of his coat pocket. Mr. Peters sighed as he walked over to Henry and pointed a finger onto the paper. As Henry signed, Elizabeth bowed her head and dabbed at her eyes with a pink cloth.

Pat turned away at that point as tears began to lace her own eyes. She didn't know if the tears were for Elizabeth's pain or for the realization that her dreams were coming true. It was a mixture of both probably, she thought, and batted her eyes to keep the tears from falling. Mark gripped Pat's hand, noticing her emotions. He smiled at her and wrapped his arm around her as she tried to get herself together.

Within a minute, Henry had finished signing the papers, capped his pen, and stuck it back into his coat pocket. He grabbed Elizabeth's hand and stroked it as he waited for Mr. Peters to look over all the pages.

"Okay," Mr. Peters said as he walked back to his seat. "Everything looks good," he said, and went through the papers one more time.

Henry and Elizabeth stood up quickly and without a word, headed for the door.

"Excuse me," Mr. Peters said, stopping the Oppenheimers just as they were about to walk out. "There's one more thing," he said as they both turned to face him. "We'll need you to have Tracy's things packed and ready to go by five o'clock this evening."

Elizabeth burst into tears upon hearing the inevitable and Henry just stood there growling. He gave a brooding look to Pat and Mark, then put his arm around his wife. "Whatever you say," he said, and escorted his wife through the door.

Pat nearly broke into tears herself as she watched them leave, but the only thing that held her back was the perking excitement she felt as Mark turned to her and planted a huge kiss on her mouth. "Hi, Mom," he said, and winked.

Pat snickered and wrapped her arms around his neck and held him tightly. "Hey, Dad."

Mark had to hurry off to take care of an electrical problem he was having at one of his apartment buildings. He wanted to get it over with quickly so that he could have the rest of the evening free to spend alone with his wife and new daughter. He dropped Pat off at the salon on his way so she could finish up with a bit of bookkeeping and promised he'd be back by four-thirty so they could go pick up Tracy.

It was Saturday and as usual the shop was packed, but as soon as Pat walked in with that big cheesy grin on her face, all business stopped.

"*Well,*" Faye said as she walked over to Pat with nervous anticipation.

Zuma followed behind Faye as they both stood in front of Pat like overanxious kids.

Slowly Pat nodded her head as Faye put her hand over her mouth and Zuma screamed, "Yes!" The three ladies laughed as they jumped up and down like cheerleaders and the rest of the shop looked on with smiling, unknowing faces. Pat jumped into Zuma's arms as Faye turned around to the rest of the people in the shop.

"Pat just adopted a child, you guys. She's a new mom!"

The entire shop screamed out and clapped as Pat flung her arms around Faye and held her tightly. Zuma ran to her hair station and picked up a comb. "Speech, speech," she said as she ran back to Pat and stuck the comb in her face.

"What can I say?" Pat said, talking into the comb as if it were a true microphone. "All I can say is that this has been a long time coming. I give all the glory to God," she said, and raised her hands in the air as the ladies in the shop all gave her a round of applause.

Sandy walked over to Pat shyly and held out her hand for congratulations. Pat slapped her hand out of the way and gave her a big hug.

"We ought to throw a party," Zuma screamed.

Faye and Sandy gave each other the eye, knowing full well about the party they were already throwing for Zuma tomorrow.

"Yeah," Zuma yelled. "Tomorrow night here at the shop," she said and turned to Pat.

Pat stuttered, then said, "Sounds good to me." Faye and Sandy both stared at her with ghastly faces.

Pat gave them both a quick wink of her eye, then turned back to Zuma. "How about eight o'clock," she said, to Zuma's delight.

Faye got hip to the program at that point. The party for Zuma was scheduled to begin at seven and now that Zuma thought the party wasn't until eight, everybody would get there before her so they could all yell "Surprise" when she walked in.

Pat waved her hand in the air to get everybody's attention. "Listen up, everybody," she said loudly.

"Ooo," Zuma said. "She even sounds like a mother now. Let me hear you say, 'Go to your room!' "

Pat nudged Zuma and waved her hand again. "Excuse me, ladies," she said as everyone quieted down. "You are all invited to the party tomorrow night," she said as shouts and claps started up again. "*But,*" she said, waving her hand again. "I'm only going to be here today for a couple hours so I need you to hang tight while I steal your hairdressers away for a brief minute."

Nobody protested. It was Saturday. They all knew they'd be at the shop for hours anyway.

"Outside, ladies," she said as she turned around and headed for the door. "You too, Sandy," she said as she walked out the shop and waited for the other three to join her.

"Uh-oh," Zuma said as she walked out the door and took a spot next to Pat. "What did we do now?"

Faye and Sandy stood in front of Pat and waited for her to speak.

Pat put on a smile to ease everyone's tension. She knew what they were thinking. Whenever there was a private counsel it usually meant something bad was going to happen. But not this time, not really.

"I've been doing some serious thinking lately," she said, looking at them all. "Tracy is only four years old and she won't be starting school for another two years," she said as she watched the tension on everyone's face turn to confusion. "I really feel that I need to spend as much time with Tracy as possible and I don't want her first years with me to be spent with a baby-sitter. So," she said, and let out a stream of air, "I've been thinking about selling the shop."

"Oh no," Faye said and put her hand to her face. Zuma's eyes seemed to brighten up.

"This won't affect any of your jobs," Pat assured them. "Whoever I find to buy the shop will just be taking over as proprietor so you don't have to worry about finding a new job."

"I'm not worried about that," Faye said softly. "It's just that I'm going to miss you," she said, and grabbed Pat's hand.

"I'm going to miss you too," she said, then turned to Zuma and Sandy. "And you guys too," she said, smiling into each of their faces. "But I've got to do this. I want to stay at home with Tracy. We both are going to need time to adjust to this new situation and I just don't feel that I can be the mom I want to be if I have to go to work every day and leave her with a sitter."

"I understand," Faye said seriously, knowing the sacrifices she had to make with her kids when she had to go to work after her husband died. She had been able to give Antoinette all the attention she needed when she was a stay-at-home mom. But all that ended when she had to go to work.

Sandy, on the other hand, couldn't understand it. She knew Pat would be making a big mistake if she gave up her career for her child. But who was she to say anything?

Zuma, too, thought Pat was being a bit hasty. There was nothing wrong with a mother working, she thought. It was certainly possible to give a child all the love and attention she needed and still have a career. But she knew Pat's circumstances were different. She had waited a long time for this child and she just wanted to make sure she didn't mess it up.

Pat cleared her throat. "I haven't even started looking for a buyer," she said. "It may take a while for me to sell the place, so for the next few months I'll still be around, but I won't be taking appointments. Just keeping track of the books and things like that."

Zuma's eyes brightened again. She couldn't believe how things were turning out for her. Just yesterday the nurse had called to confirm that she would be coming in today to give blood and urine to determine if the procedure had taken the first time and that Zuma was actually pregnant. But Zuma already knew what the results would be. It was strange, and even though she hadn't been given the final positive results, she knew she was pregnant. She just knew it. She didn't need to wait for the doctor's word. Why just last night, she'd been awakened at three o'clock in the morning with a strange craving for Häagen-Dazs ice cream and sardines. Oh yes, Zuma thought, I am pregnant. Her master plan was flowing with ease and now that Pat was talking about selling the shop, Zuma couldn't believe how lovely her master plan was coming together. She would be finished with her business correspondence classes very soon, and as planned she was going to go out and look for a shop of her own so that she could have her business under way and the money rolling in by the time the baby arrived. But now, she wouldn't have to look very far for a shop, she thought, as she turned to Pat with serious intent on her face. Pat was still going on and on about finding someone to buy the shop, but Zuma stopped her midsentence.

"I'll buy it," Zuma said directly, with a seriousness that threw Pat off.

Pat paused for a minute, then looked at Faye as they both broke out into laughter. "Okay, Zuma. Whatever you say," Pat said, and continued to laugh.

"I'm serious," Zuma said with a stone face. "I want to buy the shop."

"It takes big money to buy a business, Zuma," Faye told them. "Just because she's your friend doesn't mean she's just gonna give you the business."

Zuma eyed Faye like a peasant. A sly grin crossed her face as she turned to Pat. "How much are you asking for?"

Pat's face froze as she figured out Zuma was serious as a heart attack. "I don't know," Pat said, slowly. "About fifty, sixty grand?"

"How about thirty-five in cash up front and after I cash in my stocks and bonds at the end of the year," she said, pausing briefly to sum up the totals in her head, "I'll get you another twenty grand."

"That's fifty-five," Pat said, eyeing Zuma. "*Thousand.*"

"*Dollars,*" Faye added.

"I know, Faye," Zuma said, quickly tiring of their unspoken theory about her financial instability. "Little do you know, Miss Faye," she said, loosening her neck. "I do have a bank account and right about now it is over forty-eight thousand dollars strong," she said putting her hands on her hips. "Would you like to see my savings account statement?"

"You have forty-eight thousand dollars put away?"

"Yes, I do," Zuma replied. "I may look like some young fly-by-night, but I'm not. I've been saving for my future. It's all a part of my master plan."

"What master plan?"

Sandy snickered beneath her breath.

"Never mind that," Zuma said, and turned to Pat. "Do we have a deal?"

"Are you serious, Zuma? Don't play with me."

"Yes, I'm serious," Zuma said, raising her voice. "What? A sister can't be financially stable? What? You think I don't have goals and aspirations? What? You thought I was going to work for someone else for the rest of my life? *Please.*"

"No," Pat said, realizing that she had been making an unfair assumption about Zuma all these years. She always thought Zuma had been content being the diva hair stylist she always was. She didn't know that the girl wanted more for herself, but then again, who doesn't?

Zuma stepped in front of Pat so that her back was to Faye. She was tired of Faye's condescending attitude. "I've been saving my money ever since I turned twenty-five years old. I promised myself by the age of thirty I would have my life together. So I started saving and taking business correspondence classes so that when the time was right I could open up my own hair salon. And now the time is right," she said, waving her hands up and down. "Look, Pat. If you still don't believe me we can go down to the bank right now. I'll show you my bank statements. I'm serious about this. I want to buy the shop."

"Hmm," Pat said, impressed. "I believe you, Zuma," she said, and stuck out her hand. "This is going to work out just fine," she said as Zuma took her hand in hers and smiled. "I'm really proud of you, Zuma," Pat said, pulling her even closer and giving her a hug. "All most girls think about is finding a man to marry. But you went about it differently. You decided to get your life together."

"That's right," Zuma said, and turned around so that Faye could enter the conversation again. "I figure life is what you make it. You've got to start planning young, or else you'll be heading to forty years old and still working under someone else," she said, staring directly at Faye. She shut up when she saw Faye looking down at the ground in shame. She hadn't meant for her words to sting that much, but she did want to get back at Faye for doubting her.

"So what else is in your master plan?" Sandy asked, knowing full well that Zuma was leaving out the most important part — her baby.

"Never mind that," Zuma said, smirking at Sandy. "I'll fill you guys in on the rest of my plans tomorrow at the party."

"The rest of your plans?" Faye said suspiciously. "What else have you been hiding from us?"

"Nothing," Zuma said coyly as she smiled and patted Faye on the shoulder. The pat was more to make up for her nasty remark earlier than anything else. "Enough talk about master plans. Let's talk about this party. What is everyone bringing?"

Both Sandy and Faye began talking at the same time, trying to make up a lie that Zuma would believe, but Pat waved her hand in the air to shut them up before they messed up the plan. "Why don't we all chip in and have that soul food place you were telling me about last week deliver the food to the shop?" Pat said, and winked at Faye.

"What soul food — Oh, *that* soul food place," Faye said, catching on just in time. "Good idea. That way we can just pitch in money and no one will have to bring anything," she said, and grinned. "But I'll make the cake. German chocolate," she said, as her mouth watered just thinking about it.

"Cool," Zuma said, and clapped her hands together. "Of course you'll be bringing little Tracy?" she asked Pat.

"Of course," Pat said, grinning so wide her cheeks began to hurt. "But look, ladies," she said quickly. "Mark's going to be back to pick me up in an hour so I better get back inside and finish up my paperwork."

"Yeah," Zuma said, and looked through the window. "My client's beginning to look frustrated."

"Mine too," Sandy said, and looked through the window at the lady sitting at her manicure station.

"Guess we better get back inside," Faye said, and began walking to the door.

"Wait a minute," Pat said, and stopped everybody.

They turned to her and paused.

"Thanks," she said softly, and held out her arms.

Zuma was the first to hug her and as she kissed her on the cheek, Faye stepped in and kissed her nose. Even Sandy joined the pile without hesitation this time, and as they stood there holding one another, Pat felt an overwhelming sense of happiness. She had it all. Wonderful friends who cared about her. A wonderful husband who loved her and soon, very soon, in a matter of hours, a daughter who needed her. God is good, she thought to herself as she looked up at the neon sign above the building. Yes, she thought, and sighed, I am truly blessed.

Mark was back at four-thirty on the dot and Pat was outside the shop waiting for him. She jumped in the car, gave Mark a quick peck on the cheek, and off they went. Traffic was a doozy getting out to Glendale from Inglewood and Mark could tell his wife was getting a bit antsy. He popped in a CD to try to calm her nerves, but when he saw that the raging sounds of Aretha Franklin were only making her more nervous he realized he'd made a bad choice. He took out that CD and opted for the smoother sounds of Stevie Wonder and as they made their way through the bumper-to-bumper I-5 pileup, Stevie's "Isn't She Lovely?" came easing through the speakers. Pat tapped her fingers to the beat of the music as they got off the freeway and made their way up Brand Boulevard, and by the time they'd turned onto Tracy's street Pat was as calm as a butterfly.

The outside of the Oppenheimers' home was quiet and peaceful as usual, and as they walked across the front lawn hand in hand Pat felt a tranquility in her soul that could not be put into words. She knew the Oppenheimers would be sickened by the fact that this would be the last time they ever saw Tracy, but that was understandable. They had raised the child practically all her life and saying good-bye to her would be the hardest thing they ever had to do. But while Pat could feel for their loss, she felt an even greater security in the knowledge that she and Mark could give Tracy a better life than she could ever have with the Oppenheimers. She and Mark were going to make Tracy the happiest little girl in the world and Pat couldn't wait to start on that process.

Just as Mark was about to ring the doorbell, the door came swinging open. Henry stared at Pat and Mark briefly, then stepped back so they could walk through. The silence between the three was deafening. Pat wanted to ask where Tracy was, but she didn't want to seem too eager or too pushy. This was hard enough on Henry already, she thought as she stood gripping Mark's hand. Finally Henry stuffed his hands in his pocket and said, "Tracy will be down in a second." His eyes floated around the room and he opened his mouth to speak again. "Take care of my little girl," he said through a cracking voice as tears began to form in his eyes.

Mark quickly stuck out his hand toward Henry. "We will," he said sincerely. "I promise we will."

Henry shook Mark's hand firmly, then offered his hand to Pat. She took it softly in one hand and rubbed the back of it with her other. "Mark and I love Tracy," she said, pausing briefly to control her emotions. "And we thank you for raising her with love. You and Elizabeth have been wonderful parents."

Henry bit down on his lip and nodded his head as he took his hand away from Pat. He sighed as he turned around and walked to the bottom of the staircase. Next to the bottom step was a trio of multicolored suitcases and two large boxes wrapped with packing tape, which Henry moved to the side. "Liz," he shouted, his voice still cracking. "The Browns are here," he said, and dropped his head. He waited for a response and when none came he called out again.

Seconds later Pat heard a door open and looked up the flight of stairs. Tracy came running out of her room to the banister and leaned over it. "Hi," she screamed, and jumped up and down. "I'm ready to go," she said enthusiastically as Elizabeth slowly walked out of the bedroom and stood behind Tracy. It was obvious to Pat that Elizabeth had been crying and suddenly she wondered how or if she had told Tracy that she would be leaving their house today for good.

"Where are we going?" Tracy yelled as she came running down the steps. "Mommy said you're taking me on a trip," she yelled as she ran over to Mark and he scooped her up into his arms.

Pat frowned just a bit, knowing the Oppenheimers had not quite prepared Tracy for what was happening. But how could they, she thought. How could they bring themselves to tell her something that was so painful to them.

Mark squeezed Tracy tightly, then put her back down on the floor. Tracy then skipped over to Pat and wrapped her arms around her legs. "Where are we going, Pat?" she asked enthusiastically.

Pat looked up as she saw Elizabeth making her way down the stairs. She was crying ever so softly, trying to keep her tears to herself and not upset Tracy.

"They didn't tell you?" Pat asked Tracy as she looked down at her.

"Mommy said I was going on a trip with you, but she didn't tell me where."

"Well," Pat said, looking around to all the adults. "We're going on a trip to my house."

"Yay," Tracy screamed. "I like your house. Can we get in the water this time?" she asked and looked at Mark.

"You bet," he said, and smiled at her.

"I learned a new song at piano lessons yesterday," Tracy informed him. "I'll play it for you, 'kay?"

"Okay," Mark said, and rubbed the top of her head.

"Let's go," Tracy demanded, and jumped up and down. "Let's go get in the water."

Pat hesitated as she peered over to Henry and Elizabeth, who were in such obvious grief that Pat could barely take looking at them. Tracy demanded to go again, but Pat put her hand on her shoulder to calm her down. She couldn't take Tracy without giving the Oppenheimers a chance to say their final good-byes. They had earned that and much more.

"I think you should say good-bye to Liz and Henry before we go, sweetie," Pat said to Tracy as she rubbed the side of her face.

"Bye," she said quickly over her shoulder, then hopped her way to the door.

Henry and Elizabeth were crushed and Pat could see the turmoil written all over their faces. She reached out for Tracy and turned her around. "Why don't you go give them a big hug and a kiss," she said as she took Tracy by the hand and led her over to the Oppenheimers.

Henry bent over and picked Tracy up as she wrapped her arms around his neck. She put her mouth to his cheek and made a blubbering noise as spit shot out of her mouth. Pat winced, but quickly calmed as Henry chuckled and did the same thing to Tracy. "Bye-bye," Tracy said as Henry put her down.

Tracy hopped over to Elizabeth and held out her arms as Elizabeth bent down in front of her and wrapped Tracy up. She held her for the longest time as tears spilled out of her shut eyes. "You be a good girl," she said as she finally let Tracy go and looked into her face.

Tracy calmed as she stared at Elizabeth. "Why you crying, Mommy?" Tracy asked, and wiped a rolling tear from Elizabeth's face.

"I'm gonna miss you," Elizabeth said, and squeezed her eyes shut.

"It's okay, Mommy," Tracy said seriously. "I left Holly Hobby here to keep you company while I'm gone."

"But that's your favorite doll," Elizabeth said, looking concerned. "I'd better go get her for you."

"It's okay. I'll be back, Mommy. I'm just going to get in the water. I'll be back. You can keep her till then, Mommy."

Elizabeth took a deep breath and wiped the tears off her face. "Tracy," she said, and grabbed her hands. "You're not coming back here," she said, and put Tracy's hands to her lips. "You're going to be living with Pat and Mark from now on."

"Unh-uh, Mommy," Tracy said and shook her head.

"Yes, sweetheart," Elizabeth corrected her. "Pat and Mark are your new mommy and daddy now. They're going to take care of you and love you just like we did."

Tracy shook her head slowly, trying to figure out what Elizabeth was saying. She looked over to Henry for clarification, then at Pat. "No," she said, and looked back at Elizabeth. "I don't want to go."

"It's okay, you'll be fine," Elizabeth said as Tracy continued shaking her head.

Pat bent down and smiled in Tracy's face. "It's okay," she said, and held out her hand to Tracy, but Tracy slapped her hand away.

"No," she said, and backed away. "I don't wanna go."

Pat looked over at Mark, then stood up. "It's okay, Tracy," she said and walked toward her. "Don't you like it at my house?"

"No," Tracy snapped, and ran behind Henry. She grabbed hold of his leg and hid her face behind it.

"Tracy," Henry said, and grabbed her hand. "I thought you liked the Browns." He pulled her in front of him. "Don't you like the Browns?"

Tracy didn't know what to say. She snatched her hand away from Henry and ran over to Elizabeth. "I don't wanna go," she said, and wrapped her arms around Elizabeth's neck. "I don't wanna go."

Elizabeth stood up with Tracy in her arms and rubbed her back as Tracy hid her face against Elizabeth's neck. "Tracy," she said, trying to loosen the grip she had around her neck. "Tracy," she said again, then looked into her face. "Pat and Mark are going to take good care of you. They love you. Don't be scared," she said as she walked over to Pat and held Tracy out for her.

As Pat took hold of Tracy's waist, Tracy screamed and grabbed onto Elizabeth's blouse. "No," she yelled as Pat held the bottom half of her body, her hands still gripping and pulling Elizabeth's blouse. Elizabeth tried to pry her hands away, but Tracy was too determined.

"It's okay, Tracy. Please," Elizabeth said, and when she took one step backward, her blouse ripped straight down. Tracy almost tumbled out of Pat's grip, but Pat held on tight as Tracy switched and contorted her body so that Pat could barely manage her.

"Mommy," she screamed, flinging her arms through the air, trying to reach out for Elizabeth. "No," she yelled over and over again as Pat held on to her and looked to Mark.

Mark was dumbfounded, but he knew he had to act quickly. He opened the door to the house, then walked over and picked up Tracy's suitcases. Pat stood in the doorway as Tracy continued to yell, "No." Mark ran out to the car and put the suitcases in the trunk, then came right back and got the two boxes. When he came back again, he looked over at Henry and Elizabeth.

"She'll be all right," he told them. "She's just going to have to get used to the situation first." He turned to Pat and gave her a nod and Pat slowly walked outside as Tracy stopped yelling, "No," and began screaming at the top of her lungs. She began kicking wildly and swatting her hands through the air, hitting Pat's face several times. Mark ran ahead of them and opened the car door, but halfway there Pat fell to her knees. Tracy was putting up such a fight that Pat couldn't hold on to her anymore.

As soon as Tracy hit the ground, she took off running and screaming down the lawn. Neighbors from all around came to their front doors and peered out their windows to see what commotion had taken place on their otherwise peaceful street. But Tracy wasn't fast enough to get away from Mark. He caught up to her two houses down the street and scooped her up. Tracy tried to kick, but Mark wrapped one arm around her legs and bought her back to the car, and still Tracy continued screeching at the highest pitch Pat had ever heard.

Mark opened the front door of the car and pushed the button for the child safety locks. Then he opened the back door and put Tracy inside. Pat still sat on the ground where she had fallen with Tracy. She had watched as Mark chased her down the street, all the while trying to convince herself that none of this was happening. In her wildest dreams she would never have imagined that she would have to force Tracy kicking and screaming to leave with her. She thought Tracy loved her as much as she loved Tracy. But now she didn't know what to think. Mark helped her up from the ground and over to the car. Tracy sat in the back with her hands against the window looking toward the door of the house and the Oppenheimers who stood there, both of them now in tears. "Mommy," Tracy screamed, mashing her face against the window.

As Pat got into the car she looked over to Henry and Elizabeth and watched as they waved good-bye to their little girl. And as Mark started the car and drove off down the street, Tracy screamed as though someone was attacking her. It killed Pat to hear her like that and as they drove off, Pat too began to cry. Mark rubbed her knee as he drove cautiously. "It's just gonna take her awhile to get used to this," he said as he turned off the Oppenheimers' street and onto Brand Boulevard. "Don't worry, Pat," he said. "Everything is going to be okay."

"I know," Pat said, and nodded her head. "It just hurts."

By the time they got home and Mark opened the door to take Tracy out of the car, she had stopped kicking and screaming. Still she cried softly to herself, her small shoulders heaving up and down, as Mark walked ahead of Pat, taking Tracy by the hand and leading her through the front door. Pat stood by and watched as Mark bent down in front of Tracy and pleaded with her to stop crying. He offered her juice, cookies, pointed to the piano, even walked her through the kitchen and to the back window and pointed out to the pool. "Look, Tracy," he said, stroking her back. "It's the water. Don't you want to get in?"

But Tracy shook her head and cried harder. She had gotten so that no sound would come out of her mouth as she cried. She just stood there with her eyes shut tightly, her mouth open and the tears streaming down her face. Mark sighed as he looked back at Pat. Neither of them knew what to do. All they knew is that they had one unhappy girl on their hands and as Mark took Tracy by the hand and led her up the stairs to her room, Pat followed behind them wondering if and when Tracy would ever stop this madness.

Mark picked Tracy up and laid her across her bed. He took her shoes off, then kissed her cheek, and as he walked away Tracy clutched a pillow against her face, muffling what little sound escaped her mouth. Mark stopped in front of Pat and looked at her as if searching for some magical answer. But Pat didn't have the answer. All she could do was watch Tracy and wonder. Her cries seemed to pierce Pat's heart. They sounded so true, so utterly miserable. It pained Pat to see the child she loved in such misery and even Mark's eyes began to water as he looked over his shoulder at Tracy.

"Let's leave her alone for a while," he said, turning to Pat as he stepped out of Tracy's room and pulled the door closed.

Tracy's cries took flight again as Pat and Mark walked down the hall to their bedroom and sat down on the edge of the bed in silence. They didn't speak to each other for a while. Just sat in silence, listening to their new daughter cry herself to sleep, and after about fifteen minutes, Tracy's cries could no longer be heard. Mark got up and walked down the hall to check on her and soon came back and sat down next to Pat again. "She's asleep," he said, and sighed. "I think she's going to be all right."

Pat said nothing. She just turned to Mark and looked him in the eye and when she did she could see his uncertainty. He was hopeful, but he wasn't at all sure if Tracy was going to be all right and neither was she. "I don't know, Mark," she finally said. "Something just doesn't feel right about this," she said, and shook her head. "It wasn't supposed to be like this."

"This is normal," Mark said, and rubbed Pat's leg. "She's just a little confused right now. This is the beginning of a whole new life for Tracy."

"Normal?" Pat put her hand over Mark's. "Did you see the look on Tracy's face? Pure trauma, Mark. Trauma."

"She's just confused."

"Confused, traumatized—Call it what you want, but this is not *normal* behavior. Sadness I could deal with, pouting, the cold shoulder—I could deal with that. But Tracy's taking this much harder, Mark. This is not good," she said, and shook her head. "This is definitely not good."

"So what are you saying? Do you want to take Tracy back to the Oppenheimers."

"No," Pat said, raising her voice and jumping up from the bed. She put her hands to her face, trying to gather her senses. "I just want to do what's best for her. I love that girl. I don't want to hurt her in any way."

"So what do you think we should do?"

"I don't know, Mark," she said, frustrated. "Maybe we need to get some kind of family counseling, or talk to some other adoptive parents. I know we aren't the only ones who've gone through a situation like this."

"That's fine with me," Mark said, nodding his head. "If you think counseling will help, I'm all for it."

Pat thought for a second, then sat back down on the bed. "What does that say about us as a family?" she said and turned to Mark. "We have to get a counselor to help us relate to our own daughter? That seems so . . . so . . . unnatural."

"This isn't a *natural* situation," Mark said, making quotation gestures with his fingers. "Remember, we are Tracy's adoptive parents. There's no natural bond between us. In fact, Tracy probably has a stronger natural bond with the Oppenheimers. They aren't her natural parents either, but they've been the only parents she's ever known. The relationship we have with Tracy has to start from scratch, and if a counselor can help that along, then I say we should go for it."

Pat sat silently as Mark's comments muddled around her brain. She understood the fact that the Oppenheimers were the only parents Tracy had ever known. To take her from them would undoubtedly be traumatizing, she figured as she thought back to her own childhood and tried to imagine how it would have been if someone had come to her house one day and swept her away from her mother and father forever. Tracy wasn't overreacting at all, Pat concluded. All her tears, her screams, her kicks and cries were justified. In Tracy's eyes, she had just been kidnapped and there would be no way to make her understand that, Pat thought. She and Mark could be the best parents in the world, but to Tracy they'd never be *her* parents. They could never be Mommy and Daddy.

"Pat," Mark said, and tapped her on the shoulder. "Are you all right?" he asked, looking into her wandering eyes.

"Yeah," Pat said, and slowly nodded her head. "I'm . . . I'm all right."

"Are you sure?" Mark asked, then jumped as Tracy's voice came rolling through the air. Mark stared at Pat, then got up from the bed. "Maybe she's hungry," he said as he walked toward the door. "I'll go downstairs and make her a sandwich," he said, and hurried off.

Pat sighed as she got up from the bed and slowly walked down the hall to Tracy's room. She stuck her head inside and watched as she lay there sobbing. It was like a scene out of a movie to Pat. Somehow it all seemed unreal. Pat walked inside and over to the bed where she sat down next to Tracy and put her hand on her head. Her brown face was all flushed, her cheeks looked like stained glass, her eyelashes as if they'd been dipped in glue and pasted together. Pat stroked her head and whispered, "Ssh," but her attempts to soothe Tracy were all in vain.

Pat could see the sun was going down as she looked through Tracy's window. She had wanted to bring Tracy home, change into her swimming suit, then barbecue hamburgers outside by the pool. She thought about suggesting this to Tracy, but felt silly. There's no way a burger and a dip in the pool could take Tracy's mind off the fact that she'd just been hijacked from the only home she'd ever known.

Pat turned quickly when she felt Tracy's hand tapping her thigh. She looked down at her daughter, barely able to speak for the shock. Tracy looked up at her hiccupping, trying desperately to speak through her tears. "Pat?" she asked sweetly, staring at her with pleading eyes. "Can I go back home now?"

Pat stroked Tracy's cheek, trying to think of the right words to say. Then Mark came through the door, carrying a tray before him. He walked over to the bed, smiling, noticing that Tracy had stopped crying. Pat pulled Tracy up so that her back rested against the headboard and Mark laid the tray across Tracy's lap. "I brought you a sandwich and some chips, and a banana," he said and sat down at the foot of the bed.

Tracy paid no attention to the food in front of her. She stared over at Mark and asked him the same question. "Can I go back home now?"

Mark looked at Pat with his mouth hanging wide open as Tracy stared at him with hopeful anticipation. "Why don't you taste your sandwich?" he said cheerfully, trying to distract her, but not succeeding.

The look on Tracy's face was one of complete and utter letdown. She had done her best. She had stopped crying and asked the question as nicely as she could and still she could not have what she wanted. Frustrated, defeated tears came rolling out of her eyes as she sat on the bed looking so wretched that Mark could stand to look at her no more.

"Come on, Tracy," Pat said, trying to be perky. "You need to eat," she said as she broke off a piece of the sandwich and held it in front of Tracy's mouth, but Tracy could barely see for the tears lacing her eyes. Pat waved the sandwich in front of her, but eating was of no concern to Tracy.

Realizing this, Pat removed the tray from the bed and sat it on the floor, then she lay down in bed beside Tracy and cuddled her daughter next to her body and stroked her back. Mark stayed for the first hour as his wife lay with his sobbing daughter. But that was all he could take. He couldn't stand to hear his daughter in such pain or to see the matching emotion that spread across his wife's face.

But Pat stayed there with Tracy until she quieted down and went to sleep. Within the hour she was awake again and crying once more and Pat was there to stroke her back and try to ease her pain all over again. It went on like this all night long. Tracy would sleep for an hour or two then wake up in tears, and Pat would stroke her back until she fell asleep for the next hour or two. By morning, Pat had gotten all of maybe three hours' sleep and still, when Tracy woke up, she was crying.

Pat had wanted to take Tracy to church with her this morning, but it was obvious all her plans would have to be canceled. The day had to be spent attending to Tracy. Trying to get her to eat, watch TV, play games—anything other than crying. But everything Pat and Mark tried failed.

Tracy did tire herself out around three o'clock in the afternoon, and as Pat walked into her bedroom to lie across her own bed, she saw Mark kneeling next to the bed in prayer. She watched him and waited for him to finish and when he did, she asked, "I don't need to ask what you were praying about, do I?"

Mark shook his head and sat down on the bed and tapped the space next to him. Pat walked over and sat down and laid her head on his shoulder. "I was just asking the man upstairs to tell me what to do," Mark said, and sighed.

"And what did He say?"

"He didn't answer me yet. But He will."

Pat closed her eyes, believing her husband and trusting in the Lord, but soon her eyes popped right back open. "Zuma's party," she said, and raised her head. "We were all supposed to go." She shook her head, wondering how that could have slipped her mind.

"Just call Faye," Mark said. "She'll understand, I'm sure."

"You're right," Pat said, then thought again. "Wait a minute," she said, and snapped her fingers. "Maybe we should go."

"Tracy won't be able to handle a party right now, Pat," he said, looking at her like she was crazy.

"Maybe this is just what she needs." She stood up. "Faye's son will be there, the new girl Sandy is bringing her two kids, plus some of the customers will be there and I'm sure they'll have their kids too. Maybe this is just what Tracy needs. She needs to get comfortable with us. What do you think?"

"Whatever you say," Mark said with no sign of certainty at all.

"I knew you'd say that," Pat said as she ran to her closet and pulled out one of her oversized dashiki dresses that she always threw on when she was about to go on a quick errand.

"Where are you going?"

"I've got to run down to the liquor store to get some beer and stuff for the adults, then I've got to run down to Party World and get some things for the kids," she said as she slipped into some slide-on shoes and grabbed her purse. She stopped when she reached the door of the bedroom when another bright idea popped into her mind. "I'll take Tracy with me," she said.

"Are you sure?" Mark asked, his tone still filled with uncertainty.

"No," she said softly. "But I'll try anything. Maybe she'll feel better if she can get out of the house . . . I don't know Mark," she said, throwing her hands in the air as she headed to Tracy's room. When she opened the door she found her sitting straight up on the bed, hiccupping as if she was just ending or just about to begin one of her crying spells. Pat smiled as she walked over to the bed and picked Tracy up. She took her across the hall to the bathroom and pulled down one of the towels and wiped Tracy's face, as Tracy stared at her, still deep in misery.

Pat picked up Tracy and carried her down the stairs. Just as she was about to walk out the door, she stopped and called to Mark. "I'll be back in about an hour."

"Okay," he said, and walked all the way down. "Let me get Tracy's bags out of the trunk first."

"That's all right," Pat said, and opened the door. "We can do that when I get back."

She walked to the car and opened the door and sat Tracy down. She threw her purse onto the backseat, pushed the child safety lock button just in case, then closed the door and walked back around to the driver's side. In seconds, they were zooming down the street. Pat kept a close eye on Tracy, trying to see if the change of scenery was having any effect on her mood, but it wasn't. Pat sighed miserably as she pulled her car into the crowded parking lot at Dale's Liquor Store. She got out of the car and walked around to open Tracy's door. Tracy got out by herself and before she closed the door, Pat leaned in the car to grab her purse off the backseat. She closed the door and hit her alarm button, but when she turned around she noticed Tracy was gone. Panic hit Pat like a freight train as her head snapped from side to side looking for a glimpse of her daughter. "Tracy," she yelled as she ran behind her car, then to the front of it. "Tracy!" she screamed as she bolted down the parking lot like a crazed demon, searching, peeking, poking, and peering. But Tracy was nowhere to be found.

Pat ran inside the liquor store and straight to the counter. "Did a little girl come through here?" she asked. The man behind the counter shook his head. "Are you sure?" she asked, turning around to look for herself. She ran down every aisle of the store, then back to the front and out the door. "Tracy!" she yelled over and over again as tears ran down her face.

She took off toward the sidewalk, but saw nothing. She turned around and ran back across the parking lot. Still nothing. "Oh my God, oh my God, oh my God," she said as she backtracked her way to her car. She beat her hands against the hood as she cried, still looking around for a sign. Then, she heard a noise. At first she thought it was her own tears, but she listened again, looked around, then looked down. "Tracy?" she said as she saw the white patent leather shoe sticking out from underneath the car. She bent down for a closer look and sure enough — "Tracy," she yelled as she reached under the car and grabbed her by the hand. She pulled her out and wrapped her in her arms. If this had been any other time, Tracy would have been in deep trouble, but Pat was so glad to see her that all she could do was laugh. But when she pulled back to look into Tracy's face she could see she was the only one laughing. Tracy's eyes were still filled with tears. "Are you okay?" Pat asked, and stood Tracy up as she knelt down before her. She wiped the dirt off Tracy's dress, then took her into her arms again. She closed her eyes and thanked God that Tracy had only been hiding and hadn't run off or, worse, been carried off. She opened her eyes and looked at Tracy again, wiping more dirt from her, then looking down at her knees. She saw blood where Tracy had scraped herself on the concrete. Pat licked a finger and wiped it off, then looked over Tracy once again. "Are you hurt, honey?" she asked, concerned.

Tracy nodded her head slowly up and down.

"You are?" Pat said excitedly. "Where, honey? Where are you hurt?"

Tracy sniffled, then straightened out a finger and pointed it to her chest.

"You hurt there?" Pat said, looking at the spot Tracy indicated but seeing no blood seeping through her clothes or even a rip. "Where, Tracy? Show me where you hurt," she said again, and again Tracy pointed to her chest. Confusion swept over Pat as she put her hand on Tracy's chest. She lifted up her dress and looked at her bare chest, then dropped the dress back down. "Here?" Pat asked with frustration, and pointed to Tracy's chest once again. Tracy nodded her head and slowly but surely Pat caught on. "Your heart?" Pat said, and rubbed Tracy's chest. "You hurt in your heart?"

Tracy nodded her head and looked into Pat's eyes. Pat could do nothing but stare at Tracy. At that moment, she was Tracy. She felt what she felt, she understood it, and she knew there was nothing she could do to change it. The honesty she saw in Tracy's eyes was heartwrenching, it told the story of a child at a loss. A child from nowhere that found a family only to have it taken away by two people who claimed to love her. But if Pat and Mark truly loved Tracy they had to do what was best for her.

Pat stroked the side of Tracy's face as she felt a single tear roll down her cheek. Tracy reached out for Pat's face and wiped the tear away and Pat did the same for her. "I love you, Tracy," Pat said, looking deeply into her daughter's eyes. "Let's go home," she said and stood up. "Let's go home."

20

Zuma had made sure that her last hair appointment was scheduled for two-thirty on Saturday afternoon so that she could leave work early. But with Pat coming in and calling a private counsel and the usual Saturday walk-ins that typically invaded the shop she found herself running behind schedule. She was finishing up on her last scheduled appointment at a quarter to four, but there were still three walk-ins that were waiting on her to hook them up. But Zuma had to stick to her schedule. She had to be out of the shop by four o'clock if she wanted to keep her appointment with her doctor. Today was the day she would find out for sure if she was pregnant and nothing in the world was going to keep her from that. Not even three walk-in customers that would probably make her at least $250 richer.

She finished up her last scheduled appointment and walked her to the front for payment. She could see the walk-in customers eyeing her, wondering which one of them she'd call on next. But Zuma paid them no mind. Instead she walked back to her hair station, straightened up her countertop, then grabbed her purse and flung it over her shoulder.

"Excuse me," Faye said to her as she watched her preparing to leave. "Where do you think you're going?"

"I've got business to tend to," Zuma said, patting her pockets for her keys.

"I know you're not going to walk out of here and leave all these heads," she said, looking around at all the waiting customers.

"I don't have a choice," Zuma said, very businesslike. "I've got to go."

Faye frowned as she finished braiding a section of her client's hair, then walked over to Zuma. "I've got another two hours on my customer, Sandy's swamped with manicures, Pat's gone, and now you're just going to walk out of here? Unh-uh, Zuma. What the heck is so important that you have to leave right now?"

"That's my business, Faye," she said, opening her purse, still searching for her keys. "I've finished my scheduled appointments and I've got to go. These walk-ins are just gonna have to take their asses home. Shit, they should have made appointments like everybody else."

Faye glared at Zuma and sucked her teeth. "And you want to buy this shop? Oh, I can't wait to see how you're gonna run this place after Pat's gone."

"What is the problem?" Zuma said, raising her voice. "I'm just gonna tell them they have to come back another day."

"That's bad business, Zuma. These women have already been waiting for over an hour."

"Too bad," Zuma snapped. "Besides, they're my problem. What the hell are you bitching about it for?"

"Because you're irresponsible, Zuma," Faye shouted. "You just up and leave without warning anybody. All you think about is yourself. You didn't even have the decency to forewarn me or even tell me where you're going."

"Irresponsible," Zuma said, incensed. "You're calling me irresponsible?" she said, and chuckled a bit.

"Yes, Zuma. You," she said, and pointed at her. "You are irresponsible."

"I'm not going to argue with you," Zuma said, finally finding her keys. "I've got to go," she said, and turned around to walk out, leaving Faye standing alone and not even bothering to say a word to the walk-ins. "Now that's irresponsible," she huffed to herself, and jumped in her car.

Faye shook her head as Sandy walked over to her. "Where's she going?" Sandy asked as she watched Zuma drive away. "Oh yeah," she said, and sucked her teeth. "Today's the day she goes back to see the doctor."

"See the doctor?"

"Oops," Sandy said, and put her hand over her mouth as Faye turned questioning eyes on her.

"See the doctor about what?"

"Nothing," Sandy said nervously.

"Oh forget it," Faye said and sighed. She looked out the window to see Zuma speed away in her car and shook her head. "*Zuma.*"

Zuma blazed down the street cutting corners and speeding through yellow lights. She wanted to be on time for her four-thirty appointment and wished she hadn't wasted time quibbling with Faye. "Irresponsible?" Zuma muttered to herself as she drove. "I'm irresponsible? Please," she said, and frowned. I've been taking care of myself ever since I was eighteen years old, I've got almost fifty thousand dollars of hard-earned money stashed away, and I'm about to buy my own hair salon, she thought. How can that be irresponsible? "Jealous," she said, referring to Faye. She figured Faye was just mad because she couldn't take seeing Zuma's life come together while her own was falling apart. "Irresponsible," Zuma huffed again, thinking what nerve Faye had calling her that. She was the irresponsible one. Hell, she couldn't even keep up with her own daughter. Now that's irresponsible, Zuma thought, and shook her head. She knew one thing for sure and that was that she would never let her child run away from home. If it gets so bad that a child has to run away that means that you have not done your job as a parent. You've been irresponsible at the most important job in the world and Zuma knew for sure that she would never let that happen.

She shook off her thoughts of Faye as she turned into the parking lot at the insemination hospital. All she wanted to focus on now was getting the results of her insemination and moving on to the prenatal phase of her pregnancy. To Zuma, the prenatal phase was the most important of all. She vowed she would listen to all her doctor's instructions and follow them to a tee. She hadn't spent fifteen thousand dollars getting artificially inseminated only to have something go wrong like a miscarriage.

She smiled gloriously as she got out of her car and walked into the hospital. She got on the elevator as her mind moved ahead of her and she began making plans for what she would do after she got the good news. Since she was pregnant she couldn't pop open a bottle of champagne to celebrate, so she decided she would go to Baby Wonderland and start picking out some things for her new child. She promised herself that she wouldn't let them tell her the baby's sex from ultrasound because she wanted to be surprised. She didn't care if the baby was a boy or a girl, all she wanted was a child — period. Still she wanted to go to Baby Wonderland just to see what they had in the store. That would be the perfect way to celebrate, she thought as the elevator chimed and the doors opened.

She hurried over to the reception desk and when the nurse looked up and saw her she immediately buzzed her in.

"Miss Price," the nurse said, grinning from ear to ear. "You're right on time."

"Honey, I wouldn't be late for anything in the world," Zuma said, and clicked her fingers.

"Well let's get started." The nurse held out a hand as she ushered Zuma down the hall and into an open door. "How have you been feeling since the procedure?"

"Pregnant," Zuma said, laughing as she sat down on the edge of the examining table. "I swear I don't know what's gotten into me, but ever since I left here last week I've been having these strange cravings. One day it's ice cream and sardines, the next it's pig's feet and butterscotch pudding. Now either I'm pregnant or I'm going delirious. Which one do you think?"

"Let's hope it's pregnant," the nurse said as she began taking Zuma's blood pressure as Zuma went on and on.

"I've even started picking out names," she said, absolutely glowing. "If it's a boy — "

"Take a deep breath for me," the nurse said, cutting Zuma off.

She did, then blew out strong as the nurse smiled and unsealed the Velcro around her arm.

"Your pressure's perfect."

"Good," Zuma said, making herself comfy on the examining table. "Anyway, if it's a boy I want to name him Tiger," she said as the nurse looked at her like she was crazy. "You know, Tiger Woods, the golfer."

"I don't watch golf."

"Neither did I until Tiger came along. But anyway, I want my son to be like him. Focused, dedicated, strong."

"And if it's a girl?"

"If it's a girl, I'll name her Zuma the second."

"Zuma the second?"

"Yes," she said confidently. "Men name their sons after themselves all the time, so why not?"

The nurse chuckled and shrugged her shoulders. "I guess you're right."

"I want my daughter to be focused, dedicated, and strong too."

"Just like you."

"Just like me," Zuma said, satisfied with herself.

The nurse pulled over a tray with a bowl of cotton swabs and needles. Zuma watched as she rubbed alcohol on her right forearm and searched for a vein. She uncapped a needle, stuck it into her arm, and withdrew a tube of blood. "That was easier than last time," the nurse said.

"Oh, I'm not nervous today," Zuma explained as the nurse put a clean cotton ball on her arm and wrapped tape across it.

"Very good," she said as she labeled the tube of blood, then handed Zuma a plastic cup. "Urine sample time," the nurse said as Zuma jumped down from the table and rushed off to the bathroom. Within a minute she was out carrying a full cup of hot urine, which she placed on the tray and the nurse immediately labeled. "Okay," the nurse said as she watched Zuma hop back onto the examining table. "I'm going to run these samples downstairs to the lab. It'll take about an hour and a half to check the results, then the doctor and I will come back in and explain everything to you."

"Sounds good to me," Zuma said, making herself comfortable again.

"You can either stay here, or if you want you can leave and come back."

"I'm not going anywhere," Zuma said, and folded her hands in her lap. "I'll be right here until you get back."

"Very good," the nurse said, and wheeled her cart to the door. "See you in a bit."

"Toodle-oo." Zuma cheesed and watched the nurse walk out.

Zuma sat back against the head of the examining table and reached over to grab one of the magazines stacked next to the lamp. She opened up *Today's Mother* and began flipping through the pages until she came across an article on breast-feeding. Zuma intended to breast-feed because she thought it would be the most nutritional and natural food for her baby. But she wasn't going to be one of those women who just whipped out her boobies in public. There's a cool way and a wrong way to do everything, Zuma thought. That's why they invented breast pumps. That way when you're in private you can feed your baby from the breast, but when you go out in public you can still feed your baby natural food, but from a bottle. Mother or no mother, she thought, she was not going to be exposing herself for all the world to see. She flipped through the pages of the magazine again until she came to an article on women who had trouble losing weight after their babies were born. Zuma quickly scanned through the ladies' sad sob stories and shook her head. "If you want to lose weight, get your sloppy ass up and move around," she mumbled to herself. She didn't understand why women always complained about losing weight after birth. Pregnancy isn't a sickness, Zuma thought. Just because you have a baby growing inside you doesn't mean you can't get out and walk or swim or keep your muscles toned. And that's what Zuma planned to do. She had already talked to her doctor and he told her that it was absolutely safe to exercise while pregnant. In fact he told her that the more in shape a woman was the fewer complications she was likely to have giving birth. Zuma vowed she was not going to be one of those women who went crazy just because she was pregnant. Oh sure, she planned to continue eating her ice cream and sardines, but she was also going to get her butt moving. Pregnancy is no excuse to be fat, lazy, and funky, Zuma concluded.

She flipped through the magazine a bit more, then looked down at her watch, amazed that an hour had already gone by. She put down that magazine and picked up another, but as she flipped through it she realized it was only more of the same material she'd already read. She put the magazine down and just sat still for a moment as she thought about the wonderful future she would have with her baby. And as she thought a question popped into her head that she had never considered before. What would she do when her child became old enough to ask who her father was? Strangely enough, Zuma had never even considered that situation, but now that she did, she wondered what her answer would be.

But Zuma wasn't perplexed for long. The answer came to her quickly and surely. She'd tell her son or daughter the truth. She'd tell them that she loved them so much and wanted them so much that she got herself artificially inseminated. . . . Well, she probably wouldn't use such a big word, but she would talk to them honestly and let them know exactly how they were brought into this world.

Zuma was pleased with herself, knowing that when the time came she would be prepared to deal with all of her child's questions. The important thing is not how the child gets here, but that the child *is* here, she thought as she looked down to check her watch again. And as soon as she looked back up, the door to her room came swinging open and in walked the nurse and the doctor.

Zuma scooted to the edge of the examining table and flashed a brilliant smile as the doctor pulled over a chair in front of her and shook her hand as he sat down.

"How are you today?" he said as he opened up a file that had her name on it and sat it in his lap.

"Just fine," she said as she felt herself bubbling all over.

The nurse smiled as she stood next to the doctor and placed her hands behind her back like a soldier.

"You look anxious so I'll get straight to the point," the doctor said, and looked down at the file. "Pregnancy is a wonderful stage of a woman's life."

"Yes it is," Zuma said, all aglow.

"My job is so fulfilling to me because the women who come to this hospital are so excited about giving birth that it fills me with great joy when I can make that happen for them."

"I am excited," Zuma said, patting her hands on her knees. "No doubt about that. I've been planning for this day for years."

"However," the doctor said, closing the file and looking straight into Zuma's eyes, "it's days like this that really break my heart."

Zuma questioned the doctor with her eyes, looked over at the nurse, then back at the doctor.

"I'm so sorry to tell you, Miss Price, but the artificial insemination failed. You are not pregnant."

"What?" Zuma said softly as she slowly circled her stomach with her hands.

The nurse walked closer to her and placed her hand on Zuma's shoulder. "I know how disappointed you must be, Miss Price."

"But . . . But I know I'm pregnant. . . . I — I've been having cravings and . . . No . . . I know I'm pregnant."

"The nurse filled me in about your cravings on the way over and I think I should try to explain that for you," the doctor said, leaning forward in his seat. "Sometimes a woman can want to be pregnant so desperately that her mind tricks her into believing that she really is. Some women want it so badly that they even miss periods. The mind is a powerful tool, Miss Price. But make no mistake, we've run the tests and you are definitely not pregnant."

Zuma's heart dropped like a load of cement as she listened to the doctor in disbelief. "This can't be right," she said shaking her head. "No, this . . . this can't be right."

The doctor bit down on his bottom lip as he watched Zuma, knowing the pain she was feeling. He'd watched the pain in thousands of his patients when he'd have to tell them they were not pregnant. But it wasn't over. "Many women don't become pregnant on their first try, Miss Price. In fact, some women have to go through the procedure three or four times before they finally become pregnant. What we can do now is wait until your next cycle and repeat the process again. Now, if it doesn't take next time we'll have to run some more tests to make sure you aren't suffering from infertility and then we can — "

"We're talking another fifteen thousand dollars," Zuma said, cutting him off. She'd only set aside enough money to have the procedure done once. The rest of the money she'd saved was supposed to go toward her business. "Dammit," she yelled, then caught herself. "This was supposed to work the first time."

"You can't budget for a baby, Miss Price."

The room fell silent as the doctor and nurse watched Zuma closely, as if they thought she would lose it or cry or go crazy. But Zuma barely noticed they were there. She felt so alone, so empty. She knew these feelings well, she'd had them before. She felt like she had slipped back in time, back to the day she had her first pregnancy aborted. She'd fought so hard to lose those feelings and now they were upon her again. As Zuma sat silently, rubbing her hands over her empty womb, she realized what was really going on. Allah was punishing her. She could feel it, she knew it. He was punishing her for the baby she killed years ago. Now Zuma felt stupid. What was she thinking? How could she expect Allah to ever let her become pregnant again after what she'd done? She wasn't worthy to be a mother. Killers don't get the privilege of giving birth. She had thought having a baby that she would love and teach and respect would somehow make up for the fact that she had had an abortion. But now she knew. She knew that nothing she could do would ever make up for what she'd already done. She'd been given the beauty of life before and had disrespected it, and now, there were no second chances.

Zuma slid down from the examining table, grabbed her purse, and headed to the door.

"Miss Price," the nurse called as she and the doctor turned to face her. "Would you like to schedule the procedure for a month from now? I'm sure we'll have better results next time."

Zuma smiled and thanked both the nurse and doctor. "There'll be no next time for me," she said as a tear fell down her face. "I'm being punished."

The doctor and nurse looked at each other, trying to figure out what Zuma was talking about. She could see their confusion, but she decided not to explain. She knew what she meant, and in a peculiar way she felt almost grateful. Better to be punished here than in the hereafter, she said to herself, then looked up toward the ceiling.

21

Faye had been planning all week long to go to church this Sunday, but as luck would have it, she overslept and didn't wake up until eleven o'clock. She was usually up at the crack of dawn, but all those long, worry-filled nights she'd been staying up thinking about Antoinette had finally caught up with her. She sat up in her sofabed and grabbed the remote for the television hoping she could catch Fred Price or Creflo Dollar on cable, but she was too late.

She lay around in bed for another half hour before she decided to get up. She hadn't bothered with housecleaning since Antoinette had been gone, so she decided to take this time to straighten up the clutter that had generated over the past week. She started in the front room by cleaning off the coffee table and dusting, then she made up her bed and turned it back into a sofa. Next she hit the kitchen, washed a sinkful of dishes, and mopped, then pulled out a carton of eggs to prepare a plate of huevos rancheros. But before she started she walked to Christopher's room to get him up, but when she looked in she found his bed empty. For a split second her mind went blank as she peered around his darkened room in a panic. "Christopher," she yelled, and spun around. She opened the door to the bathroom, then walked back to the front, then turned and stopped. Slowly she walked to Antoinette's room and found her door halfway open. She stuck her head inside and found Christopher peacefully sleeping atop his sister's bed.

"Christopher," she said as her nerves relaxed and she walked over to the bed. "Christopher?" she said again, shaking his tiny body from side to side. "Wake up, sleepyhead."

Christopher twisted and turned over onto his back and slowly opened his eyes.

Faye's eyes brightened as she watched her son sit up and try to shake off his sleepiness. "Come on now," she said, and rubbed his head. "Time to get up and brush your teeth."

" 'Kay, Mami," he said as he slid off the bed and stumbled his way toward the bathroom.

Faye stood in the doorway watching as he got out his toothbrush and toothpaste. "Want some huevos rancheros?" she asked as she started to walk away.

"I want some cake!" he said, full of joy.

Faye had stayed up late the night before making the German chocolate cake for Zuma's party and Christopher had been begging for a piece ever since. She gave him the same wicked eye she'd given him last night and he knew that meant no.

"Okay. I'll have the eggs," he said, and shrugged his shoulders, then stuck his toothbrush in his mouth. "Mawbi?" he said as his mouth filled with bubbles.

"Yes." Faye turned around.

"Dun macum choo ot."

"I won't make 'em too hot," she said, and turned away.

"Mawbi!"

"Yes, Christopher," she said, and turned around again.

"Gwinis Antanet cawmin om?"

"Huh?"

"Gwinis Antanet cawmin *om?*"

"Spit."

Christopher took the toothbrush out of his mouth and spit a stream of white bubbles into the sink.

"Now what did you say?"

"When is Antoinette coming home?"

"Oh," Faye said, and walked back to the doorway. "I don't know, honey." She looked into her son's confused face. "I don't know."

"But you said she was only gonna be gone for a few days."

"I know, but . . ." Faye didn't quite know what to say. She had hoped and prayed that Antoinette would be back by now, but it was clear that her prayers had not been answered.

"She's not coming back, is she?" Christopher said softly and waited for his mother's reply. But Faye couldn't answer him. The simple fact of the matter was that she just didn't know. She didn't want to believe that Antoinette would never come home, but as each day passed she began to wonder if that's how it would be.

Chris stared at Faye a bit longer, then went back to brushing his teeth. Faye could tell he had come to his own conclusion about whether his sister would be back or not. She could tell he thought she would never return, and for the first time Faye allowed herself to believe that too. She turned away from the door and headed toward the kitchen, until . . .

"Mawbi!"

"Yes, Christopher."

"Ahmiser."

"I miss her too," she said, then continued on her way.

She walked back to the kitchen and took out a skillet, some salsa, cilantro, onions, cheese, tortillas, and chilies. She oiled her skillet and placed it on the stove, then cracked open four eggs and watched them sizzle. Antoinette used to love her huevos rancheros, she thought as she placed four corn tortillas over the eggs. Antoinette had even learned how to prepare them herself, Faye thought as she reminisced back to Mother's Day two years ago when Antoinette was in one of her rare good moods. She had made huevos rancheros and served them to Faye in bed. It was one of the last times Faye could remember when Antoinette had done something nice for her. As Faye sprinkled cheese over the tortillas she wondered if there would ever be a time when Antoinette would do that again.

She took the eggs off the stove and set them to the side as she felt a slight headache coming on. It wasn't so much pain that was throbbing in her head, but the knowledge of the fact that her daughter was never coming home. She sat down at the kitchen table and rubbed the sides of her temples as the inevitable began to sink in. Part of her wanted to cry, but part of her also felt a tiny sense of relief. She would always worry about her daughter, wonder if she was all right, if she was being taken care of and if she was happy. But now that she had given in to the reality that she was never coming home, Faye could begin to relax. Part of the reason Faye would stay up till the wee hours of the morning was because she kept thinking that at any second her daughter would walk through that door. Every sound she heard outside, every car that drove past, every cricket's chirp would send Faye running to the window only to look out and see that Antoinette was nowhere to be found. But now that she knew her daughter was never coming home she could at least begin to relax. Wherever she was, whatever she was doing, Faye had to believe that God was with her.

"She won't be back," Faye whispered to herself as she sat staring straight ahead. She pressed her lips together and whispered again, "Valle con Dios."

Christopher walked into the kitchen just as the phone rang out on the wall. When Faye didn't move to answer, he did. "Hello," he said clutching the oversized receiver against his ear. "Hi," he chirped with delight. "Fine . . . yeah . . . uh-huh . . . She right here . . . Okay, okay . . . Hold on," he said and held out the phone for Faye.

"Who is it?" she said, in no mood to talk at that moment.

"I'm not supposed to tell."

Faye rolled her eyes, thinking it must be Pat calling to check up on the party plans, but when she put the phone to her ear and said, "Hello," she was pleasantly surprised.

"Hey, Faye."

"Mr. Watson?"

"No."

Faye frowned, knowing she knew this voice. "This is too Mr. Watson."

"No," he said firmly. "This is James."

Faye chuckled and cleaned up her act. "Hello, James."

"Thank you."

"You're welcome," she said, then paused, not knowing what to say. She wanted to ask why he was calling, but knew that would sound too rude. So instead she asked, "Uh . . . How are you doing?"

"Fine and you?"

"Fine," she said, smiling intensely and waiting for him to continue with the conversation, but he didn't. "So, um . . . what have you been up to?"

"Oh, just work basically. What about you?"

"The same," she said, then paused, trying to think of something else to say. She began to feel awkward, thinking Mr. Watson must consider her a bore. But then again he was the one who called her. Shouldn't he be the one responsible for keeping the conversation lively?

"Well," he said timidly. "Has there been any word from your daughter?"

So that's what this call is all about, she thought, and sighed. "No."

"I'm sorry to hear that."

"Don't be," she said quickly. "Actually, I'm slowly coming to grips with the fact that I may never see her again."

"Don't talk like that, Faye."

"I have to be realistic, Mr. Watson. All I can do now is turn it over to the Lord."

"I guess you're right," he said. "You can't let yourself go crazy behind all this. But just remember, you did the best you could with Antoinette. You can't blame yourself."

"I know," Faye said.

"Well, what about Christopher? I saw him at school Friday. Looks like he's doing okay."

"He is, he is," Faye said, and looked at her son, who was now sticking his fingers into the huevos rancheros. She clapped her hands together to get his attention, then mouthed the words *Stop it*. "Christopher is doing just fine now, thanks to you."

"Good, good," he said, then fell silent.

"Mami," Chris shouted as Faye put her finger to her mouth and shushed him. "Mami," he said again, and bounced up and down.

Faye put her hand over the receiver. "Don't you see me on the phone?"

"But I wanna talk to Mr. Watson."

"Ssh," Faye said, then uncovered the receiver.

"It's okay, I'll talk to him," Mr. Watson said, surprising Faye that he had heard what was going on.

"Hold on a sec," she said, and handed Chris the phone.

"Hello," Chris said, almost as if he didn't know who he was speaking to. " 'Member when you had said that, uh, we, I mean you, was gonna come teach me karate?" Christopher's eyes widened with anticipation. "Uh-huh . . . Yeah . . . 'kay . . . okay . . . 'kay . . . Hold on," he said and put the phone down. "Mr. Watson said for me to ask you if he could . . . I mean if you wouldn't, um . . . um . . . Wait a minute, Mami," he said, and got back on the phone. "What am I supposed to say? . . . Oh yeah. Hold on," he said, and turned to Faye. "He wants me to ask you if you don't mind can he come over here today."

Faye was shocked and for a moment there her heart nearly stopped. "Sure," she said with excitement. But as Christopher got back on the phone, reality hit her. Mr. Watson wasn't coming over to see her. He was coming to see Chris.

Chris handed her the phone as he jumped up and down with delight. "I gotta go get dressed," he said, and ran out of the room.

Faye put the phone to her ear. "You still there?"

"Yes," he said hesitantly. "Are you sure it's going to be all right if I stop by?"

"Sure, no problem," Faye said.

"I had almost forgotten I promised to teach Chris a few karate moves."

"You don't have to do this if you don't want to. Chris will understand."

"I always keep my word," he said definitely. "Besides it'll be nice to see you again too."

Yeah, yeah, Faye thought, and rolled her eyes. That's the problem with nice guys like Mr. Watson. They have a tendency to say all the right things, making you believe they really like you when all they're really doing is being polite. Well, Faye was no fool. She could tell the difference between a come-on and a nice gesture and as usual Mr. Watson was only being polite. "Well, just remember, Chris and I have a birthday party to go to this evening."

"Oh, a party?"

"Yeah. One of the girls at the shop is having a birthday today."

"Oh, don't say birthday," he said with excitement. "Whenever I hear that word I think of cake. My mother used to make the best German chocolate cake for my birthday."

"Actually, I made one just last night for the party."

"Oh no, oh God," he said, panting. "You're not serious."

"Yes I am," she replied, and chuckled. "You can come along if you like," she said, expecting Mr. Nice Guy to come up with some polite excuse as to why he couldn't make it.

"Sure, I'll bring a change of clothes with me."

Faye's mouth dropped open. She took the phone from her ear, looked at it, then returned it. She couldn't believe he'd agreed to come to the party with her, but then again, she thought, and smirked, it would have been too rude for him to turn down her invitation. Mr. Watson was just being the nice guy again, she thought. He wasn't fooling her. "Okay, Mr. Watson," she said. "I guess I'll see you in a little while." She waited for him to say something, but he didn't. "Mr. Watson?" she said and frowned. "Mr. Watson? . . . Mr. . . . Oh," she said, and smiled. "James?"

"Yeeesss."

"I'll see you in a little while."

"Okay, Faye. See you in a little while."

Faye got up from the table and went to the counter to chop up some onions, chilies, and cilantro. She mixed it with the salsa, then poured it on top of the tortillas in the skillet and set it back on the stove to warm. Christopher came running back seconds later all hyped up in a pair of shorts and an old Penny Hardaway T-shirt.

"Mr. Watson still coming, Mami?" he asked, bouncing up and down.

"Yes, Christopher," she said, and put some eggs on a plate for him.

"You sure? When he coming?"

"He'll be here when he gets here. Now sit down and eat before your eggs get cold," she said, and set his plate on the table.

She fixed her plate and sat down across from him and watched as he stuffed food in his mouth until his jaws pumped out like balloons. "Slow down before you choke," she said. "You have plenty of time to eat before Mr. Watson gets here," she said as she tasted a bite of her food, then grabbed the bottle of hot sauce that sat in the middle of the table.

Christopher slowed down reluctantly as he chewed and looked at his mother. "Mami," he said, and eyed her closely. "Are you going to wear that when Mr. Watson gets here?"

Faye looked down at her old raggedy oversized T-shirt with a faded picture of Tweety Bird on it and her stretched-out pair of quadruple X biker shorts and raised her eyebrow. "Yes I am," she said firmly, and huffed. She always wore that outfit around the house on weekends and she wasn't about to change. What for? To impress Mr. Watson? Huh. That man ain't hardly studying me, she thought, and took another bite of her spiced-up eggs.

"Oh," Christopher said, looking embarrassed.

"What?" Faye said, and gave herself another once-over. She looked fine, she thought. She was all covered up, she was clean, and no one could even see the tiny hole she'd torn in the seat of her biker shorts. As far as she was concerned she looked decent. Decent enough for Mr. Watson or any one of her other friends.

Christopher continued eating his food, taking quick peeps at his mother out of the corner of his eye. "Didn't you say we should always try to look our best when company comes to the house?" he asked, staring at Tweety Bird.

"Yes I did, Christopher," she said, and put her fork down. "What's so wrong with the way I look today? I wear this all the time when Pat or Zuma comes to the house."

"But I thought you liked Mr. Watson."

"What?" she said, and winced. "Where did you get that idea?"

"Whenever you see him you start smiling and stuff and you be looking happy. You don't look that way around Pat and Zuma."

"Okay, Christopher," she said, dreading the fact that she had to explain this all to him. "I do like Mr. Watson, but he's just my friend. He's your friend and he's my friend. That's all," she said, swiping her hands through the air.

Christopher looked down at his food and pushed it aside.

"What's wrong now?" Faye asked and stared at Christopher as he pouted.

"Nothing."

"Talk to me, little boy."

Christopher got up from the table and walked out.

"Where are you going?" Faye asked, unwilling to believe that her son could be so bold as to walk away from her while she was talking. "Christopher," she yelled, then scooted her chair back to get up. "Christopher," she yelled again, then stopped when she saw him coming back to the kitchen.

In his hand he carried an old picture frame, which he set in front of Faye on the table. Faye sat back down and stared at the picture. It was of her and Antoine when they were newlyweds. The picture usually sat on one of the end tables in the front room and as she looked at it she became puzzled. "Why did you bring me this?"

"How come you don't look like that no more?" he asked. "You looked pretty then, Mami," Christopher said as if he were mad at her. As if she'd changed her appearance just to piss him off.

"I was much younger then, Christopher."

"But you looked happy."

"That's because your daddy made me happy," she said, pointing her finger at Antoine. "He was a good man, Christopher. There will never be another one like him."

"Ain't Mr. Watson good?"

"But Mr. Watson is not *him*," she said, pointing at Antoine again.

"But *he*," Christopher said, pointing his finger, "is dead."

Faye put the picture down and looked away from her son.

Christopher stood by her side innocently, wondering what he had said that was so wrong. When he saw his mother's hand move toward her eye he touched her on the shoulder. "I'm sorry, Mami," he said, and patted her. "Mami, I'm sorry, 'kay?"

Faye put her hand on top of his and continued looking away until she had successfully settled her emotions. "You didn't do anything wrong," she said, and turned to face him. "You just told the truth." She pulled him into her arms.

Christopher still didn't know what was wrong with his mother, and to be honest Faye didn't know either. She just got up from the table and went to the bathroom so she could be alone. She looked at herself in the mirror with disgust, realizing the true extent of how much she had let herself go. She knew she didn't look like the bodacious beauty she once was and she knew she could never look like that again. Still, she thought, as she eyed herself from the side, there was no excuse to let herself look this bad. "I've got to do something about this," she said to herself and shook her head. Being big was one thing, but being big, sloppy, and outdated was another. But what could she do? she thought, and sat down on the edge of the tub in despair. There was no way she could lose weight. She had tried and tried and failed and failed and besides, Faye was in love with food. She didn't want to restrict herself. Hell, life was too short to be worrying about counting calories. If she wanted a hot fudge sundae with nuts, then dammit that's what she wanted. But still, she thought, and placed her head in her hands, there was no reason why she couldn't do the best with what she had. These are the nineties. If they could make the biker shorts she had on in quadruple X, then they ought to be able to make a nice pantsuit in that size too. "That's it," she said, and got to her feet. "I'm going shopping." I may be big, but I don't have to look like a pig, she thought to herself as she opened the door to the bathroom and rushed out into the front room.

"Hi, Faye," Mr. Watson said, scaring her half to death.

When did he get here? she thought and moved out of the way as Chris ran by her toward the door.

"You look . . . nice," Mr. Watson said at he stared at Tweety Bird.

There he goes trying to be polite again, Faye thought to herself, and smiled. She knew she looked wrecked down to the ground, but of course Mr. Nice Guy would never tell her that.

"I'm sorry if I'm a bit too early. I just felt like getting out of the house," he said as Faye turned away from him to find her purse.

"Actually, I'm glad you're here," she said as she flung her purse over her shoulder and stuffed her feet into a pair of flip-flops. "I have to run out for a second. Would you mind keeping an eye on Chris while I'm gone," she said, squinting her right eye, too much in a hurry to realize the huge favor she was asking of him.

"Sure, no problem," he said as he followed her to the front door. "Chris and I have a lot of work to do anyway," he said, and walked over to Chris by the door. "We don't want no girls around getting in our way, do we, big guy?"

"Naw," Chris said mimicking the fierce scowl on Mr. Watson's face.

"Good," she said, and headed past them out the door. Mr. Watson and Chris followed her to the car and watched as she got inside. "You sure you're okay with this?" she asked Mr. Watson as she started up her engine.

"Hey," he said, and held out his hands. "What are friends for?"

Faye faked a smile as she backed out the driveway. Yeah, right, she thought as she took off down the street. Thanks . . . friend.

22

Sandy lit up a cigarette, sucked in a bit of air, then exhaled just slightly so that the smoke went in through her nose. She held the fuzzy cloud in her throat, then exhaled through her mouth and blew out two cloudy rings. She smiled as she took the cigarette out of her mouth. She'd been practicing that trick for days now and she finally had it mastered. It seemed there wasn't much for Sandy to do these days while she was at home but sit around and play cigarette tricks. Since Cerwin had been gone, Sandy felt as if she had no purpose. She had given up plotting her nasty schemes of revenge on Cerwin a couple of days ago. They weren't working at all, not even the phone call she made to the club in the middle of the night, disguising her voice and saying she was a terrorist and had planted a bomb underneath the stage. Tucker just laughed at her and said, "Whatever, Sandy," then hung up the phone. She gave up after that. Her schemes were only pissing Cerwin off even more and he vowed more strenuously than ever that he would never come back to her. She had wanted her schemes to get him upset — that way she would always be on his mind — and somehow she had figured that by playing these games she could make Cerwin break down and return home. But her plan hadn't worked at all.

In fact, Cerwin had made a surprise visit to the house that morning. Sandy was still asleep and when she heard the knocking at the door she jumped up all irritated, and ran to the front. She flung open the door, ready to give whoever it was a harsh tongue lashing, but when she saw Cerwin she quickly settled down. For an instant she thought he was back for good, but when he straightened his posture, cleared his throat, and asked to see his kids, she knew it was all over. A part of her wanted to refuse and slam the door in Cerwin's face, but she knew better. That would only cause more friction between them and she figured that at least if she let him in the house she would have a chance to win him over.

She stepped back and let him pass through the door, and secretly picked the sleep out of her eyes while his back was turned. She put on a smile as she watched Cerwin standing around in the middle of the floor looking as if he had never been there before. His demeanor was purely professional, and when Sandy asked if she could make him some breakfast or fix him a cup of coffee, he flatly refused and asked once again to see his kids.

"I want to take them out for the day," he told her as Sandy's eyes turned on him suspiciously. "Don't worry, I'll have them back by dusk. I'm not going to run off with them, if that's what you're thinking. That's not my style, Sandy. I just want to be with my children today."

Sandy eyed him, trying to figure out if he was being truthful, and she could tell by the look on his face that he was being sincere. Just as she was about to nod her head in agreement, David came running out of his room.

"Daddy," he screamed as he jumped up into his father's arms. Cerwin spun him around and kissed him on the mouth. "I miss you, Daddy," David said, touching his father's face as if he wanted to make sure he was really real.

"You wanna come with me for the day?" Cerwin asked as David's eyes lit up.

"*Yeah*," David said in shock, then braced himself as he looked over his shoulder at Sandy. "Can I?" he asked as he held his breath.

Sandy nodded her head, sending David into a frenzy. He kissed his father on the cheek, then squirmed until Cerwin put him down. He ran off screaming, "Oh boy," as Cerwin watched him, seeming to be on cloud nine.

"Thank you," he said to Sandy and turned to face her.

"You're welcome," she said, coldly staring back at him.

They stood in silence for what seemed forever, then Cerwin cleared his throat again. "I'm gonna go get Dalila ready," he said, pointing to the back of the house.

As he walked away, Sandy continued to stare at him. Looking at him pained her inside, but not to look would be even more painful. "I fucked up," Sandy mumbled to herself and sat down on the sofa. How did I get to this point? she thought as she leaned her head back onto the cushions and sighed. How did I let him get away? How did I end up all by myself?

The questions were purely rhetorical. Sandy knew how and why she was in the position she was in and she knew it was all her doing. Cerwin had always been good to her, had always loved her unconditionally, but that hadn't seemed to be good enough for Sandy. She needed more, but there was only so much Cerwin could give, and only so much Cerwin could take.

Within minutes Cerwin returned to the front of the house, carrying Dalila in one hand, her car seat in the other. David skipped along in front of them and ran right out of the house without a word to Sandy. Cerwin stopped for a second and turned to Sandy. "Can you help me?" he asked as Sandy stood up. "My car keys are in my pocket," he said, shaking his right leg.

Sandy walked to him slowly and reached her hand inside. She hadn't been this close to Cerwin in weeks and as she felt her way down his leg, her body began to tingle. She remembered how it felt to be held in his arms, to walk with him hand in hand, to lie naked with him and —

"You got 'em?" he asked, breaking Sandy's concentration.

"Uh, yeah," she said and pulled the keys out. "I'll go open the door for you," she said, moving in front of him and holding open the screen door as he passed through. She walked ahead of him and unlocked the car. David jumped in shotgun as she reached her hand back to unlock the rear door. Cerwin stood behind her as she took the car seat from his hand and fastened it in with the seat belt. Then she moved out of the way while Cerwin put Dalila in her seat and locked her down, then closed the door and walked around to the driver's side as Sandy backed her way toward the house.

She watched him, feeling like a child being left behind by her best friend as he started up the car. Cerwin was the only one to wave at her as he drove off. David didn't even consider her. She stuck her hand in the air as the car rolled away and as it turned the corner she walked back to the house and sat down on the steps. "I really fucked up," she said to herself again. "I can't believe this shit."

Cerwin was true to his word. At dusk, Sandy sat up on the sofa and peeked out the window as Cerwin pulled his car to the front of the house. He got out and took Dalila out of her car seat and walked her to the front door.

Sandy opened it before he could knock and Cerwin walked in shushing. "She's asleep," he whispered as he took her to the back room. When he came back out he flew past Sandy and out the door again. He unhooked the car seat and pulled it out, then opened the trunk and took out two bags of groceries. He managed everything in his arms as he walked back to the front of the car and called for David to get out. But David didn't budge. He just sat there staring down as his father called his name.

"David," Cerwin said, straining to keep a grip on everything in his arm. "Time to go now," he said. "Come on," he said as David looked at him and shook his head. Cerwin walked toward the house, looking bewildered. "I don't know what's wrong with him," he said as Sandy held the door open for him.

"Don't worry, I'll go talk to him," Sandy said and looked out to the car. "You can put those bags down in the kitchen," she said as she walked down the front steps toward David.

David could see the anger in his mother's eyes as she approached him and at the last second he reached up to lock his door, but he was too late.

"Are you trying to embarrass me, boy?" Sandy grunted directly in his face. "You're gonna have your daddy thinking you don't want to live with me."

"I don't!" David yelled, and tightened his face.

Sandy prepared herself to slap his teeth out of his mouth, but she looked over her shoulder first and saw Cerwin standing in the doorway. Instead she put her hand on David's leg and grabbed a tiny section of his skin. "You better get your ass out this car right now. Do you hear me?" she whispered through clenched teeth. David's face turned red as he tried to take the pain, but when Sandy pinched him even harder he could fight no more.

Sandy moved out of the way as David got out of the car and walked to the house with his head hanging low. Sandy followed behind him, smiling at Cerwin as if everything were peachy keen.

David walked past his father toward his room until Cerwin called out to him. "Don't I get a hug good-bye?" he said, bending down as David walked back to him. "I love you, son," Cerwin said, placing both hands on the sides of David's face. He kissed him and took him into his arms and held him for the longest time. "I'll be back to see you next week," he said, letting him go. "Would you like that?"

"Yes," David said, staring at his father as if he might not ever see him again. He stepped back into his father's arms and hugged him once again. "Love you," he said.

"Love you too," Cerwin said, and patted David on the behind as he walked away. Cerwin stood up, almost in a daze as he watched his son turn the corner toward his room. But when he heard Sandy's voice he seemed to snap out of it.

"I take it you guys had a good time today," she said. "What did you do?"

"Nothing," he said casually. "We were together. That's all that counts." He looked behind Sandy to the kitchen, then pointed. "Oh yeah," he said as he walked past her. "I stopped by the store and picked up a few things for you and the kids. I know it must be hard having to walk to the store and carry a bunch of bags home."

I guess, Sandy thought. She hadn't been to the store in almost two weeks.

"I got some formula and baby food for Dalila and some cereal and Pop-Tarts for David. Plus a few other things," he said, taking some items out of the bags. "Some ravioli, lunch meat, bread . . . You know, the essentials."

"Thanks," Sandy said, uninterested.

"Oh yeah," he said, and pulled out a piece of paper from his pocket. "Here's my new number. I found a little apartment off of Sepulveda." He handed her the paper.

Sandy's emotions were mixed. The fact that he had gotten his own apartment meant he was never coming home. But the fact that he'd given her the number gave her a glimmer of hope. Now she wouldn't have to deal with Tucker every time she wanted to talk with Cerwin.

"I've also been looking around at a few used cars for you."

"For me?"

"Yeah. For things like shopping and getting yourself to work on rainy days or if the kids have an emergency. I wouldn't want you to be stranded," he said, staring at Sandy with concern. "Okay," he said, and clapped his hands together. "I guess I'd better be going."

That's it, Sandy thought. Pick up the kids, drop them off, and leave. Is that what their relationship had come to?

Cerwin paused at the door and turned around. "I want to thank you again, Sandy," he said. "Even though we can't be together right now . . ."

Right now, Sandy thought, and perked up. Was there still some hope for the future?

"Even though we can't be together right now, I appreciate the way you're handling things. There is no one more important to me than my children."

Not even me?

"And believe it or not, you're still very important to me too."

I am?

"As the mother of my children you will always have a special place in my heart. Whether we're together or not."

What are you saying, Cerwin?

"If you need anything at all, just give me a call."

I need you, Sandy thought as she clutched the paper with his phone number on it in her hands.

"Oh, I almost forgot," he said, and stuck his hand in his pocket. He pulled out two hundred-dollar bills and held them out for Sandy. "I know you've got a job now and you're making your own money, but I don't want you to be responsible for carrying the load with the kids. I love them," he said, firmly. "And I intend to continue to take care of them. Always."

Sandy took the money out of Cerwin's hand and watched as he turned around and walked out the door and closed it behind him. She stared at the money in her hand and laid it down on the table next to the sofa. She hadn't even spent all of the last two hundred dollars he'd given her. But if he wanted to keep throwing money her way she wasn't about to refuse. She could use that money to go buy herself a sexy new dress. That way the next time Cerwin came over to see the kids she would be looking nice for him.

Somewhere in Cerwin's words, Sandy picked up on the idea that maybe, just maybe, it wasn't completely over between them. There was a chance, she thought. A tiny, minute, minuscule chance that somewhere down the line she and Cerwin would be together. Maybe not now, maybe not next year, but one day, she thought, and smiled to herself. *One day.*

Sandy checked the clock as she grabbed for a cigarette. "Damn," she whispered as she lit the cigarette and rushed off to her bedroom. She had promised Faye that she would get down to the shop early to help her set up the decorations for the party and she was already late. She opened up her closet and scanned it, then decided to just throw on her one and only pair of jeans and a T-shirt. All her dresses were too whorish and all her pants were either Lycra or had cutouts in very conspicuous places. She threw on her clothes, shook out her hair, and headed back to the front.

"David," she yelled as she dabbed out her cigarette in the ashtray, then reached for another one. "David," she yelled again, and put the cigarette down next to her matches. "Da—" she said and stopped when she saw his face peek around the corner. "Get over here," she said, and stamped her foot.

David walked over slowly, so Sandy reached out and pulled him the rest of the way. "I'm going out now," she said, seriously.

"But you don't have to go to work right now."

"Shut up and listen," she said, and frowned. "I'm going to the shop. You know what to do don't you?"

"Don't answer the phone, don't open the door, don't turn on the stove."

"That's right," she said, and pointed to the papers next to the phone. "You only pick up the phone . . ."

"If I have an emergency."

"And what do you do?"

"I call you at work," he said, and pointed to the number next to the phone.

"Good," she said, and pointed to another paper. "That's your daddy's number," she said. "If you can't get in touch with me, you call him," she said, then bent down and hovered above David's face. "You better not pick up this phone unless it's a real emergency," she said, and pointed her finger in his face. "And you call me first. Nobody else. Do you understand?"

"Yes."

"Now get on out of here," she said as she stood up and grabbed her purse. She turned out the lights in the kitchen and in the front room, then walked out the door, locking it behind her.

This was the first night in years Sandy had been out. She couldn't wait to get to the party and sit with real adults and talk and eat and drink. Her eyes rolled up in her head as she thought of a drink. She hadn't had a stiff shot of anything in as long as she could remember. She knew all the girls would ask her where her kids were, but she didn't care. She already had a lie made up if anyone should ask. Tonight was Sandy's night to get her party on and she couldn't wait to get it started.

Faye pulled into the driveway next to Blessings and turned off the engine. Christopher sat in the backseat playing with a piece of her hair she had flung over her shoulder and Mr. Watson sat next to her, trying his best not to let her catch him sneaking peeks at her, but Faye had caught on long ago.

When she'd come back home from the mall she was fully dressed. She had gone down to the Fox Hills Mall, walked directly into Lane Bryant, and rushed a saleslady who helped her pick out a beautiful linen pantsuit. When Faye went into the fitting room to try it on she was knocked out. It fit perfectly around her large frame and though it was hard to find anything that would make her look thinner, the pantsuit was so tailored that it actually exposed Faye's shape. She was amazed at her hourglass figure — it was a big hourglass — still, it was the first time in long while that Faye had worn an outfit that didn't make her look like a balloon. She was so impressed that she asked the saleslady to pick her out a shirt and some accessories and when Faye put them all on together and saw herself in the mirror she decided she couldn't take the outfit off. She slid her feet back into her flip-flops and walked out of the fitting room and to the cashier and had her ring up everything on her body. She put her old clothes in a bag and walked out of the store already feeling one hundred percent better. But with those flip-flops on her feet she looked a little odd, so she decided to run over to Macy's and buy a new pair of shoes. She anguished over a pair of flat brown crocodile shoes and a pair of brown leather heels until a guy came over and helped her make the decision. He opted for the brown leather heels, telling Faye they'd give her a bit of height and make her pantsuit hang better, then he went off into the back and brought the shoes out in her size.

When Faye tried them on, she knew he had made the right decision for her. She strolled over to the mirror and took one look at herself, then turned to him and said, "Ring 'em up." She put her flip-flops in the box, paid the cashier, then headed on about her business.

Halfway out of the store she passed by the Iman collection in the cosmetics department and was grabbed up by one of those irritating little ladies in a white jacket who are always slamming perfume samples in your face. Faye didn't even argue when the lady started fast-talking her about all the wonderful products Iman had to offer. She just sat down in the chair and let the woman go to work on her. She picked out a wonderful shade called Cocoa Dew, which she applied as foundation to Faye's face. Then she powdered her down until Faye began to sneeze, then added blush, eye shadow, and brow liner. On her mouth the lady put a wonderful shade of golden bronze lipstick, and when it was all over the woman stepped back from her and smiled like she'd just finished work on the *Mona Lisa*. Faye wasn't impressed until the woman handed her a mirror and she took a look. "Oh my goodness," Faye gasped. "Is that *me*?"

"Amazing what a little color can do, huh," the woman said, obviously pleased with herself.

Faye turned to her still gasping and pointed. "I want everything you just put on my face," she commanded. "The brushes too," she said, then turned back to the mirror, astonished at what she saw. She smiled, then raised an eyebrow, then gave a serious look. My goodness, Faye thought. I look too good.

She paid for her makeup, then got up to leave as the saleslady tried to sell her some Iman perfume. But Faye refused, then walked down to the Opium counter and sprayed herself with one of the tester bottles. She loved the smell of Opium and would always dab a bit on her wrists when she came across a sample. Still, she wasn't very big on perfume so she decided she wouldn't buy it. . . . "Oh what the heck," Faye said, and asked the Opium saleswoman to ring her up a bottle of the eau de toilette. Might as well go all the way, she thought.

Faye walked out to her car with her back straight, shoulders erect, head up, and with just enough of a smile on her face that passersby could see that she knew she had it going on. She put her bags in the trunk next to the box of party decorations she'd picked up last week, then walked around to the door and checked herself out once more in the car's window. She was in awe. She couldn't remember the last time she looked this good or felt this good. She was actually . . . cute. She was a big, beautiful babe, she concluded as she turned around still loving herself through the car's window. "There's just one thing. . . ." Faye mumbled to herself as she grabbed her long braid, which hung down her back, and pulled it over her shoulder. She took the rubber band off the bottom of it and flung it to the ground. Then she unraveled the braid, bent over, and shook out her hair. When she stood up straight her hair came flying through the air. She ran her hand through it to untangle it, then pulled a few pieces from the top forward so that they fell just over her left eye. "That's it," Faye said admiring her reflection. Her hair was beautiful and wavy from being braided so long and as Faye stood looking at herself she almost wanted to cry. Not because she looked so good, but because she felt so good. And that, Faye thought to herself, smiling with confidence, was the most important thing.

It was nearly six o'clock when she returned home, and when she walked into the house, Christopher's mouth dropped wide open. "You look pretty, Mami," he said, staring at her like he had a crush.

"Thank you," Faye said, and winked her eye. "You don't look so bad yourself."

"Mr. Watson helped me get dressed," he said, standing up and turning around for her. "He said I look *smooth*," Chris said with just a touch of arrogance.

"You do," Faye said as she looked around the front room. "Where is Mr. Watson?"

"In the bath—"

"Here I am," Mr. Watson said, stepping into the room, looking quite smooth himself all dressed up in a light brown suit, silk shirt, and matching tie. He and Faye's color scheme was right on target. Both of them looked as if they'd planned out their wardrobes together. But when Mr. Watson took a good look at Faye, color coordination was the furthest thing from his mind. His eyes nearly popped out of his head. He had a look on his face like he wanted to say something goofy, like "Hot damn!" But instead he gathered his senses and walked over to Faye. "You look . . . you look . . ."

"Yes," Faye said, feeling a tinge of embarrassment.

"You look very, very, very . . . very . . ."

"*Smooth*," Chris shouted, and giggled as he watched Mr. Watson and his mom.

"Smooth," Mr. Watson said, unable to take his eyes off Faye.

Faye figured Mr. Watson must have become embarrassed too because he kept fidgeting with his tie. "I'll go start the car," he said, still checking Faye out from head to toe.

"We'll take my car," she said, and held up her keys, but he didn't even notice. "Mr. Watson?" Faye said, and dangled the keys. "Earth to Mr. Watson."

"Oh," he said, popping out of the spell she'd put him under. "Just let me straighten up in the bathroom," he said, backing away from her. "I sort of left my things lying around," he said as he bumped into the wall. "Excuse me," he said, then briskly trotted away.

Christopher smiled at Faye with a sneaky look on his face as he followed his mother into the kitchen and stood back while she scooped the German chocolate cake out of the refrigerator.

"What you smiling at, little boy?"

"Mr. Watson gonna like you now," he said, and put his hand over his mouth.

"Look here," she said as she walked over to him. "I didn't put on all these clothes so that Mr. Watson would like me. I did all this for myself, to make me happy," she said and pointed at herself.

"You look happy when you're happy, Mami."

"Do I?" she said bashfully as Chris nodded his head. "Give me some sugar," she said as Chris planted his lips on hers.

Mr. Watson came trotting back into the room, looking like he had regained his composure. Still Faye could see he was quite taken with her, and as they drove to the shop she kept feeling his eyes on her and now that they were parked and ready to get out, she could still feel him watching her.

Mr. Watson followed her to the trunk as she unlocked it and reached in for the decorations box.

"I'll get that," he said, and beat her to it.

She closed the trunk, then walked to the front door and opened the shop. She flicked on the lights as Mr. Watson and Christopher passed through.

"Okay," she said as she closed the door behind her. "We've got about forty minutes to make this place look festive."

"I wanna help, I wanna help," Christopher said, jumping up and down as Mr. Watson set the box on a chair.

"Why don't you take these balloons and blow them up?" he said, pulling out a colorful bag and throwing it to Christopher, but Christopher couldn't hold on to them. "I see I'm gonna have to teach you how to catch too," he said as Christopher picked up the bag and jumped in the air.

"Hi-*yah*," he screamed, and kicked out his leg. Mr. Watson blocked it with his arm, then gave him a karate chop on the head.

"Okay you two," Faye said, breaking them up. "We've got work to do."

"Yes ma'am," Mr. Watson said, and saluted her. Chris mimicked him, then found himself a chair and began blowing up balloons. "What's first?"

"You grab the tape, I'll grab the streamers, and we can start hanging this stuff up on the wall."

"Got it," Mr. Watson said, grabbing the tape and following behind Faye.

"We'll start in this corner," she said, pulling over a chair, then unraveling a long piece of the streamer.

"Be careful," Mr. Watson said as Faye stepped up on the chair and propped herself against the wall.

"I got it," she said as she placed the edge of the streamer on the wall, then held out her hand. "Tape," she said as Mr. Watson cut her off a piece. "Okay," she said after taping the streamer to the wall. "Let's move on down," she said as she tried to step down off the chair and lost her balance. "Oh," Faye said, as her arm reached out for something to hold on to.

"I gotcha," Mr. Watson said and grabbed Faye by the waist and helped her to the floor. "You okay?" he asked her, still holding her around the waist.

"Yes," Faye said as she looked into his eyes. The closeness both scared Faye and mystified her. She looked at his lips and felt an overwhelming urge to kiss them. And then Mr. Watson moved closer. He looked at Faye with an intensity Faye hadn't seen on the face of a man in years. No, it wasn't intensity, Faye thought. It was passion, she concluded, as Mr. Watson's mouth got closer and closer and —

"Hey Faye," Sandy said as she came bursting through the door. "Sorry I'm late, but . . ." Sandy paused, noticing the moment she had interrupted. "I could come back," she said, and pointed her finger toward the door.

"No, no," Faye said, and whisked herself away from Mr. Watson. "We need all the help we can get." She held out her hand nervously and introduced Sandy to Mr. Watson, then took out a pack of colored markers and a huge poster board. "You can make a sign," she said, handing the markers to Sandy. "Something like, like, uh . . ."

"Happy birthday, Zuma?" Sandy said, and looked at Faye.

Faye giggled. "I'm losing my head," she said, and ran a hand through her hair.

"You look wonderful," Sandy said, and checked her out. "And your hair," she said, touching it. "Why have you been hiding these gorgeous locks?"

"It's just so hard to manage."

"Well, it's managing today, honey," Sandy said, and gave her a wink. "Go 'head with your bad self."

Faye nudged Sandy, then looked around the shop. "Where are your kids?" she said, and frowned. "Chris was looking forward to playing with David."

"David came down with the flu today," she lied, and sucked her teeth. "So I left him and Dalila with one of my neighbors."

"Oh, the lady who baby-sits for you during the day?"

Sandy stuttered for a moment, then remembered the lie she'd told everyone about the old lady across the street who watched her kids while she went to work. "Yes," Sandy said, and smiled. "That's her. She's a real life-saver, that woman."

"Oh well," Faye said, and shrugged her shoulders. "I'm sure some of the other ladies will bring their kids, and of course Pat's new little girl will be here too. I can't wait to see her," she said, and smiled as she looked toward the back for Mr. Watson. When she didn't see him she turned around in the other direction, and noticed that he was almost finished with hanging the streamers himself. "Good job," Faye said as she walked over to him. "Need some help?"

"No, no," he said, and strained to reach over. "I got it," he said as he finished hanging up the last piece. He jumped down off the chair and turned to Faye. "What's next?" he said devilishly.

Faye felt herself getting giddy and turned away from him so that he wouldn't see her face. "Oh," she said, and snapped her fingers. "The confetti." She turned back around. "We're all supposed to throw confetti in the air when Zuma walks through the door."

"Well, where is it?"

"I left it in the trunk." Faye walked over to pick up her keys.

"I'll get that," he said, following behind her and taking her keys out of her hand.

"Okay," she said. "It's a small yellow bag." She watched him walk out the door. Seconds later, she knew she needed to go help him. With all the bags she'd picked up at the mall today, it would be too confusing for him, she thought, and walked out the door behind him. She went around the car and caught a glimpse of him looking quite baffled, just as she'd expected. "It's this one," she said, surprising him and leaning over into the trunk. She grabbed the yellow bag and stood up straight, and when she did she noticed Mr. Watson was directly in front of her face. Again, she could see that look of passion in his eyes and she wondered if he could see the same in hers. She wanted to kiss him, but then again she didn't. Mr. Watson confused her. Until today, he hadn't showed any real interest in her. Oh sure, he called her, he came by the shop to see her once, but all those gestures were out of friendship, not love or anything that even resembled love. Was he just attracted to her now because she was all dressed up, her hair was down, and she had a bit of makeup on? The questions swarmed around Faye's brain, but as Mr. Watson moved in closer they faded away. All that she could focus on were his lips, until . . .

Beep, beep, beep!!!!!!!!!!!!

The sound came out of nowhere, shocking Faye and Mr. Watson so that they split apart. When Faye noticed the four-wheel-drive vehicle pulling in front of her she thought it was Pat until the tinted window came down and Mark poked his head out.

"Hey," Faye said, walking closer to the vehicle. "Where's Pat?"

"That's what I was just about to ask you," he said hurriedly.

Faye could see the distress on Mark's face even though he tried hard to keep the conversation casual. "She hasn't shown up yet."

"What?" he said and rubbed his head. "She left the house with our daughter about three hours ago. She said she was going to get some drinks for the party but I haven't seen her since."

"Three hours ago?" Faye said, and put her hand on her hip. "Well, maybe she got hung up at the mall. You know how Pat likes to go shopping."

"I don't know," Mark said, and shook his head, then smiled, trying not to let on just how worried he really was. "All right," he said, and waved. "I'm gonna run back to the house and get dressed."

"She's probably there right now waiting on you," Faye said.

"I hope so," Mark said, then rolled up his window and drove off.

Faye looked concerned as she walked back to the car and closed the trunk.

"Problem?" Mr. Watson asked, and touched Faye on the shoulder, sending a ripple up her back.

"No problem," Faye said, and started walking back toward the shop. "No problem at all."

23

Zuma had stayed in bed all day, except when she ran out to go to the liquor store to pick up two very important items. When she got back home she pulled out the first item — an at-home pregnancy kit. Zuma wanted to try one more time. *Just one more time,* she thought as she went into the bathroom, sat on the toilet, and relieved herself onto the tiny stick that came with the kit. "Doctors can make mistakes," she said to herself as she set her egg timer for three minutes. She wasn't ready to give up on her dream of having a baby just yet, even though she knew in her heart that she was not pregnant. Allah was punishing her or so she thought, but when the timer went off and Zuma checked the tiny stick for the results, she found out for the last and final time that she was not pregnant.

She dropped the stick into the trash can and went into the kitchen to retrieve the second item she had brought from the store. She had hoped she wouldn't need it, but since the pregnancy test didn't turn out like she wanted, it was time to switch to plan B — a bottle of red wine. It was the first time Zuma had ever purchased a hundred-dollar bottle of wine and when she took it out she noticed that she needed a corkscrew. "Fuck," Zuma screamed, realizing she didn't own a corkscrew. She was used to cheap wine, the kind you just twist open and drink like Boone's Farm. But she wasn't giving up so easily. She needed a drink. She needed something to soothe the pain that she felt in her heart.

Zuma paced around the kitchen until she came up with an idea. She took out a big bowl, placed it on the counter top, then found a strainer beneath the cabinet and set it inside of the bowl. Next, she picked up the bottle of wine, held it from the bottom, and smashed the neck of it against the sink until it broke off. Glass flew everywhere, including into the bottle itself, but Zuma had the remedy. She held the strainer over the bowl and poured the wine into it and watched patiently as the wine seeped into the bowl and huge chunks of glass got caught in the strainer. When the process was finished, Zuma took the bowl of wine back to her bedroom, sat down on the bed, and began drinking right out of the oversized container. The alcohol was not satisfying at first. Zuma didn't drink much and she figured one shot of the wine would get her high. But this was the good stuff, she concluded. It would take much more than a sip to melt her mind and make her feel better. So she continued to drink and drink and drink and drink as she sat on the bed waiting for the alcohol to take effect. But as she turned the bowl up over her mouth for the last time she still didn't feel any better. She was still alert, still in control, and that pissed her off. She'd spent a hundred dollars trying to get her buzz on and the shit wasn't working. "Shoulda bought some damn Boone's Farm," she yelled and got up from the bed to take the bowl back to the kitchen. But as she made it to her bedroom door, the effects kicked in and she fell to the floor.

"Uh-oh," Zuma said, and laughed as she tried to get up. The wine had snuck up on her and as Zuma struggled to get up she realized it was useless. She was able to make it up on all fours so she crawled back to her bedroom and . . .

Four hours later, Zuma woke up from her blackout and found herself sprawled out on the floor. When she lifted her head it banged against the mattress and she screamed out in agony, wondering how the heck half her body got underneath the bed. She pushed herself backward and slowly got up from the floor, still a bit groggy, but able to make it to the bathroom where she immediately pulled down her pants and handled her business. Though Zuma felt a little tired, she also felt as though she didn't have a care in the world. If you asked her what day it was she'd say "Happy Day." But actually, she thought as she stood up and pulled up her pants, it was Sunday. "Sunday, Sunday, Sunday," she mumbled to herself as she walked out of the bathroom. "There's something special about Sunday," she said as she walked back to her room and fell across the bed. "What am I supposed to be doing today?" she asked herself, and when the answer popped into her head she popped up from the bed and shouted, "Pat's party!" Immediately she patted herself down and rubbed her face, then pranced awkwardly into the kitchen, picked up her purse, and headed for the door. "Pat's party," she slurred with glee as she closed the door and fumbled around with her keys, trying to lock it. She stuck every key into the lock except the right key until she gave up. "Abracadabra," she said, and flung her hands into the air, hoping the door would magically lock itself. But when she checked it she found her little magic trick didn't work. She stared at her keys as if they were a question on the SATs until she remembered which key worked. She chuckled as she fit it into the lock and heard it click.

"Okay," she said as she turned around. Now that that ordeal was over she had to make it down the steps without falling. "Whoa," she said as she barely made it down the first stair. But after taking a couple of deep breaths, she caught on to the walking thing and made it all the way down unscathed.

She made it to her car and came across the same problem she'd experienced at the door. "Eenie, meenie, minie, moe," she said as she flipped through her keys and picked one out. Fortunately the key read Saturn on the head of it and she stuck it into the door and let herself in. She started up the engine, but had the hardest time figuring out just how to get the damn thing moving. Then she remembered something about a clutch and a gear. She stepped on the clutch and shifted the gear, but ended up rolling backward. "Uh-oh." She laughed and hit the brakes just before she crashed into the car behind her. She thought in silence for a while, then stepped on the clutch and shifted gears again and this time she was on her way. Never mind that she was going fifty miles an hour in first gear. The bottom line was that she was moving. Thank goodness Blessings was only a couple of blocks away from her home and no hills were involved in the route.

Within a couple minutes, Zuma pulled into the parking lot of Blessings, and as she drove in she looked out her side window into the shop, trying to see who was there, but the blinds on the shop were closed. When she turned back forward, she screamed out at the top of her lungs. "Oh shit," she hollered as her car banged head-on into another car. "Ooo," Zuma said, and raised both eyebrows. "I'm in trouble."

Pat would have been able to see the blue Saturn in front of her if it weren't for the bottle of Asti Spumante she had turned up in front of her face. She immediately stepped on the brakes when she felt the impact and as her car shook, the Asti Spumante spilled all over her dashiki. Good thing I didn't wear one of my good dresses, she thought, and for some reason broke out laughing. She giggled heartily until a slither of slob came dripping out of her mouth. "Gross," she said, and wiped her lips with the back of her hand. And again, for some reason that was the funniest thing that ever happened to her.

Pat finally pulled herself together enough to open her door and step out of the car. She tried to keep from laughing as she walked toward the car in front of her, but when the driver stepped out and looked into her face, she couldn't control herself. "Zuma," she said, and doubled over.

"Pat," Zuma said, and did the same.

The two stood facing one another, howling like hyenas. They both looked at each other, then looked at their cars and continued laughing like they were at the Comedy Store.

After a while their giggles died down and they looked at each other, looked at their cars, then looked at each other again. "What are we gonna do?" Pat asked timidly.

"I don't know," Zuma replied, and stared at Pat. Then suddenly she blew out air through her teeth so hard that her lips fluttered up and down and the laugh match was on again.

Pat grabbed Zuma by the hand as they walked to the door of Blessings like a couple of deadbeats. Pat put her hand on the door and said, "After you."

"No," Zuma said. "After you."

"No, no, no," Pat insisted. "After you."

Of course this caused another giggle extravaganza until finally Zuma stepped in front of Pat, opened the door, and walked right on in.

Faye was the first to notice the sloppy-looking creature standing in the doorway and she knew right away that something was up. But when she saw Pat step in behind Zuma looking just as pathetic she nearly freaked out. It took some time for the other guests to look toward the door and see the two women wobbling from side to side. But Christopher was the first to react.

"Surprise," he screamed, and jumped up and down in front of Zuma.

Zuma held up a finger and clicked it back and forth in front of her face. "You're supposed to say surprise to her," she said, and pointed to Pat as she wrapped her arm around Pat's neck.

"We fooled you, we fooled you," Chris said, pointing to the banner that hung from the ceiling and as if a timer went off the entire room of people screamed, "Happy birthday, Zuma!"

"But I . . . I thought the party was for you," she said, and looked into Pat's eyes. "We're supposed to be celebrating you and your new daught . . ." Zuma looked on the side of Pat and behind her. "Where's your daughter?" she asked seriously.

But before Pat could answer Sandy moved in. It didn't take a genius to see that Zuma was drunk out of her mind and Sandy was concerned about one thing—the baby. "Zuma," she said, and touched her shoulder. "You're drunk," she said, and put a conspicuous hand over Zuma's stomach. "What about the baby?" she whispered.

"The baby," Pat said, and looked into Zuma's eyes. "What baby?"

Zuma and Pat seemed unable to take their eyes off one another. Somehow they both knew what was going on with the other and suddenly nothing was funny anymore. Pat was the first to whimper and Zuma followed with a sniffle. It went on like this until they were in each other's arms, crying their eyes out as the rest of the people in the room looked on wondering what the hell was going on.

Faye left Mr. Watson's side and walked to the middle of the room. "Excuse us, ladies and gentlemen," she said, and held her hand in the air. She walked to the front of the room, then pushed both Pat and Zuma toward the door. "We'll be right back," she said as Sandy walked out in front of her. "Mr. Watson," she said and stood on her tiptoes so she could see him through the crowd. "Could you turn on some music?" she asked, and pointed over to the stereo system in the back of the room. "Mingle amongst yourselves," she said to everyone else as she walked outside amid whispers of "What's going on? Where's the food? What's all this talk about *babies*?"

Pat and Zuma were still holding each other and Sandy stood at Zuma's side rubbing her back. Faye walked over to Pat and immediately winced. "You two are as drunk as I don't know what," she said, and put her hands on her hips. She shook her head and looked out into the parking lot and saw their two cars jammed together. "You mean to tell me you two have been driving?" she screamed. "What in the world were you thinking? You could have killed yourselves. You could have killed someone else."

All Faye's bickering succeeded at was making Pat and Zuma feel worse and cry more. But she didn't care how they were feeling. They should feel bad for what they've done, she thought as she shook her head and continued. "And where have you been, Pat?" she said, disgusted. "Mark has been looking for you and . . . Oh my God," she said as Zuma turned away, doubled over, and began to vomit. "Mmm, mmm, mmm," Faye said as she watched Sandy move to her rescue. "This is pitiful. Two grown women drunk out of their minds. How old are you guys?"

"Please," Sandy said, and turned to Faye. "That's enough," she said as she took out a crumpled napkin from her pocket and handed it to Zuma. Zuma wiped her mouth and stood back up. "I take it the artificial insemination didn't work out," she said as Zuma shook her head.

"Artificial who?" Faye said, and squinted her eyes at Zuma. "What is going on here?"

Zuma looked at each of the ladies and decided it was time they all knew the truth. "I wanted to have a baby so badly," she said through a cracking voice. "I saved my money. . . . I thought I had it all planned out. . . . But when I went back for the pregnancy test . . . They told me I wasn't pregnant."

"Oh, Zuma," Pat said and stroked her face, but Faye was too pissed to console.

"What were you thinking?" she yelled.

"I wanted a baby," Zuma yelled back.

"Do you know how hard it is to raise a child all by yourself?" she asked wickedly. "Look at the hell I've been through since my husband died. Raising a child is the hardest job in the world and you thought you could do it alone?"

"Stop it, Faye," Sandy yelled, still trying to soothe Zuma. "What difference does it make? She's not pregnant anyway," she said as Zuma turned to her and put her head on her shoulder.

As Sandy held on to Zuma, Faye turned back to Pat. "And you," she said, and threw her hands in the air. "Where have you been? Mark has been looking—" Faye stopped and thought for a second. "Where's Tracy?" she asked, suspiciously. "Where's your daughter?"

"I took her home."

"But Mark—"

"I took her back to her foster parents."

"What?" Faye screamed and took a step back. "Why?"

"I'm not her mother, Faye. She already has a mom. She didn't want me," she said as tears overtook her and she could speak no more.

Confused, Faye took Pat in her arms and held her tightly. She still didn't quite understand it all, but she knew Pat was hurting. "It's okay," she said as two headlights flashed in her face. She looked out into the parking lot and saw Mark's car. He stopped behind the two-car pile-up and jumped out. "Mark's here," Faye whispered as Pat raised her head and looked at her husband. "Go to him," she said as Pat reluctantly put one foot in front of the other and walked away.

"Excuse me," Mr. Watson said, and stuck his head out the door. "Are you Sandy?" he asked as she turned to look at him. "There's a phone call for you," he said as Sandy patted Zuma on the shoulder and left her side.

Zuma leaned against the side of the building and put her head in her hands.

"Come here," Faye said, and held out her arms for Zuma. "Come here."

Sandy grabbed the phone from Mr. Watson and held it in her hand until he walked away. She knew who was on the other end of the line and he had better have a good excuse for calling her, she thought as she put the phone to her ear. "What?"

"Mommy," David's little voice said, shaking.

"What, dammit."

"I think I see an emergency."

"What did you do, David?"

"I know you told me not to play with your cigarettes, but—"

"But what?"

"The rug is on fire."

"*What?*"

"It's getting bigger and bigger, Mommy."

Sandy's mind went blank. There was no way for the kids to get out of the house. She'd locked them in. "David?" she said, quickly. "Call your father, right now."

"Right now?"

"Yes! Tell him to come get you right now."

"Okay, Mommy."

"Right now!" she screamed and hung up the phone. "Oh my God," she said, and looked around at the people in the room.

"What is it?" Mr. Watson asked and rushed to her.

"My kids. The house is on fire."

"Let's go," he said, and pushed Sandy's lifeless body toward the door.

They both ran out looking hysterical. Mr. Watson looked at Faye's car, but she was blocked in by the wreck.

"What's going on?" Faye said as she and Zuma let go of each other.

"My house is on fire. My kids are in there," Sandy screamed.

"But I thought your kids were across the street?"

"They're in the house," Sandy shouted and shook her hands in front of her. "Somebody call the fire department!"

"What's your address?" Faye screamed and ran toward the door of the shop.

"108 Arbor Vitae."

"Got it," Faye said and ran inside.

"I gotta get home," Sandy said, looking around not knowing what to do. She began running out of the parking lot, but Mark caught her by the arm.

"I'll take you in my car," he said. He opened the back door for her and Sandy jumped inside. Mr. Watson jumped in behind her and Zuma followed him. Pat ran around to the passenger side as Mark got behind the wheel and put the car in reverse.

"Hurry," Faye mumbled as she stood inside the shop, clutching the phone in her hand and watching the car pull out and blaze away down the street. She put her hand over her chest and tried to calm herself back down as an operator came on the line. Faye shouted frantic instructions into the receiver, then hung up the phone and closed her eyes as she prayed for the safety of Sandy's children.

"Umm . . . Faye," a voice called out from the middle of the room.

She opened her eyes to find the partygoers staring at her impatiently. Just as she was about to explain what was going on, a lady stood up and asked, "Where's the food and drinks?"

Faye shook her head and looked down at the floor, then into the lady's face. "Everybody out!" she shouted, and opened the door wide. "Get the hell out of here!"

Sandy was such a wreck that she couldn't even remember where she lived. Twice she gave Mark the wrong directions and twice they had to back track, losing precious time. "Calm down," Zuma said, and leaned over Mr. Watson. "Just tell me what street you live on."

"Um . . . uh . . . Arbor Vitae."

"Okay," Zuma said taking over. "Make a left here, then a—"

"I know where Arbor Vitae is," Mark said as he hooked a left so fast that the back end of the car almost spun out. He raced down the residential street and hooked another left. Pat let out a whimper as she closed her eyes, too afraid to look at the street. Mark looked over at her when he heard the noise she made. He still couldn't believe what she'd just told him minutes earlier, and though he could see she was in pain, he felt nothing. He couldn't even look at her he was so disgusted. She had gone behind his back and taken Tracy to the Oppenheimers without even telling him. She had gone too far. How could she, he thought? Didn't he have a say-so in the matter? Wasn't Tracy just as much his daughter as she was Pat's? Couldn't she at least have asked him for his opinion?

"Mark," Zuma yelled out. "You passed it."

Mark slammed on the brakes, reversed, then bent the corner on Arbor Vitae. He didn't need to ask which house it was when he looked down the street and saw the firetrucks and the crowd of people standing out on their lawns. He got as close as he could to the commotion, then stopped the car.

Sandy was the first one out. She noticed Cerwin's car on the street and ran toward the blazing house, until a fireman stopped her. "My kids are inside there," she screamed, looking around for Cerwin. The rest of the group caught up with her and looked toward the house as a man came stumbling out the door with a small boy in his arms. "Cerwin," Sandy screamed as he handed his son to a fireman who immediately began mouth-to-mouth resuscitation on him.

Cerwin was covered with soot and grime and as he turned to go back into the house a fireman caught him by the arm. "You can't go back in there, sir," he said as Cerwin pushed him back so hard the fireman tumbled to the ground.

"My baby girl's in there," Cerwin said, and ran back up the steps.

"Let the professionals handle this," the fireman shouted, but it was too late. Cerwin had gone back into the house and Sandy went hysterical.

"No," she shouted, flinging her body in the air as Pat and Zuma tried to restrain her. "Cerwin," she yelled. "You're gonna kill yourself."

"Calm down," Zuma said and looked across the lawn at the fireman trying to revive little David. "I hope he's all right," she said nervously.

"What about Dalila?" Pat said.

"What about Cerwin?" Sandy screamed at the top of her voice. "Somebody do something," she said, and turned to Mark and Mr. Watson.

"Where's the baby's room?" Mr. Watson asked.

"In the back of the house."

Mark and Mr. Watson conferred as they both noticed the fire must have started in the front of the house, which was totally engulfed in flames. The rear of the house was just beginning to burn.

"Do something. Get Cerwin out of there," Sandy screamed.

"Watch my back, partner," Mark said to Mr. Watson as he crept past a couple of firemen, then started running around the side of the house toward the back.

One of the firemen caught a glimpse of Mark, but just as he was about to react, Mr. Watson stepped in front of him and scrambled around, cutting off his path.

"Mark," Pat screamed when she saw him running around back. "What is he doing?"

"Oh my God," Zuma said, still keeping an eye on the fireman hovering over David's body. He's dead, Zuma thought to herself and looked at Sandy.

But Sandy paid no attention to her son. "Cerwin, Cerwin, Cerwin" was all she mumbled as she kept her eyes on the front door of the house, waiting for him to return.

The wait was too long. Everybody knew it. Pat and Sandy held each other's hands tightly as they watched for a sign of Mark and Cerwin. Zuma was the only one to see the fireman put the white sheet over David's face and take him away on a stretcher.

"Oh my . . . Yes," Sandy said and jumped up when she saw the large soot-covered man walking along the side of the house. She smiled and jumped up again, until . . . "Cerwin?"

"No, it's Mark," Pat said and put her hands over her mouth. "Mark," she screamed as she watched him walk to the front of the house. In his hand he held a tiny bundle wrapped in a blanket. He knelt down as one of the firemen rushed to him and put an oxygen mask over his face.

"I'm fine," Mark shouted and took the cover off little Dalila. "See about the baby," he demanded as the firemen turned their attention to her.

"The baby," Pat said, and looked at her closely. "I see her moving," she said, and jumped up and down. "Sandy, Dalila's moving."

"Where is Cerwin?" Sandy said as she fiercely yanked her body free of Zuma. She ran through a bunch of firemen and up to the lawn, screaming Cerwin's name.

Mark bolted up from the ground and ran behind Sandy, catching her just as she was about to run into the house.

"Cerwin's in there. We've got to get him out."

Mark took her into his arms and held her tightly. "It's too late, Sandy," he said gripping her even tighter as she tried to fight him off. "Cerwin's dead."

"No," Sandy screamed, and flung her arms toward the house. But Mark held her by the waist, whispering soothing words as Sandy struggled to get free.

"Cerwin," she hollered, finally giving up as Mark carried her off the porch. The entire house seemed to crackle and flames danced into the sky. "Cerwin," Sandy hollered again. "Oh my God. CERWIN!"

24

Faye sat at her hair station with Christopher in her arms, cuddling him against her soft breasts as he played with a balloon. It had been over an hour since she'd kicked everyone out of the shop and even longer than that since Mark and the rest of them took off like bats out of hell. She hoped everything was all right with Sandy and her children, though for the life of her she could not figure out why Sandy had lied to her. She wondered how long she had been lying. Had her kids been staying home by themselves all this time while Sandy showed up to work every day?

Her thoughts were interrupted when a knock came at the front door. She pushed Christopher up and ran to unlock it, thinking it was Sandy or Zuma or Pat, somebody with some information for her. But when she opened the door she couldn't believe her eyes.

"Mom," Antoinette said as she stood in front of her, clutching her arms across her chest, trying her best to fend off the cold night air. "Can I come in?"

Faye was at a loss for words, but she managed to step back so that Antoinette could walk through.

Christopher went nuts when he saw his sister. He ran to her and jumped into her arms, screaming her name. Antoinette's knees buckled, but she was able to hold Chris in her arms. She kissed him on the cheek, then thumped him on the forehead. "Get away from me, you little brat," she said and put Chris down.

Faye could see her daughter straining as she stood to her feet and grabbed hold of her stomach.

"Where you been?" Chris demanded. "You coming back home, Nette? Huh? You gonna come back home?"

Antoinette looked at Faye, then at Christopher. "I don't know," she said, and blew out a mouthful of air like she was the most tired girl in the world.

"Why don't you sit down?" Faye said, and motioned to the sofa with the politeness she'd show one of her clients, but minus the love and warmth a mother would show for her daughter. She watched as Antoinette waddled to the sofa, braced herself on its arm, and slowly sat down. "Christopher," she said as he followed his sister to the sofa. "Why don't you go gather up all the balloons?" she said.

"But I wanna sit with Antoinette."

"*Christopher*," she said sternly, and he walked away and did what he was told.

Faye walked over to the sofa and sat down in the corner opposite Antoinette. Part of her wanted to demand questions. Where have you been? Why haven't you called? But the other part of her wanted to take her daughter in her arms and hold her tightly and never let go. Instead, Faye sat quietly and waited for Antoinette to make the first move.

"I went to the house first," Antoinette said, looking straight ahead. "When you weren't there, I didn't know what to do," she said, and looked down at the floor. "It took me an hour to walk over here," she said, lowering her voice. "And if you weren't here I was gonna hop on a bus."

"To where?"

Antoinette shrugged her shoulders and folded her hands in her lap. "I wanted to talk to you, Mom."

"Why didn't you call?"

She shrugged her shoulders again, then slowly turned her face to look into her mother's eyes. "I wanna come back home," she said as tears ran down her cheeks.

Faye's first mind was to shout out "Yes," but she didn't, and for some reason, she was unable to look at Antoinette. All the worry, all the pain, all the fear that she'd been going through since Antoinette ran away suddenly turned to anger. Faye's breathing got faster as she tried to keep herself calm. She balled her fists together and took a deep breath. "Where have you been?"

Antoinette hesitated to speak at first and then said, "With Shock G. At his house."

Faye shook her head in disbelief, though she had already assumed that was where Antoinette had been. "You mean to tell me that boy's parents let you stay with them without asking any questions?"

"He lives with his older brother," she said, and wiped at her tears.

Faye shut her eyes as her lips began to quiver. She didn't even want to think about the lifestyle Antoinette had been living for the past week. "Why didn't you call me?"

Antoinette opened her mouth, but no words came out.

"Don't you know how worried I've been?" Faye said as her voice grew louder. "Don't you know I've been sick about this? I couldn't sleep at night, Antoinette." She balled up her fists so tight that her knuckles popped. "Do you have . . ." She stopped to keep her voice from cracking. "Do you have any idea what kind of hell you put me through?"

Antoinette's shoulder heaved up and down as she cried. "I'm sorry, Mom."

"You're sorry?" Faye said, and looked at her daughter. "You're sorry? What good are your apologies, Antoinette? You wanted to be so grown, didn't you? You wanted to live your life the way you wanted to live it. You disrespected me in every way, Antoinette," she said, pounding one fist on top of the other. "I don't know what was worse. Living with you or living without you," Faye said as she felt the veins in her neck pop out. "Why do you want to come home?" she asked, looking at her daughter with suspicion. "You were so unhappy there. Why don't you just stay with your boyfriend?" she shouted. "Why don't you and him get married, raise your child, and live happily ever after?" she asked, eyeing Antoinette's swollen belly with contempt. "Huh, Antoinette? Why don't you do that? Do you hear me talking to you? Why don't you just stay gone?"

"He kicked me out," Antoinette yelled, and covered her face with her hands. "He said he didn't want to have nothing to do with me or my baby," she said, clutching her hands over her eyes. "He said he don't want me no more. He threw me out the house and told me to never come back," she said, crying so hard that she could barely breathe.

"But I thought you said he loved you," Faye quipped. "I thought you said he was gonna take care of you. Isn't that what you told me, Antoinette? Isn't that what you said?"

Antoinette could answer no more questions. She just sat there sobbing with her hands against her face, and Faye sat there watching her as anger and pity filled her head. She reached out and moved Antoinette's hands from her face, but Antoinette didn't want to be seen. She put her hands over her face again and this time Faye slapped them away.

"Look at me," Faye said as Antoinette put her hands in her lap. "Look at me!" she said again, and waited as her daughter turned to meet her eyes. "You only get one mother in this life and that's me," she said, and put her finger to her chest. "Now I know that I made some mistakes in raising you. I know I didn't always spend enough time with you, but dammit, Antoinette, I did the best that I could," she said as tears began to form in her own eyes. "After your father died I had to be strong. I know I should have spent more time with you, but I had to *move*. I had to get with the program or else you know what?" She turned Antoinette's face back to hers. "You wouldn't have had food to eat. *You* wouldn't have had clothes on your back. You, me, and Christopher would have been out on the streets. I'm not saying I did everything right, Antoinette. But I tell you this, if I'm wrong for trying to do all I could to provide for my family, then dammit, I don't want to be right."

Faye paused to wipe her face and breathe, but as soon as she was able, she spoke up again.

"I love you with all my heart, Antoinette," she said unable to keep her voice from cracking anymore. "You are the only daughter I have and I am the only mother you have. But I'll be damned if I'm going to let you come back into my house and treat me the way you have treated me in the past. I won't have it anymore, Antoinette," she said, and raised her finger. "I will not be disrespected in my own home, I will not be ignored, and I will not tolerate your attitude," she said firmly. "*If*," she said, and looked at her daughter as if she could see straight through her, "*if* I allow you to come back home, you will abide by my rules or else you can stay your ass on the street. I've had enough, Antoinette. If you think there is anyone in this world who will do for you like I do for you, then don't bother coming back home. But I'll tell you this, no one is ever going to love you the way that I do. No one is ever gonna sacrifice for you like I do. I am your mother, Antoinette. Your mother."

Mother and daughter sat in silence, staring at each other, both knowing the truth had been spoken. Mother wanted to reach out and hold daughter, but she was afraid. It had been much too long. "Go wash your face," Faye said as she swiped at her own eyes with her fingers.

Antoinette negotiated herself to her feet, then walked off toward the rest room. But she had barely gotten away when Faye stood to her feet and ran behind her. She pulled her daughter's back against her chest and wrapped her arms around her neck. She kissed the back of her head, then her cheek, then her neck. "I love you," Mother said, and squeezed her daughter tightly.

"I love you," Daughter said, basking in the warmth of forgotten yet familiar territory.

Antoinette walked into the bathroom as the front door of the shop came flying open. Faye turned around to see Zuma stroll in as if she'd been through the worst ordeal of her life. Pat and Mark were next through the door and Mr. Watson was bringing up the rear.

"Oh God," Faye said, and put her hand to her chest. "What happened?"

"Mark got the baby out, but the little boy . . ." Zuma said and shook her head, unable to finish her sentence.

"Oh no," Faye said.

"The kid's father got caught in the house too," Mr. Watson said as he walked over to Faye and put his arm around her.

"He's dead too?"

Mr. Watson nodded his head and looked away.

"Well, where's Sandy?"

"They took her and her baby to the hospital," Pat said. "Sandy is a basket case."

"I know," Zuma said, and looked at Pat, baffled. "It's like she didn't give a damn about the kids. The only person she called for was Surgeon or Circus, or whatever his name is — was."

"Cerwin," Pat corrected, and bowed her head. "They're probably gonna keep her and the baby overnight at the hospital," she said. "I told her they could both come stay with Mark and me until they find themselves a new place to live."

"This is terrible," Faye said as Christopher walked over to her and tapped her on the leg. She looked down at him and patted his head.

"Is Antoinette really coming home, Mami?" he asked as Faye looked up and saw the confused look on everyone's faces.

"She came by a while ago," Faye said, tearfully. "She wants to come back home."

"That's great," Pat said, and clasped her hands together. "Thank God she's all right."

"Well, I hope you told her what time it is," Zuma said, and sucked her teeth. "If she's gonna come back acting a fool, you oughta kick her right back out on the streets."

"Hold on," Pat interrupted. "What's important is that she came back. You just take it one day at a time with her, Faye. You two still have a lot to work out."

"I know," Faye said, and looked behind her at the rest room door. Antoinette had been in there much too long, she thought as Pat asked where Antoinette was. "She's in the rest room," Faye said, and walked over to the door. "Antoinette?" She gave a little knock. "You okay in there?"

The door flew open and Antoinette leaned against the wall, huffing and puffing as if she were choking. "Mom," she said, gripping her stomach. "I think my water just broke," she said, and fell down to her knees.

"Oh Dios." Faye knelt down beside her. "Hold on, honey," she said, and stroked Antoinette's head.

"*Aaahhh*," Antoinette screamed out in agony. "I'm only seven months. This shouldn't be happening."

"What are we gonna do?" Faye said, looking over her shoulder.

"Let's get her to a hospital," Mr. Watson said as he and Mark ran to the rescue. Mr. Watson grabbed Antoinette's feet, Mark her shoulders, and on the count of three they both tried to lift her.

"*Aaahhh!*" Antoinette screamed out even louder than before. "Don't move me, don't move me. Put me down, put me down."

"Oh shit," Zuma said, looking on and wishing she had some popcorn.

Pat stood beside her wincing and Christopher scrambled around, trying to see yet stay out of the grown-ups' way at the same time.

"Oh, it's coming," Antoinette said as her eyes widened.

"Don't push," Faye screamed. "Not yet. We need a doctor."

"But we can't get her to the hospital."

"Y'all gonna have to do it here," Zuma said, straining her neck so that she could see everything.

"Okay," Faye said as she untied the strap that held up Antoinette's sweat pants. "Take off her shoes," she said as Mr. Watson jumped to attention. He pulled off her shoes as Faye grabbed hold of her pants and panties and pulled them down at the same time.

"Yuck," Christopher said, and curled up his lips. "She pooped on herself."

Faye propped Antoinette's legs up in front of Mr. Watson, then pushed Mark out of the way and took his position behind Antoinette's head. "Okay, honey. You can push now," she said as Antoinette howled. "Push, honey, push," she coaxed. "As hard as you can."

"Wait," Zuma screamed, and jumped up. "Don't we need some hot water and some towels or something like that?"

"Shut up," Pat said, and ran to the reception desk. "I'll call nine-one-one so they'll be on the way."

"I can see the head," Mr. Watson said, grimacing from the disgusting sight before his eyes.

"You can see the head already," Zuma yelled. "Damn, girl. You must have been in labor for hours and didn't even know it."

Faye's heart pounded from all the pressure. Just how long had her daughter been in labor, she thought, once again confirming how little Antoinette knew about the situation she had gotten herself into. But now was not the time for lectures. Faye shouted to Mr. Watson, "Put your hand on the baby's head."

"You want me to touch it?"

"Yes," she screamed. "Don't let the baby's head fall on the floor."

Mr. Watson winced as he stuck his hand under the baby's head and held it up.

"Push, mija," Faye told Antoinette. "You gotta push."

"*It hurts.*"

"I know baby, I know. But you gotta push."

"Okay, I see the chest," Mr. Watson said, coming to grips with his new job. "Ah," he said and looked closer. "Here come the legs," he said, holding on to the baby's head and torso. "Just a couple more."

"You hear that, mijita? Just a couple more pushes," Faye said. "Come on now. Give me a big one," she said as her daughter mashed her eyes together and growled. "One more," she said.

"I can't do no more."

"Yes you can."

"No, Mom. I can't do no more."

"Come on, girl," Zuma yelled, and frowned. "This ain't no time for debating."

Mr. Watson cupped his hands as Antoinette pushed with all her might, and then . . . "I got him, I got him," Mr. Watson said with joy. "No, wait a minute . . . I got *her, I got her*," he said as Pat rushed over with some clean white towels to wrap the baby in.

"What do we do with the cord?" Pat said, looking over Mr. Watson's shoulder and eyeing the thick tube attached to the baby's belly button.

"Never fear," Zuma said as she ran to her hair station and whipped out a pair of scissors. She ran back and knelt down next to Mr. Watson.

"Be careful, Zuma," Pat warned.

"I've worked wonders with these scissors before," she said, and opened them up. "Now," she cooed as the baby cried out. "Do you want an inny or an outty?" she asked. "Innies are cuter," she said and started to cut. "That way you can wear all the cool cut-off tops and show your belly button," she said as she positioned the scissors close to the baby's skin. But just as she was about to cut she stopped. She looked down at the newborn, trying so hard to hold back her emotions, but she couldn't. She thought about the baby she was supposed to have. The baby that would make her life all she'd planned for it to be. The scissors began to shake in Zuma's hand as she knelt there, wishing, silently praying that she too could be pregnant. But she wasn't. She had been pregnant once, long ago. But that was then, this was now. Tears spilled down her face as Pat came over to her and took the scissors out of her hand.

"Come on," Pat said, her eyes filling with water too. She knew what must be running through Zuma's mind. It was the same thing that was running through her own.

"The cord," Zuma said, her voice floating weakly through the air. "I gotta cut the cord." She turned to Pat. "The baby needs me to cut the cord."

"Ssh," Pat said as Zuma stood up and she held her in her arms. "The doctors can handle that," she said as Zuma laid her head on Pat's shoulder. "You just come with me," she said, walking away slowly. "Everything's going to be all right."

Mr. Watson wrapped the baby in a bundle of white towels and handed her to Antoinette.

"Oh," she said as she stared into her daughter's face. "Look, Mom," she said. "Look at her little nose."

"She's beautiful," Faye said, and wiped blood off the baby's head. "You've been blessed, mija," she said, and kissed her daughter's head. "This is truly a blessing."

Mr. Watson crawled over to Faye and looked over her shoulder at the baby. "You're right," he said, grinning. "This is a blessing."

Faye took Mr. Watson's hand as she turned to look at him. "Thank you," she said, and squeezed his hand tightly. And for the third time that evening she saw the look in his eyes, but this time she would not let the moment slip away. She leaned forward and kissed Mr. Watson ever so gently on the lips as he touched the side of her face.

Everyone could see the connection between the two, but only the incomparable Zuma was bold enough to speak up, even though the pang in her heart was almost too painful to bear. "There's a Motel Six about two blocks away," she said, and snickered through her tears. But just as soon as she said those words, her heart began to hurt again. She laid her head back on Pat's shoulder as they both stood off to the side of the room in each other's arms, trying to comfort the pain of their losses away.

Faye blushed as Mr. Watson continued to stare into her eyes even though the kiss was over. Faye looked at him, then down at her daughter and granddaughter. At that very moment, the only thing on her mind was the feeling she felt inside, and as she looked upward into what only she could see, she knew for sure that she had been blessed.

25

One week later, things were looking as if they were getting back to normal around Blessings. Pat, Faye, and Zuma had finished up their final customers of the day and were preparing to go home when Faye called the girls over to her hair station and pulled out a stack of pictures. "Here's little Faith," she said, handing both Pat and Zuma a picture.

"Oh," Pat squealed as she held the picture close to her face. "Look at little Faith. She's so tiny."

"But she's healthy as can be," Faye said, and handed out more pictures. "She was two months premature, but she's doing just fine."

"I guess Antoinette didn't get much prenatal care," Zuma said, and smiled as she passed a picture to Pat. "Next time she'd better take her butt to the doctor."

"There's not going to be a next time," Faye said, strictly. "Not at least until she's grown."

"So how's she doing?"

"Well," Faye said, and sighed. "She missed so much school this year that they won't even take her back. But next semester," she said, and raised her finger, "she's starting all over again. There's this special school for teen moms that she's already enrolled in."

"Oh really," Pat said, and took another picture.

"Yeah. They have a special program where the moms can leave their children while they go to class, and they even have advanced courses where the moms can study for a particular trade like nursing or teaching so that by the time they graduate they'll already have a job waiting for them."

"That's great," Pat said.

"Mmm-hmm," Zuma groaned. "But how are things at home?"

"Better," Faye said and nodded her head with confidence. "I can already see a change in Antoinette's attitude. Oddly enough the baby has seemed to calm her down. She's getting more responsible and more mature every day. Plus we've been seeing a counselor together. Mr. Watson . . . I mean James put us in touch with a really good family therapist and I think we're gonna be just fine."

Zuma cleared her throat and gave Faye the eye. "And how is Mr. Watson — I mean James?"

"He's just fine, Zuma," Faye said, and cracked a smile, remembering the night she kissed Mr. Watson. He drove with her to the hospital after Antoinette's baby was born and stayed by her side all night long. And ever since, he'd either called Faye or stopped by to see her every day.

"Have y'all slept together yet?"

"Zuma."

"What?"

"That's none of your business."

"Fine," she said, and rolled her eyes.

"Fine," Faye shot back.

"Good."

"Great."

"Perfect."

"Stop it," Pat said, and raised her hand as she turned to Zuma. "Now what about you?" Pat asked.

"What about me, what?" Zuma said, studying the picture in her hand.

"You know what she's talking about Zuma," Faye said. "I can't believe you hid the fact that you were getting artificially inseminated. I thought we were your friends. You could have confided in us."

"Yeah right," Zuma said, and sucked her teeth. "What happened when I told you? You went off on me, telling me what a stupid mistake I'd made. I didn't want to hear that shit."

"Wanting a baby is not stupid, Zuma," Faye said calmly. "But I still think that you don't understand how hard it is to raise children alone."

Zuma didn't like the feeling that plagued her stomach. She had kept it to herself for so long about wanting a baby that talking about it now, even though it was all over, was very difficult for her.

Faye could see the stress on Zuma's face and she realized how serious this was for her. This artificial insemination business was not some goofy stunt Zuma had pulled to bring added adventure into her life. This was serious, she concluded, and reached out a soothing hand.

Zuma felt the love from both of her friends and she knew they both cared, although they had no way of knowing the whole story behind her failed attempt to get pregnant. And Zuma would never tell them. She couldn't. Her pride was too strong and she didn't want her friends ever to look down on her the way she looked down on herself for having aborted her baby. She didn't want them to know that she so desperately wanted a child to try to make up for the mistake she'd made so many years ago. And she didn't want them to know that Allah was punishing her. No. Zuma wouldn't say a word. That aspect of her life would forever remain a secret. It was between her and Allah. Whether Zuma had a child in the years to come would all be left up to Him. Maybe he'd see fit to bless her one of these days, she thought. But until then, she'd wait and want and hope and pray.

"It'll happen for you one day," Faye said. "You are thirty years old, you're young. It'll happen for you. But there are some things you just can't plan for," she said, then smiled. "Like love," she added finally. "You can't plan for the day when a man is going to come into your life and give you the love and attention that you've been dreaming about. And the same goes for children. It'll happen when it happens. You can't plan for it. You've just got to be patient and ready when the time is right."

"And sometimes when it seems the time is right, things still may not turn out the way you've planned them," Pat said, and gave her stack of pictures back to Faye as she thought about Tracy. It seemed as though everything was going her way, but in the end everything fell apart. For her and Tracy the time was just not right. There was no way that Pat could ever be Tracy's mother. She couldn't take the place of Elizabeth, the only mother Tracy had known all her life. There was no way her heart could let her break up their union, and taking Tracy back to the Oppenheimers was the only solution. She had tried to get Mark to understand why she'd done what she'd done. Why she had to do what her heart led her to do. But Mark couldn't fathom it. He was so crushed that he left home for a couple of days to get his head together, and even though he'd been back for a couple of days, things still weren't the same between them. Pat never clearly understood how much Mark wanted a child too. And for her to return Tracy to the Oppenheimers without so much as a word to him was a total disregard of his feelings. She didn't understand his pain until he broke down and cried, pleading with her to reconsider. But it was too late. Tracy was gone. She was back where she belonged and there was nothing either of them could do to change that.

Pat sat down quietly in a chair and watched as Faye and Zuma scurried around, straightening up their hair stations and cleaning off their countertops.

"Still no word from Sandy?" Zuma asked and turned to Pat.

"Not a word," Pat said, and shook her head. "I went to see her in the hospital the day after the fire and I told her I had a room all set up at my house for her and the baby. All she had to do was call," she said, and threw her hands in the air.

"But she never did?" Faye asked, and stopped what she was doing. "She didn't even leave a message on your machine?"

"Nothing," Pat said with disgust. "And when I called back to the hospital a few days later they said she and her baby had checked out."

"I tried calling her at the hospital too," Zuma added. "I wanted to know if she needed help arranging the funeral for David and, and," she said, snapping her fingers.

"Cerwin," Faye said.

"Yeah, Cerwin," Zuma said. "But she had already left the hospital and no one knew where she'd gone."

"She doesn't have any family," Pat said.

"Just her mother," Faye corrected. "But she hasn't seen her in years."

"So what should we do?" Zuma questioned.

"What can we do?" Pat answered. "The girl has disappeared."

The ladies all stared at one another waiting for someone to come up with the solution, but no one could find it.

"Well, I'm ready to get out of here," Zuma said as she threw her purse over her shoulder and headed to the front door. But just as she got there, she stopped cold. "Sandy," she said, looking out the glass door. "It's Sandy, y'all." She looked over her shoulder at Pat and Faye as she unlocked the door and held it open.

Sandy walked in wearing the exact same outfit she'd had on the night of the fire, only over it all she wore a thick black coat. Underneath her coat and strapped to her chest was a baby holder that carried Dalila. Sandy had a blanket over Dalila's head to ward off the cold night air, and as she walked in, she took off the blanket and her coat so that Dalila wouldn't overheat.

Sandy froze as Zuma came closer to her and put her arms around her neck. Zuma hated to admit it, but she had been worried about Sandy. But as she held her, she could tell something just wasn't right. She let her go and took a step back. "Where the hell have you been?"

"Yeah," Pat said, and stood up. "You were supposed to call me when you were ready to leave the hospital. I had a room all set up for you and Dalila."

"I didn't want to put you out," Sandy said, looking down at the floor. "Dalila and I have been staying down at the Salvation Army shelter."

"The Salvation Army?" Faye scolded.

"But I told you you could stay with me. My house is big enough. You and Dalila can stay there for as long as you need."

"Thanks," she said. "But I don't—"

"No buts," Pat said, firmly. "You and Dalila are coming home with me tonight."

"I'm leaving town," Sandy announced as everyone looked at each other.

"Leaving town?" Faye asked.

"Where the hell you think you going?" Zuma asked.

"I don't know," Sandy said, and reached into her pocket. "All I know is that I've got a bus ticket and I'm getting out of here," she said, and pulled out her ticket. "I've just got to move on," she said, looking around the room. "I don't think I could stay here another day."

"But Sandy," Faye pleaded. "That baby is too young for you to be yanking her off to God knows where. Why don't you just stay here? You've got a job, you've got a place to live. What's the problem?"

"I can't stay here, dammit," she screamed. "There are too many memories. I just want to go somewhere and start a new life."

"But you'll be out on the streets."

"I've been out on the streets before."

"But not with a baby," Pat said.

"Look," she said, and stomped her foot. "I know what's best for me and I know what's best for my daughter. I've got my ticket and I'm leaving. That's final."

"Where'd you get the money for a bus ticket anyway?" Zuma asked suspiciously.

"I borrowed it from some of the volunteers at the Salvation Army. They gave me this coat and this baby carrier too."

"But what about the funeral for David and, and—"

"Cerwin?" Faye asked.

"They buried them yesterday," she said, and bowed her head. "I didn't have the money to do it myself, so the state did it for me," she said as tears fell out her eyes. "I didn't go. I heard those types of funerals aren't very nice. I couldn't take seeing Cerwin like that," she said, and quickly put her hand over her mouth.

"If you had just called one of us we could have helped out," Pat said. "Don't you get it? We are all friends. We help each other out. You don't have to go through this alone and you certainly don't have to skip town. We'll be here for you, Sandy."

"I'm leaving," she said strictly. "I have to do this for me."

"But—"

"There's nothing left to talk about," Sandy said, and wiped the tears from her eyes. "I just came by to let you all know I was leaving and to thank you all for . . . for . . . trying," she said, and grabbed her coat and the blanket for Dalila's head. "I just need to use the rest room first," she said, and hurried off without another word.

Faye, Pat, and Zuma stared at each other in shock. "Can you believe her?" Faye said.

"Let her go," Zuma said, and frowned. "There's nothing we can do for her. The girl's got issues too deep for us to understand. Just let her go. She's got to find her own way."

"But what about the baby?" Pat insisted. "It would be a different thing if she was doing this alone. But she's got a baby that's not even a year old yet. How's that baby going to eat? Where's that baby going to sleep, Zuma?"

Zuma threw her hands in the air as Sandy opened the door to the rest room, stepped out, then closed it behind her.

All was silent as Sandy walked to the door with her black coat bundled tightly around her. She tucked the blanket back over Dalila's head, then stopped when she reached the door and turned to face the ladies. "Thank you all again. You're very nice people. Even you, Zuma," she said and cut her eyes at her. "And you too, Faye," she said, and smiled in her direction. "But especially you, Pat," she said, and stared at her. "You gave me a job at a time in my life when I needed it the most and for that I thank you from the bottom of my heart."

"Wait a minute," Pat said as she rushed behind the reception desk and grabbed her purse. She dug in and pulled out a wad of cash and held it out for Sandy. "Take it," she said, and jerked her hand. "You're gonna need it for the baby."

"No," Sandy said, and shook her head. "I don't want your money, just your blessings." She put her hand on the door. "You keep your money," she said as she walked out. "You're gonna need it more than I do."

"What is her problem?" Pat said as she watched Sandy walk out the door and down the street. "I don't get it," she said, and threw her money back into her purse. "I just don't get it."

"She's got issues," Zuma said, and sucked her teeth. "She'll be all right . . . I guess."

"Let's go," Faye said, disgusted. She grabbed her purse and headed to the door. "You riding with me?" she asked Zuma.

"I guess so." Zuma cut her eyes at Pat. "My car is *still* in the shop."

"Mine too," Pat said. "But Mark's gonna pick me up. He should be here in a second."

"You know you two ought to be shamed of yourselves. I bet not ever hear tale of you all drinking and driving again, or I'll —"

"Or you'll what?" Zuma said, and opened the door.

"I don't know," Faye said, and walked out. "Just don't do it no more. That goes for you too, Miss Pat."

"Yes, Mama," Pat said. "I'll see you two tomorrow," she said as she walked behind them and watched from the window as they got into Faye's car and drove off.

Pat returned to the reception desk and checked her schedule to see that she had to be in at ten o'clock the next morning for her first appointment. She closed the book, then walked around the shop and pulled all the blinds shut. She turned out the lights in the back of the room and when she did she noticed underneath the door that the light was still on in the rest room.

She heard Mark's car pull up out front and sighed as she ran to the rest room to turn out the light. But when she opened the door she screamed. Right in front of her on the floor was Sandy's baby, Dalila. "Oh my God," Pat shouted as she put her hand over her mouth and knelt down. She picked up the baby in her arms and stared at her pale white face, wondering what in the world she was going to do. Did Sandy leave her here on purpose? she thought. But of course she did. How do you walk off and leave your child on the floor of a rest room? "*Oh my God*," she said again as she stood up with the baby in her arms.

Dalila was wrapped in a white blanket and as Pat pulled it over the baby's arms she found a single sheet of paper tucked inside. Confused, she took out the paper and saw it was a letter addressed to her.

"What is going on?" she said as she shook out the paper, held it up, and began reading.

> Dear Pat,
>
> I know you're probably in shock, but please, just hear me out. If there is one thing I know, it's that I am not fit to be a mother. I tried to be, but I failed. The only reason I ever had children was to please Cerwin. I thought it would make him love me more, but I don't think it was possible for Cerwin or anyone else to give me the amount of love I needed. No matter what people thought of him and his profession there was one thing about Cerwin no one could deny. He loved his children. And now that he's gone I know he would want to see his daughter taken care of in the best manner possible. I can't do that, Pat. I know I can't. That's why I'm leaving Dalila with you. I don't do things right all the time, but I know in my heart that leaving Cerwin's daughter with you is the best thing I can do.
>
> Please, Pat. Take care of Cerwin's baby. I know it may be difficult, but if there's anyone who can do it, it's you. You have so much love to give and so much goodness to share. Mark saved Dalila's life once, now I'm asking the both of you to save her future. Do this for me, Pat. Help me give Cerwin what I know he's wishing for.
>
>   Good-bye,
>   Sandy Dew McReiney

Pat's mind went blank. She looked down into Dalila's face as the baby gurgled and made what appeared to be a smile. Slowly, she flipped off the light in the rest room and walked out, just as Mark came rushing through the front door.

"What's taking you so long?" he said as he looked ahead to his startled wife. "What's going on?" he said as he walked to her, trying to figure out why she was carrying this baby and why she had such a look on her face.

Pat held out the note for Mark, then looked down at Dalila while she waited for him to read it.

"Is this for real?" he said, and looked at Pat, reflecting the same confusion he saw on her face.

Pat nodded her head and looked him in the eye. "What are we gonna do?"

Mark looked at Dalila and stroked a finger over her cheek. "We're gonna do what we have to do," he said, and studied the note again.

"But what if she changes her mind? What if she comes back for the baby?"

"Or what if she doesn't?" Mark said. "What if this is God's way of setting things right?"

"But if she comes back two or three years later, I don't think I could handle it, Mark. I can't have another baby taken from me again."

"We'll deal with that when or if it happens," he said, and looked at Dalila again. "But right now we've just got to take it one day at a time."

Dalila yawned, then started to cry. Pat shifted her to her other arm and bounced her just a bit. "Ssh," she said, and cuddled her until she became comfortable and quieted down. "Grab my purse?" she said to Mark as she walked toward the front door.

Mark picked up her purse, then hurried behind her and opened the door. Pat held the baby close to her chest as she stepped out into the cold and Mark locked up. Together they walked to the car and Mark opened the door for his two girls. Pat looked up at him and smiled as he closed the door, then scurried around to the other side and got in.

This, Pat thought to herself, is a miracle. She looked down at Dalila and touched her tiny nose, as she thought about Sandy, wondering where she had gone, where she'd end up, and if she was ever coming back. Dalila opened her mouth and yawned as if she didn't have a care in the world, then looked up at Pat in peaceful satisfaction. "She's so precious," Pat said softly, and as she stared down at her she suddenly didn't care about Sandy anymore. Wherever she'd gone, if ever she'd come back didn't matter. All that was important was this baby, she thought as her eyes filled with tears. For however long it lasted, Pat would take care of Dalila. She would feed her, clothe her, protect her. She would love her. She wouldn't do it for Sandy, though. She'd do it because as she sat holding Dalila, aware of all she'd been through in her own life, she was sure of one thing — this baby was a gift sent to her straight from God. "I am so blessed to have you," she said, and leaned down to place a kiss on Dalila's forehead. Of that Pat was certain. For after all, she thought as Mark started up the car and drove away, that's what children are — they are blessings.

Peace

About the Author

Sheneska Jackson was born in South Central Los Angeles and currently lives in the San Fernando Valley. She teaches fiction writing for UCLA's Extension program. *Blessings* is her third novel.